Karen

SMOKE & CRACKED MIRRORS

A York Ladies' Detective Agency Mystery

SMOKE & CRACKED MIRRORS

© Karen Charlton 2022

Visit Karen Charlton's website to learn more about her historical novels and sign up for her occasional newsletter for the latest news about her writing and public events.

www.karencharlton.com

Published by Famelton Publishing.
Cover design and illustration by Lisa Horton.
Photograph of 'The Shambles' by David Zdanowicz

Dedicated to

THE DIAMOND GIRLS

Jackie Woodhead, Lynn Butler-Ellis &

Caroline McNamara

With love.

Xxx

ALSO BY KAREN CHARLTON

The York Ladies' Detective Agency Mysteries

The Mystery of Mad Alice Lane (short story)

Smoke & Cracked Mirrors

Dancing with Dusty Fossils

The Detective Lavender Mysteries

The Heiress of Linn Hagh

The Sans Pareil Mystery

The Sculthorpe Murder

Plague Pits & River Bones

Murder on Park Lane

The Willow Marsh Murder

The Mystery of the Skelton Diamonds (short story)

The Piccadilly Pickpocket (short story)

The Death of Irish Nell (short story)

Other Works

February 1809 (short story)

Catching the Eagle

Seeking our Eagle (non-fiction)

Chapter One

York, Friday March 1ˢᵗ, 1940

Roberta 'Bobbie' Baker picked up an expensive skirt from the rack of clothes and pretended to examine it. Out of the corner of her eye, she continued to watch the elderly woman who'd pushed a fine cashmere cardigan into her shopping bag. The shoplifter's bag, like her smart coat, was a pricey item. But Bobbie knew they were both a sham, probably acquired on a previous shoplifting spree and worn to fend off the attention of the store detectives. But there was dirt under the woman's fingernails, an accumulation of wax in her ears and she reeked of cheap perfume. She didn't belong in Grainger's any more than that expensive bag belonged on her arm.

Grainger's Department Store had evolved out of a hotchpotch of adjoining seventeenth-century buildings at the corner of one of York's busiest marketplaces and it was a nightmare for the store detectives to patrol. The slim marble pillars that supported the roof often obscured their view, and there were many short flights of stairs connecting the irregular levels of the ladies' department. The shoplifters and their thieving hands often disappeared out of sight.

Thankfully, there were mirrors everywhere. In theory they were there for the benefit of the customers and reflected and maximised the light coming through the small leaded casement windows. But they also helped the store detectives. Bobbie had become adept at using them to her advantage. She knew where to stand to watch the reflection of her suspects when they disappeared around a corner or behind a rack of clothing.

The thief continued to flick through the hangers. She was waiting for something. *But what?*

—

Bobbie frowned and glanced around. Experienced shoplifters rarely worked alone; there must be an accomplice somewhere. If so, they'd chosen a good time for their thieving spree. Mr Boyes, the floor walker, was downstairs and the department manageress was in the changing rooms with a particularly demanding customer. Rosa and herself were the only staff left in this section. And Rosa was behind the glass counter, showing a heavily pregnant woman a selection of fur mantles and hats.

'They're working together,' said a soft, familiar voice by her elbow. 'Your thief is working with the pregnant girl by the counter – and she's not pregnant, by the way. That bump on her belly is a cage.'

Relief and pleasure washed through Bobbie in equal measure, but she didn't look around.

'Welcome back to York, Miss Sherlock,' she murmured, her eyes steady on her suspect. 'You've picked a good moment to reappear. How do you know about the cage?'

'Elementary, my dear Dr Watson. Her feet are too close together when she walks; pregnant women splay their feet to balance out the extra weight. Besides which, I watched her shove a silk scarf down the waistband of her skirt when I came up the stairs.'

Bobbie's lips twitched with amusement. She risked a quick glance at her petite blonde friend. Jemma looked surprisingly serene, considering what she'd been through. But she'd lost weight, a lot of weight. Her skin hadn't suffered, though. Her creamy complexion was as flawless as ever. Sprayed with freckles as a child, Bobbie had always envied Jemma her skin.

'Any minute now, I expect your pregnant shopper will cause a distraction,' Jemma continued.

'At which point,' Bobbie whispered, 'the old bat over there will slip out unnoticed with a twenty-five-shilling cashmere knit in the bottom of her bag.'

—

6

'She's left-handed, by the way – your old bat. The nails on her left hand are far more worn down and cracked than those on her right.'

'I need your help.'

'Anything.'

'Go downstairs and tell Jim, the doorman, what's happening. We've two exits at street level. If they split up, I can't follow them both. Jim's the one in the uniform. He'll grab the other one as she leaves. And by the way—'

'Yes?'

'Buy that red blouse you're holding. The colour suits you.'

Jemma smiled and slipped away from her side as quietly as she'd arrived. Bobbie resumed her passive browsing and quiet observation.

Suddenly, there was a shriek that made the hairs on the back of her neck bristle. Several of the customers glanced over in alarm at the counter. Some hurried towards the accomplice, who was bent double over her swollen stomach.

'Madam!' exclaimed Rosa. 'Are you all right? Shall I get you a chair?'

Bobbie ignored the drama and slid over to watch her quarry's reflection in one of the strategically placed mirrors. Every muscle in her lean body tightened with expectation.

The elderly woman glanced round sharply. Satisfied no one was watching, she whipped a sequined evening gown off its hanger, shoved it into her bag, then walked briskly towards the stairs.

Bobbie waited a moment before following her down the broad staircase with its gilded handrails. There was no need to rush; she couldn't accost the thief until she'd left the store.

On the way out, she caught the eye of Mr Boyes, the floor walker, over the heads of the other shoppers and gave him a nod. He'd follow her and the shoplifter. But for the next few minutes she was on her own.

—

7

The cold wind slapped Bobbie in the face when she stepped outside into one of York's busiest shopping streets and weaved her way through the crowds in pursuit of the thief.

The woman was fifty yards down Parliament Street before Bobbie caught up with her. She forgot Jemma's warning and placed a firm hand on her right shoulder. 'Stop, thief!'

The woman swung round and threw a left hook at Bobbie's face. Bobbie dodged but the shoplifter wore a ring that caught the flesh of her brow bone. Ignoring the pain, Bobbie grabbed the woman's arm, twisted it behind her back and slammed her into the wall. She threw her weight onto the woman, trapping her against the building.

A nearby group of airmen let out a cheer. 'Go for it, lass!'

'She's a thief! For God's sake, help me!'

Her prisoner struggled and let out a string of expletives. Bobbie winced at the stench of her breath and pushed harder. Her right eye stung like hell and she was half blinded by tears and blood. She'd been taught how to break a suspect's little finger if they resisted arrest, but – even now – she hesitated to use this tactic.

She heard the sound of running feet. The next second, the strong arms of Mr Boyes reached out to assist her. 'Well done, Miss Baker!' A former amateur boxing champion, he made short work of hauling the shoplifter back to the store.

Bobbie fumbled in her coat pocket for her handkerchief. 'Thanks for your help, lads,' she snapped sarcastically at the laughing airmen.

Breathing heavily and still fired up with excitement from the chase, she covered her eye with her handkerchief and followed her colleague back to Grainger's. There'd be a nice little bonus in her pay packet tonight.

Jemma stood by the entrance, her thin face flushed with anxiety. 'Your doorman got her accomplice. He's already taken her to the manager's office.'

Bobbie hesitated beside Jemma. 'I've got to go, too.'

'I know you have.' Jemma handed her a clean handkerchief. 'You'll have a nasty shiner tomorrow. I was worried about you.'

Bobbie took the handkerchief gratefully and dabbed at her brow bone. 'You know you shouldn't be. Born under the lucky Baker star, I was. How did you know I worked here?'

'Gabriel told me.'

Bobbie nodded. 'We work closely with the police. I took a young lad to the station two weeks ago and Gabriel told me you'd come home. I wanted to get in touch with you back then...'

'I know. I'm sorry, Bobbie – I should have contacted you sooner. But there's been so much to sort out. I... I needed time to adjust.' Her voice trailed away.

'I'm so sorry about what happened to Michael.'

Jemma recoiled slightly, before nodding.

'Look, I finish my shift at five o'clock,' Bobbie continued. 'Shall we get some tea and cake at Barton's?'

Jemma smiled. 'That'd be lovely. I'll meet you there.'

'And thanks, Jemma – I couldn't have done this without your help.'

'My pleasure.'

Bobbie squeezed her arm affectionately as she turned to go. 'We always were a great team.'

Chapter Two

Like many of the buildings in the centre of York, Barton's Tea Rooms was centuries old. It sagged in the middle and was only held up by its neighbours. Inside, the walls tilted and the uneven wooden floor sloped but it was comfortable and cosy, with well-spaced tables and discreet waitresses in black uniforms and crisp white aprons who glided effortlessly between the customers. Large potted ferns and aspidistras added a little extra privacy, one of the reasons it had become the women's favourite café.

Jemma was reading the 'Jobs for Women' section in the latest edition of the *Yorkshire Evening Press* when Bobbie joined her.

Despite a full day on her feet, and the nasty bruise around her eye, Bobbie looked full of energy and rather stylish. Her black hat was set at a cheeky angle over her thick dark hair, which, as usual, was trying to escape from its pins.

'I know we said tea and cake, but do you mind if I order a steak and kidney pie?' Bobbie asked, once they'd greeted each other. 'I got a nice little bonus thanks to catching those shoplifters and Mum's served us some dubious meals recently. I'm sure most of it's horsemeat.'

Jemma smiled. 'Of course, but I'll just have tea and a bun. I'm cooking for Gabriel later.' She closed the newspaper, but Bobbie had already seen the page.

'Are you looking for a job?'

'Yes – and I see Terry's are recruiting female workers.'

'Aircraft propellers.'

'Pardon?'

'Terry's have adapted part of their factory to make aircraft propellers.'

'Good gracious! Don't they make chocolate anymore?'

'Only for the troops and prisoners of war. There's not enough sugar. That's why the rest of us are eating turnips. If you don't fancy propellers, Cooke, Troughton and Simms now make tank periscopes.'

Jemma laughed and put the newspaper in her bag.

'There's always Rowntree's,' Bobbie suggested. 'I'm sure they'd welcome you back with open arms.' After she'd left school, Jemma had done a year at secretarial college before joining the confectionery company's typing pool. She was working there when she met Michael.

Jemma shook her head. 'Gabriel advised against it. Things have changed. Not everyone knows this, but they've converted the gum department in the Smarties block and they—'

The waitress arrived to take their order and both women fell silent. Careless talk cost lives.

'What were you saying?' Bobbie asked once the girl had left.

'They make fuses for landmines and pack shells with explosives.'

Bobbie snorted. 'Whoa! I thought some of their workers were turning a bit yellow. Seriously, though, apart from the explosion risk, it'll make the factory a prime target for the Jerries.'

'Exactly. I'd rather work somewhere else.'

'Do you need to work?' Bobbie asked awkwardly. 'Didn't Michael leave you… you know, *provided for*?'

Jemma swallowed hard. 'I'll be eligible to claim a war widows' pension in six months. Michael's pay from the RAF stopped almost immediately.'

Bobbie frowned. 'What are you supposed to live on for six months?'

Jemma shrugged. 'My savings, I suppose. It was hard running the electrical store without Michael. The most profitable part of the business was always the wireless repairs and Michael did those. The apprentice and I kept the store ticking over but once the… the telegram came, we knew there was no point in carrying on.' She paused for a moment and Bobbie reached across the table to squeeze her hand. 'Closing down the business we'd built together and packing up our home to return to York tore another piece off my broken heart. It felt like failure; I'd let him down.'

'You had no choice, Jemma,' Bobbie murmured. 'It's this bloody war...'

Jemma shook off the tears. 'My parents-in-law have given me a small allowance.'

'That was kind of them.'

'They said it's what Michael would have wanted and it's part of his share of the family business, but it'll stop... if... I marry again.' She struggled once more to control the emotion in her voice.

'I see. I'm sorry, Jemma, I shouldn't have asked.'

'No, no, it's fine.' It wasn't fine but she knew she'd have to get used to talking about Michael without dissolving into tears every two minutes.

The waitress reappeared with their teapot and crockery on a tray. Bobbie's face lit up at the sight of the sugar bowl. She grabbed the silver tongs, helped herself to five of the precious lumps, and placed them in the saucer beside her teacup.

The waitress humphed and disappeared, taking the sugar bowl with her.

As soon as she'd gone, Bobbie dropped one lump in her tea, scooped up the rest and hid them in her bag.

Jemma smiled. 'I didn't know you took sugar in your tea.'

'Oh, I do when I can get it. I need the energy.'

'I'm not surprised after what I saw today. Do you enjoy your job, Bobbie? I was surprised to hear you'd left the library.' Bobbie had started work at York City Library the week after they left school and, despite the old dragon who ran the place, she'd loved the job. 'Weren't you saving up to take a night-school course at the college to become a qualified librarian?'

Bobbie avoided her last question. 'Yes, Grainger's is good on days like today. But most of the time, it's dull work – and badly paid. I get half the wages of the male store detective and it's boring. Did you buy that red blouse, by the way? It'll go well with your navy suit – although I do think you need to shorten the skirt a little to bring it into the 1940s.'

Jemma smiled. Bobbie had always been the more fashionable of the two of them. Jemma's suit was good quality, and the dark, pleated skirt emphasised her slender figure, but Bobbie was right; it was far too long. 'Why did you leave your job at the library?' she asked again. 'I thought you loved it there.'

Bobbie lowered her voice. 'I guess Gabriel didn't tell you about my father's disgrace?'

Jemma frowned and shook her head.

'The Quaker Queen and I had a few disagreements after my dad got himself thrown into Armley Gaol in Leeds for three months last winter.'

Jemma nearly dropped her teacup. '*What?*'

'You know my dad worked at the carriage works?'

'Yes. He was a trade union leader, wasn't he?'

Bobbie nodded. 'Well, they were agitating for a pay rise and threatening to strike. Things got a bit heated during one discussion and "Big Bill" Baker – who'd had a barrel of drink that day – hit one of the managers.'

'Good grief!'

'Not only did he lose his job, but he also got three months for assault. He's been drinking far too much since our Frank signed up for the army.'

'Oh, I'm sorry, Bobbie. Your father was always such a passionate man – especially about workers' rights.'

'There's other words for it,' Bobbie said darkly. 'Anyway, he's had trouble finding work ever since.'

'But how did this affect you? You weren't involved.'

'Oh, you know what a small, gossipy place York is,' Bobbie said. 'The Quaker Queen soon got wind of my father's disgrace and decided she

---

14

didn't want to work with the daughter of a convicted criminal. She made my life unbearable.'

'So, you ended up at Grainger's as a store detective?'

'Yes. They're not too fussy. I think they work on the principle that it takes a thief to catch a thief.'

'But you're not a thief – and neither is your father!'

'Well, criminal then.'

'It's such a shame, Bobbie, I know how much that job meant to you.' Jemma stared at her tea thoughtfully. 'We both seem to be at a crossroads in our lives.'

Their food arrived, and while Jemma picked at her cake, Bobbie fell on her pie like a woman starved. 'I don't know where they get this meat from,' she muttered between mouthfuls, 'but it's the real thing. The pastry's melting in my mouth. You should set up your own business, Jemma,' she added suddenly.

Jemma paused with her cake fork halfway to her mouth. 'Me? Set up my own business? Doing what?'

'Whatever you fancy.' Bobbie licked gravy from her lips. 'You've got the experience now. I bet you know all about invoicing, stock control, advertising – and selling. You must know how to do it better than anyone.'

'Women don't run their own businesses.'

'That's your sister talking, not you. It's wartime – we women now do everything the men once did. All it takes is a bit of money to set yourself up. How much do you have in savings?'

'I still have my inheritance from my father. Michael wouldn't touch it. He said it was up to a man to provide for his wife and I was to save my own money and treat myself. His family set up the store for us.'

'Good, so you've got a bit of capital.'

'Running my own business would be fun. I'm used to being my own boss, and don't want to take orders from someone else. But what would I do, Bobbie? I don't have any skills apart from a bit of typing.'

'Oh yes you do.' Bobbie stopped eating and a strange gleam settled in her dark eyes. 'I know this is crazy,' she said slowly, 'but we've talked about it before. Do you remember when we wanted to start our own detective agency called Smoke & Cracked Mirrors? You should start your own agency – just like Patricia Wentworth's Miss Silver – and I'll join you.'

Jemma's smile broadened. 'That's fiction, Bobbie. In real life, women don't run private detective agencies.'

'Yes, they *do*. Come to the library on Monday afternoon and I'll introduce you to a woman who did. Monday's my afternoon off. I'll meet you at one o'clock.'

Jemma felt a strange flicker of excitement. Then her common sense sat on it. 'I have no idea how to run a detective agency.'

'Again – meet me in the library on Monday and I'll give you a reference book that'll tell you everything you need to know about becoming a PI.'

Jemma smiled. 'Are you *seriously* suggesting this should be my new career?'

'Well, if you'll have me beside you – I was rather hoping it could be *our* new career. You have the skills, Jemma. There's no one on this planet more observant – or clever – than you.'

'Apart from you,' Jemma murmured.

Bobbie shook her head. 'We need to work together. Look what happened today. I'd have only collared one of those thieves if you hadn't been there. We've always been a good team. You've got the business skills to launch an agency and it's time to put those little observation tricks your dad taught you to good use.'

—

16

'You're very persuasive. I'm intrigued. All right, I'll come – though God knows what Michael will say—' She dropped her fork with a clatter on her plate and in her rush to retrieve it almost knocked over the milk jug. 'I'm… I'm sorry… I don't know why I said that.'

Bobbie put down her knife, reached across the table and took Jemma's hand in her own again. They sat quietly for a moment.

'It'll take time, love,' Bobbie said softly. 'It must have been awful when you got that telegram.'

'It was – is.' Jemma paused for a moment to collect herself.

'How are you coping – *really*?'

Jemma swallowed hard. 'I don't cry every five minutes anymore – but some days I just don't want to get out of bed. Even dressing myself is a chore. And it's the anger, Bobbie, that worries me the most. Why am I so damned angry with the world – and sometimes with poor Michael?'

'I think that's the grief, Jemma.'

Jemma withdrew her hand and fumbled in her bag for her handkerchief. She was losing her battle against tears again.

'I'm afraid I used your hankie this morning to mop up the blood,' Bobbie reminded her. 'Here, take a napkin.'

Jemma gave her a watery smile, sniffed back the tears and declined the use of the table linen. 'I'm sorry, Bobbie. Sometimes it gets to me.'

'That's only natural, and you don't need to apologise to me – ever. If you want to talk about it, just go ahead. What happened to Michael was tragic.'

Jemma took a huge breath. 'You say "*what happened to Michael*". Sometimes I think if I knew what actually happened, I would accept it more easily.'

Bobbie grimaced and frowned. 'Didn't his senior officer tell you anything?'

17

'No. There was a name – Flight Sergeant Rodgers – on the telegram, but it happened in the middle of that terrible snowstorm in January. Half the telegraph poles were down between here and London, and most of the railway lines were blocked.'

'Yes, last winter was awful here, too.'

'When Gabriel finally got through on the telephone, Flight Sergeant Rodgers was unavailable – and the second time he tried, some woman informed him Rodgers had just been deployed on active service. The thing is, Bobbie, I don't even know where... the incident... happened.'

'Didn't the telegram...?'

'It just said he was *missing in action, presumed dead* – but he hadn't even left Britain. He was an RAF wireless mechanic – not a soldier. He'd only just finished his training and was down south somewhere. How do you go *missing in action* in England?'

Bobbie frowned. 'How do you know he didn't leave the country? Our Frank is in France, but we only know this because he managed to grab some leave before he was deployed and came home and told us.'

'Michael kept me informed where he was in his letters.'

'How did he do that? What about the censors?'

'We bypassed them. We had our own special code. We'd already worked it out between us before he joined the RAF.'

Bobbie chuckled. 'Of course, you did. I shouldn't have expected anything less from you two.'

'In one letter, he wrote *the midges are biting tonight*, which meant Scotland. In another, he told me he hoped to get a posting near York: *How is kindly Uncle Ebor? I hope to see him again soon.*'

Bobbie reached out and took hold of Jemma's hand again. 'Ebor? Oh, from Eboracum.'

18

Jemma slowed down; she felt calmer now. 'We didn't think the censors would be familiar with the Roman name for York.'

'No matter how painful it is,' Bobbie said gently, 'I think you should try again to find out what happened to Michael. You won't get any peace or be able to lay him to rest in your heart until you know the truth.'

Jemma said nothing and a moment later Bobbie's eyebrows shot up in shock.

'Oh, my God, Jemma. You don't think he's dead, do you?'

'No,' Jemma admitted. 'I don't know why, but I still think Michael is alive.'

Chapter Three

When they parted, Jemma went to catch her bus and Bobbie ambled across Lendal Bridge, trailing her gloved hand over the ornate metal parapet. Ignoring the drizzle, she paused for a moment at the centre and peered down into the swollen, heaving brown river to check its level. They'd had a lot of rain recently and everyone who lived close to the banks of the Ouse lived in dread of it flooding.

She took a moment to collect her thoughts and recap on the events of the day, which she had to admit was one of the most exciting she'd known for a while.

It was good to have Jemma back in her life, but Bobbie was concerned about her friend. Jemma's blonde, almost white, hair had lost some of its lustre and there were dark shadows below her pale-blue eyes. Shadows that didn't belong on the face of a twenty-two-year-old. Jemma's admission that she still harboured the hope Michael had survived was also worrying.

Bobbie knew first-hand the dangers of false hope. Her own mother had lost her twin brother in the carnage of the Somme in 1916 and had never accepted his death. By now, Jemma should have begun to come to terms with the loss of Michael, but she clearly hadn't.

Perhaps a distraction would help? Jemma needed a new project that would stimulate her quick and intelligent mind. They both did.

But was a private detective agency really the answer? Bobbie hadn't expected to be taken seriously when she'd first mentioned their childhood yearning to set up their own agency. It had been idle chatter, a nostalgic look back at a time when they'd shared an adolescent dream. But this crazy idea had now taken root, sprouted, and refused to wither and die.

They could make this work. She knew they could.

21

She experienced a twinge of guilt when she remembered how susceptible Jemma was to persuasion. But they were adults now and Jemma had seen and experienced more of the world than she had.

Sighing, Bobbie tore herself away from the mesmerising flow of the water and continued her walk home.

She'd show Jemma the O'Sullivan book and the magazine articles on Monday and let her think it over. Jemma could always say 'no'. If she did, then that was that. There was no way Bobbie would be able to set up the agency on her own. She didn't have a spare penny to her name, for a start.

She strolled down Tanner's Moat, past the old cocoa works. Rowntree's had moved their production to the new Haxby Road site and the tall, smoke-blackened building beside her was silently awaiting demolition. She missed the sweet smell of chocolate that used to waft around this area when the factory was operational. It had masked the stench of the river, the smell of smoke and soot from the railway station and the pervasive odour of damp.

A plane droned overhead, invisible behind the clouds. Bobbie glanced up nervously.

So far, the war had barely touched York. In fact, it hadn't really touched the rest of the country either, and some newspaper journalists were calling it the 'phoney war'. But it had changed all their lives, and everyone knew it was only a matter of time before the Luftwaffe found York.

Her neighbour, 'Little' Laurie Tipton, scurried up the road towards her in his emerald green and gold-braided hotel uniform. The trousers were a bit too long for him, she noticed. A couple of years older than her, Laurie was simple-minded and had some sort of condition that had stunted his growth, leaving him the height of an eleven-year-old. But he was a cheerful chappie, with a friendly word for everyone. He operated the lifts in the

Royal Station Hotel, a job he adored. He also, she remembered, had quite a crush on Jemma.

'Good evening, Laurie. How's your mother?'

His plain round face erupted into a huge grin. 'She's in fine fettle, Bobbie, fine fettle. A little put out by all the shortages, though.'

'Aren't we all.'

'That's quite a shiner, Bobbie. Did your dad give it to you?'

She smiled and touched her eye. The swelling had receded, but it was throbbing again. She needed another aspirin – and a mirror to inspect the damage. 'I banged it on a door at work. It's nothing.'

'It might put the fellahs off, though, if you go out dancin' tonight. Are you goin' out dancin' tonight, Bobbie?'

'Probably not. I don't want to frighten the troops – they've got a war to win.'

Laurie laughed. 'Talking of troops, I met old Ma Quigley the other day. She said their Vince were comin' home soon on leave. Not that she'll see much of him, though. He'll spend all his time with his miserable wife out in Acomb.'

'Mrs Quigley called her daughter-in-law miserable?' Bobbie was genuinely shocked.

'Oh, yes. She said he shouldn't have married her. He should have married you instead. Is that right, Bobbie? Should Vince have married you?'

'Yes, he should have.' The words were out of her mouth before she realised what she'd said.

But Laurie wasn't one to sustain a conversation for long. 'Well, I've got to go, Bobbie – I mustn't be late for work.' He puffed out his chest. 'We've some very important people stayin' at the hotel this week. They might need my help.'

'I'm sure they will. See you later, Laurie.'

She paused for a moment, trying to calm herself. It was annoying how the mere mention of Vince's name still had the power to set her heart racing and make her face flush.

Turning the corner of the street, she bumped into their rent man – an encounter guaranteed to bring any lovelorn fool back down to earth with a bang.

A burly man with long, lank, greasy hair, he had a permanent scowl that revealed his tobacco-stained teeth. 'I were just comin' t' your house. Your ma's two weeks behind wi' t' rent. She'd better have it ready.'

Bobbie's heart sank; she hated this constant lurching through poverty. Her father rarely contributed anything to the household these days and still drank too much. Her mum did two cleaning jobs to keep the roof over their heads. Frank sent home money out of his army pay and Bobbie handed over most of her wages, but there never seemed to be enough.

She reached for her purse. 'I can save you the trouble of calling round. I've just been paid; I can give you one week's money.'

'She owes me two.'

Bobbie started to replace the purse in her bag. 'Oh, fair enough. I just thought I'd save you a trip.'

He hesitated, then held out a grimy hand. 'I'll tek it. Hand it over.'

Reluctantly, she counted out the coins. 'Can you tell the landlord the roof's leaking again in the back bedroom?'

'Tell him yerself when you pay the rest you owe.'

Sighing, Bobbie quickened her step, desperately hoped her father hadn't raided her mother's battered old savings jug on the mantelpiece and gone out drinking again with the rent money.

Lost in thought, Jemma heard the clattering bus arrive before she saw it.

—

Resplendent in its maroon, yellow and cream livery, its sleek outline was spoilt by the ugly blackout shades attached to its headlights, which emitted a paltry beam.

There was only one free seat available, next to a long-faced man in a short tweed jacket and shapeless and stained flannel trousers. She accidently hit him with her gas mask as she sat down, but he ignored her apology and continued to glare out of the window.

There was a hardness about the set of his square jaw. He had untidy sandy hair and a short-clipped moustache. A faded scar ran through his right eyebrow. *A trophy from a brawl, perhaps – or the legacy of an accident?*

The collar of his check shirt was frayed and the tie carelessly knotted. It was difficult to know if his unkempt appearance was due to negligence or poverty, but the gleaming black leather camera case slung on a strap round his neck suggested the former rather than the latter.

The word *Leica* was embossed in the smooth leather. Leicas weren't cheap. She knew this because they'd sold them in the store in Middlesbrough. Jemma wondered how the owner of a Leica could be so miserable.

Perhaps it was stolen? One thing she'd learnt from Gabriel over the past few weeks was that the criminal element of the city had been slow to sign up for the armed forces since the onset of war; there were still plenty of them at large in York.

Out of the corner of her eye, she watched the man stroke the camera case in his lap with the tenderness of a lover, and noticed his fingers were stained dark with chemicals. She relaxed. He did his own developing; the camera was his.

She settled back and her attention shifted to the neatly rolled and pleated hair of the woman in the seat in front. She fingered her own soft curls and wondered if she dared copy this style. Ever since that incident when the school bully, Kathleen Young, had taunted her about her old-fashioned braids, she'd lacked confidence about changing her hairstyle.

Jemma had suffered badly from the loss of her mother when she was eleven and her father had decided the local state school was too rough for his shy, grieving and bookish daughter. He'd scraped together the money to send her to Miss Colbeck's School for Young Ladies, but her odd little ways and acute observational skills made the other girls wary. She'd found it difficult to make friends and had become the prime target for the vicious bullying of Kathleen Young and her cronies. Those first few weeks at her new school were hell, until Bobbie discovered her sobbing in the cloakroom after school. As the much derided 'scholarship girl', Bobbie had problems of her own, but she immediately took Jemma under her wing. That night, she escorted Jemma home and persuaded her bewildered father to let Jemma have her hair cropped into the stylish bob favoured by other girls her age.

Looking back as an adult, Jemma knew her elderly father had struggled with the responsibility of rearing a young girl alone, but he'd done his best. Her sister, Cecily, had already married and moved away, so he didn't receive much help from that quarter. Gabriel was always there, of course, but he only had time for his motorbikes.

The two girls became firm friends after this, and Kathleen and her chums backed off once the feisty Bobbie became Jemma's constant companion.

At the next stop, a large woman boarded the vehicle and lurched down the central aisle, distracting Jemma from her thoughts. At first Jemma thought she was drunk, but the woman's face was contorted with grief, not alcohol. She threw herself down into the now vacant double seat a couple of rows behind Jemma, put her head in her hands and burst into tears.

Her loud, ugly sobs drowned out the noisy rumbling of the vehicle's engine. The passengers fell silent and shuffled uncomfortably in their seats. Even the man beside Jemma turned his head to stare.

Another woman crossed the aisle and sat down next to the grief-stricken matron, encircling her shoulders in a comforting arm. 'There, there, love. What's the matter?'

'It's... it's my – my Dennis,' the sobbing woman stuttered. 'He's dead.'

'Ah, bless you, love. I'm so sorry. Were 'e in the Green Howards or the West Yorkshire Regiment?'

The distraught woman's reply was lost in another torrent of tears.

The man beside Jemma cursed under his breath. 'This damned war. That bloody Hitler has a lot to answer for.'

Jemma stiffened and nodded her head.

'Another poor bastard murdered by the Jerries,' he continued. 'Have you seen the length of the latest casualty list in the paper?'

'Yes. I read two newspapers every night.'

'Well, it's shockin' – that's what it is! Shockin'! And this is only the bloody start. God only knows how many poor sods like her Dennis will have to die before it's over.'

Jemma cleared her throat and braced herself. People rarely liked it when she corrected them. 'Actually, I don't think Dennis is a man.'

A pair of intelligent hazel eyes bored into her face. 'You what?'

'I think Dennis is – or was – her dog.'

His forehead puckered with confusion.

'Her coat is flecked with the short, wiry hairs of a terrier,' she continued hastily. 'I caught a whiff of ether and carbolic when she staggered past. She also has a circular lump in her coat pocket, which might be a coiled dog lead.'

'Ether?'

27

'Yes, it's an anaesthetic. My brother-in-law's veterinary surgery in Boroughbridge stinks of it. I think she's just returned from the vets after euthanising her pet. But you're right about one thing,' she added graciously, 'the Germans are to blame. My brother-in-law told us that thousands of people across the country are having their pets euthanised because they can't feed them anymore because of the rationing.'

He grimaced, then a smile spread across his lean face. 'You're a proper little Miss Marple, aren't you?'

Jemma's eyebrows twitched. She hadn't put him down as a book lover. 'Are you familiar with *The Murder in the Vicarage*?'

He never batted an eyelid. 'No, you can't lay that one at my door. I once filched a bar of chocolate from Woolies but I ain't never done in no vicars.'

Jemma tried to keep a straight face. 'But you know of Miss Marple?'

'Oh, everyone's heard of her, haven't they? She's some fussy biddy of a detective made up by that crime writer, Sherlock Holmes.'

Her mouth twitched with amusement. 'Of course, she is.'

'Come to think of it,' the fellow continued. 'You might not be Miss Marple – but your face is familiar. I never forget a face, me. Ain't I seen you down the nick on Clifford Street?' She saw his eyes flash upwards and to his left. He was trying to recall his memory of her.

'Yes, possibly. But what were you doing in the police station, Mr—?'

'Wilde, Ricky Wilde.'

'You weren't found loitering by the confectionery counter at Woolworths again and arrested, were you?'

He laughed. 'No chance! I had some official business to conduct. It were last Thursday.' He turned to her again with a quizzical expression. 'What were *you* doin' there?'

'I popped in to give my brother something. He works there.'

'Your brother's a copper? So, you're not a lady detective then?'

28

Jemma gave a short, hollow laugh. 'The chance would be a fine thing.'

'Aren't our boys in blue at York City Police keen on female sleuths?'

She remembered Gabriel telling her about the day the female leader of the Watch Committee tried to persuade York City Police they should recruit female police officers to replace the men who'd signed up. Apparently, Desk Sergeant Ackroyd had stormed into Chief Constable Herman's office, shouting that women were nothing but trouble in a police station and the rot would set in if they were let through the door.

'I think hell would have to freeze over before they'd employ women police officers,' she murmured.

Wilde laughed and jabbed his right index finger in her direction. 'I've got it. I should have seen the resemblance straight away. You're Gabe Roxby's little sister, ain't you?'

'Yes, I'm Inspector Roxby's sister – although perhaps not so little these days.'

'I'm surprised I didn't spot the likeness straight sooner,' he continued. 'You've got the same big blue eyes. Although yours are softer – he's got a glint of granite in his. He's a grizzled old git these days.'

Smiling, Jemma gathered up her basket and gas mask, ready to depart. 'In his defence, Gabriel is a lot older than me – but I'll pass on your observations to him tonight over supper, Mr Wilde.'

He laughed. 'You do that, Miss Roxby. And when he bangs me up in a cell for the insult, you can sneak me in a file hidden in a loaf of bread to saw my way out through the bars at the window.'

Jemma hesitated. 'My name's not Miss Roxby anymore. I'm Mrs James. Mrs Jemima James – but everyone calls me Jemma.'

'I prefer Miss Marple,' he said with a wink. 'So, where's your husband, lass? Why are you living with Old Gabe and makin' his supper?'

Her throat caught for a second, but her reply was steady. 'He's missing in action.'

'I'm sorry to hear that, love.' It was the pat response, but something in the soft tone of his voice and his steady gaze told her he meant it. Despite his rough edge and moodiness, this man had compassion.

'Thank you. But please excuse me – this is my stop.' She stood up and braced herself to walk down the swaying vehicle.

'Give my regards to old Gabe,' he called after her.

'I will do.' She turned back after a few steps. 'By the way, that's a wonderful camera, Mr Wilde. Is it a Leica II model?'

He laughed again and hugged the leather case to his breast. 'Sure is, Miss Marple. She's my pride and joy. Got the interchangeable lenses to go with it, too. York City Police don't know what they're missin' not having you in their ranks. I'll tell that to old Gabe next time I see him.'

Jemma was still smiling when she stepped off the bus.

Chapter Four

Jemma called into The Grey Mare, the Clifton Green village pub, on her way home, to buy Gabriel a couple of bottles of pale ale to have with his supper.

She was served over the counter by the red-headed barmaid, Maisie Langford. A few years older than Gabriel, Maisie had lost her husband in the last war. She'd brought up her baby son on her own and had never married again.

Maisie passed on her condolences as she handed over the ale, and when she saw Jemma tense and struggle to reply, she added: 'Don't worry, love. It gets easier with time.'

I suppose she'd know, Jemma thought as she trudged back to the dark cottage. *I'll have to get used to all this sympathy from virtual strangers.*

She left her shopping by the door and fumbled around with the blackout curtains before switching on the light. She sighed when she saw the familiar, well-worn furnishings and her mother's much loved mantelpiece ornaments.

Gabriel hadn't altered a thing since their father died last autumn. In fact, her father hadn't altered a thing when her mother died twelve years ago, either. The cottage was still furnished exactly the same as the day their mother breathed her last. Yes, it was comfortable and cosy – and kept scrupulously clean – but the curtains, rugs and carpets were faded and threadbare and the upholstered furniture sagged.

And it wasn't hers.

Everything she and Michael owned, including their piano, was in storage above Michael's uncle's shop in York. When they were first married, she'd done her best to make a nice home for the two of them in the flat in Middlesbrough. Most of what they had was second-hand, but she'd introduced some small modern pieces into their home – and it had been *theirs*.

Sighing again, she fetched her shopping from the front door and picked up the letters from the doormat. Two of them were for her and the first was addressed in her mother-in-law's handwriting with its occasional lapse into Cyrillic script.

She went into the kitchen, lit the fire and started the supper before settling down with a cup of tea to read her post. But the contents of Sofia's letter soon wiped the smile from her face.

The James family business was struggling. Their wireless repair shops in both Leeds and York had been vandalised several times; windows had been broken and slogans like *Go home, aliens* daubed across their windows at night. Their competitors had capitalised on the prejudice and spread vile rumours about their family, which had affected trade. *We very healthy are*, Sofia reassured her, *but no longer can we send monies*.

Jemma was more indignant about the harassment than disappointed about the cessation of her allowance. There was no one in Britain more anti-German than her parents-in-law.

She was particularly worried about Uncle Ivan, who ran the York branch of the business. A huge, hairy man with a twinkle in his eye and a kindly word and a joke for everyone, he was Jemma's favourite in-law.

She didn't recognise the handwriting on her second letter but the hand that had written it had been heavy, probably a man's.

It wasn't. It was a short terse note from her former landlady in Middlesbrough, informing her the bailiffs had been round, asking after Michael. In addition to that, the angry woman continued, they didn't believe her when she told them Mr and Mrs James no longer lived there and he'd been killed in action. Apparently, these dubious characters had cast covetous glances over her shoulder, as if eyeing up the value of *her own* furniture to pay off Michael's debt.

Debt? What debt?

Jemma read it again. Three men in dark coats and hats. Burly fellows, very ugly. Obviously bailiffs, the landlady reckoned. She had seen their type before. She had believed Michael and Jemma were a nice young couple – but not any longer. She didn't appreciate being put in this position.

The smell of burning made Jemma's nose twitch in alarm. Tossing the landlady's letter down on the table, she dashed to the oven to rescue her pie.

This was ridiculous! *Bailiffs?* She and Michael had only borrowed money from his family to stock the store. There must be some mistake. She'd telephone the outraged woman tomorrow and put her right.

She heard the front door open, and Gabriel came down the hallway and into the kitchen. He sank wearily into one of the faded old armchairs in front of the fire, removed his cap and scratched his head of curly white hair. 'Evening, Jemma.' Six foot three in his socks, Gabriel was nineteen years her senior. But some days he looked older than his forty-two years.

'Good evening, Gabriel. Have you had a good day?' She glanced at his long, lean face, looking for signs of exhaustion and trying to read his mood. Today there was a glimmer of excitement in those pale-blue eyes.

'It's been a long day, but at least we got to do some proper police work rather than clearing up the carnage after motor accidents caused by the blackout.'

'Oh? What happened?' She hung his cap on the hook, cleared the rest of the table and lifted down two plates from the old wooden dresser.

'We think we might have caught all the members of a gang who've been pilfering from the railway goods yard. One of them's offered up the rest in exchange for immunity from prosecution.'

33

'There's no honour among thieves.' Jemma drained the vegetables and wondered what ordinary people, not connected with the police force, talked about in an evening. Her father had been a police officer too, although he'd never reached the rank of inspector. 'Wash your hands. Supper's ready.'

Gabriel sat down, sniffing suspiciously at his food. 'What is it?

'It's a new recipe I found, sausage and bean pie.'

'Sausages *again*?'

'It's all they had in at the butchers.' She gazed sadly at the blackened rim of her pie. 'Unfortunately, I left it in a bit too long and the crust has caught.'

'I'm sure it'll still be delicious, although I think we'll start to look like sausages soon if we eat any more of them. Wasn't there any bacon?'

'No. Sorry.'

'Huh! The Vale of York and Malton are the biggest producers of pork in the damned country, but we haven't seen a slice of bacon for weeks now. I miss bacon for breakfast.'

'There's a new pot of dripping and fresh bread for tomorrow,' she said cheerfully. 'Anyway, I've some good news about food. Cissy telephoned this morning. She's got a side of beef – and we're invited to Sunday lunch with her and Gerald.' There was never a shortage of food in her sister and brother-in-law's home. Jemma suspected many of Gerald's farmers paid him in meat for his veterinary services.

Gabriel beamed with delight. 'Good old Cissy!' He tucked into the charred pie with relish, and she smiled. Despite his grumbling, her brother was very tolerant of her domestic shortcomings.

'We can use a few of the petrol coupons and go to Boroughbridge on the Vincent Rapide,' he said. 'What do you say to that idea?'

There was a lot Jemma might have said about the prospect of belting through the Vale of York on a chilly March day, balanced precariously on the back of her brother's motorbike. But his enthusiasm was infectious, and

—

she just smiled. 'I met an old acquaintance of yours today, by the way. A photographer, I think – called Ricky Wilde.'

Gabriel's face changed in a flash. 'Wilde? How did you meet that spiv?'

Surprised at his annoyance, she explained about her bus journey into town. 'He seemed a pleasant enough chap,' she commented.

'He's a police informer, Jemma. A grass. He keeps some dubious company, does Ricky Wilde.'

'Ah, well, he didn't mention that.'

'He wouldn't.'

'There's some treacle tart left over from yesterday. Do you want me to heat up some custard?'

After their meal, Jemma went upstairs to her room, changed into her nightdress and dressing gown and came back down with her suit skirt and her sewing box. They sat for a while by the fireside. While Gabriel guffawed with laughter at a comedy show on the wireless, she picked the stiches out of the waistband of the skirt and began to shorten it.

After the show finished, Gabriel went out to enjoy last orders in The Grey Mare.

Finally, alone, Jemma's mind returned to the two letters she'd received.

Sofia's letter confirmed what she'd known for a while. Her period of bereavement was over. She'd have to stop moping, pull herself together and get a proper full-time job. The distraction would do her good.

The note from her former landlady was more puzzling and she reminded herself to telephone the woman tomorrow.

Yawning, Jemma dampened down the fire and wearily climbed up the two flights of stairs to her attic bedroom.

The moonlight was peeking through a chink in the curtains. Conscious of the blackout, she switched off the light, picked up her hairbrush and

---

walked over to the window. A sudden impulse made her pull back the curtains and peer out over the silent village green.

The moon rode serenely through the cloudless, black velvet sky, beside a million blazing stars. There would be a frost tonight. She picked out the silhouette of the tiled canopy built over the old horse trough and the shadow of the hatted man standing next to it.

While she brushed her hair, she muttered the silly old rhyme her mother had taught her: *Moon, moon burning bright, Turn my hair silver white.* As a child, she's always assumed this fanciful bedtime ritual was the reason for her pale blonde hair.

The man by the water trough seemed to be staring in the direction of their house. She knew it was nearly closing time at The Grey Mare and the customers were drifting home. *Was he waiting for someone?*

Then the air was rent with a piercing, screeching wail that made her hands jerk and drop the brush.

Grabbing her thick woolly socks and a sweater from a drawer, she pulled them on and hauled a pair of flannel slacks over her nightdress.

Gabriel burst through the front door. 'Jemma! Air raid!'

She flew down the stairs. 'I'm here.'

'Get your wellington boots,' he yelled. 'The Anderson's flooded again.'

Two minutes later, carrying spare blankets and the flask of Rowntree's cocoa she'd made earlier in the evening, they trudged outside to their bomb shelter at the bottom of the garden.

Chapter Five

Jemma walked to her meeting with Bobbie through her favourite part of the city; the leafy, tree-lined Minster Quarter, dominated by the towering twelfth-century Gothic cathedral. The deep chime of the clock bells seemed to be welcoming her back and yellow daffodils danced beneath the ancient oaks. She felt a familiar tingle of excitement as she approached the elegant art deco library and she smiled at the memory of the hours she and Bobbie had spent here as schoolgirls. They'd shared a fanatical love of crime stories and had a favourite table upstairs in the newspaper reading room. Here, they could avoid the disapproving glare of the head librarian – or 'The Queen of the Quakers', as Bobbie had nicknamed Miss Oates – while they read, giggled and exchanged whispered comments about their stories.

She was a few minutes early and made a beeline for the fiction section to choose a new book. Daylight poured into the room from the octagonal skylights in the high plaster ceiling. The Quaker Queen was still a fixture, Jemma noted. Dressed head-to-toe in grey, with her hair scaped into a tight bun, the head librarian stood behind the vast desk, date-stamping a customer's books with her customary frown.

Jemma turned back to the shelves of crime stories and gave a little gasp of excitement when she saw *Sad Cypress*, the latest Hercule Poirot mystery from the pen of her beloved Agatha. Then she remembered how difficult she found it to concentrate on full-length novels and reluctantly pulled out an anthology called *My Best Mystery Story* instead. She read in the contents that E. Charles Vivian, another of her favourite authors, had contributed a short story, which was a consolation. She'd come back for *Sad Cypress* when she felt better.

Jemma settled in one of the curved wooden chairs at their favourite table and waited for Bobbie. The only other person in the reading room was a plump middle-aged woman at the next table, dressed in a checked wool coat and an old-fashioned green felt hat.

When Bobbie arrived, she dumped an old book and a pile of magazines on the table, then took off her coat and slid into a chair. 'How was your weekend? You've got some colour in your cheeks today.'

Jemma smiled. 'That's windburn, Bobbie. Cissy and Gerald invited us for Sunday lunch and Gabriel insisted we went to Boroughbridge on his motorbike. The rest of me is still frozen and vibrating.'

Bobbie laughed. She wore a short-sleeved cardigan over a print tea dress and exuded an air of elegant, if slightly faded, understatement. Her sturdy lace-up brogues didn't enhance the outfit but were a sensible choice for a woman who'd been on her feet all morning.

'So, how was lunch at the vets?'

'Oh, the usual. Gabriel and Gerald settled themselves with their pipes in the sitting room to discuss the dire progress of the war in France, while I listened to Cissy in the kitchen, moaning about her evacuees. She thinks it's unfair that as soon as she packed her own son off to boarding school, she had to take in two boys from Hull. The food was excellent, though. Unlike me, our Cissy's a good cook.'

'Well, she had your mother to teach her,' Bobbie said gently.

'True. Oh, and we found out a bit more about Friday's air raid. A German plane dropped a couple of bombs on the farmland near where they live – probably to lighten the load on its way home.'

Bobbie's eyes widened. 'Are Cissy and Gerald all right?'

'No one was hurt, but some horses in a field were killed. Gerald was called out to deal with the carnage.'

The middle-aged woman at the next table glanced across curiously as Jemma spoke. Everywhere you went in the city, the raid was the main topic of conversation.

'Did they get the bugger?'

'Yes, the fighter planes at Elvington were scrambled and shot it down. The pilot ejected to safety, but the Dornier came down near Easingwold.'

'Good,' Bobbie said. 'That's one less of the murdering sods up in the skies.'

'What about you?' Jemma asked. 'How was your weekend?'

'Quiet. I had an impoverishing encounter with the rent man on my way home from work.' Bobbie reached out and checked the title of the anthology in front of Jemma.

'If it's short stories you're reading, I can recommend *The Detection Medley* published last year by The Detection Club. It contains a good short story by Dorothy L. Sayers called *The Haunted Policeman*.'

Jemma smiled. 'Is your hero, Lord Peter Wimsey, the intrepid sleuth?' Bobbie had always been a huge fan of the jovial Wimsey and Sayers' effervescent style of writing, while Jemma preferred the sparsity of detail, brilliant plots and more clinical style of Christie and Freeman Croft Wills.

'Of course, he is.'

'Aided and abetted by his love, Harriet Vane?'

'She appears briefly. It's a delightful story. Descriptive, humorous – and original.'

'I'm sure it is. I'll look out for it. To be honest, since… Michael… short stories are the only thing I can manage. I struggle to concentrate on anything longer.'

Bobbie reached out and squeezed her hand. 'That's understandable, love.' Her dark eyes drifted towards the large hardback book she'd brought

---

39

to the table and she grimaced. 'But in that case, I may have been a bit a bit premature with this book by O'Sullivan…'

Jemma pulled the heavy volume towards her. Its title was *Crime Detection*. 'So, we're back to your crazy suggestion that we should set up our own private enquiry agency? This isn't a book,' she added, 'it's a doorstop.'

'Yes, it's rather extensive,' Bobbie said with a grin. 'O'Sullivan has written a good introduction to the profession. He thinks women detectives, with their intuition and unique perspective on life, are a great assent to any enquiry agency.'

Jemma said nothing. She was already scanning the list of chapter headings.

'It's American,' Bobbie continued, 'and there's a bit too much emphasis on the use of bloodhounds for my liking. But it'll give you a better idea about the role – if you can manage to read it, that is. You can just dip in and out if you're struggling to concentrate.'

'The North Riding Constabulary has a pack of bloodhound sniffer dogs,' Jemma murmured.

'These might be better for you right now.' Bobbie pushed the pile of *Pearson's Weekly* magazines across the table towards Jemma. 'Read these before you condemn the idea of a private enquiry agency.'

Over twenty years old, the magazines were badly creased, stained and in danger of falling apart. A stern-looking middle-aged woman with short dark curly hair stared up at Jemma from a black-and-white photo among the faded print. The headline above read: *The Adventures of a Lady Detective: Work in Private Houses.*

'Who's this?'

'That's Maud West, London's first female private detective. Or at least that's who she claimed to be in her advertisements. She had a rival called

Kate Easton, who also set up a private enquiry agency back in 1905. They battled it out for the title.'

'Two female private detectives – at the turn of the century? Both with their own agencies?'

'Yes. Maud West wrote regular articles for *Pearson's Weekly*. I came across them years ago. They're a bit exaggerated and lurid, but you might enjoy them.'

Jemma scanned the article while Bobbie continued talking. 'These are real women, Jemma – not fictional characters like Miss Marple or Tuppence Beresford. And don't forget, there have been female store detectives in England since the last century. Even some police forces recruit women.'

'Not in York, they don't.'

'Look, we don't have to start big, with premises and all that expense,' Bobbie said. 'We should put an advert in the paper and offer the services of two Lady Detectives to do a bit of investigation in the evenings.'

'That might work,' Jemma said thoughtfully.

The Quaker Queen entered the door at the other end of the room. The weak sunlight pouring through the tall arched windows made her spectacles flash. Her greying head swivelled towards them in disapproval and her thin nose sniffed. The woman at the next table was also staring at them, although Jemma thought she seemed more perplexed than annoyed by their chatter.

Bobbie gave the Quaker Queen a wary glance. 'I have to do a quick bit of shopping for Mum. Why don't you read these magazines while I'm gone? I won't be long. You can check out the O'Sullivan book and take it home with you.'

The Quaker Queen was now steamrollering her way towards them across the parquet floor, a quivering mass of indignation in grey flannel.

Bobbie stood up and grabbed her coat. 'I'll be back in half an hour.' She neatly sidestepped the disgruntled librarian with a cheerful 'Good afternoon, Miss Oates!' and hurried towards the exit before the old dragon complained.

Jemma grinned and bowed her head over the magazine.

Bobbie's description of the Maud West articles as lurid was correct. The woman carried a gun and seemed to spend all her time catching spies, drug barons and kleptomaniac aristocrats in country houses. The O'Sullivan handbook about crime detection was more down to earth and more honest about the job. The author described private detection as 'highly remunerative, and intensely interesting and exciting'. But he also talked of the boredom of trailing suspects, the seediness of the life of private detectives and the shady world they inhabited.

Strangely enough, this fascinated Jemma rather than repelled her.

One phrase about this branch of crime detection resonated with her: 'it assures complete *independence of thought and action.*' After running her own business with Michael for the last year, this appealed.

Was Bobbie right? Could the two of them make this work – in York?

Glancing at her watch, she realised the half hour was over. She gathered up her things and checked out the O'Sullivan book at the desk. Bobbie joined her while she was returning the magazines to the librarian.

They stepped out into the chilly street together and paused in the small square in front of the library. The street was bathed in early spring sunshine and despite the rumble of traffic, Jemma heard birds singing in the trees of the museum gardens.

'What did you think?' Bobbie asked.

'I think it's a crazy idea,' Jemma said. 'I've never heard of anything so crazy in my life.'

Bobbie looked crestfallen. 'Was it so bad?'

'Yes, absolutely ridiculous. Only nutcases would wander around a wartime city at silly hours of the day and night, following suspects and other rogues in the blackout and the freezing cold.' Jemma paused. She never could tease Bobbie for long. 'But do you know what, it also sounds like a lot of *fun*.'

Hope sprang into Bobbie's eyes. 'You mean – you'll do it?' Her voice rose with excitement.

'It also sounds complicated – and a bit dangerous,' Jemma warned.

'We're bound to make a few mistakes when we begin. We'll just have to forgive ourselves if we do.'

'I think your suggestion that we start out in a small way is best,' Jemma continued. 'We need to place a few advertisements in the papers for evening work and test the water first. Gabriel tells me this city is steeped in crime but before we invest in premises etcetera, we need to make sure there's enough business to support us.'

Bobbie squeezed her hand and smiled. 'We can do this, Jemma. Yes, we'll make a few mistakes along the way – but we *can* do this – together.' Her eyes shone with excitement.

They turned to leave – but walked straight into the green-hatted newspaper reader from the library. The elderly woman was barring their path.

'Oh, hello again,' Bobbie said cheerfully. 'Are you following us?'

'I want a word with you two.' The expression on her face was intense. 'My name's Mrs Clarissa Deburgh. I heard you talkin' about your detective agency in the library. I've got a job for you.'

Chapter Six

'So, you want us to go to Corrigan's Circus in Tadcaster – and see if we can find your husband?' Bobbie said, struggling to keep a straight face.

Jemma understood why. Mrs Deburgh's story was tragic – but quite fantastical.

They'd stepped into a cramped café to talk. It was a cheap little place with smeared windows, dirty net curtains and chipped crockery. Jemma ordered them all a cup of tea.

Across the table, Mrs Deburgh nodded and slurped her drink. Her false teeth were loose and shifted when she put the cup to her mouth. 'That's right. It were the only place the police didn't check when he disappeared. I'll give you ten bob to go there next Saturday. This'll be a start for your new business.'

Bobbie glanced at Jemma, unsure. 'Actually, it might cost more, Mrs Deburgh. There's our transport to Tadcaster to consider and the entry fee into the circus…'

'Ten bob,' the woman insisted. 'It's all I've got spare.'

Jemma believed her. Everything about Clarissa Deburgh, her chapped red hands, lined face and fraying clothes, suggested she'd endured a lifetime of hard menial work and poverty. Her husband, Jack, had disappeared nearly seven years ago. He'd been a mechanic with a good wage. His disappearance and the loss of his income would have hit her hard.

Her story would be easy enough to check out in the local newspapers kept in the library archive. Mrs Deburgh claimed the police had sent divers with huge metal helmets, weighted shoes and oxygen pipes into the River Ouse to search for Jack. An event like that would have been headline news in the small city.

45

But there was something evasive about the woman's small, crumpled eyes. She didn't look directly at either of them when she spoke, and addressed most of her comments to the milk jug.

'What makes you think...' Jemma hesitated, but she couldn't avoid the well-worn cliché. 'What makes you think Mr Deburgh ran off to join the circus?'

Beside her, Bobbie quivered with suppressed laughter.

But Mrs Deburgh was unfazed. 'He'd allus loved the circus since he were a child. Whenever Corrigan's came to York, he'd go two or three times a week. It weren't until much later – after the police investigation had ended – I remembered Corrigan's were in town the week he vanished. I were in a right state when he went missin'. I thought he were dead.'

'It must have been an awful time for you,' Jemma said kindly.

'Aye, it were.' The woman drained her cup and reached for her handbag. She pulled out a battered and creased sepia photograph from her purse and handed it across. 'That's him. That's my Jack.'

They leant over and examined the image. It was a dreadful grainy photograph of a balding man in his late forties with a pudgy nose. It would be difficult to identify anyone based on this.

'So, will you go for me on Saturday? And see if he's there, like?'

'Why don't you go yourself?' Bobbie asked. 'Why pay us to do it?'

Emotion flashed across the woman's face, but the anger wasn't directed at Bobbie. The milk jug took the brunt of it. 'Because if he *is* there – it means he deserted me, the bastard. I spent years thinkin' he were lyin' dead at the bottom of the river without a Christian burial. Folks kept droppin' hints, like they do. But I didn't want to believe he'd just buggered off. When the penny dropped, it made me angry – really angry.'

'That's understandable,' Jemma murmured.

'If he's still alive, I don't want him to think I give tuppence for his rotten old carcase – after the upset he caused. And if he sees me, he'll think I still give a damn and were lookin' for him.'

Jemma nodded and felt a wave of empathy for this worn-down and disappointed woman. Not knowing the truth was hard. 'I'm sorry for your suffering, Mrs Deburgh. I can assure you of our complete discretion in this matter. Do you want us to give him a message if we find him?'

Those small, hooded eyes flashed again. 'I don't. Meet me next Sunday morning outside Holy Trinity Church on Goodramgate at a quarter to eleven and let me know if he's there or not. And remember to bring back that photograph.' She pulled on her gloves.

'You said the circus is based in Tadcaster?'

'Aye, it's been there a while – entertainin' the troops. They won't have the petrol rations to gallivant around the country anymore. You'll find Corrigan's advert in the paper. I did.' She pushed back her chair, picked up her bag and stood up. 'You can pay for the teas.' She nodded in the direction of the waitress. 'You can take it out of the ten shillin' I'll give you next Sunday.'

She turned on the well-worn heel of her scruffy lace up shoes and disappeared out of the café.

Bobbie burst out laughing. 'Well, there goes our first client. What a stroke of luck! The patron saint of private detectives must be smiling down on us today.'

Jemma smiled. 'We've been over this before. There isn't one.'

'We'll have to invent one then. I propose: Saint Dorothy of Hell and Sayers.'

'Saint Agatha of Torquay,' Jemma countered.

'Saint Margery of Helling Ham.'

Jemma nearly choked laughing. 'We need a Catholic. What about Saint G.K. of Chester Town?'

Bobbie shook her head. 'Saint Father of Brown is better.'

'I like that. We'll keep him. And shall we call our agency Smoke & Cracked Mirrors – like we planned before?'

'Of course.'

They sat back, glowing with satisfaction and excitement.

'Seriously though, Jemma. We've just made our first mistake. Next time *we* tell the client how much we charge – we don't let them make us an offer. And we detail the expenses we expect to incur, as well. Apart from the bus fare and the teas, we've got to buy a ruddy newspaper now.'

Jemma smiled. 'Never mind. We get a free trip to the circus next Saturday. Mind you, it doesn't bode well for us in our future career that neither of us noticed we were being followed by an overweight middle-aged woman!'

'It should be fun,' Bobbie agreed.

'She's not told us everything, though. She's kept something back.'

'What? Why?'

'I don't know, but her eyes were evasive. Her husband has been gone for nearly seven years. Why wait until now to try and find him?'

Bobbie shrugged. 'All our clients will be hoarding secrets. Their morals are their own affair. Our job is to find out things. Amass information.' Her grin broadened. '*Us. We. Our* future,' she murmured. 'I like the sound of all that.'

Smiling, Jemma reached out and took her hand. 'Of course it's *us*, Bobbie. You don't think I'd set out on a crazy adventure like this without my best friend beside me, do you?'

—

48

Chapter Seven

When Jemma got home, she read some more of the O'Sullivan book in the comfort of the armchair by the fire. Then she sat down at the kitchen table with a pad and a pencil. It was time to get realistic.

The rent and rates of an office in York city centre she estimated based on the cost of their shop premises in Middlesbrough. The cost of a telephone line, gas, electricity and advertising she already knew. A secretary? No. She drew a line through that idea. That was a luxury they couldn't afford. They'd answer the telephone themselves and she'd type up the invoices.

O'Sullivan claimed launching an enquiry agency required a 'very small financial outlay', but Jemma already felt the savings she'd squirrelled away in the bank slipping through her fingers.

What about sundry items? Stationery. A brass plaque on the door with the name of the business – ooh, she liked the sound of that. A camera? Two? Yes, they'd need those. Transport and travel costs would be billed to the clients. But what about petrol rationing? How did that work for private detectives? She chewed her pencil thoughtfully.

By the time she got up to draw the blackout curtains, she'd worked out a rough estimate. In order to give both herself and Bobbie a respectable salary, the business would need to make ten pounds a week profit. She sat down again, stared at her notes and burst out laughing.

This was impossible, surely? How much demand would there be for a couple of private detectives in a small city like York? How on earth would they ever cover their costs?

She heard the front door open, closed her notebook quickly and cleared away her things.

'Evening, Jemma.' Gabriel threw down his cap, ran his fingers through his white curls and slumped into his armchair by the fireside. But he nearly jumped up again at the sight of her old brassiere lying on her sewing box. 'Good grief! What's that thing doing there?'

'I'm going to use the cups to make shoulder pads to bring my navy jacket into the 1940s. I saw the tip in a *Make Do And Mend* leaflet.'

'Well, put it away. It'll put me off my food. What's for supper tonight?'

She laughed. 'Toad-in-the-hole, but I've made an onion sauce to go with it.'

'That sounds exotic. Are you still working your way through *One hundred things to do with a sausage*?'

'I am.' She set the table and served the food. 'The Yorkshire pudding looks a bit stodgy – but at least I haven't burnt it.'

'I can't wait. This surfeit of sausages – the butcher's not tricking us, is he? These aren't sausage dogs he's selling, are they?'

'I sincerely hope not. Come on, it's ready.'

'I had to lock up your new friend, Ricky Wilde, this afternoon,' he informed her a few minutes later.

Jemma paused in surprise with her fork halfway to her mouth. 'Why? And he's not my friend. He's just a man I met on the bus.'

'The silly idiot was caught by the military police, taking photographs of the Dornier the RAF shot down last Friday near Easingwold. He's in the cells in Clifford Street, waiting for his appointment with a magistrate on Monday. He'll get a hefty fine.'

'It must be difficult for a press photographer to earn a living in wartime.'
Gabriel frowned. 'Why?'

'Haven't you noticed? The newspapers are half the size they used to be, thanks to the paper shortage. The *Yorkshire Evening Press* is down to six sheets. Fewer pages mean less need for photographs, I presume.'

'No, I hadn't noticed. But as for Wilde, why can't he join up like the rest of the men his age? It would make my life easier if he did,' he added darkly.

Jemma just smiled. 'Treacle tart and custard for pudding?'

'How big was this tart you baked?' he asked suspiciously. 'It seems to be going on for ever.'

It wasn't until later, when they were sitting beside the fire listening to big-band music on the wireless, that she broached the subject at the forefront of her mind. She was sewing as usual, and Gabriel had lit his pipe.

'Do you know of any private detectives in York?'

'PIs?' He thought for a moment and exhaled a billowing cloud of smoke. 'Well, there's old Will Sharrow. He's got an office on Low Ousegate.'

'What's he like?'

'Scruffy and stooped, I suppose. Why?'

'Do you put much business his way?'

Gabriel eyed her suspiciously. 'Our paths don't tend to cross much. His business mostly seems to involve serving writs on debtors and stalking adulterous husbands.'

'So, you've never worked with him?'

'He's given us a couple of tip-offs over the years. One of them involved a drugs ring and was helpful. Why this sudden interest in Sharrow? You've not got some crazy idea about employing him to find out more about what happened to Michael, have you?'

'Good heavens, no. It's nothing. I saw Bobbie again in the library—'

'Ah, Bobbie's behind this, is she?'

'We were talking about Miss Marple and Tuppence Beresford and wondered what it would be like to be a real private detective.'

Satisfied, Gabriel sank back in his chair. 'Well, it's nothing like your stories. For a start, every time I see Sharrow, he seems to have a new set of bruises on his face. His is a world of sleaze, shadows and secrets.'

—

51

'I imagined it to be more about divorce and blackmail – with the odd missing person thrown in for good measure,' she said airily.

'Exactly. His clients will be as untrustworthy and sleazy as the people they want him to investigate.'

Jemma laughed. 'Sounds a lot like the police witnesses you deal with.'

Gabriel shrugged. 'It's an unsuitable job for a woman.'

'In that case, I'll cross it off my list of possibilities,' she joked.

'Are you looking for a job?'

She nodded and told him about the letter she'd received from Sofia. 'This prejudice and harassment is unfair. Michael's family have done everything possible to blend into the British way of life since they arrived in England. They even Anglicised their family name, for heaven's sake.'

Gabriel nodded sadly. 'It is what it is, I'm afraid, Jemma. The war in France is going badly; there's real fear about a German invasion. A colleague of mine down in Towcester had to pull an enraged mob off a tramp they thought was muttering away to himself in a foreign language. The poor old fellow had lost his marbles and was speaking gibberish. He didn't know who he was, or how to speak English anymore – all he could do was play the piano. They didn't know whether to imprison him as a foreign spy or send him to the mental asylum.'

'None of this is any excuse for the bigots to whip up hysteria about innocent foreign nationals.'

'True. Did I tell you Chief Constable Herman had received several threatening letters at the station?'

'What? Addressed to Herman-the-German?'

'Something like that – his name is the problem. Like your father-in-law, Herman risked his life fighting against the Germans in the last war, but these people don't remember that.' Gabriel sucked on his pipe and enveloped them both in a swirling cloud of pleasant-smelling smoke.

'Well, without my allowance from the James family, I can't support myself.'

'I'm sorry.'

'It's fine. Please don't worry about it, Gabriel. It's time I sorted out my life and moved on.'

Gabriel tapped out his pipe in the grate, stretched and yawned. 'I'm going up, Jemma. I've got a busy day tomorrow. We've some new recruits. Two retired police officers have been enticed back to duty to ease our shortage. One of them has a false leg.'

'Oh, heavens! He'll be useful chasing criminals down Parliament Street!'

'There's plenty of other things he can do back at the station – and I'll take all the help I can get. Mind you,' Gabriel continued, 'I don't envy them coming back into the force at their age. War or no war, I wouldn't do it. In fact, I'll quit the force once the war ends. I've had enough of the hours and the low pay.'

Jemma was shocked. 'But what about your pension?'

Gabriel made a disparaging noise. 'It'll be a pittance.'

'But you'll be bored. You're too active to sit at home and potter in the garden growing vegetables.'

Gabriel had rented an allotment at the start of the war, following the 'Dig for Victory!' campaign, but he was hardly ever there. He spent all his time at work. There wasn't even a woman in his life at the moment as far as she knew, although there'd been a steady stream of them visiting the house in the past. Her brother was a confirmed bachelor, married to his job.

'Oh, I don't plan to be idle. I'll be too busy in the pub.'

'What? You plan to spend your days drunk in the pub?'

—

'No, not drinking, silly. Running it. I've always fancied myself as the landlord of a quiet country pub. Somewhere out in the dales, away from the city.'

Jemma raised her eyebrows. 'I never knew you had an ambition to be a publican. Would you lease the freehold or sell up the house, take your share and buy it outright?'

Gabriel paused. 'My share?'

'Yes, you know – of this house.'

'Jemma, I own this place. It's mine.'

Jemma's stomach lurched. 'What? When did that happen? Did you buy it from Dad?'

'No. Dad never owned this house.'

'But I thought…'

Gabriel shook his head. 'Just after Mum died, the landlord gave us notice to leave because he wanted to sell it. Dad had just paid for Cissy's wedding and needed his money for your school fees. So, I took out a loan from the bank, sold my favourite Triumph and used my savings. Neither of us wanted the upheaval of moving home – and we didn't think it would be good for you.' He gave her a quizzical glance. 'I thought you knew this?'

Jemma squirmed in her seat. 'No, I, I didn't. Dad never said.' She'd always assumed that she, Cissy and Gabriel owned the house jointly; that it was their family home, and she had every right to be here. But it wasn't and she hadn't. She was a freeloader, living rent-free on the charity of her brother. She was more indebted to Gabriel's kindness than she knew.

Her thoughts shifted to her father, and she sighed. His health had been failing for years, and when Michael suggested they move to Middlesbrough, she'd been reluctant to go. But her father had insisted she put her own happiness and her husband first. A few months later, he'd died quietly in his sleep.

———

54

Jemma had been devasted and bitterly regretted leaving York. Gabriel and Cissy sorted out the funeral and the finances between them and gave her a cheque for one hundred pounds, which they said was her inheritance. Jemma had been too distraught to enquire further or ask to see her dad's will.

Then Michael's disappearance had eclipsed everything else in her life.

'I'll start paying you something for my keep.'

Gabriel stood up and stretched. 'Don't be silly, Jemma. I've told you before, I don't want any money from you. I'm off to bed.' He paused when he reached the door and looked back. 'I'll try again to track down Flight Sergeant Rodgers, if you like. I know you still want answers about Michael.'

'Thank you, Gabriel. Good night.'

Once he'd gone and she heard his weary tread on the creaking wooden stairs, she went to the dresser and pulled out O'Sullivan's book. Gabriel's revelation had unnerved her; she was less financially secure than she'd thought. It was more important than ever to make Smoke & Cracked Mirrors work.

When she finally went upstairs, she picked up her hairbrush and walked in the dark towards the window. The back of her neck tingled in alarm and she stopped abruptly. For one unnerving moment, she thought someone was standing beside the wooden beams supporting the canopy over the old water trough. Then the clouds cleared above, and soft moonlight flooded the green. No one was there. Her overactive imagination was playing tricks on her again.

'Get some sleep, girl,' she chided herself. 'You've had too much excitement today.'

Chapter Eight

Jemma dressed in her comfortable slacks and an old jumper for her trip to York Central Library.

It took her less than half an hour in the old newspaper archives to track down the story of Jack Deburgh's mysterious disappearance. Their new client had told them the truth. The middle-aged mechanic had simply vanished into thin air and his disappearance triggered an extensive police search. A witness saw a drunk man answering Deburgh's description staggering beside the Ouse and police divers searched that part of the river.

She jotted down the newspaper description of the missing man and realised they should have asked Clarissa Deburgh for more details about his appearance and stature when they interviewed her yesterday. *Mistake number two.* They'd be more thorough next time.

Next time? Would there be a next time?

She flicked to the back of the newspaper in her hand and scanned the old advertisements. There weren't any for private detectives, and as far as she could remember, there never had been. How did Will Sharrow get his clients? She knew many private detectives were former police officers and used their old contacts in the force to acquire business, but if Sharrow did get help from York City Police, then Gabriel knew nothing about it. She thought of the advert she'd promised Bobbie she'd place in the papers today. Dare she be so bold?

Her fingers tapped on the pile of old newspapers and she wondered if they'd reported on the inquest. Then she remembered there wouldn't be an inquest. No dead body, no inquest. In fact, according to British law, Clarissa Deburgh wouldn't be able to declare her husband dead until seven years after his disappearance. That date would fall in about two weeks. *Is*

that why she's decided to make one last attempt to find him? Before his life
was officially expunged from the records?

She had another flash of empathy for the woman. For years, Mrs Deburgh had lived in limbo as neither a wife nor a widow. That's how Jemma had felt since the telegram.

'Lost in action' could mean anything.

What if Michael was a prisoner of war and came back one day? Stranger things had happened. She tried to imagine her excitement at receiving a *second* telegram that told her he was still alive, and allowed herself to daydream about their reunion…

Sighing, she abandoned her fantasy, packed up her bag and returned the newspapers to the librarian on duty.

Then she left the building and headed in the direction of the *Yorkshire Evening Press* offices on Coney Street.

Nothing ventured, nothing gained.

The offices were in a tall medieval building that backed on to the River Ouse. Despite the constant risk of flooding, this was a convenient arrangement for the proprietors, who still had their paper delivered in bulk by barge. The offices themselves were a labyrinth of small dark interconnected rooms, each on a slightly different level. They smelled of tobacco smoke and paper, with a slight whiff of the river.

Jemma nervously dictated their advertisement to a balding, bespectacled man with ink-stained fingers. His face remained impassive as he wrote the words on a form, as if hearing about a female detective agency was something that occurred every day. But she felt embarrassed, pretentious almost.

She fumbled in her purse for the coins to pay for the advert, turned to hurry out and walked straight into her elderly – but sprightly – neighbour, Miss Frances Rawlings.

Fanny wore paint-splattered slacks beneath a dirty old coat, an outfit that belied her comfortable wealth and betrayed her passion for art at the same time. Beneath a bright green silk turban, her pale face crinkled into a broad smile and her intelligent grey eyes sparkled with amusement.

'Hello, young Jemma! I'd heard you were home. How are you, my dear? And how's your gorgeous brother?'

Jemma smiled. This flamboyant spinster was one of her oldest and most trusted friends. Despite being nearly seventy, Fanny had always flirted outrageously with Gabriel. 'He's well, thank you, Fanny, and so am I.'

After her mother's death, Jemma had often sought comfort with Fanny. Talking nineteen to the dozen, Fanny would give the grieving child a cup of milk and a biscuit, sit her on a stool in her studio and let her watch while she daubed colour across a new canvas and brought a beautiful scene to life. Her paintings were highly prized by collectors throughout the north.

'And what are you doing here? Did I overhear you placing an advert?'

'I've started a new business venture.'

The old woman's bushy grey eyebrows rose in surprise. 'That sounds interesting. You'll have to call round and tell me all about it.'

'That'd be lovely, Fanny, thank you. I'll come round soon, I promise.'

A bony, age-spotted hand reached out to squeeze Jemma's arm. 'I heard about your loss, my love, and I'm sorry for it – especially so soon after the loss of your poor father. Michael was a kind and very special young man. Such a tragic waste. How are you coping?'

'I have good days and bad days still.'

'Take long walks and spend time in the garden,' Fanny advised. 'The sunshine is good. It worked for me when my fiancé died.'

'I never knew you were engaged to be married, Fanny.'

'Oh, good grief. Yes – to poor Henry. But it was over forty years ago – the typhoid got him. You'll get over it, my love. When the time is right, the pain will ease. Take little steps, baby steps.'

Jemma gave a rueful smile. Did launching your own business count as a *baby step*? She thanked Fanny for her advice, promised to see her soon and stepped outside into the windy street. She cast a wary glance at the blanket of grey scurrying clouds above.

Fanny's remedy for a broken heart would have to wait; spring sunshine was still a long way off. As if on cue, it started to rain again.

The newspaper printed their advertisement in the evening edition. Unable to contain her excitement, Jemma met Bobbie at the staff entrance of Grainger's after she'd finished work. 'Come with me to Barton's for a cup of tea. I've something to show you.'

'I've no money,' Bobbie protested.

'It doesn't matter – I'll pay.'

Bewildered, Bobbie fell into step beside her. Once they were seated at a table in the café and the drinks were ordered, Jemma pushed the newspaper in front of her friend.

SMOKE & CRACKED MIRRORS

York's Ladies' Detective Agency

Every kind of detective work undertaken

With secrecy, discretion and speed.

Divorce Shadowing, Insurance Fraud

Investigation and Mystery Solving.

Evening work preferred.

Bobbie's eyes gleamed in the soft light. 'It's fabulous! I love the bit about *mystery solving*. What made you think of that?'

'Clarissa Deburgh,' Jemma confessed. 'I wanted to use the line *missing person investigations undertaken*, but I thought *mystery solving* covered more kinds of cases.'

'It's great! We're now officially in business!'

'This advert will run every night for a week,' Jemma continued, 'and I've placed the same one in the *Yorkshire Post*. It's got a wider circulation.'

Bobbie grinned. 'Knowing our luck, our next case will be in Bradford! But well done, Jemma. If it doesn't drum up some business for us, I don't know what will. Why did you use a post office box number for written responses? I thought you had a telephone at home?'

Jemma glanced away and picked up her cup. 'That's Gabriel's telephone – he had it installed so the station could contact him quicker in case of an emergency. I'm not sure how he'd feel if I used it as a business line.'

'It sounds to me like you've not told him about our new venture.'

Bobbie's sharp, dark eyes met hers across the table. Jemma sighed; she knew a denial would be useless. 'You're right. I haven't told him – yet. I want to see if we can make a success of it first. He doesn't think it's a suitable job for a woman.'

'Does that worry you?'

Jemma paused for one imperceptible moment before she shook her head. 'No, I'm more determined than ever to make our new business work. We'll solve mysteries and help people, Bobbie, with or without the assistance – or blessing – of anyone at York City Police.'

Bobbie frowned, unconvinced. 'Are you sure everything's all right at home? You haven't fallen out with Gabriel, have you?'

'It's not that. It's something else.' She told Bobbie about her shock discovery that Gabriel owned the roof over her head.

—

'Well, it could be worse,' Bobbie said cheerfully. 'If he was married, you might be sharing that house with a resentful sister-in-law.'

'I suppose so.'

Bobbie smiled. 'Gabriel's right about one thing. We're going to have to tell a lot of lies, visit places decent young women would normally avoid, and probably end up in all sorts of scrapes. Any reputation we have for respectability will fly out of the window once our friends and neighbours find out what we're up to!'

'I know,' Jemma said. 'But just think of the *fun* we'll have!'

The next evening, Jemma saw the man lurking by the old water trough again.

She went into their front room, or *parlour*, as her old-fashioned mother used to call it, and noticed there was a chink in the curtains, a clear blackout infringement. Crossing the dark room with practised ease, she raised her hand to close the curtain and froze on the spot.

There was no mistake this time. A man was hiding in the shadows beneath the canopy, his gaze fixed on their home. She held her breath, waiting for him to move. Or to turn away. Anything. He didn't.

She hurried back to Gabriel in the kitchen. 'Gabriel, there's a man outside on the green watching our house.'

'What?'

'I've seen him before. He just stands there. I don't know who he is or what he wants. You can see him out of the parlour window.'

Irritation flashed across her brother's face. He put down his pipe, switched off the wireless and disappeared into the hallway. Jemma held her breath and waited, conscious of the ticking of the old clock on the mantelpiece.

When Gabriel reappeared, he went straight to the drawer in the dresser where he kept the German Luger pistol their father had brought back as a souvenir from the last war. Tipping the old box of ammunition out on the dresser, he loaded it.

Jemma gasped. 'Is that necessary?'

'I've upset a lot of crooks in my time, Jemma – and imprisoned even more – but one thing they all have in common is cowardice.' He blew down the barrel of the pistol to remove any dust. 'One look at this, and he'll be running for the hills.'

'So, you think it might be some nutcase criminal with a grudge against you?'

Gabriel shrugged. 'Harassment like this is common for police officers.' He grabbed his jacket and headed for the front door. 'Just trust me – and stay here.'

Jemma ignored his instructions and dashed into the front room to watch through the window.

She was just in time to see a black, man-sized shadow dash across the green in the direction of Clifton and disappear into the gloom. She heard Gabriel shout and watched him give chase, but she knew it was hopeless. Their stalker was over a hundred yards ahead of her brother and it was easy to vanish into the back alleys, nooks and crannies of those crowded, unlit streets.

She waited anxiously for Gabriel to reappear before she closed the curtain and went to meet him in the hallway. It was a relief to know her imagination hadn't been playing tricks on her, but it was unnerving to think someone had them under observation.

'I scared him off.' Gabriel threw the pistol down on the hall table and pulled off his jacket. 'The bastard legged it as soon as I left the house. You

---

63

were right, Jemma – he's up to no good. We need to ask the neighbours if they've seen him before.'

'Gabriel—'

'I'm sorry, but you'll to have to take extra care in future. Make sure the door is always locked. This sort of thing goes with my damned job, I'm afraid.'

'Gabriel – it might not be anything to do with your work.'

'What?'

Quietly, she told him about the angry letter she'd received from her former landlady in Middlesbrough. 'I don't understand it – Michael's only debts were with his family.'

In the gloom of the darkened hallway, she sensed rather than saw Gabriel wince.

'Let's go into the kitchen,' he said quietly.

'I telephoned the landlady the next day,' Jemma continued hastily, 'to explain her mistake, but she was adamant that the men who'd visited her were bailiffs.'

'Did they mention the nature of the debt Michael owed them?'

'I don't think they had chance. She said they didn't believe her when she told them Michael was missing in action and I think she flew off the handle at that point. They wouldn't have been able to get a word in edgeways. She's a very fiery woman.'

Gabriel sank into the armchair by the fire and ran his long fingers through his hair, a gesture she knew meant he was thinking. She perched on the edge of the chair opposite. The incident had left them both rattled.

'Firstly, I don't think the bloke outside was a bailiff. That's not how bailiffs operate. They usually muscle their way into a house to take back items of property to the value of the debt.'

'So, we're back to your theory that this man is something to do with a case you solved?'

'Not necessarily.'

'But Michael wasn't—'

'Let me finish, Jemma.' He paused again to collect his thoughts. His broad face was creased with exhaustion and worry. Eventually, he threw up his hands. 'Look, I don't know what the hell is going on. And unless I manage to corner this bloke, we won't find out until he makes his move. And that's what bothers me, his next move. Hopefully, I've scared him off, but you must keep the doors locked and avoid going out after dark alone.'

She nodded glumly and hoped that would satisfy him. Promising to stay indoors at night would be a big problem for a woman with a fledgling enquiry agency.

'I'll see if we can spare a constable to watch the house for a while, in case he comes back,' Gabriel continued, 'and he can ask the neighbours if they've seen any strangers in the area. But you need to be alert – I can't be here all the time to protect you. As for Michael, we'll have to redouble our efforts to find out what happened to him – I got nowhere with my latest enquiries.'

'I'll write again to the ministry.'

'And Jemma,' he added gently, 'ask them if they knew of any undischarged debts Michael may have accrued.'

'What?'

'You may have to brace yourself for more bad news. A man's death can sometimes bring all sorts crawling out of the woodwork. Michael seemed a decent fellow – everyone liked him. But let's be honest, you barely knew him or his family when you married him, and you were both very young and naive.'

———

'I knew him well enough,' she protested, 'and he didn't just *seem* a decent man, he *was* one – he *is* one.'

He regarded her sadly across the hearth, his tired eyes full of compassion. 'All men have secrets, Jemma – and many have a nasty gambling habit.'

'Michael has never been near a bookie's or a dog track in his life!' She stopped, overwhelmed with anger and grief.

Gabriel said nothing. His expression never changed.

She bid him a tearful goodnight and stumbled up the stairs.

Chapter Nine

Jemma weaved her way around sandbags stacked against the wall of the parade of shops and nervously entered the post office. Their advertisement had run for the past three nights in the newspapers, but this was the first time she'd dared to check if there had been any replies.

It's too soon, she told herself. *Don't build up your hopes.*

Jemma felt wretched this morning. She'd barely spoken to her brother since their argument about Michael and the heavy silence at mealtimes was hard to bear. She found it difficult to forgive Gabriel for suggesting Michael may have been a secret gambler. His lack of faith hurt her.

But he'd been as good as his word about organising a regular police patrol outside their home. She's seen the beat constable several times on the village green. Their mysterious stalker seemed to have vanished.

Gabriel had a rare day off today and had gone out on his motorbike. When he said he wouldn't be back for supper she'd felt a flash of relief but that had now subsided into guilt.

It's too soon for a reply, she told herself, when the postmistress checked the scruffy pigeonhole on the back wall bearing Jemma's number.

But it wasn't.

There were two letters waiting for Jemma to collect.

The first was a plain white envelope with a stiff and officious typed address. It was postmarked 'Leeds'. The second letter was from York and came in a thick, creamy envelope that smelled faintly of perfume. The address was written in blue ink from a fountain pen in a beautiful, swirling cursive.

Trembling with excitement, she hurried home and sat down at the kitchen table to read.

—

67

She opened the typewritten letter first. There was no letterhead, no company name, and it was short and to the point.

Dear Madam,

I read your advert in the Yorkshire Post with interest. I suspect your organisation may be able to assist one of my clients. Please telephone me on the number below for further information.

Yours faithfully,

Terence King

There was a Leeds telephone number at the bottom of the letter but no other clue about the identity of the writer or the company he worked for.

She resisted the urge to rush to the phone, and instead turned to the second letter, the one postmarked York.

It was written by Mrs Isabella Banyan, who gave her address as The Spinney, on Albemarle Crescent. Jemma knew the street. It was in one of the wealthiest, leafiest areas of York, just off the Tadcaster Road by the racecourse. The properties here were an eclectic mix of old farm cottages and rambling private villas, hidden from prying eyes behind rows of flowering trees, sets of double gates and long red-brick walls.

To whomever it may concern, (wrote Mrs Banyan).

If you are who you claim to be, I may have an assignment for two of your female operatives on the evening of Saturday next, the 16th.

Meet me at Betty's Tea Rooms on Monday 11th at half past noon to discuss the details. Phone the house and leave a message to confirm you'll attend this appointment.

I rely on your complete discretion with my staff. Simply leave your name with them so I know how to address you when we meet.

68

Neither of these prospective clients had given much away, Jemma thought. But that wasn't a surprise. Both would want to interview her first before they trusted her with their business.

She just hoped Mrs Banyan intended to pick up the bill for anything they ate or drank at Betty's. One of the most glamorous and expensive restaurants in York, Betty's owners had recently enjoyed a cruise on the *Queen Mary* and had designed the interior based on the opulence of the ship.

But Mrs Banyan had one of the best addresses in York and *staff*. This might be a lucrative contract.

Terence King was more mysterious. He was clearly a businessman, with *clients*, but the lack of a company name or any indication of his position within the company suggested a man who played his cards close to his chest. *A cautious lawyer, perhaps?*

'Time to find out,' she said to herself. Grabbing her notebook and a pen, she went to the telephone in the hallway and lifted the receiver.

She telephoned The Spinney first and left a message with a maid that *Mrs Jemima James would meet Mrs Isabella Banyan as requested, at Betty's Tea Rooms at half past twelve on Monday 11th*.

Next, she asked the operator to connect her to King's number in Leeds.

Her call was answered abruptly by a secretary: 'King's. How can I help?'

While Jemma waited to be put through to Mr King, she tried to imagine what he looked like. She decided he was a hunched, elderly man with wispy grey hair.

But the male voice that came on the line suggested he was far younger and rather attractive. There was humour in his tone when he asked: 'Is that the owner of Smoke & Cracked Mirrors, York Ladies' Detective Agency?'

69

Straightening up, Jemma tried to sound her most business-like and officious. 'It is. My name's Mrs Jemima James. You're Mr King, I presume? How can I help you?'

'You claim you do insurance fraud detection? Do you have a camera?'

'Yes,' she lied. 'A Leica II. What's the case, Mr King?'

'It's the usual story, I'm afraid. One of my Leeds clients has an employee who sustained injuries while at work and has claimed considerable damages. They've reason to believe he's exaggerated the situation – he goes out dancing every Friday. They would like evidence of him enjoying himself to present at the hearing.'

'Dancing? At a dance hall in Leeds?'

'No, he's not stupid enough to frolic on his own patch with the court case pending. We've heard reports he comes up to York to a place called the De Grey Rooms. Do you know it?'

'Yes, it's next to Bootham Bar and the theatre. It's the most expensive dance hall in York.'

King laughed. 'Well, the claimant expects a substantial payout from my client. He's obviously decided to start spending it already.'

'What's his name? And please describe him for me.'

'Steady your horses, young lady. Tell me about yourself and your organisation first.'

'There's two of us running Smoke & Cracked Mirrors: myself and Miss Roberta Baker.'

'How old are you?'

Instinctively, she added a few extra years. 'We're both twenty-five. Bobbie has years of experience as a store detective and I've... I've experience with York City Police.' She kept her fingers crossed that he wouldn't ask in what capacity; she suspected that being the daughter of a police sergeant and the sister of an inspector wouldn't count.

'Mrs Jemima James and Miss Bobbie Baker...' He rolled their names around his tongue and savoured them like a vintage whisky. 'So, what brought young ladies with such delightfully alliterative names into private detection?'

'We've wanted to set up our own agency for a while – and the time seemed right. I take it you'll want photographic evidence of this man on the dance floor at De Grey's? Is there anything else?'

'No, that should cover it. Several clear photographs of Mr Eddie Chambers tripping the light fantastic is what we require. How much do you charge?'

Jemma braced herself for rejection. 'Six shillings an hour – each. And there'll be expenses, transport costs, the entry fee – and drinks for the evening. We'll need to blend in with the rest of the clientele. In fact, we may have to take a couple of our male operatives with us as dance partners, to keep up the charade.'

Male operatives? Where the hell had that idea come from? She desperately hoped Bobbie knew a couple of men who'd accompany them.

King's reply, when it came, wasn't what she was expecting. He laughed. 'Well, you're cheaper than the other bloke.'

'What other bloke?'

His tone took on that teasing note again. 'Oh, don't tell me you just launched a new business, Mrs James, without checking out your competition first?'

'Oh, you mean Will Sharrow with the office down on Low Ousegate?' She remembered Gabriel's description of the stooped and scruffy PI. 'I don't think dancing's his forte. He'll stick out like a sore thumb at De Grey's.'

'That's what I thought – and no one would suspect a couple of glamorous young ladies like yourself and Miss Baker of being private detectives. Very well, Mrs James, the assignment is yours if you'd like it. You can bill me for four staff for the evening – but go steady on the alcohol. We've got a month yet before the court case, so if he doesn't turn up next Friday, you can try again the following week. I'll send a photograph of Chambers to your post office address – and a retainer. I imagine you'll want a retaining fee in advance?'

Jemma almost kicked herself at the omission. It was the first thing O'Sullivan had suggested private detectives ask for. 'Yes, please, ten shillings should cover it.'

King gave her a detailed description of both Eddie Chambers and his dancing partner, then wished her the best of luck and rang off.

Mistakes number three and four, Jemma thought as she replaced the receiver. *Check out the competition – and always ask for a retainer.*

But she found herself grinning from ear to ear.

She'd done it. Smoke & Cracked Mirrors had its first official assignment.

Chapter Ten

Bobbie was startled to find Jemma waiting at the staff entrance of Grainger's for the second time that week. 'What's the matter?'

'I've got news, exciting news. And this time we'll have a celebratory drink in a pub! We've got clients!'

'Fantastic! But I'll buy them – I've just been paid.'

The colourful and beautifully tiled pictorial of three wading birds above the entrance to the Three Cranes belied the cramped, rough interior of the ancient pub. Hard wooden furniture wobbled on the uneven flagstone floor and willow-patterned plates and faded photographs of York decorated the dirty walls. Popular with the local market traders, it was smoky and stank of stale ale. But it was warm, and the alcohol was cheap.

'Isn't this place supposed to be haunted?' Bobbie asked, when she returned from the bar with two port and lemons.

Jemma winked. 'Aren't they all? Every place over fifty years old in York has a resident ghost, usually a Roman centurion or a mad monk. The tourists love it.'

'Tell me what's happened.'

Jemma told Bobbie about Terence King and Mrs Banyan.

Bobbie clapped her hands together in glee and held them tight over her chest. 'I knew we could make this work! Did Mrs Banyan give you any indication about the work she wants us to do?'

'No. She simply booked us for the evening. I assume I'll find out more at the meeting on Monday.'

'I'll try and come along too, when I've finished at Grainger's. Monday's my half-day off, remember? I bet it's a kleptomaniac.'

'A what?'

73

'Her problem. One of her well-heeled house guests has been stealing the family silver and she wants us to mingle with the guests at her next soirée and find the thief.'

Jemma laughed. 'We'll see. I just hope we're not too tired on Saturday. We'll be dancing the night away at De Grey's the night before. Which reminds me, I'd better go and buy a camera, although where or how we'll get the photographs developed, I don't know. By the way, do you know a couple of reliable men who can accompany us to De Grey's?'

Bobbie's answer surprised her. 'What about your new friend, Ricky?'

'Who? Oh, you mean the newspaper photographer?'

'It would save us some expense if he loaned us his camera, and you said you thought he does his own developing. Perhaps he'll let you borrow it?'

Jemma frowned. 'I haven't seen him since the day we met. The last time I heard, he'd got himself arrested.' She remembered how tenderly Ricky Wilde had held his Leica. 'I doubt he'd loan something so precious and expensive to a virtual stranger.'

'In that case, invite him to come with us for the night and pay him to take the photographs.'

'Oh, I don't know, Bobbie – Gabriel said he mixes with a bad crowd.'

Bobbie shrugged. 'I'm not sure we can afford to be too fussy at this stage. Building up a group of reliable and useful contacts is more important than their social circle. Besides which,' she added with a smile, 'how can he resist a night out on the tiles with two gorgeous young things like us?' She tossed her head in an exaggerated way to emphasise her point – and half her hair fell out of its pins.

Jemma laughed. 'I'll think about it.'

Jemma felt better as she walked towards the bus station. The rain had stopped, and her fledgling business was beginning to flap its wings.

Three bombers droned across the ice-blue sky above. They flew low, seemingly skimming the minster towers by mere inches. She exhaled with relief when she spotted the concentric rings on the wings and the fuselage; they were British. There was something comforting about the permanence of the honey-coloured medieval minster, whose soaring towers dominated the city skyline. It had been a symbol of stability in a fractious world for seven centuries and had survived plague, pestilence and several attacks by the Scots. *Please God, don't let Hitler raze it to the ground.*

She heard the familiar, vibrating roar of a motorbike coming up the street behind her. It was Gabriel in a leather helmet and goggles on the Vincent Rapide – and he had a passenger.

Oblivious to his open-mouthed sister on the pavement, he braked hard and drew up behind a bus waiting at the stop. The woman riding pillion fell forward against his back and clutched him tighter. She wore an old leather air force jacket and a pair of flying goggles from the last war, which made her look like Amy Johnson.

Gabriel checked out the road ahead, opened the throttle and veered past the stationary vehicle with a loud roar and the unmistakable whiff of oil and exhaust fumes.

Jemma just had time to see the mane of red hair streaming behind the woman before the pair disappeared around the corner.

It was Maisie Langford, the barmaid from The Grey Mare.

Jemma burst out laughing. How had she not seen this coming? The clues had been there for a while. Gabriel's regular late-night trips for last orders at the pub. The abandoned allotment. And his sudden desire to leave policing and run a country pub – no doubt with Maisie, an experienced barmaid, by his side.

She wondered how long they'd been together. And why, oh why, hadn't he told her there was a new woman in his life? Was she so fragile Gabriel

75

thought she couldn't bear any more shocks or surprises? But she was pleased for her brother and hoped this relationship lasted longer than the others.

She shook her head and smiled at the irony. A few days ago, she'd silently agreed with Bobbie it was a good thing Gabriel was a confirmed bachelor and she didn't have to share his cottage with a resentful sister-in-law.

She didn't know Masie very well, although she'd always thought she was a kind woman. Hopefully, she'd treat Gabriel – and herself – kindly if they got married and set up home in the cottage. She suspected Maisie wasn't the type of woman to throw a grieving, penniless sister-in-law out on the street.

And if the pair of them did want her to leave? Well, that was a problem for another day. Nothing was going to spoil today.

Pulling her coat tighter around her shoulders against the wind, she smiled and continued to the bus station.

Gabriel came home late that night. She heard him quietly let himself into the house in the early hours of the morning. But he was up and dressed in his uniform when she went down to the kitchen for breakfast. He'd made himself a quick slice of bread and dripping and was about to leave.

'Good morning,' she said sweetly. 'Did you have a nice day off, yesterday?'

'Yes, thank you. I had a good run up to Settle. The weather was bracing – and wet – but the scenery fantastic.'

'Were the two of you looking for a pub to run together, by any chance?'

He eyed her warily across the kitchen table. 'The two of us?'

'Yes, I saw you with Maisie.'

76

There was a short pause, then she added: 'You should bring her round to supper one night. I'd like to get to know her better. I can make coq au vin with some chicken and the bacon Cissy gave us. I'm good at coq au vin.'

Gabriel relaxed and laughed. 'No offence, Jemma, but I'd like to get to know her a bit better myself before I inflict your cooking on the poor woman. I don't want to put her off.'

'Charming!'

He grabbed his jacket and made a beeline for the door. 'Besides which,' he yelled over his shoulder, 'if you use my precious bacon in some fancy French casserole, I'll lock you in a police cell. See you later.'

She laughed and made a pot of tea.

Chapter Eleven

Jemma met Bobbie at the staff entrance of Grainger's after she'd finished her shift, and thrust a packet of pilchard sandwiches into her hand. 'I knew you wouldn't have time to eat anything before we caught the bus to Tadcaster. I hope these help.'

Bobbie looked weary after a day on her feet in the store, but her eyes lit up at the sight of the food. Both women wore slacks and sensible shoes, ready for their trudge around the circus. The bus took them down the Tadcaster Road. They peered out of the steamed-up window, trying to catch a glimpse of Albemarle Crescent and the home of Mrs Banyan.

Corrigan's Circus was pitched in a large, muddy field on the outskirts of Tadcaster. Dowdy and dull, it bore no resemblance to the glittering, brightly lit palaces of magic Jemma remembered from her childhood. There were no coloured lights swinging around the awning of the big top, and even the glitzy stars on the dodgem cars had been painted over in matte black to comply with the blackout requirements. But there was the same unmistakable smell of wet canvas, manure, musty straw and warm animals.

'We're a bit early,' Jemma said as they approached the entrance booth.

'Good, we need to snoop around a bit.'

'How are we going to handle this?'

'Straight up, I think,' Bobbie suggested. 'If Jack Deburgh's there, let's just walk right up to him. It's been seven years since he disappeared, and if he *has* run away to join the circus, there's no reason for him to suspect his wife has renewed her attempt to track him down.'

Jemma nodded. 'I've been thinking. I doubt the circus let him stay for free. He'll have had to work for them – and he's a mechanic.'

'Exactly,' Bobbie said. 'Leave the talking to me, I've got an idea.'

A heavily whiskered bloke stood in the pay booth. 'You're too early for the performance,' he said gruffly.

'We know. It's deliberate,' Bobbie replied. 'My dad asked us to call and see an old mate of his who works with you: Jack Deburgh.'

'Eh?'

'Your mechanic – Jack.'

Jemma held her breath. Somewhere, in the distance, a horse neighed.

'Oh. You mean Dobbo? 'E'll be busy – we've got a broken truck. You'll 'ave to wait until after t' show.'

'My dad and Dobbo are old friends,' Bobbie persisted. 'Dad's sent a message for him.' She gave the man a dazzling smile. 'Perhaps Dobbo has mentioned him? Big Bill Baker from York?'

'Can't say as 'e 'as. Look 'ere, I ain't supposed to let anyone in early in case they tek sommat.'

Bobbie laughed. 'Do we look like a couple of thieves? Go on, let us in – we've got to catch the bus back to York straight after the performance.'

The man's dull eyes weighed them up. 'All right then. I'll tek you.' He turned around and yelled at a scruffy young lad of about eleven, who was larking about with some other children nearby. 'Joey – watch the booth!'

They followed the man through a maze of old caravans, animal cages and tents.

'I see you didn't evacuate any of your children,' Bobbie said.

Their guide gave Bobbie a surly look. 'What fer? We live on wheels. If owt 'appens bad from the Jerries, we just strike camp and bugger off.'

The occasional chink of light gleamed weakly between the curtains in the caravan windows, but it was very dark. Something large and invisible growled in one of the cages nearby and music drifted their way from the big top. The small band was warming up. Jemma narrowly avoided tripping over a guy rope.

'It must be hard to get spare parts for your motors and petrol, these days,' Jemma said.

The fellow shrugged. 'Dobbo does what 'e can to keep us goin', and if we can't get petrol, we put paraffin in t' tanks.'

We must be getting close now, Jemma thought with a tingle of excitement. Mind you, there was no proof that this circus mechanic called *Dobbo* was the missing Jack Deburgh.

'Where's his caravan?' Bobbie asked hastily.

The man pointed ahead. 'It's the one on the end – but he'll be workin' on one o' trucks behind.'

Bobbie stopped in her tracks and pointed back the way they'd come. 'Your son has just called you.'

'Eh?'

'The lad called Joey who you left in charge. He ran out from behind that tent back there and shouted something. It sounded like "Da".'

'I bloody 'ope not,' the bloke said. ''E ain't mine – there'll be 'ell to pay if 'e did that. Can yer find yer own way from 'ere?'

The two women reassured him they could, and he trudged back towards the pay booth.

'Well done, Bobbie – that was brilliant!' Jemma whispered. 'Especially that last lie! Let's split up now. You go and watch the caravan and I'll find the mechanic. I'll meet you at the entrance to the big top when the performance starts. Don't break an ankle falling over something in the dark.'

Bobbie nodded and they separated. Jemma veered around the back of a caravan. She found herself in the middle of a tightly packed group of lorries and vans. The smell of crushed grass mingled with that of leaking oil.

The weak flash of a torch beam directed her steps. A small boy of about six stood on a low stool at the front of a large lorry, fumbling with a torch.

The bonnet was raised, and a man bent over the engine. She shifted further down the narrow gap between two lorries, desperate to get a closer look at his face.

''Old it steady, lad,' the man grumbled from beneath the bonnet.

'Hurry up, Dad, I'm cold,' the little lad complained.

'Nearly there.'

Jemma heard the screech of twisting metal.

'Just another couple of twists. There – that's it. Done.'

The man straightened up and Jemma got clear sight of his profile in the torchlight. His bald head, pudgy nose – and the smile – were familiar. It was definitely Jack Deburgh.

Father and son turned around when a little girl appeared out of the gloom and toddled towards them. She was followed a few paces behind by a slim, dark woman with an old army greatcoat casually thrown over her spangled leotard, tights and boots.

'Daddy!' shrieked the little one.

Jack Deburgh slammed down the bonnet, wiped his oily hands on an old rag and scooped up the little girl into a big hug.

Jemma hands itched for a camera.

'She couldn't wait for you to come back,' the woman said, laughing. 'She thought she were missin' out on sommat.'

Deburgh laughed. 'Let's get back inside the caravan while Mummy goes to work. It's cold out here.'

The family walked off in the direction of their caravan and Jemma edged after them, sticking to the shadows cast by the vehicles. She wasn't in time to see Deburgh take the children inside, but she heard the door open and shut and watched the lithe figure of Deburgh's woman stride off towards the big top.

———

Bobbie slid out of the shadows to join her. 'It's definitely him, isn't it?' she whispered.

'Oh, yes. Quite the family man, isn't he?' Jemma snapped sarcastically. 'What a charming little group.'

Bobbie laughed quietly. 'No one said we have to like the people we deal with. Come on, let's mingle with the crowds and enjoy the circus.'

The big top was packed with service personnel in uniform. The seating tiers rose around the sawdust-strewn ring like a wrapping of khaki and air force blue. Everyone – including Bobbie – was determined to enjoy themselves. But Jemma struggled to laugh at the clowns and the antics of the little dogs with frilled collars or appreciate the horseback acrobatics. Her mind kept drifting back to Deburgh's abandoned wife in York.

Bobbie's right, she thought, *I've got to be more detached. Our job is to find out information, not feel sorry for the clients.*

Jack Deburgh's woman came into the ring with a male partner and swung herself up to the trapeze, distracting Jemma from her thoughts. Stage make-up was caked on her face and despite her athletic and daring performance, Jemma realised the woman was a lot older than she'd originally thought. Early forties, perhaps? The appreciative audience rose to their feet at the end of the show and nearly brought the canvas roof down with their applause.

The grizzled man in the pay booth was still there, counting out the takings, when they left, but they mingled with a large crowd and he didn't notice them.

'Well, that was fun,' Bobbie said, 'and an easy way to earn money.'

But the excitement of the evening wasn't over yet.

As the bus approached the outskirts of the city, the driver pulled over to the side of the road and switched off the engine, throwing them into total darkness and silence. The passengers looked up in surprise.

———

83

He turned around and yelled down the aisle: 'There's a raid over York. We're stayin' put until it's finished.'

Everyone groaned and Jemma craned her neck round the seat in front, half expecting to see the city skyline glowing orange with fire. To her relief, the only sign of attack was the powerful searchlights from the anti-aircraft guns raking the black velvet sky for enemy bombers. The lights had alerted the driver to the raid.

Some of the passengers started to complain, their voices filled with anxiety for their loved ones.

'You can walk from here if you want,' the exasperated driver told them, 'but this company vehicle ain't goin' anywhere until the all-clear sounds. We're a couple of miles out of the centre.'

'What do you think?' Bobbie asked.

Jemma stared ahead and tried to weigh up the odds. She couldn't see any explosions or hear the ack-ack of the anti-aircraft guns. Was it another false alarm?

'Yes, let's walk. At least it'll keep us warm. We'll freeze to death on this bus otherwise.'

They went outside and heard the unmistakable droning wail of the air-raid siren in the distance. There was no pavement and the group of passengers stuck together for safety. Everyone had one eye on the black sky above – and the other on the road ahead. There were other dangers out here beside bombs raining down on their heads; fatal motor vehicle accidents had more than doubled since the blackout began.

A few clouds scurried across the sky, blocking out the moonlight. The cold breeze rustled through the long grass and the hedgerows at the side of the road. A dog fox barked in a distant wood.

No vehicles overtook them on the way into York, although several came out of the city, packed with white-faced families fleeing the raid. They also passed several parked cars with people huddled beneath blankets on the back seats.

'They're called trekkers,' Bobbie told Jemma. 'They're frightened of air raids and sleep in cars away from built-up areas.'

For some reason, Jemma thought of the conscientious objectors Gabriel had recently escorted to tribunals in Leeds. Most of them had been from York's thriving Quaker community. They claimed it was religious principle, not fear, that kept them from signing up for the army. That may be true for them, Jemma reasoned, but fear was a constant and unwelcome companion for many in wartime Britain. She'd smelled it in the sweat of the people crammed into the public air-raid shelters in the centre of town – and it was here, now, in the back of these freezing cars.

'I'll run those adverts again next week,' she told Bobbie.

Bobbie linked her arm through Jemma's. 'Are you sure? It'll put a dent in your savings – but I'll pay you back when I can afford it.'

'Yes, I'm sure. I've enjoyed tonight – I feel like I've come alive again. You were right – private detection is exciting and fun.'

Bobbie stumbled in the dark, winced and clutched Jemma's arm tighter. 'It's also tough on the feet, especially after standing around in a shop all day. Thank goodness I'm off work tomorrow.'

'There is one thing I'm still worried about.'

'What's that?'

'The *acting*. The role of a private investigator often requires the detective to elicit information from people by assuming a different persona. I'm not as confident as you. I don't think I can do what you did tonight with the man at the pay booth. I might be too awkward to be convincing.'

Bobbie shook her head. 'Of course, you can do it! Don't you remember how you were praised for your performance of Benedict in our school play?

—

85

It's just the same – just think yourself into the role you've adopted, and you'll come across genuine enough.'

'I only worked so hard at Benedict because you were my Beatrice and I didn't want to let you down,' Jemma confessed. 'Plus, we only got the roles because we were the only two in the class who could handle the Shakespearean English.'

'That's true,' Bobbie said, laughing. 'Our classmates were a bit dim, weren't they? Especially that bully, Kathleen Young.'

Jemma smiled, grateful for Bobbie's light-hearted good humour. 'What happened to her when we left school?'

Bobbie shrugged. 'I saw in the newspaper she married an air force officer last year.'

Jemma's mind drifted back to the present. 'We said we'd meet Clarissa Deburgh outside Holy Trinity just before eleven tomorrow. But I can do it if you want to stay in bed and have a rest.'

'I wouldn't miss it for the world.' Bobbie stifled a yawn. 'I can't wait to see her face when we tell her about Dobbo's life with Bendy Wendy and the little 'uns.'

Thankfully, the air raid siren stopped just as they reached the outskirts of the city. The crowd around them let out a sigh of relief when the all-clear sounded.

'Thank goodness for that,' Bobbie said. 'I thought my eardrums were going to burst.'

Exhausted and agitated, people drifted out on to the streets and gathered in groups to discuss the raid. Others scurried home. It had been another false alarm. Everyone had been trapped in the shelters for several hours, but the city was safe for another day.

The two women parted at the station. No buses were running, and Jemma braced herself for a weary trudge back up to Clifton.

'See you at church!' Bobbie called cheerfully, as she turned and waved goodbye.

Chapter Twelve

The fifteenth-century church of the Holy Trinity was located in a small, secluded, leafy churchyard, tucked away behind Goodramgate. To access the churchyard, Jemma passed through a crumbling red-brick archway tacked on to the uneven whitewashed walls of buildings that had served as artisans' workshops in the fourteenth century.

Apart from the parish notices hung on a board on the rusty black metal gate, there was nothing to indicate the church was there and most people walked straight past it. But not today. There was a service at eleven o'clock and several groups of people entered the gate. Clarissa Deburgh obviously intended to be part of that congregation.

Jemma checked her watch, waited for Bobbie by the archway and realised how much she missed the sound of church bells on a Sunday morning. They'd been silenced for the duration of the war and would only ring again in the event of a German invasion. She sighed with relief when Bobbie raced round the street corner, tendrils of unruly dark hair flying behind her.

'Sorry,' Bobbie gasped. 'I went to the wrong Holy Trinity. You know? The one on Micklegate? There's too many blooming churches in this town!'

Jemma gave a wry smile. 'Well, York is the ecclesiastical centre of the north.' She waited a few seconds for Bobbie to catch her breath and smooth her hair back into place. 'Don't worry, you're not late. Let's find our client.'

The sound of the city was muffled when they stepped through the gate. A short alley between the buildings led to the small, peaceful graveyard in front of the church. Bathed in weak spring sunshine, golden daffodils

---

danced in the breeze beneath the trees. Above them, birds chirped on the branches amid the new leaf growth.

Clarissa Deburgh was waiting for them in front of one of the crumbling graves, decked out in her Sunday best black coat and hat. 'Well?' she asked, as they approached.

'You were right, Mrs Deburgh,' Jemma said as she handed back the grainy photograph of Jack Deburgh. 'Your husband *is* living at the circus. He works there as a mechanic.'

Despite her previous protestations about her lack of feeling for the man, Mrs Deburgh was visibly moved. Her face flushed and her lips tightened to hold back the furious outburst writhing inside her. Her gloved hand shook as she fished in her handbag to find her purse. She still couldn't speak when she pulled out a ten-shilling note and handed it across to Jemma.

'There's more bad news, I'm afraid,' Jemma continued. 'Your husband appears to be living with one of the circus performers – and they've a pair of small children.'

'Ha! The lyin', cheatin'...' She fell silent.

A young couple ambled up the path towards the church and glanced curiously in their direction.

Mistake number five, Jemma thought. *Letting the clients choose the place for a meeting.* This churchyard was far too public to deliver such bad news; their agency needed a private office.

'Well, that's it, then, isn't it?' Mrs Deburgh exclaimed bitterly. 'I'm goin' to have to move now, aren't I? Mind you, I've often hankered after a small boardin' house in Bridlington. No doubt the bugger will still try and find me, now there's money comin'.'

Jemma frowned – and then the truth hit her like a blinding flash.

'You shouldn't feel you need to be hounded out of your own home,' Bobbie said. 'There's no shame in this attached to you. He's the one who's guilty of desertion, adultery – and wasting police time. He should be arrested for the trouble he's caused.'

The agitated woman's small eyes narrowed. 'Aye, well, I suppose I could allus threaten him wi' the police if he came back to bother me for the cash.'

Bobbie's brow furrowed in confusion. 'I'm not sure he'll want to come back, Mrs Deburgh. He seems very settled with his new family over in Tadcaster.'

'You don't understand the half of it, young woman.'

Bobbie didn't. But Jemma did.

'If you get a lawyer, we can serve him a writ for divorce,' Bobbie continued.

Shock flashed across the woman's eyes and her face contorted with anger. 'Divorce! What kind of a woman do you think I am?'

Her reaction stunned Bobbie into silence.

'The novelist Agatha Christie divorced her first husband,' Jemma said quietly.

Mrs Deburgh rolled her eyes to the heavens and regained her brisk, no-nonsense manner. 'I always thought Mrs Christie were no better than she ought to be – especially after that fuss about her vanishin' to Harrogate. No. Decent Christian women don't get divorced. I'm happy to be a widow.'

Bobbie opened her mouth to correct the woman about her marital status, but Jemma stopped her with a gentle squeeze on her arm.

Mrs Deburgh glanced towards the low stone porch of the church. 'Anyway, it's time I went t' service. Thank you for the trouble ye've gone to – and good luck for the future. I saw your advert in the paper and I think it's a good one. No doubt you'll do well.' She turned on the worn-down

—

91

heels of her shoes, pulled back her shoulders and, mustering as much dignity as she could manage, disappeared inside the church.

'Well!' Bobbie exclaimed. 'What was that about?'

Jemma smiled. 'The life insurance policy.'

'The what?'

Jemma took Bobbie's arm and led her back out into Goodramgate, away from prying eyes. 'I've only just worked it out, but that's what it's been about all along, the life insurance. There's obviously a policy in Jack Deburgh's name, which will pay out once he's declared dead in the next few weeks. She's worried the cheeky sod will turn up to try and claim a share of the money.'

Bobbie laughed and shook her head in disbelief. 'Do you think she knew all along that he'd run off to join the circus?'

Jemma thought back to the newspaper reports she'd read about the police search and shook her head. 'Not initially, no. But once she'd worked it out, her heart hardened, and she kept her suspicions to herself. No doubt the insurance money will be a substantial amount, especially if she continued to pay the premiums.'

'And you think she was worried Dobbo would reappear and demand his share?'

'Yes, that's why she employed us. She needed to know if her suspicions were correct, so she could plan her response.'

'Good grief!' Bobbie laughed. 'Another mystery solved by Mrs Jemima James. Mind you, I think we ought to join her in Holy Trinity. I feel I need purifying after that!'

Jemma smiled. 'Let's settle for a cup of tea instead.'

'Everywhere's closed. It's Sunday, remember?'

'Yes, but the Methodist church has an earlier service than Holy Trinity and it serves tea in the church hall at eleven, mostly to the forces. Let's sneak inside and buy a cup.'

'Thank goodness for all the churches in York,' Bobbie said with a wink.

Chapter Thirteen

Jemma was early for her appointment with Mrs Banyan in the elegant tea rooms of Betty's Café.

A slim waitress in a black dress with a white collar and a pristine white bib apron led her up the broad staircase to the Belmont Room. Jemma paused to check her hair in one of the many large, tinted mirrors that lined the walls of the staircase. The soft hum of conversation, gentle laughter and the chink of delicate bone china drifted through the restaurant door towards her.

Following Bobbie's advice, she'd rolled, pleated and pinned her hair into the latest style. Her new red blouse went well with her altered navy suit. The shorter length of the skirt left her knees a bit chilly, but she felt confident she looked the part of a modern, professional businesswoman. She'd eschewed her usual sensible black walking shoes for this meeting and was wearing her high-heeled wedding shoes, which she'd spent yesterday afternoon dyeing navy to match the suit.

A gleaming grand piano stood idly in one corner of the Belmont Room, amid a flurry of exotic potted plants and ferns. Glass panels etched with tropical trees, foreign beaches and towering volcanic mountains separated the tables. Everything, from the walnut panels lining the walls to the comfortable open-weave rattan chairs, was designed to evoke the luxurious spirit of a cruise ship gliding through warm tropical waters.

Mrs Banyan's table stood beneath a beautiful marquetry panel depicting geese flying across a lake, and Jemma spent a moment or two admiring the artistry before glancing around at the rest of the clientele. It mostly consisted of off-duty air force men accompanied by York's ladies of leisure.

The waitress brought a tall, elegant, dark-haired woman in a glossy mink coat and beautifully feathered hat across to the table. She arrived in a haze of exquisite French perfume and held out her hand, still encased in its kid-leather glove.

'Good afternoon, Mrs James.' Her voice was refined, without a trace of the local northern accent. 'My goodness, it's a cold day.'

Jemma agreed about the weather, shook her hand, and sat down nervously while Mrs Banyan divested herself of her coat and handed it to the waitress. She wore a blue silk dress with matching sapphire earrings glinting in her earlobes.

Beneath the face powder, there were faint lines at the corners of Mrs Banyan's mouth and eyes. Her dark glossy hair was beautifully curled, but it was touched up at the temples to cover the grey. She was probably in her mid-thirties.

'It's a pleasure to meet you, Mrs James.' She picked up the coloured menu card. 'I fancy a buttered teacake. Would you like one? I'm afraid these blasted shortages mean there are no longer any cream-filled fancies or rich chocolate cakes to be bought at Betty's, but they still manage to rustle up a delightful teacake.'

Jemma wasn't sure she'd be able to swallow anything just now, but she nodded and thanked her hostess.

'Excellent! Please don't take offence, Mrs James, but you look like you could do with fattening up a little. You're very thin.'

Jemma gulped at her forthright manner. 'My colleague, Miss Baker, should be with us shortly. Would it be possible to order an extra cup of tea, please?'

Mrs Banyan's smile was brittle. 'How delightful! The more the merrier. We'll have tea and buttered teacakes for three, please, Edna. Add it to my account.'

96

Once the waitress left, her new client turned her dark eyes on Jemma and scrutinised her shrewdly. 'How exciting your detective agency sounds. Do tell me about it. Is it just the two of you? You and Miss Baker?'

'Yes, that's right.' She gave Mrs Banyan the same information she'd given to Terence King the week before.

'And Mr James? Is he also part of your organisation?'

The directness of this personal question took Jemma by surprise. 'No, he's missing in action,' she stammered.

The woman's voice softened. 'Oh, I'm sorry to hear that. My husband is Colonel Banyan of The Queen's Own Royal West Kent Regiment. I know how hard and uncertain life can be for the wives of our brave troops.'

Her sympathy seemed genuine, but Jemma didn't want to answer any more questions about Michael. 'Can you tell me something about the work you wish us to do for you next Saturday?'

She paused as Bobbie arrived, flushed and ruddy-cheeked from the cold air outside. Jemma introduced her.

'My apologies for my late arrival,' Bobbie said as she sat down. 'I've just finished another job for our agency.'

'I'm delighted to hear you're so busy,' Mrs Banyan said with a cynical twist to her lips. 'However, please be aware for the future that I'm a stickler for punctuality.'

'Mrs Banyan was about to explain to us her problem,' Jemma said quickly.

Bobbie nodded impassively. If she was offended by the rebuke, she didn't show it. She'd also made an extra effort with her appearance for this meeting. Her unruly hair was tamed and she wore a smart bottle-green dress slightly flecked with fawn-coloured swirls, which suited her dark colouring. The dress had wide lapels and she wore it with a matching fawn-coloured cable-knit cardigan.

—

Mrs Banyan sighed and tapped the long rose-pink nails of her right hand on the table. Her face creased with concern. 'I'm afraid it's quite a delicate problem.'

'You can rest assured of our complete discretion.' Jemma pulled her notepad and pen out of her handbag and placed them on the table.

'And there's nothing you can say that will shock us,' Bobbie added.

'Well, I sincerely hope so – because I want you to spy on my younger brother's fiancée and there will be the devil to pay if he finds out I've employed you.'

'Don't worry – he won't,' Bobbie reassured her.

Jemma raised her pen. 'I like to start at the beginning, Mrs Banyan, and take notes as I go along. Please tell us about your brother and his fiancée.'

'Have you heard of Anston and Brierly, Architects?'

'Yes,' Jemma said, 'they've an office on Coppergate. Weren't they the architects behind the design of the Cocoa Works on Haxby Road?'

'That's right. Well, my father is Andrew Anston, the founder of the company. My brother, Teddy, is also an architect and property developer, and he works for the family firm. I know I'm biased but my little brother is a poppet and everyone who knows him adores him. Like our wonderful king, he's suffered with a stutter since childhood and has always been a bit tongue-tied around people – especially women. I'd always assumed that one day he would settle down with one of *our* crowd, someone who's known him a while and is sympathetic and tolerant of his speech impediment. So, you can imagine my surprise when I came back to York last autumn and discovered he was courting a racy stranger from Leeds.'

Jemma frowned. 'I thought The Spinney in York was *your* address?'

'No, I live down in Kent with my husband. The Spinney is my family home, my father's house. When this damnable war was declared last

September, rather than evacuate the children, I brought them back to York for safety.'

Jemma nodded. 'I've heard it's difficult down on the south coast at the moment – everyone fears an imminent invasion.'

'Anyway, that's when I first met my brother's young floozy, Miss Helen Urwin. I've been unhappy about the relationship for a while but when they announced their engagement two weeks ago, I decided it was time to act and either expose the harpy for the fraud she is or put my mind at rest once and for all. I need to know more about this woman and her background.'

Their tea and teacakes arrived, and the waitress poured the steaming beverage from a silver teapot into the delicate china cups. Generous helpings of real golden butter were melting into the lightly toasted teacakes.

Bobbie helped herself to three lumps of sugar. 'Are you worried Miss Urwin might be a fortune hunter?' she asked.

Mrs Banyan shook her head. 'No. She has a considerable fortune of her own. I find it difficult to trust the woman. I can't quite put my finger on it but there's something wrong. She's travelled extensively in England and over on the continent during the last few years. To listen to her talk, her life has been an endless round of parties in Paris, London, on the Riviera and in Switzerland. She only returned home to England because of the threat posed by the Germans. I don't understand why such a vivacious creature wants to settle down in a northern provincial city with my tongue-tied little brother.'

'How old is she?' Bobbie asked. 'Maybe she wants a family.'

Mrs Banyan waved her beautifully manicured hand dismissively. 'She's twenty-seven, a year older than Teddy. And there's something else – despite her foreign travel, she has the most atrocious French accent I've ever heard. She claims to have been taught by a governess, but if this is true, the woman did an awful job.'

'You suspect she might be lying?'

'Good God, yes. I believe she lies about a lot of things. My intuition tells me she's not the woman she claims. Her dress sense is appalling; she has no taste. In addition to this, she has bold eyes.'

'Bold eyes?' Bobbie paused with her teacake halfway to her mouth.

'Yes, apart from when she looks at me, of course. When she looks at me, her eyes narrow.'

'That's squinting,' Jemma said. 'It means she doesn't like you. Each squint lasts for about an eighth of a second and is an instinctive reaction. It evolved to stop us seeing things we don't like and usually indicates anger or displeasure.'

It was Mrs Banyan's turn to pause with her teacake halfway to her lips. For a moment, Jemma thought her tongue had run away with her again, but her client laughed.

'Well, this confirms what I've suspected about Helen for a while. But what an interesting little thing you are, Mrs James. Where on earth did you learn that? From some private detective manual, perhaps?'

'No, my father taught me. He was a police sergeant.'

'When is the wedding to take place?' Bobbie asked.

Mrs Banyan looked surprised at the question. 'It's to be in June – but if you're planning to buy a new hat, Miss Baker, it'll be a small family affair.'

Bobbie smiled. 'I wasn't angling for an invitation, Mrs Banyan. I just wondered how long we'd got to save your brother from making the biggest mistake of his life.'

Mrs Banyan visibly relaxed and took another sip of her tea. *This must be as awkward for her as it is for us*, Jemma thought. Especially as there's two of us and only one of her.

———

'We're hosting their engagement party at The Spinney on Saturday,' Mrs Banyan continued, 'and Helen will stay overnight in our guest room.'

'Ah, Saturday,' Bobbie said. 'That's what you want us to do – come to the party and watch her.'

A small smile twitched at the corners of their client's mouth. 'Yes, but before you iron out the creases in your party frock, Miss Baker, you need to know that I want you to come along as hired help – waitresses. It's quite normal to employ casual waitresses for events like this. No one will think anything of it. It's not silver service – all you'll have to do is carry around the plates of canapés and top up the champagne. Do you think you can manage that?'

'Definitely,' Jemma replied.

'And can you provide your own uniforms? A black dress and white apron and cap.'

'Yes, I'm sure we can. But what else do you want us to do while we're there?' Jemma asked. 'Apart from keeping our eyes and ears open, of course.'

Their client hesitated for a moment, then lowered her voice. 'I want you to slip away while Helen is busy downstairs, go into her bedroom and find the black engagement diary she keeps in her handbag. Once you have it, make a note of all the appointments she has lined up for the next week or so. I want to know *exactly* what she gets up to when she's not with my brother.'

'Do you suspect there might be another man in her life?' Bobbie asked.

Mrs Banyan shrugged and the movement made her dark silk dress ripple and shimmer. 'I don't know. Helen has had more freedom in her life than most young women of our class, so it wouldn't surprise me.'

'If we did find evidence of another man, your brother will have second thoughts about marrying her,' Bobbie suggested.

101

'Exactly,' Mrs Banyan said.

'And if we don't find any suggestion of impropriety,' Jemma added, 'at least you will know you did everything in your power to safeguard your brother's future happiness.'

Mrs Banyan looked impressed. 'What a clever little thing you are, Mrs James. I'm so pleased you understand my predicament.'

Jemma wondered about the long-term future of this assignment; it had the potential to last far longer than one night. 'Are her appointments likely to be in Leeds?'

'I don't know where they'll be. She's currently renting an apartment here in York. She sold her family home in Leeds last summer – that's how she met my brother. His property development company bought the old place – it's a rambling old mansion in Roundhay. They're turning it into luxury flats.'

'Once we make this list of Miss Urwin's movements and assignments over the next few weeks, do you want us to shadow her and see whom she meets?'

Mrs Banyan put down her napkin, pushed away her plate and gestured to the waitress. *She's ready to leave*, Jemma thought.

'Let's see what happens on Saturday, shall we? Telephone me at the house at six o'clock on Sunday to report what you've discovered. Teddy and Helen will be out, and my father usually takes a nap at six, so I should be able to converse with you in private. Now, shall we talk about your terms and conditions? You may find out nothing, of course, but I do feel it's worth a little investment.'

Jemma pulled out the contract she'd typed up the previous day and handed it across the table. Mrs Banyan accepted their terms without quibbling, signed the contract using an expensive tortoiseshell fountain pen and handed over the ten-shilling retainer without a fuss. Jemma made a few

---

more notes about the exact location of Miss Urwin's bedroom in the house and asked for a description of the young woman.

'Not that you'll be able to miss her,' Mrs Banyan said tartly. 'Her clothes clash, her jewellery is too showy and she's rather loud after a glass of champagne. She hangs on to Teddy's arm like she owns him.'

Bobbie frowned. 'Is there anything else you can tell us that's unusual about Miss Urwin?'

Mrs Banyan gave a short laugh. 'What? Apart from the fact she's not invited any friends or family to her own engagement party?'

'Good grief! That's odd.'

'Yes, I know. She's an orphan with no siblings. While I understand she may have lost touch with her friends while she was out of the country, I still find it difficult to believe she doesn't have an aunt or a distant cousin floating about somewhere. The guest list consists of our family, friends, business colleagues and their wives.'

'How strange,' Jemma said.

'And there's one other thing,' Mrs Banyan said when the waitress arrived, weighed down with her fur coat. 'Whenever she talks about visiting London, she always says "going down to the big city".' She stood up and allowed the waitress to help her into her coat.

'Why's that odd?' Bobbie asked.

Mrs Banyan waved the waitress away and picked up her gloves and her bag. 'Because people in my social set,' she said, with a pointed stare at Bobbie, 'would say "going up to town".'

Chapter Fourteen

Bobbie laughed quietly when Mrs Banyan swept out of the restaurant. 'Well, she put me in my place all right. She reminds me of that bossy socialite Marie Van Schuyler in *Death on the Nile* – except she's younger and less jaundiced.'

'You didn't hear her earlier. Apart from being a *strange little thing*, I'm also far too thin, apparently.'

Bobbie mimicked their client's voice and tone perfectly when she said: 'People in my social set would say *going up to town*, Miss Baker – and please be aware for the future *I'm a stickler for punctuality.*'

'Well, at least she's genuine in her concern for her brother and she's happy to employ us.'

Bobbie suddenly became serious. 'Do you think she's right to be worried about this Helen Urwin? She's not given us much to go on: a slip of the tongue when talking about London, and *bold eyes.*'

'You've forgotten Miss Urwin's complete lack of friends and relatives. Whatever her faults, I think Mrs Banyan is an astute woman with keen intuition. She senses a mystery here.'

'Ooh, deception thy name is woman.'

Jemma smiled. 'I think the quote is *frailty, thy name is woman*. But you're correct. Ever since I found out the shocking truth about the deception practised by Beryl Stapleton in *The Hound of the Baskervilles*, I've harboured a sneaking suspicion that we females are the most duplicitous sex.'

Bobbie eyed her with concern across the table. 'You've obviously not met enough men. But, either way, The Spinney – here we come! Why did you say we had our own waitress outfits?'

Jemma shrugged. 'I just thought it sounded more professional. We'll use our earnings to buy you a uniform. There's an old black dress of my mother's that'll do for me; she was a maid when she was younger. O'Sullivan claims the only change of clothes a private detective will need is a different coat and hat, but I suspect we may need to start acquiring a few costumes for different roles.'

'I didn't know your mother was in service.'

'Yes, and she kept her dress for some reason. No one ever throws out anything in our house.'

'It'll be rather old-fashioned,' Bobbie warned.

'If I get my sewing box out, I'm sure I can adjust it.'

'Don't buy me one,' Bobbie said hastily. 'I've had an idea. I can probably provide my own.'

Jemma was relieved. 'Thanks, Bobbie.' Earlier that morning she'd picked up the ten-shilling postal order sent by Mr King from the post office. With the money from their two female clients, they now had one pound and ten shillings in the kitty. But this wouldn't go far if they had to buy costumes – and she was about to reorder the newspaper advertisements.

'I intend to search for an office this week for Smoke & Cracked Mirrors,' she announced. 'It'll look more professional if we have our own premises, a telephone line – and business cards with our names and contact details. We'll need to save all the money we can.'

Bobbie's eyes lit up with delight and she reached across and squeezed her hand. 'Oh, Jemma! This is so exciting!'

Jemma smiled and pushed back her chair to stand up. 'You may feel differently in a few minutes. I want you to come with me to try and persuade Ricky Wilde to come with us to the De Grey Rooms on Friday – and bring his camera along. I think meeting him will be quite an experience for you.'

Bobbie was on her feet in an instant. 'How did you find him? Did you get his address from Gabriel?'

Jemma tutted. 'We don't need help from the police. We're private detectives.'

They entered the *Yorkshire Evening Press* offices and Jemma led the way up the narrow, uneven wooden staircase to the top floor, where the photographers worked.

The bearded man with ink-stained fingers who met them at the door told them Ricky Wilde wasn't there.

'Can you give us his address, please?' Jemma asked.

The man frowned. 'I'm not sure I should give out the personal details of the staff.'

'Oh, please do,' Jemma pleaded. 'It's urgent. He promised to take some portrait photographs of my friend, Bobbie, and her sweetheart – but he's been called up to the front line. There isn't much time.'

'Yes, please give us the address,' Bobbie said. 'I want this photograph before he leaves me.' Her lip trembled. 'I may never see him again.'

Eventually, the man agreed and shuffled off to find Wilde's home address, and a few moments later they were hurrying through the streets to his lodgings.

Nervousness gripped Jemma's stomach in a tight ball. If she couldn't persuade Ricky Wilde to help them on Friday in the De Grey Rooms, she wasn't sure how they'd manage Mr King's assignment. 'If he's not there, I've typed out a note explaining everything, and I've given him the phone number of my house. But I hope he doesn't have to use it. The last thing I need is Gabriel overhearing me making arrangements to go to a dance hall with Ricky Wilde. He thinks he's a bit of a spiv.'

Wilde lived in the top-floor rooms of a house on Hetherton Street. His landlady said he was in and let them upstairs. The stairwell was in need of a coat of paint and the thin carpet on the landing was badly worn.

A wireless was blaring in the room off to the right and they could also hear the sound of male voices. Jemma knocked on the door and stepped back.

Wilde's hazel eyes blinked with surprise when he saw Jemma and Bobbie standing on his threshold, then a broad, cheeky grin spread across his face. 'Why, if it ain't little Miss Marple!' His sandy hair was uncombed, and he looked as scruffy as ever in a grubby and frayed shirt beneath an old and rather ugly tank top.

'And friend,' Jemma said. 'This is Miss Bobbie Baker.'

'You didn't bring that Hercule Parrot fellah, then?' he asked with a wink.

'We need your professional help, Mr Wilde. May we come in?'

He glanced over his shoulder and rubbed the faded scar in his eyebrow. 'Well, it's a bit of a mess, lass, but if you don't mind the clutter?'

'We're not here to judge your domestic skills.'

He chuckled and stepped back to let them in. 'Thank God for that. Mind out for the Canuck, though – he ain't seen a real woman in weeks. Here, Don! We've got lady visitors.'

Wilde wasn't joking about the mess. Jemma wrinkled her nose against the stink of cigarette smoke, unwashed laundry and male body odour as she entered.

The main room was used for both living and sleeping and an archway led to a small scullery kitchen. Apart from a crumpled bed in one corner and a battered wardrobe, hung on the outside with clothes on hangers, there was a small table and two rickety chairs. Everything was piled high with dirty laundry. A battered settee stood in front of gas fire, separated from it by a filthy rug and a small coffee table covered with newspapers, unwashed plates and cutlery and an overflowing ashtray.

But it was the good-looking fair-haired young man in a dazzling, white, open-necked shirt and beige slacks who drew their eye. He rose from the settee and switched off the wireless. 'Don't listen to Ricky, ma'am – I'm both harmless and house-trained,' he said in a soft transatlantic accent.

'This is Don Hudson, ladies,' Ricky said. 'Or should I say, Flight Lieutenant Hudson. Don, this is Miss Marple and her friend, Miss Baker.'

'Miss Marple, huh?' Don asked. 'I thought she was a little old biddy.' Despite his fair colouring, he had really dark eyes, heavily fringed with black eyelashes. They twinkled with humour.

Jemma smiled and reached out to shake his hand. 'It's Mrs James – Jemma. And this is Bobbie.'

'I prefer Miss Marple,' Ricky said. 'Watch yourself, Don. This one can work out your wicked life story just by lookin' at you for a few seconds.'

'You overestimate my abilities, Mr Wilde,' she said, with a smile.

Ricky took their coats and hung them on the overcrowded hooks behind the door. He whipped the laundry off the rickety chairs, dumped it on the bed and carried the chairs over to the seating area in front of the gas fire. 'Can I get you anything to drink, ladies? I've got tea – or some fine Irish malt whiskey if you're in a party mood?'

Jemma settled herself on the edge of one of the uncomfortable chairs and politely declined his offer. She didn't trust the cleanliness of anything in this bedsit.

The two men sat back down on the settee and waited.

Jemma cleared her throat. 'Since we last met, Mr Wilde—'

'Call me Ricky.'

'Ricky, then. Since we last met, Bobbie and I have set up a private enquiry agency.'

Wilde whooped with delight. 'Well, I'll be damned! Not that Smoky Mirrors outfit I've seen advertised in the paper?'

'Yes, that's the one. Although we prefer the title Smoke & Cracked Mirrors.'

'I bet you'll do a roarin' trade.' He turned to Don and jabbed a finger in Jemma's direction. 'She's a damned good little detective, this one.'

'Anyway, we've got a client who wants us to go to De Grey's dance hall on Friday and get photographic evidence of a young man embroiled in an insurance claim.'

'Oooh, someone's been a naughty boy!'

'At the moment, we don't own a camera between us, so we need a photographer.'

'And a couple of dance partners for the night,' Bobbie added.

'We'll pay you for your time, of course,' Jemma added hastily, 'and for the development of the photographs.'

Wilde whooped again and thumped the grinning Canadian on the back. 'Looks like we've got ourselves a date for Friday, mate!'

'Are you both available?' Bobbie asked.

'You can count me in,' Wilde said, 'and Don's takin' a bit of leave from bombin' the Jerries.'

'I'd be delighted to accompany you ladies,' the Canadian drawled, 'if you want me to.'

Jemma opened her mouth to thank him, but Bobbie was there first. 'Perfect! We'll meet you both outside the De Grey Rooms at seven thirty. Don't forget your camera, Ricky.'

'I won't, lass.'

'Are you billeted in York, Lieutenant Hudson?' Jemma asked.

He pointed towards the door. 'Yes, across the hallway there. There's not enough room for us all at RAF Linton. I met Ricky on my first night in York.'

'And we've been best mates ever since,' Wilde added, 'despite the fact he speaks funny.'

The women laughed again. They chatted for a while longer and Lieutenant Hudson told them about his home back in Ontario, which sounded both chilly and remote. Jemma and Wilde discussed a price for the photography and developing.

'The drinks are on us for the night,' Jemma said. She held back from mentioning the hourly fee Mr King had offered to pay their escorts; Ricky's fee for the photography and developing was high.

Wilde winked. 'Maybe not. We'll see about that. It ain't right for lasses to pay for the drinks.'

'At least let me pay for our entrance fee. This is a business arrangement, Ricky.'

He waved away her protests and offered to show them his darkroom, which was situated at the far end of the small kitchen. Jemma declined and suggested to Bobbie it was time to go.

'Just one last thing, Ricky,' Jemma said as they rose to leave, 'please don't mention a word about us or Smoke & Cracked Mirrors to my brother, should you chance to meet him.'

'What? Doesn't Old Gabe like the competition, eh?' He tapped his nose with his grubby forefinger. 'Mum's the word, Miss Marple.'

It was a relief to be back outside in the fresh air after the stuffiness of Ricky's bedsit.

'Well, that was a stroke of luck!' Bobbie said. 'Friday night is going to be a hoot! That Canadian's a dreamboat! Did you see those eyes?'

Jemma smiled. 'You seem rather taken with him.'

'Do you blame me? He's the best-looking man I've seen for years! And Ricky's quite a character, too. He'll be great fun.'

'We must keep it professional,' Jemma warned gently. 'Remember: we're there to do a job.'

'Spoilsport.'

'I'm pleased Ricky noticed the advert – and Clarissa Deburgh mentioned it yesterday too.'

'A lot of people have seen it. One of the shop girls at Grainger's told me about it on Saturday. I had to hide my smile when she suggested I should apply to you for a job.'

Jemma hesitated when they reached the busier main road of Bootham. 'I know this is your afternoon off, Bobbie, but do you want to come with me to the estate agents to look for offices to rent?'

'Wild horses wouldn't keep me away.'

Chapter Fifteen

Several weary hours later, Jemma arrived home to a deserted house, feeling slightly dispirited. She and Bobbie had viewed several offices in the centre of York, but they'd been either too expensive or completely unsuitable. Still, she wasn't in a rush and there were plenty of other estate agents in town.

She bought fish and chips for supper on her way home, although she had doubts about the chippy's claim it was fish. Since half the trawlermen of Britain had signed up for the merchant navy to try to beat the German sea blockade, there'd been a terrible cod shortage. Rumour had it, the nation's favourite supper was mostly whale meat these days.

She put the food on a low heat in the oven to keep warm and rushed upstairs to the little lumber room opposite her own bedroom. She still had one job to do tonight, and she wanted to do it before it got too dark. Finding an old black dress in a room full of junk with no light wouldn't be easy.

She battled her way through a mountain of broken furniture and boxes of rubbish until she found the old suitcase containing her mother's clothes. She dragged it out on to the landing and opened the lid. The toxic smell of mothballs made her reel.

Her eyes watered as she rummaged through the clothing. The black fabric of her mother's old uniform was too old and delicate to wash; she'd have to hang it out on the line to air. It was also dreadfully out of date, with a high neck and long mutton sleeves fringed with frayed, yellowing lace. She could remove the lace and open up the neck a little but there wasn't much she could about those Victorian sleeves. She suspected the garment might rip to shreds if it was subject to any exertion, but it only had to last one night.

She stroked the material gently and wondered how many exhausting hours of service this dress had seen before her mother had got married and left her job. Her parents had been happy together and they'd had four children initially, but their life hadn't been easy. They'd lost two of their sons to a diphtheria outbreak in 1910, and nearly lost Gabriel in the same outbreak.

When Jemma was born in 1917, her parents were already in their forties. Gabriel often teased her about being the 'afterthought'. But her parents had called her 'their little miracle' and her war-weary father said her cherubic smiles were the only thing that lifted his spirits in those dark days following his return from the trenches...

The snell of burning jerked her out of her reverie.

Rushing into the kitchen, she found Gabriel bending over the oven door, trying to extinguish a small fire. 'For God's sake, Jemma! You're supposed to take chips out of the damned newspaper before you put them in a gas oven!'

'Sorry!' She scurried past him with the dress in her arms, heading for the washing line in the garden.

He wrinkled his nose. 'What's that dreadful smell?'

'Mothballs. It needs airing.'

Gabriel was still scowling when she returned. He pointed to her battered typewriter at the far end of the kitchen table. 'And what's that thing doing there?'

'I brought it down to type out some job applications,' she lied.

This silenced her grumpy brother for the moment. She set the table, found the vinegar, and they sat down to pick their way through the remains of their charred supper.

'Have you had any luck?' he asked.

'I've got a bit of casual waitressing lined up for Saturday night. It might lead to some more work,' she said vaguely.

'Waitressing? That's not using your talents or your education, Jemma.'

She shrugged. 'It's only temporary. I'm still exploring my options.'

He grunted. 'By the way, Maisie has invited us both round for supper on Friday night. You said you wanted to get to know her better...'

'I'm afraid I can't. I'd love to meet Maisie properly – but maybe another night next week? I'm going dancing with Bobbie on Friday.'

Gabriel rolled his eyes but didn't look too disappointed. 'And Cissy rang,' he added. 'They've got a pork joint for Sunday lunch. We're invited to Boroughbridge.'

Jemma hesitated. She knew she would be exhausted after two late nights on the trot – and she'd hoped to take the bus to Middlesbrough on Sunday to fetch her car back to York.

'Actually, the hotel mentioned there might be more work with them on Sunday. Why don't you ask Cissy if you can take Maisie instead? I'm sure she and Gerald would love the opportunity to meet her.'

Gabriel hesitated with his fork halfway to his mouth and a strange look in his eye. Both of them knew from experience that introducing any of their friends to their sister came with an element of risk. Eventually he nodded. 'All right, I'll suggest it. But you'll regret missing out on the food. You'll need all the stamina you can get if you're going to take up a career in waitressing.'

If only you knew, Jemma thought with a smile.

Bobbie raced home and caught her neighbour, Little Laurie Tipton, just as he was setting off for work at the Royal Station Hotel. Resplendent, as usual, in his oversized uniform, his eyes opened wide with surprise to find her, breathless, on his doorstep. 'Evenin', Bobbie. You all right?'

115

'Yes, thank you, Laurie,' she gasped. 'I need to ask you a favour.'

'What?'

'Jemma and I need a waitress's outfit each for Saturday night. Is there any way you can borrow a couple from the hotel?'

His eyes narrowed with suspicion. They were slanted, like a cat's. 'What? *Steal* them, you mean? I can't do that, Bobbie. I'm trusted at the Royal Station Hotel – I never steal nowt.'

'No, not steal them, just *borrow* them for the night. We'll return them to you straight away on Sunday morning – and you can put them back. No one will notice.'

His face puckered with indecision. 'I don't know, Bobbie. Mrs Higgins might not like it if I take anythin' off the rack. I'll have to ask her first.'

'Is she the hotel housekeeper?' He nodded. 'Does she just leave the uniforms in the changing rooms?'

'Oh, yes, there's a full rack of them. The waitresses come and go, you see – those waitresses don't have much loyalty. Not like me.'

'*Please,* Laurie.' Bobbie held her breath while he made up his mind.

'Did you say Jemma will bring them back on Sunday morning?'

'Of course, she will. We both will.'

'So, you'll bring Jemma *here* – to my house?'

Bobbie forced herself to stop grinning. She'd pitched her request in the right way; Laurie was still infatuated with Jemma. 'Yes. We'll come in for a cup of tea.'

Laurie grinned from ear to ear. 'That would be good. Ma enjoys a bit of company – and she said a while back she'd like to meet Jemma because I often talk about her. I'm not goin' to steal them uniforms, though, Bobbie. I shall ask Mrs Higgins first. I'm trusted at the Station Hotel, I am. I've got to go.'

'Thank you, Laurie!'

'By the way, Bobbie,' he said over his shoulder. Despite the gathering dusk, she could still see the sly, cheeky gleam in his slanting eyes. 'Mrs Quigley told my ma that Vince is back in York on leave this weekend.'

Two days later, Jemma found the perfect office space above a shop on Grape Lane.

It had its own front door on to the street, which meant she'd be able to place a brass plaque on the door bearing the name of their agency. The door led straight up a staircase to a large office with an archway into a smaller kitchen with a sink. Both rooms were unfurnished, apart from the black Bakelite telephone sitting on the dusty bare floorboards of the main office. And both had large, sash windows overlooking the narrow, cobbled street below.

Jemma tried to assess the size of the office, while wondering if the roll of carpet she'd left in storage at Uncle Ivan's shop would be big enough to fit.

The landlord, a cheerful balding man with a paunch overhanging his trousers, read her mind. 'You'd have to furnish it, of course – but there's room for expansion. Let me show you something.'

He led the way back to the landing and unlocked another door. It led into a smaller back room which overlooked the grimy alley known as Coffee Yard at the rear of the buildings. This room was stacked with old tea chests. 'I use it for storage,' he said, 'but if you want it, I'm sure we can come to an agreement.'

Jemma nodded. If she and Bobbie ever needed a waiting room for the stream of troubled clients she hoped would beat a path to their door, this extra space had potential. But not right now. There'd been no more response to her newspaper advertisements this week and the rent the landlord wanted for the two other rooms was at the top of her budget. The corporation business rate for these premises was also eye-watteringly high.

117

She wandered back towards the grimy window of the main office. Cyclists whizzed along the street below. She felt a draught, but she had a good pair of thick curtains in storage.

Her brain was calmly assessing these rooms – but the rest of her was in turmoil. Glorious, heart-racing turmoil.

This was a great location. Thanks to its notorious history, everyone in York knew Grape Lane. Once part of the city's red-light district and famous for its brothels, someone in the past with an excess of moral indignation had changed the lane's name from Grope to Grape.

But terms hadn't been agreed yet and she knew she needed to hide her excitement from the landlord. 'How soon do you plan to let these rooms?'

The landlord hesitated. 'They're available now – there's another fellow interested, but he can't take on the lease until next month. I promised him first refusal.'

Jemma gave a tiny smile. She would prefer to wait a few more weeks until she was sure there was more demand in the city for private detectives, but the wrangling over money had commenced. 'And if I could rent them sooner?' She struggled to keep her voice neutral, businesslike.

He grinned. 'Well, I suppose if you move in next week, you can have them.'

Next week? Jemma had a vision of her hard-earned cash writhing in horror in the bank vault, but she dismissed it. She knew she was being hustled, as the Americans called it, but this place was too good to lose. He wanted her to sign a six-month lease, but she managed to barter him down to three.

When she left her new office, Jemma finally understood the meaning of the expression 'walking on air'. Beneath her feet, an imaginary iridescent cloud carried her along the pavement, rippling with repressed emotion and humming with undischarged electrostatic energy. She remembered the Van de Graaff generator Michael had once shown her and how, when they placed their hands on it, their hair had defied gravity and stood on end. She touched her hat lightly, half expecting to find it floating two inches above her head.

Three months.

She had three months to prove herself.

She would have to live on her savings and the rent, rates and other bills would take nearly every other penny she had. But this was her opportunity to change her life for ever. For the better.

When she turned into Stonegate, she heard Michael whisper in her ear: *Carpe diem.*

Chapter Sixteen

'Wow! Do we look great, or what?' Bobbie twirled in front of the full-length mirror in Jemma's bedroom and the full skirt of her shimmering, dark-green satin dress flew out around her shapely legs. 'It's just such a shame we have to take those ugly bloody things to De Grey's.' She pointed to their gas masks.

Jemma smiled and agreed. She was nervous but Bobbie's enthusiasm was infectious. Her friend looked truly glamorous tonight. Her dress, with its low sweetheart neckline, was a second-hand bargain from a local jumble sale but it clung to her curvaceous figure as if it had been made for her. She'd finished off her look with a matching pair of green satin court shoes and a sequined snood, interwoven with artificial black flowers, to hold back her hair.

'The shoes pinch,' Bobbie confessed, 'but they were an end of range bargain from Grainger's, and I used my staff discount. I can suffer them for a night.'

Jemma's own white and pale-blue dress, with its cute short sleeves and floaty hem, was an old favourite. It fell in soft pleats over her bosom before gathering into a high, V-shaped waist and flaring out over her hips in loose folds. Bobbie had pleated and rolled her silvery blonde hair and embellished it with a spray of little blue artificial flowers that reminded her of periwinkles. 'I've got some flowery blue earrings somewhere,' Bobbie said, reaching for her bag.

'Don't worry, I'll wear the pearls Michael bought me.'

Bobbie laughed. 'Ooh, listen at you – posh lady with her pearls! I remember your first pair of earrings – large gold hoops made from cheap metal that made your earlobes turn green overnight.'

'I've changed a bit since then.' Jemma clipped the tiny pearl clusters to her ears and fastened the single strand of lustrous pearls around her neck.

'They're sweet,' Bobbie said.

'Husbands have their uses,' Jemma joked. 'They're also rather generous with the French perfume on birthdays. Here, have some.' She lifted her cut-glass perfume bottle from the dressing table, squeezed the rubber pump and sprayed them both with a sensual and exotic haze of patchouli, carnation and vanilla.

'Gorgeous!' Bobbie exclaimed. 'Now let's go and wow those guys!'

De Grey's was an elegant, white-rendered building with a wrought-iron balcony running the full length of the dance hall on the first floor. The faint strain of big-band music drifted down to where Ricky and Don waited for them on the pavement.

Don looked fabulous in his blue uniform with its gleaming gilt buttons, winged badges and peaked cap. Ricky had made an effort, too. He'd shaved, polished his shoes, slicked back his fair, floppy hair into a recognisable style and found a clean shirt to wear with his suit. His Leica swung casually on its strap over his left shoulder. The only odd thing about him was the long red-leather box sticking out of his jacket pocket.

The two men greeted the women with a peck on the cheek like old friends. Ricky offered Jemma his arm and they led the way into the spacious, richly furnished entrance hall.

Jemma slipped Ricky a ten-shilling note to pay for their entry fee. The sound of a Louis Armstrong jazz classic met them as they swept up the circular staircase.

The candlelit dance hall was smoky, but not unpleasantly so. It was early but the hall was nearly full, and the well-sprung dance floor was crowded with couples. Others sat at the low tables, which were covered with pristine white tablecloths with pretty little lamps glimmering in the centre. The cocktails they held gleamed like the contents of a jewel casket. Meanwhile, the bar on the far wall, with its neon lights and rows of glasses suspended above the heads of the bartenders, glowed like a crystal cave.

The two women settled at a vacant table while the men went to order drinks. Jemma's eyes scanned the swirling mass of bodies on the dance floor, looking for their insurance fraudster. Terrence King had sent her a photograph of Eddie Chambers as promised, and she was confident she'd spot him easily. Besides which, she figured the 'injured' man would stand out like a sore thumb in his civvies. Like Don, most of the men were in uniform. But there was no sign of Chambers – yet.

Her foot began to tap to the seductive beat of the music. There was time to enjoy themselves before they had to focus on their assignment.

The men returned with their beers, and port and lemon for the women. Ricky whipped the cover off his Leica and pulled the strange red-leather box out of his jacket pocket. It contained a flashlight attachment. He screwed the pole with the bulb to the side of his camera. 'Smile, Miss Marple! We need to look like we're here for a good time.'

Jemma, Bobbie and Don raised their glasses and shouted 'Cheers!' as Ricky stepped back and took their photographs.

When he'd finished, the band struck up Glenn Miller's popular tune 'In the Mood'. The four of them took to the dance floor, with Ricky partnering Jemma. He was surprisingly light on his feet. His hip-swinging was a bit overdone, she thought, but not embarrassingly so.

They swapped partners after a while, and it was when Jemma danced with Don that the tempo changed. The pleasant, mellow trill of the clarinet filled the air and led the saxophonists and other musicians into the slower Cole Porter song 'Begin the Beguine'.

Don pulled Jemma closer, crushing her against his broad chest, and she felt his heartbeat beneath the stiff cloth of his uniform. As they drifted around the dance floor, she realised with a jolt she hadn't been this intimate with a man for months. Like the different ends of a magnet, she was repelled and attracted at the same time by the closeness of his muscular body and his unfamiliar masculine scent.

To distract herself from this uncomfortable feeling, she focused on what she could learn about Don from his appearance. This wasn't easy when a man was sporting a regulation forces' haircut and a uniform. However, just below the collar of his shirt she thought she saw the small rise of a chain beneath the material. *A religious medallion, perhaps?* Maybe a crucifix or a St Christopher? *Was he a Catholic?*

And when she glanced up at his face, she saw the faintest twitch in the corner of his left eye. Her father had taught her that an eye tic often indicated a traumatic experience in childhood or adolescence, like the death of a parent or a sibling. But Don was in the air force and must have a gruelling flying schedule. The tic probably indicated nothing more ominous than exhaustion.

'What do you think of De Grey's, Don?'

'I think it's a swell joint. You and Miss Bobbie are gracious ladies to let us join you in this show. Mind you, I don't need much of an excuse to come out and bend an elbow with Ricky. Time tends to drag when I'm not in the air.'

'Bend an elbow?'

He grinned and fine lines crinkled around those gorgeous dark eyes. 'Drink. Your food isn't up to much in this country – but your beer is great.'

She smiled. 'I take it you're not flying your aircraft tomorrow?'

He shook his head. 'It's the last day of my leave. I'll be off out on another show the day after.'

That was the second time he'd used the word. 'Show?'

'A mission.'

124

'What do you fly, by the way? Is it a Whitley bomber?'

He grinned again. 'It's a secret. If I tell you, Jemma, I'll have to kill you immediately.'

She laughed. 'Well, I'm afraid your secret's out. Your Whitley bombers look and sound like a plague of locusts when they leave base. Every schoolboy in York with a dog-eared aircraft identification book knows what you're hiding in those hangars.'

'Shh,' he said with a wink, 'don't let the Jerries hear you.'

They twirled again and when they slowed once more, she asked him the question that had been puzzling her since they first met. 'Excuse my nosiness, Don, but I'd love to know why you're here – in England – helping us.'

'What? Apart from the attraction of such beautiful female company?'

She laughed. 'Yes, apart from that. What made you leave your family in Ontario and come to fight for us?' *Did he have a family back home? A wife, perhaps? Children?* She estimated he was about thirty – certainly old enough to have both.

'I was born in London. My family emigrated to Canada when I was a child. When war broke out, I felt I wanted to help. I fly commercially back in Canada. So, I signed up for a posting back to the old country. I wasn't the only one. There are thousands of us over here now and the Royal Canadian Air Force is a strong presence alongside the RAF. Unlike me, most of them weren't born here.'

'That's... that's very loyal of you.'

'True, but then again only an idiot would fail to see the threat Hitler poses to peace and the stability of the entire world.' He wasn't smiling now. His eyes glittered with anger. 'The Nazis must be stopped.'

'It's a pity the Americans don't seem to see it the same way as you.'

'Oh, the Yanks see it all right. They'll be along soon enough – they just don't want to join in the fight yet.'

Reassured, Jemma leant against his chest and enjoyed the sensation of their bodies swaying together. Previously, she'd dismissed the foreign airmen she'd seen in the city as a loud, swaggering, overconfident bunch with too much money and time on their hands, but Don seemed different, intelligent and more thoughtful.

Eddie Chambers had entered the dance hall with a woman on his arm. Her heart skipped a beat and she stiffened. 'I'm sorry, Don, but we're going to have to find Ricky. Our insurance fraudster has just arrived.'

Don followed the direction of her gaze. 'Are you sure?'

'Yes, there's no mistaking that lean face and those shifty hooded eyes.'

'He doesn't seem to be limping, the sly devil. Do we have to go right now? I'm enjoying myself.' He'd made no attempt to loosen his hold on her waist.

Jemma smiled. 'We can wait until he takes to the floor with his partner – or until this dance finishes. My client wants photographs of him actually *dancing*.'

Chapter Seventeen

Jemma and Don took a few more turns around the dance floor before he led her back to the table, where Bobbie and Ricky were deep in discussion about American music.

Jemma leant down between them. 'Don't both look up at the same time – but Chambers is here. He's dancing with the blonde woman in the cerise and black dress.'

'That's an understatement if ever I heard one,' Bobbie said, after a casual glance in Chambers' direction. 'That's not *dancing*, that's *gyrating*.'

Jemma nodded. Terence King had been right to suspect the man was a fraud. Chambers was throwing himself and his partner all over the place, in perfect control of every one of his limbs and with a suppleness most of the other men would envy. Jemma hesitated, unsure what to do next.

'What's *cerise*, when it's at home?' Ricky asked.

'Bright pink,' Bobbie informed him.

Now he had his mark, Ricky swung smoothly into action. 'We need more photographs as a souvenir of this evening – and this time I need the dance floor in the background.' He reached for his Leica, checked the flashlight attachment, fiddled with his aperture, then stood up and moved back. 'Smile, folks.'

Grinning, they allowed him to position them around the table. Every time Chambers and his woman whirled past behind them, Ricky snapped a photograph.

It took time, and the forced smile on Jemma's face made her jaw ache. She desperately wanted to turn around and see if Chambers had noticed Ricky and the camera, but she didn't dare move. At one point, Ricky stepped back into the path of a man with a tray of drinks. Fortunately, none were spilled, and the guy shrugged off Ricky's apology.

When he'd finished, Jemma relaxed. Chambers hadn't noticed anything. Bobbie and Don went back on the dance floor and Ricky sat down and pulled a new roll of film out of his pocket.

'Do you think you got a clear shot of his face?' Jemma asked.

Ricky winked at her. 'Stop fussin', Miss Marple. You've got a professional here. It's all on film. You can relax now.'

She laughed. 'Were my nerves so obvious?'

'I'll say – you've barely touched your drink. You shouldn't worry so much.' Ricky changed the film and snapped the camera shut. 'This is easy money for you gals. No one would ever suspect either of you of being a PI. As Don said earlier, you're both far too pretty.'

She blushed. 'I'll have to remember to thank him for the compliment.'

'And another thing, Miss Marple—'

'Yes?'

'If you ever need my help again – you've only got to ask, right?' His sharp eyes locked with hers across the table. 'I don't care what your stuffy brother says about this set-up – I think what you girls are doin' is swell, and provided we can agree terms, I'm happy to help, OK?'

'Thank you, Ricky – that's a relief. Can I buy you a drink?'

'No. I'll get you and Bobbie a cocktail to seal the deal. Mind you,' he added with a glance at the dance floor, 'it looks like she might be a while yet before she's back.'

Jemma followed his gaze, half expecting to see Bobbie in an intimate clinch with Don Hudson, but she wasn't. A khaki-clad serviceman had interrupted their dance and whisked the flushed and excited Bobbie away to the far side of the dance floor. Jemma caught a glimpse of the soldier's face; it was Vince Quigley.

Ricky rose to his feet and made his way towards the bar. En route he pulled out his camera and started taking sly shots of the insurance fraudster and his partner in the bright pink dress.

Don arrived back at their table. He took a swig of his beer then pulled out a silver cigarette case and offered Jemma one of his Sweet Caporal cigarettes.

'No, thank you.'

Chambers and his partner swirled past once more and Don's eyes followed them. 'I guess you're glad he showed up and Ricky got those shots?'

'Yes, I am.'

'Well, personally, I think it's a shame.'

'Why?'

'I understand from Bobbie your client offered to pay you for two evenings here. It would have been a great excuse to do this again. Mind you, we still can. Your client will never know if we dragged this assignment out another week.'

Jemma relaxed and smiled. 'I don't think that would be very professional, Don. I want to impress him with our efficiency. I'm not sure who he is, but I suspect he might use us again.'

He grinned. 'Well, in that case we'll just have to make the most of tonight. After all, the evening is still young.'

His deep voice was soft and his accent seductive. Jemma remembered how she'd always loved the faint Slavic lilt in Michael's voice.

Don reached out and took hold of her hand. 'It's time to enjoy yourself now, sweetheart.' There was no mistaking his meaning.

Jemma withdrew her hand sharply. 'I'm sorry, Don. I don't want you to get the wrong impression – about me, or tonight. I'm only just finding my feet again... I... I lost my husband a few months ago.'

He nodded. 'Bobbie told me he's missing in action. I'm sorry for your loss, Jemma, and if there's anything I can do to help, don't hesitate to ask.'

She shuffled uncomfortably in her seat, struggling for a reply that would do justice to Michael's memory without dampening the party mood.

But Don hadn't finished. 'In fact, she told me the unusual circumstances of his disappearance – and how the military left you in the dark. It reminded me of something that might help.'

'What?'

'I don't want to build your hopes up...' – he glanced around to check no one could overhear him – 'but your husband isn't the first wireless mechanic to mysteriously disappear out of the ranks of the RAF – or the Royal Canadian Air Force – and go up to Scotland. It's all very hush-hush, of course.'

She sensed his hesitation. 'Don, please. I'm desperate for information. If you know anything, *anything* at all...'

He took another drag of his cigarette and leant closer. 'There's a rumour they're training a new unit in Scotland. Your husband didn't speak any other languages besides English, did he? That guy of ours they took was a French Canadian from Montreal.'

Jemma felt like she'd been doused with a bucket of cold water. 'Yes.' Her voice cracked. 'Michael spoke five languages.'

'Five?'

Jemma reeled them off automatically while her mind tried to make sense of this alarming new information. 'Michael was born in Kiev. The Ukrainian dialect is his mother tongue, but he learnt to speak Russian when he was young – and German. When his family emigrated to Britain, he learnt English here and French at grammar school.'

'Your late husband was a Ruskie?' She registered the shock in his eyes.

'Was. His family fled the Bolsheviks after the last war. He was a child when he arrived in England – like you, when you went to Canada. He's a naturalised British citizen.'

'He must have been one hell of a smart guy to manage all those languages,' Don murmured. 'I've never even heard of Ukrainian.'

'He was – is – a smart guy.'

A special operations force consisting of bilingual and multilingual wireless experts?

This could only mean one thing: Michael had been dropped behind enemy lines and was spying for his country when he went *'missing in action'*.

If this was a new, top-secret task force, then it explained why information had been so hard to get. She desperately wanted to discuss this with Gabriel. Did her brother have any contacts in the Secret Service who would help them? Gabriel's rank in the police force counted for nothing with the military. But maybe he knew someone who could help?

Spying. She sucked in her breath as a new and horrible thought came to her. There were rules protecting prisoners of war, as laid down in the Geneva Convention – but did those basic safeguards also apply to men slinking about in enemy territory in the shadowy world of espionage? Or did the Germans just shoot British spies once they'd caught and tortured them?

'Jemma?' Don was trying to get her attention. 'I'm sorry if I've distressed you – but Bobbie said this information might help.'

Jemma snapped back into the real world and felt a rush of gratitude. The last thing she wanted was a romantic entanglement with a man whose home was on the other side of the planet, but she sensed Don's loneliness. He deserved her friendship, if nothing else. She needed to make an effort.

The piano and bass played the slow, seductive opening bars of Billie Holliday's 'I Wished on the Moon'.

She put on her most dazzling smile and stood up. He rose with her.

'I'm fine,' she lied. 'Let's dance.'

Chapter Eighteen

Vince startled Bobbie when he appeared out of nowhere and cut into her dance with Don. It wasn't just the surprise of seeing him either. The army had changed him. His thick chestnut hair had been shorn back to almost to nothing and there was a new and ugly scar snaking round the left-hand side of his head. But the twinkle in his blue eyes behind his spectacles and that slow, easy grin were unmistakably Vince.

He pulled her towards him, and she leaned happily against the scratchy material of his uniform, although she closed her eyes when she caught sight of his wedding ring. Instinctively, they locked together and picked up the steps of the dance.

'Lovely to see you again, Bobbie,' he whispered in her ear. 'You look fantastic.' The side of his face nuzzled against her own in affection. She breathed in his familiar scent. Her heart lurched with nostalgia for her childhood playmate and sweetheart.

'Are you here with Jemma tonight?' he asked.

'Yes. And some friends. Is Susan not with you?'

He shook his head. 'No, she'd already made plans and didn't want to change them. I surprised her when I turned up without warning.'

Bobbie examined his face for any sign of resentment. After so long away from home, he must have been disappointed to discover his young bride was too busy to spend the evening with him. But he looked as calm and unperturbed as ever. Behind his glasses, his eyes were glazed from the beer but shone with contentment. It took a lot to upset Vince.

'Do you still work at the library? Did you ever take that librarian course?'

'No, I left the library.' She changed the subject quickly. 'How are the Royal Engineers? Have they sent you to France yet?'

'No such luck. I'm based at Chatham in Kent and spend most of my time training apprentices to build new runways and civil defence barriers for the beaches on the south coast.'

She smiled. 'I remember those miniature bridges and pistons you used to build – and those damned bilge pumps.'

The music slowed, and he pulled her in tighter, grinning. 'Yes, I loved my bilge pumps.'

'You were obsessed with them, weren't you? What was that all about?'

He laughed and shrugged. 'I don't know – I guess I liked the sound of the word *bilge*. I was stunned when you brought that library book home and showed me what one actually looked like. I'd been building them wrong for years. Once a fool, always a fool, I guess.'

'What do you mean?'

He let go of her waist for a moment and tapped the scar on the side of his head. 'I'm still an idiot. I had an altercation with a slab of concrete while telling my apprentices about the importance of safety.'

She laughed, then grimaced. 'Sorry, Vince, that must have hurt.'

'Not as much as my pride did.'

'I guess it's another one of your nine lives spent.'

He shrugged in that easy, familiar way of his and grinned again. 'I think I'm down to my last life now.'

'Well, make sure you treasure it. Were you badly hurt?'

'I was out cold for twenty-four hours – and woke up with the biggest hangover I've ever known.'

'What? An even worse hangover than the one we shared after we stole your mum's cooking sherry and drank the lot?'

He winked. 'Yes, even worse than that. We were a right pair of scamps, weren't we?'

'The Tanner Street terrors.'

They grinned at the shared memories. In those back streets by the river, their school uniforms doubled as their playing out clothes. Vince, the only grammar school boy, and Bobbie, the scholarship girl at a private school, stuck out like sore thumbs among the other children. The local bullies made a beeline for them and they quickly realised there was safety in sticking together – and fun. Always a bit of a tomboy, Bobbie clambered up the stunted trees down by the riverbank with the same ease as Vince, and never fussed about getting filthy while playing beside the railway track. Other times they would go into town to watch parades and Bobbie would make him laugh by inventing scandalous stories about the civic dignitaries leading the processions.

Later, Vince would find bits of junk and build a set for the action of these stories. These usually contained complicated bridges, random pistons, flat-bottomed river dredgers and his beloved bilge pumps.

'We had a good childhood, didn't we?' he asked.

She nodded. 'Innocent games.' Things became less innocent when they grew older, of course, but she didn't want to dwell on that.

The song ended and the drummer began to thump out the lively, foot-tapping opening beat of Benny Goodman's 'Sing, Sing, Sing'. By the time the trumpets had joined in the cacophony, they were swinging around the dance floor.

Jemma and Don whizzed by, laughing, and a group of soldiers – Vince's mates – laughed and cheered when they whirled past. Someone wolf-whistled.

'They're idiots,' Vince said, grinning. 'Ignore them.'

The dance ended too soon but Bobbie was glad of an opportunity to catch her breath. 'That was fun!'

'Sorry about your toes, Bobbie. Are they still intact?'

'I think so. How much leave have you got?' she asked.

135

'Just a few days,' he murmured. 'Officially, I'm still sick, but they said I might as well stop cluttering up their hospital ward and recuperate at home until Monday.'

Vince showed no sign of tiring of her company and when the band struck up a slower, more graceful dance, he pulled her close again.

They passed his drunken friends once more and one of them yelled out: 'Atta boy, Vince!'

'They're old chums from university,' Vince explained. 'But they've all signed up now. It was lucky I came home when I did – heaven knows when we'll see each other again.'

Bobbie fought back her unease. She'd always been jealous of those years he'd spent away at university in Sheffield, and the people – especially the women – he'd met there. Once he'd left her to her humdrum life at the library, and soared into a more intellectual orbit, she'd felt inadequate and awkward. She'd worried how this new life would change him.

But when he'd returned with his degree, he was the same old Vince, apart from sporting a pair of spectacles. Or so she'd thought.

For a few brief, wonderful months they'd resumed their easy, affectionate relationship. She'd started to hope. Hope and dream – that it could lead to something more.

He nuzzled against her face and neck again. 'It's good to see you, Bobbie.'

She closed her eyes and tried to block out the rest of the world as she swayed in his arms. 'You too, Vince.'

His friends called out that they were leaving and wanted Vince to go with them. The dance ended and the band announced an interval. Vince led her off the floor. There was an excited buzz of conversation, but it was easier to talk now the music had stopped.

'It's been wonderful meeting up with you again, Bobbie… and I'm sorry, I haven't asked about you. How are you? And your family?'

'We're fine. Frank's in France with the Green Howards – and I've started a new business venture with Jemma.'

'That sounds interesting. Perhaps you'd like to write to me at Chatham and tell me about it? I like getting post.'

'Yes, of course. I'll get your address from your mum.'

He paused for a moment, then asked: 'And your dad?'

'Oh, he's fine,' she said quickly. 'He's out of work – but at least he's out of prison now.'

He nodded, leant forward and kissed her on the cheek. 'I'm so sorry about all that, Bobbie. I know how hard it must have been for you and your family.'

No, you don't, she thought sadly. *You didn't stick around long enough to find out.*

'Come on, Vince!' one of his friends yelled. 'Bring the lass with you, if you want.'

Bobbie held her breath. *Would he ask her to go with him?*

If he did, she'd go. To another dance hall. A pub. The ends of the earth. Hell, damn it. She'd even go a hotel room if he asked…

'I've got to leave, Bobbie.'

Her disappointment was crushing. 'I know you have.'

'It's been lovely.' He leant over, kissed her again, then walked out of her life once more. Back to the war. Back to his wife. Back to God knows what.

Would she ever see him again?

For a few brief, romantic minutes, she'd been back in his arms. But now, as she stood there fighting back the tears, reality washed over her like the icy black waters of the river in flood.

She'd lost more than her job at the library when her father disgraced himself and was sent to prison.

Chapter Nineteen

The two women met at Bobbie's house to prepare for their assignment at The Spinney.

'There's a small problem with my waitress uniform,' Bobbie said as Jemma took off her coat in the narrow hallway. 'I might need your sewing skills.'

'What's happened?'

'Well, I asked Laurie Tipton—'

'Little Laurie?'

'Yes. I asked Little Laurie to get us a couple of uniforms from the hotel, which he was quite happy to do because he's still got a tremendous crush on you. But the sneaky little monkey has only brought us one, which he insists is for you.'

'Well, I've got my mother's old dress in my bag, so you can wear the one he provided. He'll never know.'

'The problem is, the little pervert has your measurements down to a T. He must have been sizing you up for years, Jemma. The uniform will fit *you* perfectly but I'm struggling to get it over my bust.'

Jemma laughed. 'I'm sure we can sort something out.'

Bobbie's home was cramped, cluttered with faded old furniture and smoky from the coal fire. But it was warm and a delicious smell emanated from the kitchen, which made Jemma's stomach rumble. Mrs Brown welcomed her and insisted they sat down for a bowl of vegetable broth before they went to work. She showed no curiosity about why the two of them had suddenly taken up waitressing and Jemma felt she seemed distracted and more careworn than before.

But it was the difference in Bobbie's dad that shocked Jemma the most.

'Big Bill' Baker had always seemed a giant of a man to Jemma when she was a child. Loud, confident and proud, he'd dominated every room with his presence and his argumentative conversation. A staunch Labour supporter and union man, his anger with the politicians and the bosses always simmered below the surface.

Now he was slumped down in his chair by the hearth and seemed to have shrunk into himself. His broad face was mottled red from the drink and his hand shook when he stirred the coals in the grate with the poker. He only became animated when she asked after his son. 'Frank's battalion is with the British Expeditionary Force in France,' he told her proudly.

'Isn't that on the front line? It must be dangerous out there.'

Mr Baker laughed. 'Aye, he's seein' plenty of action. My boy will be kicking those Jerries right up the arse.'

Jemma didn't doubt it. Bobbie's older brother had been a tough, unruly young man when they were young, and a bit of a bully at times.

'I send him a parcel when I can,' Mrs Baker reassured her vaguely.

Jemma hesitated. She knew the news from France wasn't good and the Allies were struggling to hold back the invading German army. She didn't doubt Frank's courage for one minute, but even a battalion of tough back street Yorkshire lads didn't stand a chance against the relentless surge of Hitler's panzer divisions as they rolled across the continent. 'Don't you worry about him?'

'Nonsense! He's got the "luck of the Bakers", has our Frank. He'll be fine.'

Jemma didn't reply. When she thought back to everything that had happened to Bobbie and her family over the past year, this so-called luck of the Bakers didn't seem much of an asset.

Bobbie rose from the table. 'We need to get ready, Jemma.'

'I take it they don't know about our new venture,' Jemma said when they entered Bobbie's small room.

Bobbie shrugged. 'I'll tell them when I'm ready. My dad has a nasty habit of ruining my life. Smoke & Cracked Mirrors is safer if he doesn't know it exists.'

Jemma tactfully changed the subject. 'Your dad seems quite relaxed about Frank being out there on the front line.'

'We're not allowed to think the unthinkable. So, we don't. Now, let me show you this damned uniform.'

The two of them spent the next twenty minutes trying to squash Bobbie into the black dress Laurie had provided.

'Good grief, when did you grow these bazoomers?' Jemma giggled as she snipped away at the centre seam with a small pair of nail scissors. 'There. I can't go down any further if you want to retain any sense of modesty. Can you breathe?'

'Just about.'

Jemma put a stitch in the top of the lowered neckline. 'Hopefully, this should hold it. Just don't exert yourself too much or there'll be an explosion. I'll sew the seam back up tomorrow before we return it to Laurie.'

Bobbie eyed herself in the mottled old mirror on the dressing table. 'Aren't I showing too much cleavage for a waitress?'

Jemma handed her a freshly laundered and starched high-bibbed apron. 'If you wear this high and don't lean over, no one should notice.'

Bobbie tied the apron so high the bib almost reached her neck. 'This dress is too short,' she complained. 'I look like a trollop.' Her eyes widened when she saw Jemma's own dress.

'Wow! Mutton sleeves – how Victoriana!'

Jemma pulled on the uniform and the two of them paused to examine themselves in the mirror. They burst out laughing.

'We look a right pair of clowns,' Bobbie said. 'I look like a tart and you look like something voluminous from last century that's just washed up on the banks of the Ouse.'

Jemma smiled and tied her own apron round her waist. 'It's only for one night. We'll survive.'

Bobbie pulled a white cap over her hair, tucking in a few loose strands. 'It's a good job Don and Vince can't see us. They'd be running for the hills.'

Jemma glanced at her curiously. Bobbie had left De Grey's soon after the interval and Ricky had walked her home. Jemma had enjoyed a couple more dances with Don before she'd asked him to find her a taxi. He'd asked her to go out for a drink with him when they parted, but she'd politely declined.

'Was everything all right last night? You seemed upset when Vince left.'

Bobbie reached for her lipstick. Her expression in the mirror was blank but Jemma sensed she was on the verge of a confidence.

'Vince and I became very close when he came back from university last summer,' Bobbie said quietly. 'I'd always loved him and hoped he felt the same way. But it didn't last.'

'I'm sorry to hear that, Bobbie. He got that great job at Stubbs Engineering, didn't he?'

'Yes.'

'What went wrong?'

'Susan Stubbs is what went wrong – his boss's daughter. She decided her father's brilliant new engineer would make her a great husband. She pursued him relentlessly.'

Jemma frowned. 'What did her family think about this?'

'I don't know the ins and outs – and this is gossip, you understand – but I think there'd been some trouble with Susan in the past. She's a bit flighty and her father wanted her to settle down.'

'And Vince? What did he think?"'

'I'd like to think that gentle, easy-going Vince was tricked into marriage with Susan before he realised what had hit him.'

Jemma hesitated and picked her words carefully. 'Marrying his boss's daughter will advance Vince's career.'

Bobbie shrugged and removed a tiny smudge of lipstick from her front tooth. 'I suppose so. And once my father disgraced himself, well that was that for us, wasn't it?'

'What?'

'Everything happened at the same time. Vince disappeared from my life after my father's arrest. Six weeks later, he walked down the aisle with Susan.'

'That's appalling! When did Vince become such a snob?'

'I don't blame him. How can I? I'm still racked with shame about my dad. Why on earth would a man with such a glittering future tie himself to a woman whose father was a prison inmate—' Her voice caught, and Jemma squeezed her hand.

'That must have hurt, but I think you need to stop making excuses for Vince, Bobbie. I suspect he's an ambitious man.'

Bobbie thought for a moment, then sighed. 'You're right. If I'm honest with myself, he was pulling away from me even before Dad was arrested... The affection he showed me last summer was probably just part of the euphoria of finishing his degree, returning home and starting his job.'

'You deserve someone with more integrity,' Jemma said, 'if he'd really cared for you, he would have stood by you.'

Bobbie shrugged, put the lipstick back in its case and stepped back, finally satisfied with her appearance. 'We've got a busy night ahead. Are you ready?'

Jemma nodded.

'Come on. It's time to start our investigation into Miss Helen Urwin.'

Chapter Twenty

Their taxi to The Spinney took them through large wrought-iron gates and up a long driveway, past mature lawned gardens surrounded by fruit trees and herbaceous borders.

Bobbie whistled with appreciation when she saw the large red-brick house with its modern bay windows and towering chimneys.

'Mrs Banyan said her father designed and built it himself,' Jemma whispered.

Bobbie headed for the impressive arched entrance with double timbered and panelled front doors, but Jemma grabbed her arm. 'No. It's the servants' entrance for us.'

The back door led into a warm and busy stone-flagged kitchen where Mrs Banyan, in an elegant full-length, dusky-rose silk evening gown, was directing the staff. Over her shoulders she wore a matching taffeta bolero, beautifully embroidered and decorated with sequins. She showed no hint of recognition when they entered the kitchen. 'Ah, I see the casual waitresses have arrived, Mrs Higgs.'

The elderly woman she addressed looked up from a tray of vol-au-vents and gave them a welcoming smile. Wiping her greasy hands on her apron, she pointed to a small cloakroom. 'Take your coats off, dearies, and hang them up in there. What are your names?'

'I'm Ann and she's Mary,' Bobbie replied.

When they returned, Mrs Banyan was drawing a pair of dusky-rose gloves up her arms – a perfect match for her gown. Her eyes glittered with distaste when she saw their uniforms. 'Goodness, how *last-century!*' she said to Jemma. Her long, thin nose twitched. 'Is that mothballs I can smell?'

Jemma stared down at her feet and addressed her shoes. 'Might be.'

Mrs Higgs leant towards her mistress, tapped a finger on her forehead and said in a hushed tone, 'I think she might be a bit simple, ma'am.'

'Oh, my God,' Mrs Banyan replied. 'Why is it so hard to get decent staff these days? And you, young lady—' She swung round on Bobbie. 'I think you grew out of that uniform years ago.'

'Sorry, ma'am,' Bobbie said with a submissive bob.

'I'm sure they'll be fine, ma'am.' Mrs Higgs said. 'No one notices the staff at events like this.'

Mrs Banyan sighed wearily. 'I suppose so. Can you give them their instructions, please, Mrs Higgs?'

'Will do, ma'am. You go and enjoy your party.'

Mrs Banyan turned on her elegant silver heels and departed in a cloud of perfume. Jemma bit back a smile. This may not be Mrs Banyan's home any longer, but when she was in residence, she ran her father's house as if she owned it.

Mrs Higgs introduced them to the two other staff, a harassed housemaid called Daisy and a young footman called George. Like them, George had been hired for the evening. 'Daisy here will greet the guests at the door and take their coats,' Mrs Higgs informed them. 'Your job is to top up the drinks and take orders for cocktails. George will make the cocktails, and you will serve them – along with the canapés. When they're ready to do the speeches, congratulating the young couple on their engagement, you need to take round the trays of champagne. All right?'

Bobbie and Jemma nodded and right on cue, the doorbell rang.

Bobbie picked up a silver tray of ruby sherry in crystal glasses and Mrs Higgs handed Jemma a tray of tiny salmon and watercress sandwiches.

They followed the maid out into the hallway and caught their first glimpse of Helen Urwin.

Tall, dark-haired and pale-skinned, with a dusting of freckles over her powdered nose, she wore a flowing lime-green evening gown with a beaded and sequined bodice. Incongruously, she'd paired the lovely dress with a pair of garish crimson shoes and a chunky, reddish-brown carnelian necklace. Her large dark eyes flickered nervously over the guests as they arrived.

Beside her stood her fiancé. Sandy-haired, portly and bespectacled, Teddy Anston looked gentle but seemed overwhelmed by the occasion; a thin sheen of perspiration glistened on his high forehead. Helen repeatedly touched Edward's arm for reassurance and the many glittering bracelets on her wrist jangled every time she moved.

She was a good-looking woman, Jemma decided, but not classically so. Her mouth, with its vivid carmine lipstick, was too big and so was her nose. *Handsome, rather than pretty.* She was also incredibly thin, and her bony shoulders poked out from beneath the fragile silk of her gown.

The large, oak-panelled hallway was soon filled with elegant women, divesting themselves of their furs, and dapper men in black tie. Everyone was laughing loudly, including Helen Urwin.

Bobbie and Jemma flattened themselves against the wall next to a huge aspidistra in a Chinese vase on a wooden pedestal.

'When they start the speeches,' Jemma whispered to Bobbie, 'that'll be a good a time for us to snoop around upstairs. Everyone will be in the drawing room.'

Bobbie nodded then stepped forward when Mrs Banyan gestured for her to circulate among the guests with the sherry.

For the next two hours, Jemma hardly saw Bobbie, although she overheard her laughing with Mrs Higgs in the kitchen. They were run off their feet. In keeping with her new persona as a 'simpleton', Jemma avoided conversation with the other staff.

147

The guests filled most of the reception rooms on the ground floor, including the conservatory with its beautiful black-and-white tiled floor and exotic plants. It was a mild evening and several of the male guests disappeared into the rear garden to smoke cigars. The only children present were Mrs Banyan's two young daughters, who raced round the rooms in their frilly pink dresses, engrossed in some game of their own.

Jemma only had one close encounter with Helen Urwin, when she handed her a vol-au-vent from a silver platter.

'Delicious!' Helen exclaimed as she delicately wiped a flake of puff pastry from her lips with a beautifully manicured nail. 'I don't know how Mrs Higgs manages to produce such gems with these dreadful food shortages. Apart from Aggie Black who cooked for us in Leeds, she's the best cook I've ever come across.' She leant across and placed an affectionate hand on her fiancé's arm. 'Teddy, *darling*, do you think we can steal Mrs Higgs away from your father when we move into our home? Do you think he'd mind awfully?'

Edward Anston's plump face broke into an indulgent smile. 'I... I... do... do think he might mind, he stammered. 'Mrs Higgs has... has been with the family *for ever.*'

'Have you found a suitable house yet, Teddy?' asked one of the other guests.

'Yes,' the young man replied. 'It's nearby – on Blenheim – and... p... perfect for our needs.'

Helen squeezed his arm tighter. 'It's a *gorgeous* house. Six bedrooms, private and modern, with all the latest gadgets. You and Sarah *must* come and visit us when we move in...'

Frowning, Jemma glided away towards another group of guests with her platter. Her first impression of Helen Urwin and Teddy Anston was that they were just like any other happily engaged young couple, excited about their future life together. Yes, Helen seemed fraught with nerves – her voice was high-pitched, and sometimes her laughter rang false – but there could be many reasons for that. Not least, the constant critical scrutiny she received from her future sister-in-law.

Mrs Banyan was a polite and gracious hostess. She spent most of the evening ensuring the comfort of her elderly father and chatting politely with the young couple's friends and work colleagues. But every time her eyes fell on Helen, her smile faltered, her dislike resonating across the high-ceilinged room.

As Jemma returned to the kitchen, she passed Bobbie in the corridor, carrying a tray of champagne flutes. Bobbie gave her a small wink and whispered, 'Not long now.'

The footman handed Jemma another tray of flutes and her hands trembled with excitement as she circulated among the guests once more. Finally, the last glass was lifted from the tray and Mr Anston Senior called for the guests' attention.

Jemma slipped out of the room and met Bobbie in the main hallway. They raced up the central staircase, thankful for the thick carpet that silenced their steps.

Mrs Banyan had given them directions to Helen Urwin's bedroom but when they approached the door, Jemma paused and held Bobbie back. 'There aren't any more staff here than the ones we've already met, are there?' she whispered. 'We don't want to go into Helen Urwin's room and find her maid in there.'

'No, Mrs Higgs said Helen gave her maid the night off once she'd styled her hair. She's gone to the cinema for the evening.'

'Good. Did you get the maid's name?'

'Lou – Louise Wilcox.'

Satisfied no one else was around, Jemma tried the door handle.

It was locked.

'Damn!' Bobbie hissed in disappointment. 'Foiled at the first attempt.'

Jemma pulled a keyring of spiky objects from her pocket. 'It's a good job I thought to bring these.'

'What the devil are they?'

With an enigmatic smile, Jemma chose one of the slim prongs and inserted it into the lock. A few seconds later there was a satisfying click and the door swung open.

'Dad and I spent a lovely winter afternoon together one year. He wasn't keen to play with my dolls, so he taught me how to pick locks instead. He was so impressed with my skill, he gave me this set as a Christmas present.'

Bobbie laughed. 'I should have known.'

The room was in darkness, but the blackout curtains were closed. Bobbie went to the bedside table and switched on a lamp.

'We're looking for her black diary,' she reminded Bobbie. 'It'll probably be in the handbag she uses during the day.'

But Bobbie was distracted by the pile of books on the bedside table. 'Austin Freeman, Edgar Wallace – and another Austin Freeman. This woman's been indulging in an orgy of crime.'

'Just like us,' Jemma said as she walked round the bed. *Where the devil did Helen Urwin keep her handbag?*

'Mrs Banyan had better be nice to her future sister-in-law. Austin Freeman's books are full of ingenious plots about how to poison your relatives.'

Jemma pounced on a shell-shaped crocodile-skin bag on the dressing table stool and pulled out a slim black diary. 'It's here.' She removed a small notebook and pen from her uniform pocket. 'I'll make a note of her appointments. You keep watch on the landing. Sing out if anyone comes.'

Bobbie disappeared and Jemma took the diary over to the lamp.

There was nothing personal in the little black book; Helen Urwin simply used it to record engagements. Apart from a forthcoming dentist's appointment, the entries consisted of a name next to a time. Most seemed to be evening social events. Jemma listed them carefully on her notepad. The appointments petered out after about four weeks, so she flipped back to the previous two weeks and made a note of those entries too.

Once she'd got enough information for Mrs Banyan, she replaced the diary in the bag. As she did so, she caught sight of an envelope among the make-up and other clutter. She pulled it out. It had already been slit open and read.

It was a letter from the Royal National Lifeboat Institution in Scarborough, thanking Miss Urwin for her generous donation to their charity of one hundred pounds.

Sighing, Jemma dropped the letter back in the bag. It was getting harder and harder to dislike Helen Urwin and suspect her of mischief.

She backed out of the door, inserted her lock pick and locked up the room.

Bobbie was waiting for her at the top of the stairs. 'Did you get everything?'

'Job done,' Jemma replied with a wink.

Chapter Twenty-One

Bobbie and Jemma returned the waitress uniform to Little Laurie the next morning and joined him and his elderly mother for a cup of tea. Then Jemma dashed through the rain to the bus station and caught a bus to Middlesbrough to collect her car.

Tired after two late nights on the trot, she found driving back in the rain very stressful. In addition to this, her car heater was broken, her feet were frozen, and the screech of the windscreen wipers grated on her frazzled nerves. She sighed with relief when she pulled up outside the cottage and dashed indoors. She had just enough time to settle herself with a cup of tea before phoning Mrs Banyan with her report.

Once the grandfather clock in the hallway finished its sonorous chiming, she rang the number. Mrs Banyan answered the call herself. 'Good evening, Mrs James. Were you able to carry out your mission, as instructed?' She sounded tense, Jemma thought – and excited.

'Yes. Thankfully I remembered to bring my lock pick. I needed it – Miss Urwin had locked the bedroom door.'

'You had to break in? Good grief! What exactly is that woman trying to hide?'

'I don't know,' Jemma confessed. 'Shall we go through her diary entries and see if they give us a clue?'

'Yes, fire away. I've a pen and pad here.'

Methodically, Jemma reeled off the list she'd made in her notebook.

Mrs Banyan was able to identify almost every engagement. Carol and Bob were the couple her brother and Miss Urwin played tennis with on a Saturday. Hazel and George were friends with whom they were due to dine. *Lloyd's at 7 p.m.* on Friday meant cocktails with the Stroughton-Reevells.

In the end, they were left with only three unidentified engagements – *Mattie Dickinson* at 11 a.m. on Thursday and two mysterious entries for the following morning: *Martins at 10.30 a.m.* and *N.W. at 11 a.m.*

'Mattie Dickinson, Mattie Dickinson...' Mrs Banyan muttered. 'It's familiar but I can't quite place it... Oh, good heavens!'

'Have you worked it out?'

'Yes! It's Mrs Dickinson's hair salon on Low Petergate – that's where she has her hair done. Oh, damn the woman, with her casual ways – it's so disrespectful! Did you hear her last night talking about Aggie Black, her former cook?'

'Yes, I did.'

'It's an irritating lack of respect. One should always call the staff *Mrs*. Mrs Higgs, Mrs Black, etcetera. Anything else is just downright rude.'

'What about these appointments for tomorrow morning, Mrs Banyan? Have you any idea where they could be and who they're with?'

'No, I haven't.'

'There's no apostrophe in "Martins",' Jemma remarked.

'I'm afraid that means nothing to Helen,' Mrs Banyan snapped. 'I've already explained to you, her education has been substandard.'

'I wonder if it's Martins Bank on Coney Street?'

'Oh! You clever young woman! Yes, of course it is. I once saw a cheque she wrote out. It's where she banks.'

'Which just leaves us with "N.W." half an hour later.'

'Yes, that's a mystery I can't fathom. It seems odd it's the only one written in initials.'

'May I make a suggestion? It looks like she'll be at the bank on Coney Street at half past ten tomorrow. Why don't I wait for her there, then follow her to this appointment with N.W.? I've a car in case she takes a taxi.'

154

There was a short silence. 'What an excellent idea – I had no idea you drove. Are you quite sure she won't recognise you from last night?'

'As Mrs Higgs said, no one remembers the staff from events like that.'

'Very well, I'll pay you to spy on her – or shadow her – or whatever you people call it.'

Delighted, Jemma grew braver. 'And what about the appointment with the hairdressers on Thursday? I can book into the salon at the same time and listen to her conversation with Mrs Dickinson. Women tell their hairdressers all sorts of things.'

'No, I don't think that's necessary. I doubt she'd confess to her hairdresser the kind of scurrilous information I want and I'm not going to pay for you to sit there and watch her have her hair dyed.'

'She dyes her hair?'

'Of course she does! Women that pale are not natural brunettes.'

'I've had some ideas about how we can move this investigation forward, Mrs Banyan. I think it would help if I went back to her family home in Roundhay in Leeds and made some discreet enquiries with the neighbours. We need to build up a picture of what's happened to Miss Urwin over the last few years, and Leeds seems the logical point to begin. I know your brother and his company bought the house from her last year – can you get me the address?'

'That may be possible, but let's see what happens tomorrow with the shadowing, shall we? You can call me back tomorrow night at the same time with your report.'

'Certainly.' Jemma realised with a sigh of relief that she'd have her own office and telephone line by then. The telephone exchange had promised to reconnect her line sometime in the afternoon. 'Good night, Mrs Banyan.'

'Good night, Mrs James – and please, do send me your bill for last night. I like to keep my accounts up to date.'

Jemma replaced the receiver, and, despite her exhaustion, a quiver of excitement rippled through her. She had an ongoing case, which offset her disappointment that no one else had replied to her advertisements last week. And on top of this, she was taking ownership of the office tomorrow.

It would be a busy day, shadowing Helen Urwin in the morning then dashing to Grape Lane to clean the place out before Uncle Ivan brought her furniture round. But launching a successful new business was never going to be easy and Bobbie had promised to use her half-day off to help. Jemma had given her the spare set of keys.

In fact, a small celebration with Bobbie wouldn't be out of place. Suddenly she had an idea.

Full of renewed confidence, she picked up the receiver again and called the house where Don and Ricky lodged. Their landlady answered the call and Jemma asked her to fetch one of the men downstairs to the telephone.

It was Don who took the call. 'Hello, Jemma,' he said. 'How lovely to hear from you again.' His accent sounded even more seductive over the telephone.

'Hello, Don. I'm calling because tomorrow will be a special day for Bobbie and I and, if you and Ricky are available, I'd like you to come out and celebrate with us.'

'What's the celebration? Do I need to bring champagne?'

Smiling, she explained about the new office and gave him the address and telephone number.

'That's great news! We'll meet you girls there about six thirty and go to one of your great British pubs.'

'That'd be lovely. Thank you.'

She replaced the receiver with a sense of satisfaction. This wasn't the private date he'd wanted but it was an assignment that made her feel comfortable. She knew she had to start socialising again, but she had to do it her own way.

Outside, she heard the unmistakable roar of the Vincent Rapide. Gabriel was home. She hurried into the kitchen to light the fire, grateful that Gabriel would have returned from Cissy's with a full stomach, and she didn't have to cook anything tonight.

She was still on her knees in front of the hearth when Gabriel burst through the front door and slammed it behind him. She heard him go into the parlour and head straight for the whisky decanter on the sideboard. 'I'm in here, Gabriel!' she called. 'I've just got back myself – I'm lighting the fire.'

There was no reply.

Frowning, she washed her hands and went into the parlour.

Gabriel sat in the dark, still wearing his thick leather coat, scarf and the sturdy boots he used for his motorcycle. He had a large tumbler of whisky in his hand and even in the gloom she could see his face was white with anger.

'What's happened?'

'Our Cissy,' he hissed, 'that's what's happened.'

'Oh dear. Let me sort out the blackout and you can tell me all about it.' She drew the curtains, switched on a table lamp and sat down opposite him.

'How bad was it?' she whispered. 'What did Cissy do?'

Gabriel swallowed the last of his drink, reached for the decanter and poured himself another. 'She's upset Maisie – badly.'

'How?'

'You need to understand Maisie means a lot to me, Jemma.'

'I do. And that's wonderful news. I think she's lovely – and if you love her, that's fantastic.'

'I don't just love her – I've asked her marry me.'

Jemma squealed and clasped her hands in delight. She was about to stand up and hug her brother when he added: 'She hasn't said "yes" yet.'

Jemma sank back down into her chair. 'Is there a problem?'

'She wants to be sure first.'

'But what's there to be sure about?' Jemma was genuinely baffled. Her brother was a decent and well-respected man with his own home and a well-paid job that gave him both security and standing in the local community. They also had their ambition, didn't they? To run a country pub together. Provided Maisie could tolerate freezing to death on the back of his blessed motorbike and had strong teeth that wouldn't dislodge with the vibration, she shouldn't have any objections, surely?

'She wants to know if my family will accept her and both her sons. Cissy reacted badly – and showed herself up for the blithering snob she is – when she learnt about Tom.'

'Tom?' Jemma was lost. 'I thought her son was called Harry. He's in the Yorkshire Regiment, isn't he? Who's Tom?'

Gabriel stared at her. 'Don't tell me you've lived in Clifton most of your life and you didn't know that Maisie Langford had another boy – a ten-year-old son – called Tom.'

'I didn't. I never knew she married again.'

'She didn't marry the father. Tom is a ba—. He's illegitimate. The result of an unfortunate fling. You honestly didn't know about this?'

Reeling with shock, Jemma steeled herself. Was this why Gabriel had been so secretive about his relationship with Maisie? 'I'd no idea, Gabriel. I've had very little to do with Maisie – or The Grey Mare – over the years. I'm not a drinker… or a village gossip.'

He paused, then grunted. 'That's true enough. You're not a gossip. You live in a peculiar little world of your own.'

'Am I allowed to ask about Tom's father?'

'Long gone. He left Maisie in the lurch when he found out she was pregnant.'

Jemma winced. 'Poor Maisie. She didn't deserve that after losing her husband in the last war. What a hard life she must have had.'

Gabriel swirled the whisky round his glass. 'Yes, she's had a tough time raising both boys on her own with the gossip swirling around her. But she's not bitter. In fact, she's the warmest, most loving woman I've ever met. Unfortunately, other people aren't kind to women who have illegitimate children – as we found out again today when our Cissy was told about Tom.'

'I'm so sorry, Gabriel. Was Maisie very upset?'

'Yes. I think she's ready to call the whole thing off with me. You're my last chance to show her that someone in my family is compassionate and normal.'

'Normal? You think I'm normal?'

He observed her coolly across the hearth rug. His anger was fading, and she thought she saw him repress a small smile. 'Well, perhaps *normal* is pushing the definition of the word a bit far. But you're something Cissy is not: you're kind-hearted. That's why it's so important you're on your best behaviour tomorrow night.'

Tomorrow night?

He saw the surprise on her face. 'Don't tell me you've forgotten we'd rearranged supper at Maisie's for tomorrow night?' he snapped.

'No, no, of course not.'

Damn. She'd have to cancel the celebration with Don, Bobbie and Ricky.

'I'm at work until just after six, but I'll come straight home. I'm looking forward to it. Going to Maisie's, that is.'

He took another sip of his drink. 'Are you waitressing again?'

'Yes, that's right.'

'So, it went well today – the waitressing?'

'It was fine.' She rose to her feet. 'I'll make us a cup of tea.' There was so much to think about. If Maisie accepted Gabriel's proposal – and she sincerely hoped Maisie would – then everything would change. Maisie would move into the cottage – with her son. With both sons. It was going to be different – and crowded.

'I don't want to alarm you, Jemma,' Gabriel said, as she hurried towards the door, 'but while you were out *waitressing*, somebody brought Michael's car down from Middlesbrough and parked it outside our front door.'

She pulled up sharply. 'Oh, you recognised it?'

'I should do. Michael and I spent a full afternoon under the bonnet one day last year, trying to fix the carburettor.'

'Yes, a friend from Middlesbrough drove it down and dropped it off for me today. I thought it might be useful in my search for a proper job. Would you like a toasted teacake with your tea?'

Chapter Twenty-Two

Once Gabriel left for work the next morning, Jemma loaded her car with her typewriter and the sundry items she'd need for the new office, then drove into York. By nine o'clock she'd rebooked the advertisements at the newspaper office, using Smoke & Cracked Mirrors' new address and telephone number. Half an hour later she was at the printers, collecting her brand-new letterhead, receipt books and the business cards she'd ordered for herself and Bobbie. This gorgeous new stationery, inscribed with her company name and address, gave her a lovely thrill. It even smelled fresh and exciting.

She put her parcels into the car and drove to Coney Street, parking a short distance from the four-storey half-timbered bank. She grabbed her bag and joined the crowds on the narrow pavement. The ancient clock jutting out from the crumbling stone walls of St Martin-le-Grand church told her it was nearly ten thirty. She'd timed it perfectly.

Helen Urwin strolled down the pavement towards her, in a brown fur coat and small feathered hat, carrying the same crocodile-skin bag Jemma had rifled through two nights before. She walked beneath the overhanging eaves of the bank and disappeared inside.

Jemma pulled her navy hat lower over her face and fell into step a few paces behind her.

She'd wondered if the *Martins 10.30 a.m.* in the diary had signified an appointment with a bank manager or was just a memory aid. It seemed it was the latter. Helen walked across the tiled floor to the high wooden counter and addressed the teller: 'I'd like to withdraw fifty pounds from my account, please.'

Jemma's eyebrows twitched at the amount. She took a seat at a small side table, picked up a pen and pretended to fill in a deposit slip. From the corner of her eye, she watched the young assistant count out the notes and seal them in a plain brown envelope. Helen put it in her handbag and left.

Jemma screwed up the deposit slip, pocketed it and followed her outside.

Only fifteen minutes remained before Helen's appointment with the mysterious *N.W.*, and Jemma was relieved to see the woman made no effort to flag down a taxi. In fact, she walked slowly, pausing often to glance in the shop windows. The meeting with *N.W.* must be nearby.

Jemma stayed close because of the crowds and at one point, when Helen stopped abruptly in front of a dress shop, Jemma almost walked into her. With a pounding heart, she kept her eyes straight ahead and veered around the woman with only inches to spare. She pulled up outside the next shop window, an ironmongers, and pretended to examine a selection of gardening implements. The window reflected the street behind and a few moments later Jemma watched Helen Urwin's reflection walk past her own. The woman showed no concern or recognition.

When she reached the junction with Museum Street, Helen crossed the road, walked towards the river and descended the steps that led to the tree-lined river walk that ran between Lendal Bridge and Ouse Bridge.

Jemma slowed down; it would be hard to lose sight of her there. A popular spot for young lovers, there were wooden benches beneath the trees where people sat and watched the river barges, tugs and pleasure craft sailing by.

By the time Jemma descended the steps, Helen Urwin was standing about twenty yards away, talking to a young man who'd risen from a bench to greet her.

Thin, red-headed, and dressed in a cheap flashy suit, which seemed to have one leg slightly longer than the other, he had a sallow complexion pitted with acne scars. He was several years younger than Helen and definitely not part of her posh social circle. They sat down on the bench together, facing the river.

There was a vacant bench further along and Jemma walked slowly towards it. She wouldn't be able to overhear their conversation from there but at least she could watch them out of the corner of her eye. Grateful for her sensible soft-soled shoes, she held her breath as she passed behind the couple and heard the man say: 'Our Alma is unhappy with the food rationing.' He had a strong West Riding accent, Jemma noted. *Someone Helen knew from her time in Leeds, perhaps?*

Jemma settled herself on the vacant bench, fastened her coat up tight against the stiff breeze, and pulled out her notebook and pen. She busied herself making notes for Mrs Banyan, while sneaking the odd sideways glance at the couple, who continued to chat like old friends. The odd word of their conversation – and their occasional laughter – drifted down towards her on the breeze, but she overheard nothing that made any sense.

What was apparent, though, was that they were relaxed and comfortable with each other, like old friends. Both kept their hands to themselves and there was a gap of several inches between them. This was no lovers' tryst.

Friends. That's what they were. Friends.

Her client might be disappointed, but Teddy Anston would be able to take his fiancée to church without fear; this strange young man was no threat to their union. However, Mrs Banyan would still want to know N.W.'s identity.

Jemma had a couple of hours before she was due to meet Bobbie at the new office, so she decided to follow the young man once they parted. If he led her home or to a workplace, she'd soon be able to find out his name. York's annually compiled street directories and electoral registers were a mine of useful information and co-workers could always be bribed or tricked into giving away his name. Mind you, the electoral register would only be useful if he was old enough to vote. Jemma tried again to estimate his age and decided he was somewhere between nineteen and twenty-four.

The gentle warmth of the sun on her face was relaxing and she enjoyed the tranquillity. This spot wasn't exactly scenic; the industrial river barges moored downstream at the Marygate Landing and Rowntree's derelict old factory spoilt the view. But there was something mesmerising about the repetitive tightening and sagging of the mooring lines of the barges as they shifted with the current; something hypnotic about the grace of the swans gliding past and the flow of the wide brown river.

When the couple finally rose to their feet, Helen Urwin leant forward and kissed the young man affectionately on the cheek. Then she reached into her handbag and gave him the brown envelope full of money she'd collected from the bank. It was still sealed. Then she turned to walk away.

'Thank you,' he called after her.

'It's my pleasure, Neil,' she called back.

Neil. He was called Neil.

Neil lit a cigarette and stared thoughtfully at the river for a moment, while Helen Urwin retraced her steps back up onto Museum Street. Eventually he threw his stub onto the ground and walked back in the same direction. Once he reached Museum Street, he turned towards the railway station.

Jemma's heart sank. *What on earth would she do if he caught a train?* Buy herself a ticket and follow him to God only knows where?

He turned off into one of the narrow streets surrounding the station, mounted the steps of a boarding house and disappeared inside.

A small café stood on the opposite side of the road, with large windows overlooking the street. Jemma ducked inside, found a window table and ordered a cup of tea, grateful for the chance to warm up for a few minutes. She had no idea how long she would have to wait until Neil reappeared, but she needed some time to think. Shadowing someone was a longer, more complex game than she'd imagined. She'd only allowed herself a few hours. Had she just made mistake number six?

The boarding house proprietors should have his home address in their register but persuading them to part with that information might not be easy.

A few moments later, Neil reappeared on the steps of the building – this time with a small suitcase in his hand.

Abandoning her drink, Jemma left the café and slipped into his wake. He headed straight for the railway station. It was time for her to make a decision: exactly how far should she follow him?

York station's curved, smoke-blackened glass roof, held up by rows of ornate pillars, towered over the lines like the dome of a cathedral. A cacophony of noise reverberated beneath that roof: slamming carriage doors, bells, whistles, the rumble of loaded barrows and porters yelling 'Mind your backs!' Sulphurous smoke and steam from the panting engines swirled everywhere, mingling with the smell of hot oil.

The entrance was crowded with soldiers, some standing around in small groups, others sitting on their bags, cigarettes dangling idly from their fingers. Neil went straight to the inspector at the barrier and Jemma closed in behind him. This was a desperate situation and the time for discretion was over.

Neil handed the inspector a return ticket and over the clamour of the station announcer heralding the arrival of the next train for Grantham and King's Cross, Jemma heard him ask, 'Which platform for t' next train t' Leeds, mate?'

The guard punched the ticket with his clipper and checked his pocket watch. 'Platform six – but you'll have to run. She's about to leave.'

Neil shot off through the barrier towards the footbridge and Jemma found herself face to face with the frowning railway official. 'Ticket, madam.'

'I, I haven't got one,' she stammered, 'but I need to get that train to Leeds. Can I buy one on board?'

'No. No ticket, no journey.'

'Please?'

Neil disappeared from sight into the crowds.

'No, madam. Next, please...'

Disappointed, Jemma backed away and drifted over to the ladies' room. There wasn't enough time to buy a ticket before the train left. The decision had been taken out of her hands.

But the game wasn't over yet. She still had a chance to find out Neil's full name and address – but she needed to lick her wounds and refuel her courage before she took that step.

In the relative peace of the ladies' room, she splashed water on her face and regarded herself critically in the mottled mirror above the cracked hand basin. *Could she pull this off?*

What was it Bobbie had said about playing a part? *Just think yourself into the role you've adopted, and you'll come across genuine enough.*

'Nothing ventured, nothing gained,' she muttered. Pulling off her wedding and engagement rings, she dropped them into her purse. She reached for her lipstick and comb and tidied up her appearance. If she was going to act the part of a desperate young woman in love, she might as well go dressed for the role.

She felt her heart pounding in her chest as she retraced her steps to Neil's boarding house. She knew she was flushed, but that was an advantage. It was a nervous, excitable role she was adopting.

A plain middle-aged woman carrying a duster and wearing a headscarf and apron answered the door. 'Yes, love?'

'Is Neil here, please? I need to see him.'

'Neil?'

'Yes, Neil from Leeds. He told me he stayed here last night.'

'Ah, you mean Mr Watts. I'm sorry, love, but you've just missed him. He's checked out and left.'

Jemma allowed herself to look crestfallen. 'Oh, no. I desperately wanted to catch him before he went.' She glanced down at the ground, shook her head sadly and, after a short pause, let out strangled sob. It had the desired effect. The landlady reached out a comforting hand. 'Are you all right, love? What's happened?'

'I've lost his address,' Jemma wailed. 'He gave it to me last night and *begged* me to write to him. He's about to sign up, and you know how much our lads need our letters to keep them going. I so wanted to catch him before he left – it was my last chance to get his address again.'

A broad grin spread across the woman's face. 'Sweet on him, are you?'

'Oh yes – he's the most amazing man I've ever met!' As soon as the words were out of her mouth she wondered if she'd overdone it, but the woman just laughed.

'Well, there's no accountin' for taste, I suppose. I thought he were a surly, skinny little bugger and I were wonderin' why he weren't in uniform, but step inside, lass, I might be able to help you with the address.'

Jemma's innocent blue eyes widened in surprise and delight. 'You know his address? Oh, thank you – that's kind of you.'

'Don't worry about it.' The woman led the way down a narrow hallway, which stank of fried onions. 'I were in love meself – once.'

A tatty, much thumbed guest register lay on a small table at the end of the hallway. The woman skimmed through it and prodded a fat finger at an entry. 'Here we are: Mr Neil Watts, 14 Gordon Terrace, Roundhay, Leeds.'

167

'Yes, that's him!' Jemma exclaimed in glee. She pulled out her notebook, copied down the address and reached for her purse.

The woman laughed. 'Get away with you, lass! I don't need payin'. You get home and write your letter.'

The woman wished her good luck as she let Jemma back out into the street.

Grinning with delight, Jemma bounced off towards Grape Lane with a new spring in her step.

Chapter Twenty-Three

Bobbie had already let herself into the empty office, lit the gas fire and was washing the windows when Jemma arrived. 'We've a working telephone!' she announced. 'The exchange people have come and gone. Where've you been?'

Jemma gave her a hug. 'Shadowing Helen Urwin.' She glanced around the bare but sparkling room with a pang of guilt. 'Thanks for this, Bobbie.'

'My pleasure – I just want to help out in whatever way I can, whenever I can.'

'You must be exhausted. You spend every spare minute you've got helping me with this business.'

'That's because it's *our* business.'

'I must get to a solicitor and ask him to draw up a partnership agreement.'

Bobbie waved a dismissive hand. 'Don't waste the company funds on lawyers just yet. There's plenty of time for that when we're making regular money. So, what happened this morning?'

'Let me fetch the kettle, tea and milk in from the car and I'll tell you about it. I'm desperate for a cuppa.'

'The mystery deepens!' Bobbie announced fifteen minutes later as they relaxed with their tea. 'Why would an upper-class snob like Helen Urwin want to mix with a spiv like him – and give him money?'

'I don't know. But let's hope Mrs Banyan shares our curiosity. I'm to phone her back tonight at six.'

'Zdrastuyte!' bellowed a deep masculine voice from down on the street. 'Zdrastuyte, little golden bird!'

'It's Uncle Ivan!' Jemma turned to the window in delight, threw up the sash and leant out. A huge man in overalls, with a bushy grey beard and sideburns, stood on the pavement below, next to a large van. 'Zdrastuyte! We're up here, Uncle – we'll come down now.'

'Ha!' he replied. 'I should have known it would be up the stairs – thanks to God you didn't want the piano!'

Uncle Ivan had brought one of the young men from the shop to help, and for the next hour the four of them hauled the contents of his van up the narrow stairs. Uncle Ivan tacked down the carpet before they brought up the rest of the furniture, which included a bookcase, armchairs for the clients, a bureau and the small dining table Jemma intended to use as a desk. It was hard, sweaty work but Uncle Ivan kept them laughing with a string of jokes. He flirted shamelessly with Bobbie, calling her sweetness and 'little honey'.

Once the boxes of kitchen utensils, the lampshades and lamps and sundry office equipment were upstairs and everything was in its place, Jemma stood back to admire their handiwork. The bare office had sprung into life and was cosy and inviting. She knew it needed proper office chairs for the table and a filing cabinet, but it would do nicely for the moment.

She was pleased to see some of her – their – possessions in use once more, but it was happiness tinged with sorrow. She paused by Michael's favourite armchair and stroked its upholstered wing.

'I can still see Mykhail sitting there.' Uncle Ivan's voice caught as he spoke. 'Not a day passes without I cry for that boy.' He sighed and addressed his next comment to Bobbie, as if to draw her into the conversation. 'Sometimes depression, she chases after me like a shadow or – like a faithful wife.'

Confused, Bobbie smiled politely.

Ivan's brown eyes glistened, and Jemma reached out a comforting hand.

Michael's loss had never been hers alone to bear. Apart from the devastating grief his disappearance had caused his parents and his brother,

Ivan had also been distraught. Michael had always enjoyed a wonderful relationship with his loud, exuberant uncle, especially during the years of his apprenticeship in the family business in York.

'Those potted ferns were a good idea,' Bobbie said tactfully, trying to fill in the emotional silence that had descended on the room. 'It's more like a parlour than a business office. That'll put nervous clients at ease.'

'Ha! Those blahoslovennyy plants!' Uncle Ivan exclaimed. 'You've no idea how pleased I am to see their backs. "Keep my plants alive for me, Uncle Ivan," she says. What am I? Some peasant from the fields of the Donbass?'

The two women laughed. There was a short pause, then Jemma pressed one of her new business cards into Ivan's large, hairy hand. 'What do you think about my new business venture?'

He threw up his hands and grinned through his beard. 'What do *I* think, little golden bird? What *I* think is no consequence. As the great Dostoyevsky says, every man – and woman – must have an aspiration and choose one of the many paths of life that presents themselves – and desire that alone.'

'What do you think Michael would have said?'

'Ahh, Mykhail, Mykhail,' he murmured. 'He once say to me: "You know our little Jemma is cleverer than me, don't you, dyad'ko?" And I say: "Ha! How is that possible? You are the smarty pantaloons of the family".'

The women giggled.

'I think you will do well, little bird – and you too, sweetness.' He gave Bobbie's shoulder a gentle pat. 'I know how you torture yourself with self-doubts, but as the great man says, "you never reach any truth without making fourteen mistakes and likely a hundred and fourteen". Now, I fetch you those cameras from the lorry. I've the latest Kodaks from America.'

———

171

Bobbie turned to Jemma in surprise when he left the room. 'What's this about cameras?'

'He's found me a couple of simple pocket cameras, and sold them to me at cost.'

'Ooh, exciting! And what was that about faithful wives? He wasn't proposing, was he?'

Jemma laughed. 'Sorry to disappoint you, but I don't think so – he's a confirmed bachelor is Uncle Ivan...' She grimaced. 'Mind you, as I've just learnt, there's no such thing.'

She told Bobbie about Gabriel's hope to marry Maisie – and the trouble Cissy had caused.

'Good for Gabriel, championing Maisie like this,' Bobbie said firmly. 'He's a man in a million, your brother. Although I have to say, Jemma – your sister is a mean cow.'

Jemma nodded in agreement. 'I'm supposed to go to Maisie's for supper tonight and pour oil on troubled waters. Quite frankly, I'm dreading it. What exactly am I supposed to *do* and *say* to persuade Maisie to marry Gabriel?'

Bobbie laughed. 'Gabriel must be desperate to have roped you into this scheme.' When Jemma's face fell, she added: 'Just be your lovely self, Jemma. All Gabriel wants is for Maisie to feel welcomed into the family.'

Jemma nodded thoughtfully. 'By the way, I'd invited Ricky and Don to come out and celebrate with us today, but once Gabriel reminded me about supper at Maisie's, I phoned Don back and cancelled. He said he and Ricky may call this afternoon anyway. Don's got a few hours off. I hope Ricky brings the photos for Mr King.'

Ivan reappeared with two packages in his hands. While they unwrapped them, he explained that the Kodak Vigilant Junior Six-20 was the latest design in folding pocket cameras. He spent some time showing them how to use it.

'What a fantastic piece of equipment,' Bobbie said. 'They're far more discreet than that monster Ricky uses.'

'They're still a little big for my coat pockets, though,' Jemma said.

'Oh, toss out your gas mask and carry them in the box,' Bobbie suggested. 'It's about time those cumbersome things had a use.'

When Ivan left, Bobbie headed for the little kitchen. 'I don't know about you, but I'm desperate for more tea. I'll put the kettle on while you type out your invoice for Mrs Banyan. After all the money you've spent this week, we'd better try to claw some back.'

'Did someone mention tea?' shouted a familiar voice from the landing. The door, already slightly ajar, swung open to reveal Ricky and Don. The two women exclaimed in delight, pulled off their dirty aprons and rushed to greet them.

'Forget the tea,' Ricky said, pointing to the bottle in Don's hands, 'our Canuck has something far better for a celebration like this!'

Bobbie squealed and took the bottle from Don. 'Champagne! And the real French stuff, too! How the devil did you get hold of this, Don?'

'The officers' mess at the base is well stocked.'

'This is kind of you,' Jemma said, 'but I'm afraid I don't have any champagne flutes – or any glasses. I never expected—'

Don winked. 'We kind of predicted that. Do you have some cups?'

'I'll fetch out the best china,' Bobbie said proudly.

'You've got china cups for your clients, Miss Marple?' Ricky's fair eyebrows rose in mock surprise. 'Wow! You sure know how to treat folks well.'

'The tea set was a wedding present,' Jemma mumbled.

But Ricky wasn't listening. His eyes scanned the room, taking in every detail. 'Well, this is a great set-up, Miss Marple. Ooh, Kodaks.' He moved towards the cameras on the table.

'This is a swell joint,' Don said. 'Very professional – and comfortable.'

'Thank you,' Jemma said shyly. If he was disappointed about their cancelled trip to the pub, it was well hidden behind his smile.

The next few minutes were hilarious as Ricky and Don fussed about, opening the champagne. Bobbie produced the flowery china cups and they toasted the future of Smoke & Cracked Mirrors.

Don smiled, turned to Jemma and raised his dainty cup for a second toast. 'To new beginnings, Jemma?'

His words, and the broader suggestion they contained, sent a wave of guilty anticipation swirling through Jemma. Being near Don confused her. She smiled back, clinked her cup against his and said: 'Yes, to new beginnings.'

He looks pale, she thought. There were shadows below his eyes and the twitch in the left one was more pronounced.

'Got a few presents for you, Miss Marple.' Ricky pulled a large brown envelope out of his jacket pocket and handed it to her. Inside were the photographs of Eddie Chambers.

She spread them across the table, and everyone gathered round to look. Ricky had done a superb job. The insurance fraudster was caught in sharp relief against the background of De Grey's, laughing as he whirled around the dance floor with his partner.

Ricky pulled out another envelope. 'And here's an extra one for you girls, an office-warming present from me.' It was a beautiful photograph of Jemma and Bobbie dressed up to the nines, relaxing at their table at De Grey's with a cocktail. They were leaning towards each other with a conspiratorial smile.

'The pair of you look as thick as thieves,' Don observed.

'That's a gorgeous photograph!' Bobbie exclaimed. 'When did you take it?'

'When you weren't looking. Always the best way. Put it in a frame and stick it on your wall somewhere.'

'It's wonderful – they're all wonderful – thank you so much, Ricky.' Jemma reached for her petty cash tin and paid Ricky the amount they'd agreed.

'Thank *you*, Miss Marple.' Ricky pocketed the money, downed the last of his champagne and turned to Don. 'Right, now, mate, it's time to work.'

'Work?'

'Of course! You didn't think we'd turned up here just to booze, did you? We guys have come to lend a hand with any jobs you need doin'. First things first, did you know your doorbell ain't workin'?'

'I didn't.'

'We'll fix that now. We've brought a couple of screwdrivers and a few other tools. Is there anything else you need doin'?'

Jemma pushed a large, flat parcel towards him across the desk. It was the brass plaque she'd had engraved with the company name. Ricky removed the brown paper and whistled appreciatively as the light bounced off the gleaming metal. 'That's classy. Do you want it up by the front door?'

'Yes, please.'

The two men disappeared downstairs, and Bobbie went into the kitchen to wash the cups, while Jemma typed out the invoice for Mr King and popped it into an envelope with the photographs of Eddie Chambers. She fed another sheet of her letterhead into the machine and billed Mrs Banyan for the work so far.

Bobbie checked her watch and reached for her coat. 'The post office is still open, I'll take them. Remember to phone Mrs Banyan at six – I'll tell the chaps not to disturb you for a few minutes.'

Jemma thanked her and at precisely six o'clock she picked up the telephone receiver.

Mrs Banyan listened in silence while Jemma told her how she'd watched Helen Urwin withdraw fifty pounds from Martins Bank and give it to the young man she'd met on the river walk. 'His name's Neil Watts and he lives at Gordon Terrace in Leeds. I followed him to his boarding house and got those details from the proprietor. I estimate he's somewhere between nineteen and twenty-four years of age.'

'Hm, he seems a bit young to be her lover.'

'That's what I thought too, and quite frankly I don't think he's her type. He looked rough and from the little I heard he sounded working-class. He had a broad West Riding accent, and his suit was cheap and badly fitted. The boarding house was one of those grimy ones by the station favoured by travelling salesmen.'

'Could he have been a blackmailer? Was she paying him off for something, perhaps?'

'I wondered about that, but they were too relaxed and friendly with each other. Not that they were behaving like lovers,' Jemma added quickly. 'She kissed him on the cheek like he was an old friend.'

'Good grief! Well, his Leeds address supports your theory. Is it the same part of Leeds where Helen used to live?'

'Yes, Roundhay.'

'They may have met when she lived there.'

'All roads seem to lead back to Leeds,' Jemma said, wincing at her own unintentional pun.

'Yes, they do.' There was a short pause while her client made up her mind. 'Very well, Mrs James. I've thought about the suggestion you made last night about broadening the scope of this investigation, and I agree – you may pursue our investigation in Leeds. I raided my brother's files while he was out and found a solicitor's letter written during the sale of Helen's property, which contains her former address. I think you should make some discreet enquiries with the neighbours. While you're in the area, see what else you can discover about Mr Watts.'

'Thank you.'

'I'll pay you for another week.'

Delighted, Jemma noted down Helen's former address, and the name and address of her solicitor. As she explained to Mrs Banyan, the more information she had about Helen Urwin, the better.

'I've just moved into an office on Grape Street,' she told her client. 'Let me give you the telephone number and address.'

'I'll take the telephone number,' Mrs Banyan said tartly, 'but please don't expect me to visit you there. A woman of my standing can't afford to be seen walking into the seedy office of a PI.'

Slightly abashed, Jemma gave her the number and promised to phone her back in seven days with an update.

But when she replaced the receiver, it was with a strong sense of satisfaction. Personally, she had a sneaking suspicion the money Helen Urwin had given to Neil Watts was nothing more than another charitable donation. But time would tell, and she had more work for the next week.

177

Chapter Twenty-Four

Once Ricky and Don finished their jobs, Ricky taught the two women how to use the different lenses provided with their new cameras and the four of them lingered, chatting.

Inevitably, Jemma was home nearly an hour later than she'd planned. She found a terse note from Gabriel on the kitchen table:

I couldn't wait for you any longer. Make your way round to Maisie's immediately.

She dashed upstairs, changed into a clean blouse and ran a comb through her hair before taking the short walk across the dark village green to Maisie's cottage.

Her smiling hostess answered the back door, and the delicious smell of a casserole greeted Jemma. Pans of vegetables simmered on the gas stove in the narrow kitchen.

'I'm so sorry I'm late,' she said as she removed her coat.

'Oh, don't worry, Jemma. Our Tom's not back yet either.'

Jemma followed her into the adjoining room. Maisie wore a pair of high-heeled shoes with her smart brown patterned dress, which seemed an odd choice of footwear while cooking supper. Her thick auburn hair was rolled and pinned back but the steam in the kitchen had left it a bit limp.

The small dining room was dominated by the table, where Gabriel sat flicking through the newspaper. He was wearing a blue check shirt with a thin grey tie; the two colours enhanced the hard, glacial blue shimmer in his eyes beneath his frowning brows. 'Good evening, Jemma. I'm glad you've finally found the time to join us.'

Maisie laughed as she took Jemma's coat away. 'I've told her not to worry, Gabriel. I haven't served up yet. Take a seat, Jemma, our Tom won't be long.'

Jemma slid into the seat at the opposite end of the table to her grumpy brother. The table was set with a crisp white tablecloth and pretty crockery with a flower pattern.

'It's a wonder our supper isn't spoilt,' Gabriel hissed.

'It's hard to spoil a casserole, Gabriel,' Maisie said cheerfully as she returned from the hallway. 'It's only belly pork and a bit of seasoning, Jemma. That's all I could get at the butcher's. Do you like belly pork?'

'I love it – and it smells delicious. Is there anything I can do to help?'

'I wouldn't let her in the kitchen, Maisie,' Gabriel warned.

Maisie laughed and pointed to a large modern cabinet, the only other piece of furniture in the room. 'Can you get the cutlery out of that drawer for me and finish off setting the table, please? I do hope Tom gets back soon – oh! Here he is.'

A draught of cold air wafted into the room as a grubby, freckled young lad with fat, rosy cheeks and his mother's auburn hair came through the back door.

'About time too. Good grief – you're filthy, son! Take those boots off on the mat and wash your hands.'

Drying his hands on a ragged old towel, Tom hurried into the dining room. 'I got the last of the potatoes in, Uncle Gabe, and planted the carrots under the cold frame like you told me.'

Gabriel pushed aside his paper, reached into his pocket for some loose change and smiled. 'Good lad. How much do I owe you for this week?'

'Two bob.'

'So that's what happened to the allotment!' Jemma exclaimed. 'Tom's been digging it for you.'

'Not just digging it,' Gabriel corrected, 'he's *managing* it. He's my allotment manager.'

Beaming with pride, the young lad pocketed the coins and slid into the seat beside Jemma. He smelled of fresh air and earth. 'It's looking great, Uncle Gabe. There's still the beans to plant though.'

'Yes, and we'll get some salad crops and radishes under those cold frames once we plant the carrots out,' Gabriel said.

'At this rate you won't have to buy any veg this summer, Mum,' the lad called out to the kitchen.

'That'll be really wonderful, Tom.'

Jemma held out her hand. 'I'm Jemma, Gabriel's sister.'

The boy took her hand awkwardly. 'Yes, I've seen you around. Pleased to meet you, Miss.'

'Oh, call me Jemma.'

Maisie brought in a large casserole dish and placed it in the centre of the table. She whisked away the scruffy towel her son had dropped next to his plate and said, 'Can you find the salt and pepper, please, Gabriel?'

Gabriel rose and retrieved the condiments from a shelf on the cabinet. Jemma noticed he was wearing carpet slippers – he was as comfortable here as in his own home, she thought, smiling.

And it wasn't surprising. Despite being a bit of a squash, the room was homely and nicely furnished, with pretty curtains drawn across the window. Black-and-white photographs of Maisie's two boys and her late husband in his uniform took pride of place on the mantelpiece, along with little china ornaments that reflected her warm personality and obvious love of cats.

The next few minutes were a flurry of hot plates and serving spoons. A contented silence fell as they ate. Maisie had simmered the cheap meat in a sauce made of stewed apples and herbs, and it was delicious. Still flushed and hot from the kitchen, Maisie undid the top button of her dress in an effort to cool down and wriggled in her seat as she kicked off her high heels under the table. Jemma smiled down at her plate. Her brother's girlfriend had made a lot of effort to impress her tonight, although the uncomfortable shoes were perhaps a step too far.

The arrival of young Tom and the food softened Gabriel's mood. He chatted comfortably with the lad for a while about their shared allotment and their fellow gardeners.

'It's impressive to see someone your age helping out so much with the war effort, Tom,' Jemma said.

The lad's cheeks glowed with pleasure. 'I collect salvage too. The WVS has organised a competition at the schools to see who can collect the most. There's big prizes and I want to win one. Do you have any salvage in your house, Jemma?'

'Salvage?'

'Yes. Paper, old saucepans, frying pans and coat hangers. That sort of thing.'

Jemma's mind drifted across Clifton Green to their cluttered home, and she realised it was bulging at the seams with scrap metal. 'Yes, there's an old canary cage in the attic and I'm sure I can find you loads more. Come over on Sunday and I'll see what I've got. In fact,' she added mischievously, 'your Uncle Gabe has the remains of a motorbike engine under his bed. I'm sure that's salvage.'

Tom was delighted, but the faces of the other two adults were a picture.

'That's the engine of my first Triumph!' exclaimed Gabriel, nearly choking on his food. Meanwhile, Maisie said in disbelief, 'You keep an old motorbike engine beneath your bed?'

'I've told him for years that garden sheds are the place for souvenirs,' Jemma said airily. 'To be honest, Maisie, our house needs sorting out. Neither of us have done anything to our parents' room since Dad died and it's such a shame. It's the biggest bedroom in the house.'

She glanced over at Tom, who'd resumed his assault on his food and had lost interest in the adult talk. 'That bedroom needs redecorating and some modern furniture.' In for a penny, in for a pound, she thought. 'There's plenty of room in there for someone to *grow*, if you know what I mean,' she added, with a wink and a nod of her head at Tom.

Maisie and Gabriel said nothing. Their faces were impassive, but their silence gave her the confidence to continue.

'It needs someone to make the decision to start on the refurbishment. I can run up a new pair of curtains on my sewing machine – that would help – but the room desperately needs redecorating.'

'Jemma is a good needlewoman,' Gabriel said generously.

'Then there's the parlour.' Jemma was on a roll now. 'That also needs modernising. As a room, it's underused but it has a lovely fireplace and would make the perfect place for anyone who wanted some *privacy.*'

'I confess I'd never thought about any of this,' Gabriel said, after a moment. 'Perhaps I should make more of an effort with the house.'

Maisie leant forward, smiling. 'Well, I'd love to help you, if you do, Gabriel.'

'You would?'

'Yes, of course I would. We should do it together. We can make a start on the bedroom on Wednesday afternoon, if you want?'

'Wednesday? So soon?'

Gabriel looked like he might choke again but Maisie had picked up Jemma's enthusiasm. 'Yes, we can strip it out,' she said, 'and I'll help you choose new paints. It's such a pity Harry isn't at home. He could have built you some new cupboards.'

'Is your elder son a carpenter?' Jemma asked.

'Oh yes, he makes furniture over at Ledshams. He's dead good with his hands is our Harry. He can fix anything. He built me that cabinet over there.'

'That's lovely,' Jemma said. 'I noticed how smoothly the drawer opened when I fetched the cutlery.'

'Do you remember him at all, Jemma? I know you went to different senior schools, but you may have known Harry at Clifton primary.'

Jemma shook her head. 'I think he's a couple of years older than me. And I didn't care much for boys at that age!'

Maisie laughed and turned back to share more ideas about the redecorating with Gabriel.

After a delicious pudding of apple pie and custard, Jemma helped Maisie clear away and wash up the pots while Gabriel and Tom remained at the table, deep in conversation about motorbikes.

It was a delightful evening and later, when Jemma and Gabriel walked home together, he stopped to light his pipe and thanked her for her kindness to Maisie and Tom. The streets were pitch black but every now and then the moon sailed out from behind the scudding clouds and bathed everything in its silvery light.

'It's not hard to be kind – they're both lovely. I hope she accepts your marriage proposal, Gabriel. She'll make you happy. And for the record, when Maisie moves in, I'll give her some money for my board and lodging while I remain living with you.'

'I've told you before, Jemma, I don't want your money.'

'I won't be giving it to you,' she replied sharply. 'I'll give it to Maisie. She'll be in charge of the household and the expenses when she becomes your wife.'

He chuckled. 'That's me put in my place.'

'Seriously though, Gabriel, I hope you meant it when you said you'd make the effort to redecorate and refurbish the house. If you want Maisie and Tom to feel welcome, you need to make it more attractive. At the moment, it's a shrine to the memory of Mum and Dad, an Edwardian mausoleum.'

She couldn't see his face, but she heard his strangled exclamation. 'It's not that bad, surely?'

'It *is* that bad. A nice home is important to a woman because they spend most of their time there. Maisie needs somewhere she'll be proud to entertain her friends while you're at work. And that means refurbishing the parlour as well.'

He was silent for a moment. The sound of big-band music and the loud hum of drunken chatter rose to a crescendo then subsided as someone opened, then closed, the door of The Grey Mare.

'I don't want to spend money on the house,' Gabriel confessed, 'especially if we sell it after the war and buy a pub.'

Jemma sighed. 'This damned war will go on for years, Gabriel. You and Maisie need to live for now – in the present – and Tom needs a cheerful and comfortable home in which to grow up. Mum and Dad's bedroom would be perfect for him – and for Harry to share when he's home on leave. If you want to persuade Maisie to be your wife, you need to appeal to her maternal instinct, the love and care she has for her sons.'

She stopped in her tracks. About twenty yards ahead of them, the huge domed crown of a mature beech tree was silhouetted against the moon. Beneath its dense branches, a man stood in the shadows.

Gabriel saw him the second after Jemma. Swearing under his breath, he strode across the muddy grass towards him. Instinctively, Jemma followed.

'What are you doing here? Who are you?'

The man jerked. Whether it was out of shock at Gabriel's aggressive tone or whether he was checking his impulse to run, Jemma couldn't tell. Then he laughed. 'Nothing, guv'nor. Just havin' a pee. Ain't no law against it.' His accent was alien, southern. 'Been boozin' in the pub all night – you know how it is afterwards.'

Jemma hovered nervously behind her brother, trying to see the man's face below the brim of his hat. But the traitorous moon had disappeared behind another cloud, taking its light with it.

'If I took you back to The Grey Mare,' Gabriel snapped, 'would the landlord recognise you? And for the record, I'm a police inspector and there's by-laws in York against urinating in a public place if it causes offence.'

'Weren't in The Grey Mare.' He waved his hand in the general direction of Bootham. 'In one of the other boozers. Off-duty copper, are you? Out with your missus?' The man touched his hat in Jemma's direction. 'Apologies for any offence, missus.'

'I ask you again,' Gabriel barked, 'who are you?'

'No one important, officer. Just passin' through.' He turned and started to walk towards the city centre.

Gabriel started after him, but Jemma reached out and caught his arm. 'No, Gabriel. Leave it. He's not a debt collector from Middlesbrough with an accent like that.'

Gabriel stopped and they watched the man disappear into the gloom.

'Did you get a good look at him?' she asked.

'Not really,' he confessed, 'and I didn't recognise his voice.'

'Good. Then he's no one you've arrested or convicted. He's probably just some travelling salesman in town for the night.'

Shrugging, Gabriel turned and the two of them walked back to the house in silence, each lost in their own private thoughts.

Was it a coincidence, Jemma wondered, that they seemed to be under observation again now Gabriel was asking questions about Michael's possible connection with a top-secret government force?

Chapter Twenty-Five

The next morning, Jemma called into her new office before setting off for Leeds. It was exciting to see the place again and know it was theirs. The telephone rang almost as soon as she sat down at her desk.

'Good morning, Smoke & Cracked Mirrors, York's Lady Detective Agency.'

The caller was a middle-aged man who spoke with military crispness.

'Ah, good morning, ma'am, my name's Newton, Captain Howard Newton. I saw your advert in the *Yorkshire Evening Press* last night, and I would like to book an appointment tomorrow to discuss a sensitive matter.'

Jemma reached for the diary. 'Certainly, sir. I'm Mrs James, the proprietor of this agency. What time would suit you?'

'About ten, if you please. The thing is, darn it, I may need your assistance later that afternoon, as well.'

'I'm sure one of our operatives would be available tomorrow afternoon. Can you tell me anything about the nature of your problem, Captain Newton?'

'I don't want to discuss the matter in too much detail over the telephone – it's a sensitive case.'

'I understand. Please let me reassure you of our complete discretion. Anything discussed in this office stays in this office.'

'Good-oh. Well, the truth is, Mrs James, I'm being blackmailed, damn it – and need help. But I'll tell you the rest tomorrow. Grape Street, isn't it?'

'That's right. There's a plaque beside the door. Just ring the doorbell and I'll come downstairs and let you in.'

'Fair enough. Cheerio for now.'

Jemma could barely contain her delight when she wrote the appointment in the diary.

189

Jemma easily found Helen Urwin's former home on Dalton Grove in the leafy suburb of north Leeds, near Roundhay Park. It was an area of quiet streets, lined with mature oaks and elms and large rambling villas. The city's wealthy Victorian industrialists had sought refuge here from the smog and grime of the Industrial Revolution, although they hadn't escaped it entirely. The sandstone buildings, which would have originally gleamed like honey in the weak spring sunshine, were now smoke-blackened and grey.

Helen's house was situated at the head of a small cul-de-sac that rose away from the main road. Surrounded by a large stone wall and extensive mature gardens, it was a small, square mansion, three storeys high, with gabled attic windows on the roof and huge stone bay windows on either side of the large oak door.

A removable metal barrier had been erected across the entrance of the gravel drive between the two stone gate pillars, and a large board placed beside it advertised *Anston Construction*. In the distance, Jemma saw two workmen sawing a piece of timber.

She hesitated and glanced around the street. She'd always known this wasn't going to be easy and that the old house, now empty of its contents and people, wouldn't provide her with any clues about the enigmatic woman who used to live there.

She needed to speak to a neighbour, but this was no working-class back terrace where everyone else knew your business and you spent the day gossiping over the backyard wall. The rest of the houses on the street stared back at her, their façades blank and impenetrable, and she wondered about the friendliness of their occupants.

Across the street, a middle-aged woman in a faded turban and apron came outside to put something in a metal dustbin. She glanced at Jemma and smiled.

The charwoman or a housekeeper, perhaps?

Jemma hurried across, conscious that this might be her only chance to glean information. 'Good morning. I'm sorry to bother you, but I'm looking for a woman called Mrs Agnes Black. She's a relative of mine and she used to work at that big house.'

The woman's greying eyebrows gathered together in a frown. She was plump, with a broad, creased face. 'Aggie? I'm sorry, love, but she hasn't worked there for years. She retired over to Dewsbury to be with her brother.'

Jemma sighed sadly. 'Oh dear, I'm so disappointed – and Mum will be too.'

'You're a relative, you said?'

'Yes, my mother and Agnes are cousins – distant cousins. They lost touch years ago when Mum moved up to Middlesbrough, but I came here with Mum once and met Aunt Agatha. I live in York now – and Mum asked me to look her up.'

'York! My goodness – you've come a long way for nothin', you poor lass.'

Jemma shivered theatrically as a breeze fluttered round her neck. As she'd hoped, the woman took pity on her, and continued, 'And you look nithered. Never mind. Step inside, I think I've got Aggie's address somewhere – we still exchange Christmas cards. If you give me your address, I'll send Aggie's to you.'

'Oh, thank you!'

'In fact, I were just about to put the kettle on. You can join me if you like and warm yersen up.' She gestured her thumb at the upper storeys of the house. 'The Brownings are out playin' golf.'

'This is really kind of you.' Jemma followed the woman round the back of the house and into the spacious kitchen. 'Are the Brownings your employers?'

'Aye, that's right. I'm their housekeeper. Mr Browning, he were a solicitor,' she said proudly, 'but he's been retired fer the last few years and the two of them live on the golf course these days. Take a seat, lass, while I put the kettle on and find a pen. My name's Edna, by the way.'

'I'm Mary Smith.' The kitchen was homely, bright and painted a pleasant shade of pale lemon, with green check curtains at the window and a pot of hyacinths on the windowsill. The table still had a fine film of flour in places and the smell of baking lingered in the air.

This was clearly Edna's private domain in the house and had been for years. Her favourite spot appeared to be a faded and lumpy armchair in one corner, surrounded by magazines and a pair of reading glasses. Jemma sat on a chair at the table while Edna filled the kettle and lit the gas stove. 'Did you know my Aunt Agatha for very long?'

'Nigh on ten or twelve years. She'd often pop across to have her tea break wi' me – and sometimes I'd go over there.'

'My mother said Auntie worked there for years and the family were lovely people. They were called Urwin, weren't they?'

'Yes, that's right. Mr and Mrs John Urwin – but they're all gone now.'

Jemma looked shocked. 'Not all dead, surely?'

'No, no. Well, old Mr Urwin, yes – he's dead. He died of a stroke back in '34. His wife, God bless her soul, passed many years before. But their daughter's still alive – somewhere. Aggie were with them fer about twenty years. It broke her heart when the daughter shut up the house and laid off the staff.'

'That's sad.'

Edna pulled open a kitchen drawer and rummaged through it. 'Yes, she gave them the best years of her life, Aggie did, and she were booted out with barely a "thank you". She never got a proper pension, or a decent pay-off, either.'

Jemma frowned. Such meanness seemed out of character for Helen Urwin.

'Mind you,' Edna continued, 'Aggie will tell you about that herself when you meet her.' She pulled out a chewed biro and a scrap of paper. 'When you see her, you'll give her my regards, won't you?'

'Of course.'

Edna slid the pen and paper across the table. 'Write your address down there, lass. I'll send you Aggie's address in Dewsbury.'

Jemma wrote down *Mary Smith* and the office address in Grape Lane, while Edna mashed the tea. This was a lucky break. Making contact with Agnes Black would be useful – especially if the former cook held a grudge about her measly pay-off.

'So were the Urwins bad employers?'

Edna shook her head. 'No, he weren't so bad, Mr John Urwin. It's just his daughter who upset Aggie. Mr Urwin were in manufacturin', but don't ask me what they made. Mr Browning would know, if he were here. He used to be their solicitor.'

She paused while she set up a tea tray with a couple of cups, the sugar bowl and a milk jug, and Jemma made a mental note: Browning wasn't the name of Helen Urwin's current solicitor, according to the information she'd received from Mrs Banyan last night.

'The Urwins were an old family firm and his mother – Naomi, she were called – was one of the Whartons from Adel. You've heard of them, I suppose? The Whartons? Rich family. They own that big chain of menswear shops.'

Jemma had heard of the Whartons and knew they were a famous Jewish clothing manufacturing company as well as retailers. So, Helen Urwin was the grand-daughter of a jewess.

Edna reached for a cake tin. 'You'll take a scone wi' yer tea, I hope? I made them fresh today.'

'Yes, please. You were saying that the Urwins were a family firm. Was it a big family?'

'Not anymore. Mr Urwin lost two brothers in the last war. His youngest brother weren't married, but the eldest one had a young wife and four bairns. But Mr John saw them all right when he took over the company. They didn't want for owt.'

'I'm pleased to hear it,' Jemma murmured. 'Do they live in Leeds?' This was the kind of information she needed for Mrs Banyan. If Helen Urwin had four first cousins and an aunt, why on earth hadn't she invited any of them to her engagement party? 'And did Miss Urwin get on well with her cousins?' she added hastily. 'They must have been about the same age.'

Edna laughed, sat down and reached out a mottled hand for the margarine and a knife. 'What a lot of questions you ask, young woman!'

Jemma checked herself; she needed to be more careful. 'I'm sorry, it just sounds such a fascinating story – and my mum will want to know. She was close to Aunt Agatha at one point and so sorry when they lost touch.'

Edna slid the plate of scones across the table towards Jemma. 'Well, I don't know where the aunt lives, but the family were close.' She jabbed her knife in the direction of Helen Urwin's former home. 'The children used to play with each other in the garden.'

'Being an only child must be lonely.'

'I suppose so,' Edna conceded. 'But Miss Helen were allus busy with her swimmin', her tennis and her hockey. She were a great swimmer. At one point there were talk of her joinin' the Olympic swimming team.'

'Really? That's impressive. She must have been very fit.'

'Aye, big, strong, strappin' girl – broad in the shoulders and across the chest.' Edna patted her own ample bosom to emphasise her point. 'She'd have done well in them Olympics.'

Jemma blinked. She sipped her tea and thought back to Helen Urwin's flat chest and the thin, angular shoulders poking out beneath her silk dress. The woman must have lost a lot of weight and muscle tone over the past few years. *Had she been ill?*

'It were her mother who got her into the sport,' Edna continued. 'Mrs Urwin were delicate and favoured the fresh sea air. Every summer, she'd take Miss Helen to Whitby for a couple of months and the girl learnt to swim in the sea. Your Aunt Aggie used to enjoy them summers, with only Mr Urwin left in the house to care for – and he were hardly there, of course.'

'I think it must have been in the summer when Mum brought me here to meet Agatha – there was no one else around. It must have been lonely for Mr Urwin, though.'

'Oh, he were never lonely,' Edna said with a smirk, 'if you know what I mean.'

Jemma's eyes widened. 'Really? Did he have other women?'

But Edna shook her head, refusing to be drawn down that particular route. 'I wouldn't like to say. There were rumours.'

'So, what happened when Mr Urwin died? How did Aunt Agatha end up losing her job?'

'That were sad, that. Miss Urwin were about twenty-one at the time – and, of course, had just come into her money. She announced she planned to tour around the country and possibly go abroad for a bit. She took her maid and swanned off. She kept Aggie on at first, to look after the place – and the gardener – but about six months later, she wrote and informed them she were shuttin' up the house and they would be paid until the end of the month. Just like that. No pension or pay-off or anythin'. They never saw her again.'

'Poor Aunt Agatha! When did this happen? Back in 1934 when Mr Urwin died?'

'No, he died in December of '34. Aggie lost her job the followin' year.'

'It's amazing Miss Urwin just went off like that. I'd never have the courage to go abroad – even with a maid. Aunt Agatha told Mum about their maid called Lou. She said she was a nice girl. Helpful.'

Edna's eyes narrowed and she shrugged. 'I don't recall her name – but she were an uppity piece of work. Thought she were better than she was, with ideas above her station. Aggie weren't keen on the baggage, but Miss Helen were fond o' her.'

Edna paused and observed Jemma across the table. 'What did you say yer name were again? Smith? It's funny but Aggie never mentioned any family called Smith.' Her eyes shifted up to the left as she tried to recall a conversation with her old friend.

'Yes, that's right – Smith.' Pushing for the name of the maid had been a question too far; Edna was beginning to smell a rat. 'Mum and Agatha were second cousins, distantly related, but they were close as children and young women.'

'Oh, that'll explain it, I suppose.' She didn't sound convinced.

Jemma drained the last of her tea and reached for her bag and gas mask. 'I really appreciate the help you've given me, Edna – and thank you for the tea and scone.'

'Don't worry about it, lass, I've enjoyed the company.'

'Please send me that address soon. I can't wait to meet Agatha again after all these years and get the gossip. Mum's dying to know how she is.'

Edna showed her out and Jemma scurried down the road with her mind whirling.

She'd parked her car around the corner, out of sight of the street. She slumped down into the seat, pulled out her notebook and wrote down everything she could remember from the conversation with Edna.

Helen Urwin's dramatic weight loss was a mystery. So was her apparent estrangement from her family and her abrupt dismissal of the loyal family staff. Bobbie said Helen's current maid was called Louise Wilcox. Jemma had toyed with the idea of tricking or bribing Louise into revealing some information about her mistress. But they needed to find out how long she had been employed by Helen. If she was a recent appointment and had only served Helen since her return to England, she wouldn't be much help. Her instincts told her Agnes Black in Dewsbury would be more helpful.

Chapter Twenty-Six

Jemma spent the next few hours sitting in her car, watching the home of Neil Watts and wishing she'd had her car heater fixed.

Gordon Terrace consisted of two rows of houses, facing each other across the street. It was behind a parade of shops on the main arterial route that cut through Roundhay and wasn't far from Helen Urwin's former home. But the two houses couldn't have been more different. The paintwork on the door and window frames of number fourteen was peeling with age. Dirty, ripped net curtains hung at the windows and the small front garden was overgrown with weeds and full of junk, including a dented metal dustbin, a broken mangle and a rotting wooden washboard. A crumbling low wall separated the garden from the street and the gate hung off its hinges.

Jemma glanced at the other houses, which were neat and well maintained, and wondered how popular the Watts family were with the neighbours.

Not that she saw many neighbours. A couple of housewives came back with their shopping and a young mother took her child out in a perambulator. The street was quiet – and exposed. There was nowhere to hide or loiter for any length of time without attracting attention, even in her car. She wondered how many pairs of eyes were already watching her.

She ate her sandwiches, poured a cup of tea from her flask and sighed with boredom. O'Sullivan had been right about the tedium of shadowing.

At one point, a mysterious hand opened the door of the Watts' house to let out a small Jack Russell terrier. Jemma left her car and ambled along the other side of the road, hoping to catch a glimpse of the rest of the person, but there was no one there. The owner had simply opened the door and left the dog to its own devices. Disdainful of its own cluttered front garden, it came out into the street, entered next door's garden and did its business on their small patch of well-tended lawn.

An hour later, several groups of schoolchildren appeared, drifting home. Two young girls of about ten and twelve, accompanied by an older boy, headed for the Watts' house. All of them were freckled and had the same vivid red hair as Neil Watts. The scowling lad picked up a stone and hurled it at a passing car.

She checked her watch and decided to go back to York. Neil Watts was probably out at work and she didn't have the time or the patience to sit and wait for him to return today. She'd come back first thing in the morning and follow him to work.

Then she remembered her appointment with Captain Newton at ten o'clock and frowned. She'd have to come back the day after instead. Running this agency single-handed wasn't easy.

Bobbie had volunteered to call in at the office every day after work to help out, so Jemma expected to see her when she returned just after five.

What she didn't expect was for Bobbie to be waiting for her on the doorstep, wide-eyed and shocked.

'We've got a visitor upstairs,' she whispered dramatically.

'Gabriel?' Jemma asked in horror.

'No, our dear old school friend, Kathleen Young – or Mrs Pulleyne, as she's now known.

She saw the advert in the paper last night,' Bobbie continued, 'and walked in off the street about twenty minutes ago. When she recognised me, she nearly walked out again – but I've persuaded her to stay and made her a cuppa. I was just about to try and wheedle her problem out of her when I heard your car pull up.'

Jemma took a deep breath and hurried up the stairs.

She'd have recognised her old nemesis anywhere. Kathleen's thick mousy hair was tinted blonde now and rolled into a modern style, but the small eyes that narrowed at Jemma's approach were exactly the same – and no amount of lipstick could enhance that tightly pressed, mean little mouth.

She might be grown up, but she still hasn't grown a chin... Jemma had no idea where this random thought came from, but she was grateful for it and smiled. 'Hello, Kathleen, how lovely to see you again.' She sat down at her desk and pulled off her gloves.

'I'll get you some tea, Jemma.' Bobbie disappeared into the kitchen.

'Well, Jemima Roxby! Fancy that! I should have realised once I met Roberta that you wouldn't be far behind. The two of you always were inseparable, weren't you?'

Yes, luckily for me, we were – especially when you were around.

'How are you, Kathleen?' she said sweetly. 'I understand you're married now?'

The woman bristled with pride. 'Yes, to Group Captain Ian Pulleyne. He's based out at RAF Elvington and we've a beautiful house out at Fulford. You married that boy from the wireless repair shop, didn't you?'

Jemma flinched at her rudeness but kept her face straight. 'Yes, I'm Jemma James now. My husband also joined the RAF when the war broke out.'

Kathleen frowned and waved a languid hand around the office. She hadn't removed her gloves and clutched her handbag tightly on her lap. One wrong word and she'd flee. 'And your husband... he doesn't mind you doing... this? Working as a private detective? I don't have to work, of course. Unlike you, we're comfortably off.'

Jemma gave her a sweet smile. 'He's never complained. Bobbie and I've been in business for a month or so now. We offer our clients a discreet service. People come to us with all sorts of problems.'

Kathleen frowned and Jemma sensed her inner battle. 'So, what's discussed in this office is never repeated elsewhere?'

'Never. We're completely confidential. How can we help you, Kathleen?'

'I'm not sure you can. I do have a little problem, but it's probably just my imagination.'

Bobbie returned with Jemma's tea and slid into another chair at the table. Neither she nor Jemma said anything. In a few moments Kathleen would either start to gabble to fill the awkward pause – or she'd get up and leave.

'I've had a strange fancy recently... but I suppose it's just part of the mood swings of being pregnant.'

'You're expecting?' Bobbie said. 'Oh, how wonderful! Congratulations!'

The woman flushed with pleasure. 'Yes, the baby won't arrive until autumn, but we're both delighted, of course.'

Jemma also congratulated her and added: 'It's well known that the hormonal changes experienced by a pregnant woman can result in some fanciful thoughts. Tell us what's the matter, Kathleen, and we'll see what we can do to put your mind at rest.'

Kathleen sighed and said peevishly: 'Oh, very well. I don't suppose I've much choice, have I? York's not exactly overflowing with private detectives. It's my husband, Ian. He has an important job within the RAF that takes him out of the house at strange hours of the night and day. He tends to be a bit secretive at times.'

'He must be very busy,' Jemma said, 'an important man like him – in worrying times like these.'

'Yes, he goes out often – especially on a Tuesday and a Thursday night – to the officers' mess at Elvington. But when I phoned up last Thursday –

the girl said he wasn't there. In fact, she sounded rather cagey. I'm sure she was hiding something.'

We're in the middle of a war, Jemma thought. *The RAF are cagey about everything.*

'Does he drive himself to the base?' Bobbie asked.

'No, he always takes a taxi at seven p.m. He used to come home by nine thirty, but he stays out later now. But I'm sure it's nothing to worry about.'

'Would you like us to follow him to the base one evening, just to put your mind at rest?' Jemma asked.

'Yes, exactly. That's exactly what I want.'

'Then please let us help you, Kathleen. This is a list of our fees.' She pulled a copy of their terms and conditions from the pile of papers on her desk and slid it across the table.

'Good grief! You charge this much?'

'Yes, but I'm sure it'll only take a couple of hours.'

Kathleen chewed her lip, unsure.

'Think of the comfort it'll bring you, Kathleen,' Bobbie said.

'Very well. Do you want this retaining fee now?' She reached into her handbag and pulled out both her purse and a photograph of a good-looking man in a uniform. 'This is Ian.' Her eyes narrowed and scanned their practical slacks and flat, comfortable shoes. 'There's no need to dress up for this assignment, by the way. That'll just attract his attention. Wear those scruffy clothes you've got on.'

Ignoring the insult, Jemma made a note of their address and asked for more details about Group Captain Pulleyne and his movements. She offered to start work for Kathleen on Thursday. She would park on the street near their house and follow his taxi.

Once she'd left, Jemma and Bobbie stood together at the window and watched her hurry away down the chilly street.

'Well! Who'd have thought it!' Bobbie exclaimed.

'She must be really worried about her husband's fidelity,' Jemma said thoughtfully. 'Otherwise, why on earth would she let *us* take on this case? She always despised us.'

'You're endowing her with too much sensitivity. Kathleen's skin is as thick as a rhino's. We're inconsequential – just pawns to be used to get her what she wants.'

Jemma smiled. 'You're very cynical today.'

'I've been re-reading *The Murder of Roger Ackroyd*.'

'Ah, the unreliable narrator. Do you think Kathleen's trying to lead us up the garden path?'

'I don't think any of our clients are trustworthy. Every one of them adjusts the truth to suit themselves.'

'I disagree. I think Mrs Banyan has been honest with us. She's not easy to work with, but I think she's straight.'

'So, you're happy to take Kathleen's case?'

Jemma smiled. 'I'm happy to take her money – there's a difference.' Her smile faltered as a worrying thought crossed her mind. 'I just hope I don't get caught with a camera in my pocket near the airbase.'

'I doubt his taxi will lead you to Elvington. He'll be off to see his mistress. I mean, would you stay faithful to a woman like her? She must be awful to live with. It's the baby I feel sorry for.'

Jemma laughed. 'Business is looking up, Bobbie – in fact, we're a bit too busy. I'm working on another new case tomorrow, for a Captain Newton, who's being blackmailed – and shadowing Neil Watts in Leeds will be a long job.'

Bobbie's eyes lit up in delight and surprise. 'We've got *another* new case?'

They sat down and Jemma told Bobbie about her telephone conversation with the captain.

'Well, that's decided it.'

'Decided what?'

'I'm owed some time off from Grainger's – I did a lot of extra hours there over Christmas. I'll take a few days off from the store and lend a hand. You've taken on too much for one person, Jemma. I'll come and help.'

'Oh, Bobbie! Are you sure? That'd be wonderful! I never expected things to take off so quickly.'

'Absolutely sure.' Bobbie stood up, then reached down to switch off the fire. 'In the meantime, grab your coat and let's go home. I don't know about you, but I'm shattered – and I promised Mum I'd walk the dog tonight.'

Chapter Twenty-Seven

Jemma arrived early at the office the next day, determined to give the Helen Urwin case some more thought before her appointment with Captain Newton. She opened up her notes from the previous day and reread them, trying to work out her next move.

Shadowing Neil Watts was on hold for the moment and questioning the Urwins' former cook depended upon whether, or not, Edna sent her Agatha's address. The only other lead left to explore was Helen's mysterious family, but without their address it would be difficult to find them. Urwin was a common name and Leeds was a massive city.

Mr Browning, the family's former solicitor, might know where they lived, of course, but Jemma hesitated at the idea of enlisting his help. No doubt he was intelligent and shrewd; he'd see through her lies immediately and demand to know what was going on.

What about the famous Jewish clothing manufacturers and retailers? Could the Whartons help her in any way? She tapped her pen beside her notebook and an idea came to her.

Grabbing her coat, hat and gas mask, she left the office and hurried the short distance to the library. In the reference section she found an old copy of *Who's Who in Yorkshire*. There was a brief entry for Mr Urwin in Roundhay and dozens of entries for the extensive Wharton family. Jemma scanned through them, looking for someone who may be a spinster aunt, distantly related to Helen's Jewish mother. She found a couple and settled on a woman called Esther Wharton, who, if she was still alive, had an address out in the wilds of Wensleydale.

Returning to the office, she drafted a letter in longhand to the Urwins' former solicitor, then fed a piece of her gorgeous letterhead into her typewriter.

207

Dear Mr Browning,

I act on behalf of the executors of the estate of the late Miss Esther Wharton of Hawes in Wensleydale. They wish me to locate the descendants of the late Mrs Naomi Urwin née Wharton, wife of Thomas Urwin and mother of Mr John Urwin, of Dalton Grove, Roundhay, Leeds.

    I understand Mr John Urwin and his brothers are now also deceased. However, I hope you may be able to shed some light on the current whereabouts of their descendants.

    I believe the three brothers had at least five children, who are all the grandchildren of Mrs Naomi Urwin. There was a sizeable bequest left for the family in Miss Wharton's last will and testament and they are her legitimate heirs.

    I know you have since retired from legal practice and I apologise for any inconvenience this may cause you. Please telephone me at the above number, if you prefer.

Yours sincerely,
Jemma James (Mrs)
Proprietor

She knew from the O'Sullivan book that it wasn't unusual for private detectives to be employed to track down missing relatives named in the wills of the deceased. Of course, Mr Browning may smell a rat if his housekeeper had already let slip that a strange young woman had been in the vicinity asking questions about the Urwins.

    But it was worth a try.

Captain Howard Newton, a small, smartly dressed man of about fifty-five, with a silver-tipped walking cane that matched his silver hair and moustache, and his black hat balanced at a rakish angle, arrived bang on ten o'clock. Jemma was glad she'd worn her navy suit and red blouse for this meeting. Kathleen's comments yesterday about her scruffy appearance had stung.

He shook Jemma's hand firmly, wiped his booted feet on the mat and limped up the stairs behind her, chatting pleasantly about the damp weather. Jemma made him a cup of tea while he sank into the armchair opposite her desk.

She warmed to the man immediately. Unlike their other clients, he was relaxed, and his blue eyes twinkled with boyish mischief.

'Thank you for finding the time to see me, Mrs James.'

'It's my pleasure, Captain Newton. How can I help?'

'Well, as I explained on the telephone, I'm being blackmailed by a man called Shaun Flynn, whom I knew in the last war.'

'How did you know him?'

'He was an orderly at the hospital where I was sent to have my leg patched up after my, er, accident. He was a decent chap – or so I thought – and his friendliness made those dark days more bearable. He's Irish and, well…' – he broke off and gave her a wink before continuing – 'you know how the Irish can talk. He spent a lot of time with me during my recovery. After four years in the trenches, I was grateful for his cheerfulness. He told me he hoped to train as a doctor after the war. I left the army once the war finished and returned to my old job in an insurance firm, but we kept in touch. I offered him whatever help and advice I could – and on one occasion sent him some money.'

'Did he ever study medicine?'

He sighed heavily. 'No, I don't believe he did. I think he found an easier career, extorting money out of the likes of me. Anyway, he disappeared out of my life for many years – as people do. Last year, when war broke out again, I was recruited by the local territorial army as an instructor. This was announced in the local paper and Flynn suddenly reappeared with his blackmail threats.'

'What exactly is he blackmailing you about?'

Captain Newton paused and took a sip of his tea. A shadow passed over his face as he replaced the china cup on its saucer. 'Do you have any family who fought in the last war, Mrs James?'

'Yes, my late father was in the machine gun corps and my brother was a motorcycle dispatch rider with the Royal Engineers Signal Service in the final year.' She softened her voice, conscious of his sudden hesitation. 'Neither of them talked much about their experiences, but I gather it was horrific.'

'Yes, it was.' His bright eyes dulled at the memory. 'During the Spring Offensive after Ypres, myself and the few men left alive under my command retreated, as per instructions. We took shelter in the cellar of a building. There were French ambulances outside loading up the injured. Unfortunately, our building took a direct hit from a shell. I wasn't hurt but the last of my men were killed or badly wounded.'

'I'm so sorry.'

He paused again and Jemma held her breath.

'At that point, I decided I'd had enough of war. I pulled out my revolver and shot myself in my leg.'

'I see,' Jemma stammered.

'I'm not proud of what I did, Mrs James.'

'No, I can see that.' Jemma swallowed hard. 'What happened next?'

'I managed to drag myself outside to one of the ambulances, who took me to a French dressing station and on to Rouen Hospital. I was later shipped back to England.'

Jemma tried to imagine the courage and sheer desperation needed to actually shoot yourself. Gabriel and her father had always been disparaging of men who'd taken the 'coward's way out' as they called it. But sitting here now, with one of those 'cowards' in front of her, Jemma wondered if that was too harsh. The last war, with its relentless horror and bloodshed, had driven many men to insane acts. One thing was for sure, though – Bobbie's theory that most of their clients were unreliable narrators of their own story was flying out of the window. No one in his right mind would confess to an act like this unless it were true.

'It was carnage out there, Mrs James,' Captain Newton continued quietly. 'Fortunately for me, no one questioned my injury or how I'd received it.'

'Until Flynn turned up?'

'Yes. He spent a lot of time scouring patient notes and realised there was an anomaly in my description of what had happened. But he was sympathetic, and I was grateful for his discretion. Unfortunately, during our later correspondence, I thanked him in writing for his kindness and discretion and he's still got the letter.'

'Is this what he's using to blackmail you?'

'That's right. If the truth comes out, Mrs James, I'll be court-martialled and disgraced and I... I don't think I deserve it. I do valuable work for the current war effort with the territorials.'

Jemma frowned. 'How on earth does Flynn think he'll make this work? Blackmail is against the law and an imprisonable offence. He can't expose you, without incriminating himself.'

'Ah, but that's where his mysterious accomplice comes into the picture.'

211

'His accomplice?''

'Yes, a man called Evans, whom Flynn claims is another veteran from the trenches. If I don't pay Flynn the money, then Evans will trail me until I'm in sight of a local police constable. At this point, he'll attack me, shouting that I'm a coward. He'll insist he was in the cellar in France and saw me shoot myself. He intends to cause a disturbance and the constable will have no choice but to arrest him. Once Evans appears in court before the magistrate the next day, he'll denounce me from the dock, laying bare my cowardice and publicly ruining my reputation.'

'Good grief! That's a devious plan!'

'Yes, no one would ever expect he's part of a blackmailing gang. In the inevitable fuss that will follow my disgrace, Flynn and Evans will get away scot-free with their crime.'

Jemma frowned. 'Not necessarily. His account can be challenged – he would have to prove he was in that cellar in France at the same time as you.'

Captain Newton shook his head sadly. 'I fear by the time I've hired a lawyer, the damage to my reputation would already be done.'

'Well, how can I help you? Do you want me to try to get that letter back from Flynn?' O'Sullivan's book had been full of good suggestions about how to retrieve such documents – unfortunately, not all of them were legal.

'That would be wonderful, Mrs James – and I'd give you twenty pounds if you retrieved it. Flynn always carries it around with him in a brown leather bag and taunts me with it every month. But no – that's not why I'm here.'

'It's not?'

'No, my immediate concern is to find out if Evans really *does* exist. I've never seen him, you see. Flynn is always alone when he collects my money and I suspect he's just invented Evans to scare me.'

'What will you do if Flynn is lying, and he doesn't have an accomplice?'

'I plan to stand up to him. I won't pay him any more money. I'll brazen it out when he next tries to extort cash from me and send him packing with a flea in his ear.'

Jemma's frown deepened. She saw several problems with this plan. 'So, you want me to follow Flynn and see whom he meets – if anyone?'

'Yes. When I saw your advert, I thought: Bingo! Who would ever suspect they're being followed by a female private detective?'

Jemma smiled. 'I hope you're right, Captain Newton. The future success of this company depends on that. However, I hope you've realised that although Flynn may not have an accomplice at the moment, there's nothing to stop him acquiring one in the future. It would be better for you if I can steal back the incriminating letter from under Flynn's nose.'

Captain Newton shook his head. 'No, I couldn't possibly ask you to put yourself in such danger. Flynn's a big, rough chap – and don't forget he claims to have Evans by his side.'

'We'll see what happens.' Touched by his chivalry, Jemma pushed a copy of their terms and conditions across the table. 'These are the fees we charge, Captain Newton.'

He leant forward in his seat and read the sheet, his eyes gleaming with excitement. 'I'm meeting Flynn in King's Square at eighteen hundred hours tonight to give him another ten pounds. Can you be there to follow him?'

'Six o' clock? Yes, I can, and I will.'

When she took him back downstairs and let him out of the building, she had the impression that, despite his limp, he walked with a lighter step. The old soldier was looking forward to going into battle once more.

The telephone was ringing as she went back up the stairs. It was Terence King.

'Good morning, Mrs James. I just wanted to thank you for those excellent photographs of our insurance fraudster – and for such a speedy resolution to the case, and not dragging it out for the second week. There's a cheque in the post.'

'It was our pleasure, Mr King. I'm glad we could help.'

He laughed. 'Yes, it looks like you had lots of fun at my company's expense – but I don't begrudge you a penny of it. And taking along that American was a nice touch.'

Jemma smiled but didn't correct him.

'You seem very relaxed in that setting,' King continued, 'and you and Miss Baker are a couple of good-looking young women.'

'Thank you,' she stammered, blushing at the compliment.

'In fact, I've another job for you this Friday, if you're available?'

More work? Jemma could hardly believe her ears. She grabbed her pen and her notebook. 'Yes, we're available.'

'One of my clients in Leeds, an industrialist, is entertaining a wealthy American investor this week. His name's Van Cleef. Have you heard of him?'

'No, I haven't.'

'Well, he's in Yorkshire discussing a big investment that might result in a contract worth hundreds of thousands of pounds.'

'What exactly—?'

He cut her off abruptly. 'You don't need to know any more about the nature of their business. Unfortunately, my client thinks one of his competitors is trying to steal the contract from under his nose and his anxiety hasn't been helped by the fact that Van Cleef has booked himself

214

into a hotel in York for the night on Friday. He claims he's going to historic York to do a little sightseeing, but we think he might be meeting a rival.'

'Which hotel?'

'The Royal Station Hotel. Do you know it?'

'Yes, very well. It's a smart hotel, favoured by wealthy businessmen.'

'Is it the kind of place where two classy young women, like yourself and Miss Baker, would go for a drink on a night out?'

Not if we wanted some fun, Jemma thought. The Royal Station Hotel bar had a reputation for being expensive but rather dull. 'Yes, we can call in there and have a few cocktails. I take it you want us to get into conversation with Mr Van Cleef, charm him a little and try to find out what he's doing there and who he's meeting?'

'Exactly. I hope you'll do whatever is necessary to get this information. If you don't strike lucky on the Friday night, you might have to follow him around for a bit on Saturday. He's due back in Leeds on Sunday – but we've no idea where he plans to bed down on Saturday night.'

'We'll find out.' Jemma's calm and confident tone belied the fact she was almost shaking with excitement. Mind you, King's suggestion that they '*do whatever is necessary to get this information*' had made her eyebrows rise. *Who the devil was Terence King – her fairy godfather or her pimp?*

'Excellent. The usual rates apply, I assume, Mrs James?'

'Of course.'

'If you find out anything on Friday, I'll be in my office until noon on Saturday. Otherwise, please contact me first thing next Monday morning. Good day to you.' He rang off abruptly.

Jemma replaced the receiver and felt a surge of mixed emotions. She was delighted to have yet another new case, but how on earth was she going to manage this workload over the next few days?

Their patron saint, Father of Brown, must have sensed her anxiety because the next minute she heard familiar footsteps outside on the landing. The door opened and Bobbie waltzed into the room, flushed with the cold and grinning from ear to ear.

'Guess what? I've got the rest of the week off work – and next Monday! I'm all yours until Tuesday. Where do you want me to start?'

Chapter Twenty-Eight

Bobbie shivered in the cold breeze as she leant against the end wall of Gordon Terrace and peered around the corner at the home of the Watts family.

It had taken her two hours, a bus and a tram to get here from York and the daylight was already fading. This was a blessing, however, because – as Jemma had warned her – the street was very exposed. The windows of the two rows of terraced houses looked straight across into each other's living rooms and bedrooms and she knew it was only a matter of time before she attracted attention.

She took a short walk around the back of the terrace to warm up and found a slimy cobbled alleyway full of dustbins. She counted along the row until she came to number fourteen. A warped wooden gate leant on its hinges in the middle of the damp and crumbling brick wall. Peering through a crack, she saw the Watts' rear yard was also full of junk. But there was a sturdy outhouse in there, locked tight with a shiny metal padlock.

By the time she returned to her vantage point, a group of children had come out to play on the street, including the red-headed boy and the two girls whom Jemma suspected were Neil Watts's younger siblings. Bobbie heard them shouting to each other and soon worked out their names: Alfie, Alma and Edith.

Alma? Jemma had overheard Neil Watts talking about an *Alma* when he was with Helen Urwin on the river walk. Exactly how well did Helen know this family?

The Watts kids were a rough bunch, preferring to push and shove each other about and throw things. Bobbie watched helplessly as they bullied the small girl from next door and made her cry.

Twenty minutes later, a fat, balding man in a grubby shirt, with his belly hanging over his stained trousers, opened the door of the Watts' house and let out the Jack Russell terrier. It trotted out of their garden and through the gate of number twelve, on the same route Jemma had witnessed the previous day. Only this time, when it squatted down to do its business, the owner of number twelve, a large, middle-aged woman in an apron and hair curlers, came out with a bucket of icy water and hurled it over the dog. It scurried back round to its own home, yelping in shock.

The Watts children raced across, roaring in protest and using language that made Bobbie's eyebrows rise. Alfie, the ginger-haired lad, repeatedly kicked the woman's garden gate and the noise brought the fat balding man back to the doorstep. The two adults proceeded to hold a lively slanging match in front of the kids. *Forget 'Love thy Neighbour'*, Bobbie thought, *there's no love lost here.*

The man called the children back inside and slammed the door behind them.

A few moments later, a thin young man answering Neil Watts' description sauntered down the street and entered the house. Bobbie checked her watch. It was nearly six o'clock. *Was he returning from work?* It might be a good idea to return first thing tomorrow morning and follow him to his workplace.

He carried a large black carpet bag, which swung at his side with ease, apparently empty. *What did he use it for?* she wondered.

The next person to appear was a tall, stooped man with a money satchel thrown over his shoulder and a notebook and pencil in one hand. He went methodically from house to house, knocking at the doors and taking money from the householders.

Bobbie smiled; she recognised a rent man when she saw one. The fellow seemed friendlier and more approachable than her own rent collector back in York. Occasionally, he paused to chat a while with the tenant before moving on to the next house with his strange lolloping gait. Her eyebrows rose in surprise when he missed out the Watts house.

She checked the loose coins in her coat pocket, waited until he'd finished the street then hurried across the road towards him. 'Excuse me, may I have a word with you, please?'

The man glared suspiciously at her from beneath a pair of bushy eyebrows. 'What d'you want, lass?'

'My name's Miss Smith and I'm here on behalf of Leeds Corporation about the complaints.'

'What complaints?'

'The complaints the other residents have made against the Watts family at number fourteen. You know, the noise, the mess – the trouble they cause.'

He glanced over his shoulder at the Watts' house and laughed. 'That don't surprise me. It'll be her next door – Mrs Sheils – who's been complainin', I suppose?'

'That's right. I assume you've held this job for quite a while?'

'Twelve year,' he said, 'but I don't know how you expect me to help?' He licked his lips, and an avaricious gleam entered his eyes. 'My memory ain't what it used to be.'

'Oh, I'm happy to pay you.' She pulled out a couple of silver half crowns from her pocket and let them glint in her palm. 'I'm authorised to pay a small fee for information.'

'Yeah, right.' He took the coins and pocketed them.

'I noticed you collected rent from every house in this street – but not from number fourteen. Why's that? Doesn't this terrace belong to the same landlord?'

'I used to collect at number fourteen – but they own it now, see? Bought it from Mr George, my boss, a few years back. That upset the Sheils woman. She were askin' Mr George to evict them. Fat chance of that now.'

'The Watts family own their own house? Mr Watts must have a good job.'

'Which Mr Watts?' the man said with a sneer. 'The fat old drunk – or his spiv of a son? Neither of 'em have ever done an 'onest day's work in their life. No, old man Watts came into some money about four years ago,' he continued. 'An inheritance from his aunt, he said. He were a bit of a wheeler-dealer afore that, but now spends his time in the boozer.'

'How many children are there in the house? Mrs Sheils complains about the racket constantly.'

He shrugged. 'Dunno. Maybe five? It's the youngest lad, Alfie, who's the biggest problem – he's a nasty piece of work, that one. He tried to set fire to Mrs Sheils' house once by shovin' a burnin' rag through the letter box. It's a wonder they weren't burnt alive in their beds.'

'That's awful!' Bobbie exclaimed. 'No wonder she complained to the corporation. Was he ever charged with arson?'

'His dad boxed his ears, but the police weren't really interested in the little sod. Should have been sent to borstal, if you ask me.' He shuffled impatiently, eager to leave.

'Thank you, you've been very helpful. Do you know how long they've lived here?'

He shrugged again. 'For as long as I've been collectin' on this street – and before. I heard Mrs Watts moved here on her own when she were widowed wi' her eldest girl – who were a bad piece of work too, by all accounts. Don't know what happened to the first husband. Watts is her second. The other kids are his.'

'The older girl you've just mentioned, does she live here too?'

He shook his head. 'Look, lass, I've got to get goin' and finish my round.'

Bobbie thanked him and chewed her lip thoughtfully as she watched him lollop across the street to the houses on the other side. She still needed more information. Once he'd vanished into the gloom, she went through the gate and up the short flight of steps to the door of Mrs Sheils' house at number twelve.

Chapter Twenty-Nine

Mrs Sheils answered her knock almost immediately. She was chewing and wiped a smudge of grease from her chin with the corner of her apron. The smell of roast meat wafted out of the door on the warm air and made Bobbie's stomach rumble.

'Can I help you, love?'

Bobbie spoke quietly, conscious that the front door of the Watts' house was only a few yards away. 'My name's Miss Smith. I've been sent by Leeds Corporation to investigate the complaints about the family next door. I need to see if there's enough evidence to prosecute them under existing by-laws.'

Mrs Sheils swung the door back with a delighted flourish. 'About time too! Get yourself in here, lass! I'll give you yer evidence!'

She led Bobbie into a dining room dominated by the table on which the remnants of the family supper were still visible. A large crucifix and several images of saints hung on the walls. Two little girls were just climbing down from the table. Bobbie recognised one of them as the child Alfie Watts and his sisters were bullying.

Mrs Sheils shooed the children out of the room and poured Bobbie a cup of stewed tea from a large brown pot. 'Them's my granddaughters,' she explained. 'My son's daughters. Their poor mother's dead – bless her – and their father's gone to war, so I've took 'em in.' She crossed herself when she talked of her dead daughter-in-law.

'That's very good of you. I'm sure your son must be very grateful.' Bobbie accepted the tea and complimented Mrs Sheils on her lovely home. She took a seat and pulled out her notebook and pen.

For the next ten minutes, Mrs Sheils regaled her with the litany of horrors she'd suffered over the years at the hands of her neighbours. Her chubby

223

face flushed when she spoke about the attempted arson and how the Watts children had hurled a dead cat over the back wall into her yard. Leeds Corporation also came in for a lot of criticism for ignoring her complaints. Bobbie made notes and let her talk.

'It's a nice street this,' Mrs Sheils insisted, 'full of decent, honest, hard-working folk – but, as God is my witness, that family are a disgrace.'

'I can see that,' Bobbie murmured. 'It must be upsetting to live next door to them. How many of them are there in the family?'

'Him and her – and four bairns. She's hopeless with the kids. I can hear old man Watts yelling through the wall sometimes – and he doesn't spare them the belt – but it don't seem to curb their behaviour. It's the youngest lad who's the worst – the little devil.'

'I thought there were originally five children?'

'Aye, well, her eldest lass, Gladys, is in service. Though how she got a respectable job, I don't know – she did a stretch in prison, did that one. She used to work at the infirmary and stole the pension books from some dying old women and claimed the money. It used to be Gladys and the eldest lad, Neil, who caused the trouble on the street – proper pair of tearaways they were. But he's settled down now and passed the baton on to the little sod called Alfie.'

'That's awful,' Bobbie murmured. 'How long have you lived here, Mrs Sheils?'

'Thirty-five years. Arthur and I moved here when we were first wed. It were a lovely street then. We raised all our bairns here.'

'You've never thought of moving somewhere else, somewhere less troublesome, perhaps?'

Mrs Sheils frowned. 'Why should I be forced out of me own home? It's them that should go! Even when we realised she were a floozy and she scandalised the neighbourhood, I stood my ground and told Arthur we were stayin' put. He said he didn't like livin' next door to a prostitute, but I stood my ground.'

'I'm sorry, who's the prostitute?'

'Her – the mother! Dora Watts! The mother. Gladys's father were her fancy man. He'd just turn up here and swan inside like he owned the place.'

'So, when did she marry Mr Watts?'

'That were a few years later, when the fancy man grew tired of her. The brats came thick and fast after that and she pretended she were respectable like, now she were *Mrs Watts*. But I tell you what, Miss Smith – God watches everything, God knows the truth about that woman's sin.' She jabbed her finger towards the dividing wall between the two houses to emphasise her point.

'What was your neighbour's surname before she married Mr Watts?'

'Mellor. Dora Mellor.'

Mrs Sheils told her about the time Alfie Watts had stuck a bunch of rats in her outdoor privy, but Bobbie had had enough of hearing about the disreputable little brat. Gathering up her things, she checked her watch and used the time as an excuse to leave.

But Mrs Sheils didn't give up so easily. Before she showed Bobbie out, she extracted several promises from her about the future action Leeds Corporation would take to resolve her problems. All were promises Bobbie knew she couldn't keep.

She hated giving the woman false hope and sighed with a mixture of guilt and relief when she stepped back out into the cold street. Jemma had said earlier that she felt awful about all the lies she'd told this week. Bobbie could see her point.

Without the street lamps, the road was pitch black. She fumbled in her bag for her small torch with its tissue paper filter.

A door opened and closed nearby. Neil Watts left his house and walked towards her, carrying his large black carpet bag, which now appeared to be bulging with something heavy.

Bobbie held her breath and continued to rummage in her bag.

'Evening.' He politely tipped his hat.

'Good evening,' she murmured.

Racked with indecision, she hesitated. She was tired and it was dark and miserably cold. Her natural impulse was to find a tram and start the two-hour journey back to York – but this was an opportunity too good to miss. *Oh, bugger it.* She fell into step behind him.

Watts led her to the nearby tram stop on the main road. The shelter was full, and Bobbie loitered at the back of the crowd until the tram rumbled over the metal tracks towards them and screeched to halt. Bobbie slid into the narrow seat behind Watts and when he asked the conductor for a ticket to Harehills, she did the same.

The vehicle sped up after a while, causing the windows to rattle. She grabbed hold of the metal bar on the back of the seat in front as the tram swayed from side to side. They must be travelling through the same large area of parkland she'd seen on her earlier journey to Roundhay. She'd no idea where Harehills was, but this route was taking them back into Leeds city centre.

When Watts left the vehicle, she followed and found herself standing outside a large art-deco-style cinema, in a busy area of back-to-back terraces and factories. She knew from the broken glass crunching beneath her feet, the drunk slumped in the bus shelter, and the noisy gang of youths on the other side of the busy road that Harehills was a rougher part of the city than Roundhay. The smoke-blackened buildings were tightly packed, almost claustrophobic, and traffic waited impatiently in the road, nose to tail. Noise was everywhere, from the snarling of the pack of semi-feral dogs gulping down the contents of an upturned dustbin to the trams squealing round the corners and the horns of the frustrated van drivers.

She followed Neil until he entered a large, three-storey public house called the Fforde Grene, whose ancient name seemed anachronistic with its modern box-like exterior. She hesitated; the old taboo about the loose morals of women who went into pubs was dying out but women on their own still attracted the wrong type of attention.

'What's the worst that can happen?' She stepped down a side alley, repinned her hair and reapplied her lipstick in the dark. No doubt it was all over her teeth, but she'd have to live with it.

The Fforde Grene was huge, blandly decorated, stank of stale ale and was already packed with customers, many of them soldiers. Bobbie hesitated in the foyer and glanced into the two rooms either side of the door, trying to spot Neil Watts. A few rough-looking men crouched around a low table in one of the bars cast curious glances in her direction. Apart from a blowsy-haired, big-busted woman laughing with a group of soldiers, Bobbie was the only female on the premises.

The bar was manned by a great hulking fellow in a grubby shirt, who was drying glasses on a filthy tea towel. In front of the bar, there was a solitary unoccupied wooden stool. A glossy-coated Labrador slept on the floor beside it. Crossing her fingers that the dog was friendly, she sauntered across the sticky carpet towards the stool.

'You look a bit cold, lass,' yelled one of the blokes at the table. 'Come over here and sit in my lap for a while. I'll soon warm you through.'

'Sorry, mate,' she quipped cheerfully. 'You'll have to join the queue.'

The men roared with laughter and even the surly bartender cracked a smile. The noise woke the slumbering dog, who raised his head. Bobbie bent down to stroke him. 'I'd like a port and lemon, please,' she said. 'Does this lovely dog belong to you?'

———

227

'Aye, lass.' The barman's pride in his mutt was evident as he reached for a glass. 'Best dog I've ever owned. Friendly with the punters.'

She slid on to the bar stool. 'What a beautiful coat he has.'

The barman smirked. 'He's well fed.'

'My mum's got a dog but it's not easy to get them meat any more with these damned rations.'

The barman poured her drink and slid it across the bar towards her. 'So, where you from, lass? Not from these parts wi' an accent like that.'

'I'm here to visit my mother – but I needed some fortification first.'

The barman grinned, revealing a mouthful of irregular nicotine-stained teeth. 'Like that, is it? Live locally, does she?'

'Yes, on Harehills Lane.' She raised the glass, said 'Cheers!' and took a large gulp. Her starved stomach gurgled as the liquid filled it. 'Where's your privy?' A trip to the lavatory was a good excuse to snoop around the premises.

He gave her directions. Leaving her drink on the bar, she took a leisurely walk around the pub, which consisted of a series of interconnecting bars and lounges, all swirling with tobacco smoke and loud with conversation and laughter. A dance band was setting up its equipment in the corner of one of the larger lounges.

There was no sign of Neil Watts.

Dejected, she returned to her drink and her stool. *Where the hell had Watts vanished to?* She'd checked out every room in the sprawling pub. The only place she hadn't been was up the broad staircase, blocked by a sign on a chain that read *Private*.

The barman was serving another customer, but once he'd finished with him, he sidled back towards Bobbie. 'You want another drink, lass?'

'No, thanks, I've got to get off to my mother's.'

'You got some cash on you?'

'Yes,' she replied cautiously.

'D'you want to take yer old mum some meat fer her dog?'

For a split second, Bobbie was flummoxed. Then the truth dawned. 'Oh, yes. Yes, please.'

'Go up the stairs to the room on the right. But mum's the word, remember?' He tapped his nose in a conspiratorial gesture.

'Thank you.' She downed the last of her drink, grabbed her bag, hurried back out into the hallway and ran up the staircase. When she knocked on the door of the room, a gruff male voice bade her 'enter'.

She nearly choked when she saw Neil Watts and another man sitting at the table, and it wasn't just the heavy fog of cigarette smoke that made her cough. The muscly and heavily scarred and tattooed man sitting with Watts had a menacing scowl. Beside him, Watts looked like a spindly ginger twig. She panicked for a moment and wondered if she'd bitten off more than she could chew.

Watts glanced at her coldly, without a glimmer of recognition. In front of them, scattered across the surface of the scratched wooden table, was a mountain of tin cans and two overflowing ashtrays.

'How can we help you, lass?' the big man asked once she'd stopped coughing. His cigarette bounced between his thick lips as he spoke.

'The barman sent me,' she stammered. 'He said you might have some meat for my mother's dog.'

Watts nodded and reached for a pile of tinned ham. 'How many do you want?'

She fumbled in her bag for her purse, desperate to get out of the room and praying that Watts wouldn't recognise her. 'I'll take two.'

The transaction complete, the tattooed man told her he'd skin her mother's dog alive if she breathed a word to the authorities.

Nodding, she backed out and almost fell down the stairs in her haste to leave. It wasn't until she was safely back on a tram heading for the city centre, with two cans of black-market ham hidden in her bag for Timmy, that she finally allowed herself to relax and smile.

Chapter Thirty

King's Square was so named because it was alleged to be the site of a Viking palace, but it had never been a glamorous part of the city centre. For centuries it was dominated by a small church, which eventually crumbled into disuse and was used as a holding pen for animals about to be slaughtered by the Shambles market butchers. As a child, Jemma had always begged her mother to avoid the area because she loathed the squeal of the terrified animals and the smell from the insanitary piles of entrails and pools of coagulating blood on the cobbles.

The church had been demolished a few years ago but, macabrely, the corporation had used some of the old gravestones to pave the area. Jemma hated standing on the dead, which meant she still found herself gingerly picking her way towards the warped old bench in the corner. King's Square had always been a place where you had to watch where you put your feet.

She was early for the assignation between Captain Newton and his blackmailer. A cold breeze stirred a pile of rubbish in the centre of the square. She was glad she'd changed out of her suit into her warmer slacks and a jumper. She'd a funny feeling she was in for a long night and had phoned Gabriel at home before she'd left the office to tell him she was working late.

He sighed heavily. 'I won't be here for supper either, Jemma. I've just been called back into the station. Maisie and I have started the decorating in Dad's room, but I'll have to leave her to it. Four German seamen have escaped from the POW camp on York Racecourse.'

'Good grief! Are they dangerous?'

'They're unarmed – but desperate – and only one of them speaks English. We need to find them before the general public start to panic.'

'Good luck! And I'll see you tomorrow.'

By the time Captain Newton and Shaun Flynn arrived in King's Square, it was all but deserted. The two men approached from different directions, and the old soldier limped towards his blackmailer, his stick tapping on the cobbles, while Flynn stood his ground. Flynn wore a black leather overcoat and a black hat. His hat was pulled low, and the light was fading but Jemma could just about see his midnight-black hair, his smirking face with sharp-edged aggressive bone structure and his swarthy complexion. Captain Newton had warned her Flynn was a big, broad-shouldered man, but rather than be deterred about the size of her quarry, she was pleased. It would be easy to follow such a tall man. And this was all she had to do: follow him, see if he led her to the mysterious Evans, and perhaps take a photograph or two.

Her client and Flynn had a brief conversation, during which Flynn laughed and patted his large brown leather bag.

That must be where he keeps the letter Captain Newton wrote him, Jemma thought. She couldn't hear what they were saying, but she sensed Flynn was goading the old man. The captain's rigid posture and grim expression suggested it took every ounce of his self-restraint not to smack the fellow over the head with his walking stick.

Eventually, her client removed his wallet from his inside coat pocket and handed over a banknote to the blackmailer.

Flynn tipped his hat in an insolent gesture of thanks, turned on his heel and sauntered off down towards The Shambles.

Jemma rose to her feet and without a glance at Captain Newton, whom she knew was watching her, set off in pursuit. Her successful shadowing of Helen Urwin a few days ago had boosted Jemma's confidence and she strolled confidently after Flynn, who led her down The Shambles, York's oldest – and narrowest – medieval shopping street. Lined with wooden beamed Tudor buildings, the jutting upper storeys were so close they almost touched and cast the cobbled street below into semi-darkness, but she never lost sight of him.

Flynn crossed over the river on the Ouse Bridge and seemed to be heading in the general direction of the station. He turned down Railway Street, where most of the abandoned and derelict properties were boarded up awaiting demolition, leapt up the steps of the Great Northern Hotel and disappeared inside.

Jemma followed him into the small, bland foyer of the hotel and stood a few yards behind him at the reception desk.

A mousy and bespectacled young girl sat behind the desk.

'Good evening, Colleen.' Flynn had a strong Irish accent. 'Faith! And what a glorious day it is, to be sure, and how lovely you look.'

The girl blushed. 'The weather's been miserable today, Mr Flynn, and I've told you before my name's Claire. How can I help you?'

He placed his bag on the desk in front of her. 'Will you be a darlin' and keep this old bag safe for me a while?'

She stood up and reached for it. 'Certainly, sir. Are the contents valuable?'

'Most definitely, Colleen – and too precious for me to lose. Which oi'll most certainly do after a quart or two of your excellent Yorkshire ale.' He turned and made his way over to the staircase.

'Have a nice evening,' the receptionist called after him. She was about to turn to take the bag into the back office when Jemma stepped forward.

'Excuse me, would it be all right if I sit and wait for my friend here? He's one of your guests.'

The girl waved in the direction of the two battered chairs in the corner of the foyer. 'Help yourself, love.'

Jemma sank into a chair next to a large fern in a pot and picked up one of the newspapers scattered on the low table in front of her. Flynn had been stroking his stubbled chin when he mounted the stairs. She suspected he'd gone up to his room for a shave before he went out to the pub. *Is that where he'll meet Evans?* she wondered. *In a pub?*

She also wondered why he'd left his bag containing Captain Newton's letter in the care of the hotel office. Had the hotel had a spate of thefts from their rooms? Or didn't he want to leave such sensitive content where a nosy chambermaid might read it?

Twenty minutes later, Flynn bounded back down the stairs, freshly shaved and fastening his coat over a clean shirt. Jemma rose and slipped out of the door after him.

There was very little daylight left but she trailed him easily. He retraced his steps across the river and entered one of the public houses on Spurriergate. Time to change into her other coat and hat. She stopped abruptly in her tracks and glanced round, looking for somewhere to change.

An old, stooped man with his hands in the pockets of his grubby brown coat bumped into her.

'Sorry,' she stammered, stepping back.

But he stepped closer, so close she could smell his breath and see the scowl on his lined face. 'You will be, lass, if you go any further. Don't make a fuss – you're coming with me.' A pair of small brown eyes glared at her from beneath thick, greying eyebrows.

'I don't think so! What do you want? Go away!'

The hand in his coat pocket pushed something hard and metallic into her side. 'I've got a gun – see? And if you don't do what I say, I'll bloody well use it. Now turn around and walk back down towards the river.'

Jemma's legs nearly gave way in shock. She opened her mouth to protest but her throat was bone dry. 'What the hell...?' was all she managed to stammer.

He jabbed her again with the gun. 'Move!'

Silently, she started walking. She glanced desperately around Spurriergate, looking for help – but the dark street was deserted.

Was this Evans? Had he found her before she'd found him?

They turned on to Low Ousegate and he told her to stop outside a plain door next to a boarded-up shop.

'You're a bloody idiot,' he snarled, fumbling with a key to the door.

'Don't think I'm coming inside there with you!' she exclaimed. 'This is kidnap! Have you any idea who my brother is?'

'I know who your damned brother is.' He shoved her inside. 'It's for his sake I'm lockin' you up. Now get up those stairs!' He pushed her again.

'Who are you? How do you know Gabriel?' She tried to hold her ground, but now they were off the street he pulled the gun out of his pocket and jabbed her towards the stairwell, which stank of mouldy old carpet and damp.

Terrified, and close to tears, Jemma stumbled ahead of him up the stairs. What an idiot she'd been to ever think she could succeed at this game. Was this guy someone Gabriel had arrested and imprisoned? Did he hold a grudge? Oh my God, what the hell did he plan to do with her?

When they reached the first-floor landing, her kidnapper opened the door into a small, windowless outer office and switched on the light. There was another door on the opposite wall, presumably leading to the main office that overlooked the street.

He kept the gun trained on her and strode over to the skirting board behind the desk. Reaching down, he pulled out the telephone wire and plucked the telephone off the desk. 'You'll stay in here until I decide it's safe to let you out. You've no idea of the danger you're in.' He turned towards the door, taking the telephone with him.

'Why? Why are you doing this? Are you Evans?' she cried out.

He turned and confusion flickered across his face. 'Who the hell is Evans? It's Flynn I'm saving you from.' He left with the telephone, slamming the door behind him.

As soon as he'd gone, Jemma tried the door to the main office, but it was also locked. She thought about screaming for help but knew it was useless. She was trapped in an inner office above a boarded-up and abandoned old shop in an empty building.

Desperate for a clue to her whereabouts, and why she was here, she tried the desk drawers and the drawers in the filing cabinets – but everything was locked tight. Whoever worked in this bland, featureless office was both security conscious and tidy. There wasn't even a diary or an address book on the desk.

Slumping down into a chair, she tried to make sense of her predicament.

Her kidnapper said he wasn't Evans and didn't seem to know anything about him. His comments about Gabriel, whom he obviously knew, didn't make sense.

Was he connected to the men who'd been watching their home? Her stomach lurched with alarm at the thought.

Calm down. He'll be a plain-clothes detective who works with Gabriel and was also following Flynn. But then again, why would a police detective lock her in an office in York city centre?

Her eyes fell on the wastepaper basket beneath the desk. There was some rubbish in it.

Dropping to the floor, she pulled it out and went through the screwed-up receipts and tatty scraps of blotting paper. At the bottom was a sheet of discarded carbon paper.

Holding it up to the light, she peered at the faint imprint of a covering letter for an invoice for services rendered to a man named Wilson, and there at the bottom were the words: *Yours sincerely, William Sharrow, Private Detective.*

'You silly, silly girl,' she muttered to herself as relief washed through her. Why hadn't she realised? She was in Low Ousegate and Gabriel had told her Sharrow had an office there.

She remembered Terence King's words: '*Don't tell me you just launched a new business, Mrs James, without checking out your competition first…*' Well, she hadn't. But obviously Will Sharrow had checked her out. Mistake number six had come back to haunt her. And just to make her feel even worse, her eyes spotted another line on the carbon paper. Sharrow was charging his clients ten shillings an hour – not six.

But why did her rival want to keep her away from Flynn? She sat back on her heels, with the sheet of carbon paper still in her hand, and chewed her lip thoughtfully.

There was only one explanation. Sharrow was also shadowing Flynn. He'd spotted her doing the same thing and intervened to get her out of the way. Was Flynn blackmailing someone else in York? One of Sharrow's clients?

She thought back to Flynn's jaunty attitude with the hotel receptionist and his excitement about going out for a drink. He was in the mood for a celebration, which suggested he'd had a successful and lucrative day. She remembered the captain's words when she'd asked him about Flynn's plans to retrain as a doctor: *he found an easier career extorting money out of the likes of me.* The more she thought about it, the more likely it seemed that Captain Newton wasn't Flynn's only victim.

But if Sharrow was following Flynn on behalf of one of his own clients, what on earth did he hope to achieve? Surely, he knew Flynn kept the incriminating evidence from his victims in the leather bag he'd left with the hotel receptionist?

—

237

For the first time that evening, Jemma's mouth twitched and curled into a smile. Obviously, Sharrow didn't know this. But she did. Her smile broadened as a crazy idea came to her about how to turn this dire situation to her advantage. It was brazen and audacious, but if she got Ricky's help, she might be able to pull it off.

And then the air-raid siren exploded with its terrifying, screeching banshee wail.

Horrified, Jemma leapt to her feet and tried the outside door once again. She rattled the handle and screamed: 'For God's sake! Someone help me! I'm trapped up here!'

But it was useless. *Dear God, could her day get any worse?*

Rushing back to the desk, she dropped to her knees and crawled beneath it with her bag. She placed her hands over her ears and tried to calm herself down.

It'll be another false alarm. It'll be another false alarm.

Of course it would. This couldn't be the day the Luftwaffe finally found their mark and blew York to smithereens. She couldn't be this unlucky.

She laughed hysterically at the irony of her situation. When she and Bobbie had discussed the potential hazards of their new venture, not once did she imagine her life may be endangered by a fellow private detective, someone who was supposed to be on the same side.

More grim thoughts shot through her mind. Apart from Sharrow, no one knew she was here – and Gabriel wasn't coming home tonight. If she was killed, how long would it be before her brother even noticed she was missing? Would they be able to identify her body among the rubble?

Her eyes filled with tears when she thought about Gabriel's grief; he didn't deserve this. Reaching for her bag, she pulled out a handful of her business cards and pushed them down the front of her blouse into her brassiere. It was stupid, she knew, but maybe some would survive...

Please God, let someone find me if I die.

Suddenly, she saw a pair of trousers legs striding across the room towards her. Sharrow was back and she hadn't even heard him open the office door above the wail of the siren. He reached down and hauled her to her feet.

'Get out! Get to the bloody shelter!'

She didn't need telling twice. She was down the dark staircase in a few seconds and stumbled outside into the black street.

'Run!' yelled Sharrow.

But she spun round to face him before she left. 'I'll see you tomorrow – *Mr Sharrow.* Don't think you're getting away with this atrocity!'

Chapter Thirty-One

Leaving Sharrow gawping on the doorstep, Jemma hurtled down Coney Street towards Ricky's house, pushing her way through the tide of people dashing for the public shelters.

Above her head, powerful searchlights on the outskirts of the city raked the night sky for enemy bombers. Jemma's ears strained to hear the ack-ack of the anti-aircraft guns over the rise and fall of the wailing siren, but they remained silent. The streets were full of ARP wardens. 'You're going the wrong way, lass!' one of them shouted after her.

Jemma ignored him and continued to run. She knew being out in the open was dangerous. Apart from the risk of a direct hit and flying debris, the sadistic Luftwaffe pilots liked to drop out of the sky and strafe people on the streets with machine-gun fire. But the air raid could work to her advantage. She had to get to Ricky before Flynn returned to his hotel.

Only when she turned, breathless and panting, into Ricky's street did it dawn on her that Ricky might also have taken cover. But she was here now; it was too late to turn back.

The front door to Ricky's house was slightly ajar, as if someone had left in a hurry. She didn't bother to knock but raced up the stairs and pounded on the door to his flat. There was no answer and for a moment her heart sank – then she remembered his darkroom at the far end of his scullery kitchen. If Ricky had been developing photographs when the raid started, there was no way he'd risk damaging the exposure by opening the connecting door to the kitchen to leave.

She tried the handle, found the door unlocked and entered the cluttered bedsit just as Ricky walked into the room from the other side, wiping the chemical stains from his hands with a cloth.

241

Shock flashed across his long face. 'Miss Marple! What the hell are you doin' here?'

She tried to speak but was too out of breath.

'For God's sake, lass, take a seat.' He pushed a pile of newspapers off a chair and onto the floor and gestured for her to sit down. 'What's happened?'

'I need your help, Ricky,' she gasped. 'I'm desperate!'

And then the siren stopped.

'Thank God for that!' they said in unison.

Beneath the long continuous note of the all-clear, Jemma told Ricky about her commission to shadow Shaun Flynn and asked for his help to retrieve the bag containing Captain Newton's letter. He growled angrily when he heard how Sharrow had frogmarched her at gunpoint to his office and locked her inside, but he laughed when she explained her plan. 'My God, Miss Marple, you're a devious little old biddy! Old Gabe should be grateful you've never turned to crime. The York coppers wouldn't stand a chance.'

'It's not stealing – the contents of that bag aren't rightfully his. Will you help me?'

''Course I will. You poor lass, what a hell of a night you've had!'

'Can you fake an Irish accent?'

He laughed and launched into an exaggerated Irish brogue. 'Tok like a bog dweller? To be sure, to be sure I can.' His demonstration made her cringe but there was no turning back now.

'Come on. Let's make this telephone call before my landlady gets back from the shelter.'

It took ages for them to get through to the Great Northern Hotel. Ricky turned to her, frowning. 'It just keeps ringing.'

'Keep trying. They might not have returned from the air-raid shelter yet. And remember,' Jemma added, 'he called the receptionist "Colleen".' She fished out her hankie and handed it across. 'Put it over the receiver to muffle your voice.'

Ricky's posture stiffened when his call was finally answered. 'Hello there, me darlin',' he drawled. 'Will that be young Colleen, I'm tokkin' with? Good. It's Mr Flynn here. Oiv found myself stuck at the other side of town after the raid and I was hopin' you could send me bag over in a taxi. You remember? The brown bag oi left with yer good self? That's right. Charge the taxi to me bill. Yes. Send it to the Half Moon Hotel, on Blake Street. Thank you, me darlin'.'

Ricky put the phone down and grinned. 'I'd love to see the fellah's face when he finds out his bag's gone, *and* he's been charged for the taxi that whisked it away!'

But Jemma wasn't ready to celebrate yet. Too much could still go wrong. Flynn might walk back into the Great Northern just as the hotel staff were dispatching his bag.

She groaned as another problem flashed through her mind. 'What if the staff at the Half Moon ask for identification in the name of Flynn before they release the bag to you?'

Ricky smirked and tapped his nose in a conspiratorial gesture. 'Easy,' he said. 'But this'll cost you extra – and not a word to your brother and his mates, all right?'

She followed him back upstairs and watched curiously as he pulled a small, buff-coloured cardboard booklet out of a drawer and reached for a pen. 'What did you say this fellah's name was again? I'll make up an address.'

'A forged ration book?'

'You never saw it, Miss Marple.'

243

Jemma stammered out Flynn's name and took a seat while Ricky falsified the document. 'There's no rush,' he said cheerfully. 'Either that bag will turn up at the Half Moon, or it won't. Either way, we've done our best for your client.' He went off to the bathroom, whistling.

But Jemma was still agitated. What if Flynn found out what they'd done and followed the taxi containing his precious bag to the Half Moon?

When Ricky returned, he'd shaved and run a comb through his untidy sandy hair. Pulling on the smart coat and hat he'd worn for their night out at De Grey's, he shepherded her out on to the landing. While he locked his door, Jemma glanced across at Don's room. 'Where's Don tonight?'

'Hopefully airborne and blasting those damned Jerries out of the sky.'

She blurted out the next question before she could stop herself. 'Is he married, Ricky?'

Ricky gave her a quizzical glance over his shoulder as they descended the stairs. 'He's not told you then?'

She shook her head and held her breath. Part of her didn't really want to know.

'Yes, he's married and has two small kids back in Canada.'

'Oh.'

They stepped out into the street. Jemma shivered and pushed her hands into her coat pockets. Was it her imagination or had the temperature plummeted?

'Doesn't stop a bloke from being lonely, though, and wantin' a bit of female company to take his mind off the job,' Ricky said. 'Especially a job like that. One of his mates bought it the other day – and he was gutted. Don't judge him too harshly.'

'I know, I know.' She fell into step beside him and had a desperate desire to change the subject. 'What about you, Ricky? Are you walking out with anyone?'

He gave her another amused, quizzical look. The moonlight lit up his grin. 'I wouldn't exactly describe it as *walking out*, Miss Marple, but yes – there's a couple of lasses in my life. None who'll miss me too bad, though, when I leave.'

'You're leaving? Have you signed up?'

He shook his head. 'The regular army won't have me – medical reasons – but there's a rumour they want to recruit war photographers from Civvy Street.'

She was hit by a pang of regret, reached across and squeezed his arm. 'I'll miss you if you go, Ricky. But good for you, wanting to do your bit for the country.'

'Humph,' he said, embarrassed. 'I ain't made up my mind yet.'

They reached Blake Street and stopped opposite the two-storey Georgian terrace containing the hotel. The blackout curtains made it look deserted, but a man came out of the main door. Above their heads, the three golden globes of a pawnbroker's sign creaked in the wind. 'Do you think it's in there?'

Ricky stepped confidently into the road. 'Only one way to find out. Wait here.'

She grabbed his arm. 'Take care, Ricky – this Flynn is dangerous.'

He tapped the faded scar running through his eyebrow and grinned. 'Don't worry, lass. I've been playin' with the big boys since before you were born.'

Jemma watched him enter the hotel, then stepped out of the wind into the shadowy doorway of the pawnbrokers. She stamped her feet in an effort to keep warm and relieve some of the tension built up inside her.

Five minutes later, Ricky sauntered back across the road – swinging Flynn's brown leather bag by his side and grinning from ear to ear. 'Piece of cake, this private eye business, Miss Marple.'

Jemma laughed and hugged him before the two of them hurried back to his bedsit.

Ricky cleared a load of junk off his settee, and she sat down. Opening the bag, she delved into the contents. Stuffed among some personal clothing items of Flynn's were three bundles of papers. She quickly found Captain Newton's letters, but her exhausted brain struggled to make sense of the rest of the contents.

Ricky handed her a whiskey. Ignoring the dirty glass, she gulped it down. 'What's the matter, Miss Marple?'

'My client's documents are here – and this is a hotel receipt for Flynn and a woman called Mrs Harrison. But there's also a pile of letters here from a Harrogate vicar called Slingsby to a young man, whom I assume is his son. I'm not sure what they're about.'

'Pass them here.'

Jemma handed over the reverend's letters gratefully.

For a few minutes, Ricky read in silence, then his square jaw set hard, as if in distaste. He reached over to top up her glass. 'Have another swig of your drink, Miss Marple – you might need it.'

'Why?'

'Firstly, it looks like your blackmailer were out to extort money from *three* people – not two – while he were in Yorkshire. This hotel receipt compromises Mrs Harrison – she's clearly spent the night at this hotel with Flynn and my guess is she doesn't want her husband to know about it. And this vicar is a friend of Dorothy's. A queer.'

Jemma sat back in shock. 'Good grief. So, Flynn *has* made a career out of extortion and blackmail.'

'Looks like it. And he's a smooth-talkin' cad if he's conned this woman into a hotel and persuaded this young man to part with these letters.'

'He may have stolen them.'

Ricky shrugged. 'Either way, homosexuality is a crime punishable by jail. Could that Sharrow fellow be workin' for both the queer vicar and the woman?'

'I don't know...' Jemma stammered. 'I need more time to think. I plan to confront Sharrow tomorrow in his office – but I need to understand what I've got here first.'

He passed back the bundle of papers and grinned. 'Go home, do some knittin' and get some sleep, Miss Marple. You'll work it out tomorrow. But one thing's for sure...'

'What?'

'Where there's muck there's brass. You're sittin' on a fortune here. All of those folks will pay you big money to get back that evidence. And trust me, lass, you've earned it.'

Chapter Thirty-Two

There was no sign of Bobbie when Jemma let herself into the office just before nine the next morning, but Jemma wasn't surprised. Bobbie would have had a late night after her stint in Leeds and was probably catching up on her sleep. Jemma could have done with a couple of extra hours in bed, too, but she knew from experience that sleep was a luxury when you launched a new business.

Beside which, Maisie had arrived early at the cottage to continue with the decorating and Jemma would have felt a fraud lying in bed while her brother's girlfriend was working so hard in the room below. There was no sign of Gabriel, whom she assumed was still out looking for his escaped prisoners of war.

Jemma peeked into the half-stripped bedroom on her way out of the house and complimented Maisie on how much they'd accomplished so far. Without the heavy old curtains and the dark, sagging wallpaper, the room was surprisingly light and sunny. The clutter on the windowsill and the dressing table had vanished and the contents of the drawers and the wardrobe had been removed, along with the old mattresses from the two single beds. Jemma offered to pick up a roll of light-blue fabric from the market to make curtains.

There were letters waiting for Jemma on the doormat of the office. Two of them contained cheques: one from Mrs Banyan and one from Terence King. He'd used his company cheque book to pay them this time, which gave his company address on Albion Terrace, Leeds.

The third letter was addressed to *Mary Smith*. She opened it with a mixture of surprise and relief; it was from Edna in Leeds, and contained a kind note and the Dewsbury address of Agatha Black. Jemma wondered if Agatha had a telephone. Not everyone had one installed but if she did, then

Jemma might be able to find her number in a directory in the library. It would save them some time – and petrol – if she could telephone.

Grabbing her coat and hat, she went across to the library.

There were several telephone directories in the reference section. Unfortunately, they didn't include one for Dewsbury, although there were several for Leeds. A sudden thought came to her and she trawled through them, looking for any reference to Terence King's business. She smiled when she found it: *King's Private Enquiry Agency, Albion Terrace, Leeds.*

The mystery of her fairy godfather was solved: he was another private eye.

When she returned to the office, she telephoned Captain Newton and asked him to call round at eleven o'clock. Then she telephoned Sharrow's secretary to arrange a private appointment with her gun-toting rival for later that afternoon. All this, along with a trip to the bank to deposit the cheques and her important search for curtain material, would fill her day until it was time to follow Kathleen Pulleyne's husband.

She was revisiting the contents of Flynn's bag when Bobbie stamped up the stairs and burst wild-eyed and furious into the office. She threw a newspaper down on the desk in front of Jemma.

'I'll kill that bloody Ricky!' she yelled. 'Have you seen last night's paper?'

Jemma glanced down at the large black-and-white photograph of Bobbie swirling across the dance floor of De Grey's in Vince Quigley's arms. Above the picture was the headline: *Keep Calm and Carry on... Dancing: York revellers ignore the German threat. Courage, Cheerfulness and Resolution will bring us Victory.*

She smiled. 'It's a beautiful photograph of you, Bobbie. Ricky's captured the light bouncing off your cheekbones. You look like Vivien Leigh. I can understand why the editor chose to use it.'

'Humph! Vivien Leigh with bushy hair.' Bobbie threw herself down in the chair opposite and unbuttoned her coat. 'That's not the point, Jemma. Vince is a married man. Look – you can even see his wedding ring! What if someone shows this to his wife? My parents gave me this when I got back from Leeds last night – half the city will have seen it!'

Jemma bit back her laughter. 'You're only dancing, Bobbie – and it's Vince who's married, not you.'

Bobbie was unconvinced. 'I'm still going to skin Ricky alive when I see him! How dare he make a bit on the side from freelance newspaper work while we've employed him for the evening? And with a photograph of *me* too!' She rose and stomped off into the kitchen. 'Do you want a brew?'

'Yes, please. And actually, after the help Ricky gave me last night, you might have to forgive him.'

Alert to the change in Jemma's tone, Bobbie popped her head round the doorway. 'Why?'

'Things didn't go quite as planned when I was shadowing Flynn. I needed Ricky to help me out.'

Bobbie brought in the tea, then flicked through the bundles of letters belonging to Mrs Harrison and the Reverend Slingsby while Jemma recounted the events of the night before. Her anger against Ricky was rapidly replaced by fury against Sharrow. But that subsided when she learnt how Jemma and Ricky had turned disaster into triumph. 'You clever, clever girl! Well done for pulling that off! Gosh, I wish I'd seen Flynn's face when he discovered he'd been outfoxed! So, the mysterious Evans didn't exist after all?'

Jemma shrugged. 'I don't know – but it doesn't matter now we've retrieved the incriminating evidence. Captain Newton promised to pay me twenty pounds for the return of his letters, and I intend to make Sharrow pay me at least ten for the return of *his* client's letters.'

'Ask him for more,' Bobbie said with a wink. 'Mrs Harrison and the vicar have been very, very naughty.' She handed Jemma a sheaf of handwritten notes. 'Sorry about the poor handwriting. I scrawled these on the bus on the way home last night. The Watts family are the neighbours from hell. The eldest daughter has done time in a juvenile prison for conning dying old ladies out of their pension books and our charming Neil Watts is a black marketeer.'

Jemma frowned and picked up the notes. 'Did you find out anything to connect them to Helen Urwin and explain why she gives them money?'

'No, but old man Watts came into an inheritance from an elderly aunt a few years ago and bought their house. I wondered if Helen Urwin was behind this. If so, she's got poor judgement when it comes to charitable causes.'

Jemma's frown deepened. 'But why would she be so generous to these awful people? What are we missing here, Bobbie?'

'I honestly don't know – but there has to be a connection somewhere.'

'Maybe Helen Urwin's old housekeeper can help us.' Jemma slid Agatha Black's address across the table. 'I hate to ask you to do this, Bobbie, after traipsing halfway round Yorkshire yesterday, but I haven't got much petrol left. Can you get a bus to Dewsbury and see what you can find out?'

Bobbie grinned and reached for her coat. 'I'll see you back here later. By the way, dump that leather bag and Flynn's socks in the river before you get accused of theft. Those letters weren't his – but technically the bag and other contents are.'

Captain Newton was delighted to get his letters back and happily gave Jemma twenty pounds, along with payment for the other expenses (mostly Ricky's) that she'd incurred. She left the money and cheques secure in the office while she did her shopping. She had a strong suspicion her trip to see Sharrow would make her even richer and she might as well take everything to the bank at the same time.

Following Bobbie's advice, she took a slight detour down a side alley on her way to Sharrow's office and dumped Flynn's bag in a metal dustbin.

A chubby, grey-haired and grey-suited secretary sat in the outer office where Jemma had been imprisoned the night before. She eyed Jemma coldly and led her through to the main office, where Sharrow, in an open-necked shirt and tank top, sat slumped behind his desk. 'Mrs James to see you, Will.'

Without waiting for an invitation, Jemma sat down at the desk with her handbag on her knee and stared straight into his small, piggy brown eyes. He shifted his gaze away from hers. 'Well, good morning, Mr Sharrow. How nice to meet you under normal circumstances.'

He grunted and eyed her warily. He looked old, exhausted and a poor advertisement for their profession. Years of working as a PI had taken it out of him, but she had no sympathy.

'I'm not here to harangue you about your disgusting behaviour last night – I'm here to do business,' she informed him curtly. 'However, I want to make it quite clear that if you ever try a stunt like that again, I'll file charges against you with the police.'

'Flynn would have thumped you if he'd spotted you spying on him. He's hit women before – I've seen it.'

'You're assuming he would have noticed me. Female private detectives are rare and unlikely to attract attention, don't you think? The truth is that you wanted me out of the way because you were shadowing Flynn for your client, whom I assume he was also blackmailing.'

He grunted again.

'Anyway, to business. I have in my possession a bunch of letters from the Reverend Slingsby in Harrogate…'

'Who the hell's that?' He had the same confused frown he'd worn the night before when she'd mentioned Evans.

She changed tack. 'And a hotel receipt – belonging to a Mrs Harrison, whom Flynn was blackmailing.'

He sat up straight now. 'How the hell did you get that?'

'I've no intention of discussing my methods with you, Mr Sharrow. I'm here to discuss how much you'll pay me to hand over the hotel receipt.'

'The bastard compromised her. He charmed her, took her out for a meal at a remote hotel and pretended his car had broken down. They had to stay the night. She'd insisted on separate rooms, but it didn't matter. They weren't itemised on the bill, and it looks like she slept with Flynn.'

'How unfortunate for Mrs Harrison. How much will you pay to get back the receipt?'

'Soon after that, Flynn started waving the hotel bill under her nose,' Sharrow continued. He wanted her to soften, to feel sorry for the woman. 'He threatened to tell her husband.'

'I imagine she's promised you about thirty-five pounds to retrieve this hotel receipt?'

'Twenty,' Sharrow snapped.

'Very well, let's settle for thirty, shall we? That's fifteen pounds each.'

'Twenty-five.'

'You seem to forget, Mr Sharrow, that I went to great trouble and expense to retrieve these documents.'

'We'll split the difference at twenty-seven. I'll give you thirteen pounds and ten shillings.'

Jemma held out her hand. 'Deal.'

Sharrow's secretary glanced up from her typewriter when Jemma left his office.

'Gosh, he's a grumpy old so-and-so,' Jemma complained. 'Is he always like that?'

The elderly woman shrugged. 'He has been for the last twenty-six years, since I married him.'

Blushing, Jemma beat a hasty retreat.

Bobbie returned to the office about an hour later.

'I hope you had a more successful day than me.' She sank back into the chair and gulped down the tea Jemma plonked in front of her.

'Did you have any luck with Agatha Black?'

'I'm afraid not. I was met at the door of her house by her brother. I'm afraid Miss Agatha Black died of a stroke last month. This line of enquiry is, literally, a dead end.'

Chapter Thirty-Three

Jemma shifted uncomfortably in her car and pulled an old blanket over her coat. She'd booked the car with its broken heater into the garage for repairs the next day; tonight, she'd just have to put up with the chill.

At seven o'clock exactly, a taxicab pulled up outside the Pulleynes' smart Victorian villa. A tall man left the house with an overcoat slung over his air force uniform and climbed into the waiting cab. When it pulled away, Jemma turned the ignition key – but was horrified when the car gave a series of rapid clicks and refused to start.

'No, no, no!' She waited a moment and tried again. Thankfully, the engine roared into life. She exhaled a huge sigh of relief and the condensation from this immediately fogged up her windscreen. Cursing beneath her breath, she set off in stealthy pursuit of the taxi. There wasn't much traffic on this quiet country road, but things became more stressful when the taxi turned towards the city centre and another car shot out of a junction and placed itself between them. Jemma's eyes strained to keep the cab in sight. This wasn't the road to the officers' mess at the Elvington airbase. Group Captain Pulleyne had lied to his wife.

Five minutes later, the taxi turned into Coney Street and came to a halt outside a modern art gallery. Jemma overtook the stationary vehicle and pulled into the kerb a few yards ahead on the other side of the road.

Using her mirror, she watched Pulleyne leave the vehicle and ring a doorbell next to the gallery door. It was opened a few moments later by a gorgeous blonde woman clearly unconcerned about the blackout rules. Backlit by the blazing light in the gallery, Jemma had a good view of her high heels, the shimmering chiffon dress and the brightly coloured silk scarf draped round her shoulders. Her welcoming smile would have lit up a Hollywood film studio. She kissed Ian Pulleyne on the cheek, then backed into the gallery and led him inside.

Jemma was surprised by the sudden pang of sympathy she felt for her old nemesis. Kathleen Pulleyne may be mean-spirited and cruel, but she was also pregnant, and her marriage was crumbling round her ears.

Jemma turned her car round so she faced towards the art gallery. Placing her camera beside her on the seat, she made a note of the time and location in her notebook then reached for her flask. While she sipped her hot tea, she tried to remember what she knew about the shops on Coney Street.

Like most of the main shopping streets in the city centre, Coney Street was a tightly packed hotchpotch of mismatched buildings from the past four centuries. Everything at street level was a commercial business and most of these establishments used the rooms upstairs for storage, office space or living quarters. The blonde woman must live above the gallery. But who was she? A quick perusal of the electoral register in the library should reveal her identity.

Jemma waited to see if Group Captain Pulleyne reappeared and wondered how long the gallery had been in business; she'd never seen it before. But then again, it wasn't the kind of place she'd visit. Modern art didn't interest her. She preferred fine art and the exquisite portraits and landscapes painted by her neighbour, Fanny Rawlings.

Taking her bag and her camera, she left the car and strolled towards the gallery for a closer look. There wasn't much to see because blackout blinds were down but there was a small brass plaque screwed into the wall over the entrance. It read: *Miss Cynthia Ravenscar, Proprietor.* Well, that solved the mystery of Pulleyne's glamorous mistress.

She heard voices and movement from within. Turning swiftly, she crossed the street and stepped into the shadows cast by the overhanging upper storey of a florist's.

The door to the art gallery opened. Ian Pulleyne stepped out and lit up a cigarette, leaving the door wide open behind him and light flooding out into the street. Jemma stepped further back into the recessed entrance of the florist's and pulled out her camera.

Pulleyne frowned, checked his watch and glanced back inside the building. 'Leave it, Cynthia, or we'll be late.'

The lights went off and the blonde woman sailed out of the shop, swathed in a white fox fur. Once she'd locked the door, Pulleyne pulled her into his arms and kissed her tenderly. Unable to believe her luck, Jemma raised the camera and clicked.

She'd been worried the flash would alert the couple to her presence, but they were too engrossed in each other to notice or care. She risked a second photograph – and a third.

Finally, they broke apart and strolled off down the street, hand in hand. Jemma fell into step behind them. They strolled through the quiet Minster Quarter, where the branches of the trees shivered in the breeze above Jemma's head, and entered the exclusive Dean Court Hotel. An impressive red-brick Victorian building with towering gables and bay windows in elaborate stone mouldings, the hotel also had an expensive restaurant overlooking the magnificent west door of the minster.

Jemma gave the couple a few minutes to find their table before going in herself.

The liveried doorman cast a frowning glance at her slacks and unglamorous shoes. 'It's patrons and guests only, ma'am.'

'Oh, please! I just want to nip to your lavatory. I'm expecting a baby – and you know how it is for us women. I'm desperate!'

Something flickered in the man's eyes and he nodded curtly. 'All right, just straight in and out – don't linger.'

She hurried inside and followed the signs for the ladies' lavatory until the doorman turned away. Then she doubled back, found the restaurant and peered inside the doorway.

Group Captain Pulleyne and Cynthia Ravenscar were sitting at a discreet candlelit table in the corner, holding hands and staring into each other's eyes.

Jemma had everything she needed for her client. It was time to go home and make some curtains.

Chapter Thirty-Four

Gabriel was in the kitchen when Jemma came down the next morning and she realised with a shock she hadn't seen him for two days. 'How are you?' she asked. 'And did you catch your escaped prisoners of war?'

'Finally,' he said with a grunt of satisfaction.

'That's a relief,' Jemma said. 'Well done. Where were they?'

'We caught up with them at a fireman's hut beside the York-Hull railway line. They planned to stow away on a freight train heading for Hull docks and then get a boat back to the continent.'

'Well done – but you look exhausted. Can you get some rest today?'

'I'm all right,' he said. 'To be honest, Jemma, it's been the most exciting couple of days I've had for ages and it's been a real tonic. You won't believe some of the humdrum situations we deal with on a day-to-day basis. A woman turned up at Clifford Street police station yesterday with a brown leather bag containing men's socks, which she'd found in a city centre dustbin. She wanted to know if there was a reward for finding it.'

Jemma's hand trembled as she cut herself a slice of bread and spread dripping on it. She lowered her head to hide her expression. 'How strange.'

'Yes, it was.'

'Did anyone report the bag and socks missing?'

'No. By the way, Maisie's invited us both to supper tonight.'

'I'm afraid I'm working again tonight, Gabriel.'

'Still waitressing?'

'That's right. But I'll be home tomorrow night. Sorry, but I've got to dash now. I'm late.'

'Serving breakfasts now, are you? Well, have fun. I'll see you tomorrow.'

Jemma called at Ricky's and gave him the film containing the photographs of Pulleyne and Cynthia Ravenscar to develop. Then she took her car to the garage and was half an hour late arriving at the office. She heard the telephone ringing as she climbed the stairs and quickened her pace.

Bobbie was already there and had answered it. She nodded as Jemma dashed through the door. 'One moment please, Mr Browning. I'll pass you over to Mrs James.'

Jemma threw her bag and gas mask on the nearest chair, grabbed the receiver and introduced herself.

'Ah, good morning, Mrs James,' said a cheerful male voice. 'It's Alistair Browning here. You wrote to me about your search for the descendants of Mrs Naomi Urwin.'

'That's right. Thank you for getting back to me so promptly. Do you have any information that might help me?' She scrambled around the desk, grabbing a pen and her notebook.

'I've some information,' he said, 'but not a lot. I was the Urwin family solicitor for over twenty years, and worked for Naomi Urwin's husband, Thomas, as well as for her son, John. But I retired from practice a couple of years ago and anything I know may be out of date.'

'I'll be grateful for anything you can tell me. Miss Esther Wharton's last will and testament is a complex and extensive document and it's not been easy tracking down the Urwin beneficiaries.'

'Quite so. I may be able to help you with at least one branch of the family – the widow and children of Harold Urwin, who was Naomi and Thomas's eldest boy.'

Jemma mimed a silent cheer and gave Bobbie a thumbs up. These were Helen's aunts and cousins.

'As you already seem to know, Thomas and Naomi Urwin had three sons – Harold, John and Richard. Harold and Richard perished in the last war.

Richard died unmarried, but Major Harold Urwin left a wife called Anne and four young children. The family lived in Moortown in Leeds. I know this because Thomas Urwin asked for my professional help to set up a trust fund to provide for the widow and children, who were his grandchildren.'

Jemma nodded. This was exactly what Edna had told her.

'I have their last known address. It took me some time to find it in the old files.'

Jemma raised her pen. 'I'm very grateful for all the trouble you've gone to, Mr Browning.'

'Well, Mrs Anne Urwin is a lovely lady – and I'm happy to help. But I have to warn you, Mrs James, this address might not be current. I heard a disturbing rumour a few years ago that the family had fallen on hard times and had to move to a smaller property. I've no idea about the veracity of this statement – I haven't worked for any of the Urwins since 1935.'

Jemma swallowed hard. 'Why was this rumour disturbing, Mr Browning?'

'I'm not prepared to comment further, except to say that Anne and her children were adequately provided for in the trust set up by Thomas Urwin and it was honoured by his son, John, during his lifetime.'

'I understand,' Jemma stammered. She didn't, but she wanted to keep him talking. 'Before you give me the address, Mr Browning, what about the descendants of Mr John Urwin himself? I believe he was your friend and neighbour. He had a daughter called Helen, didn't he? What happened to her?'

His tone hardened. 'I've no idea of Miss Helen Urwin's current whereabouts. After her father died, she shut up the house, dispensed with my services and went abroad. The family home on Dalton Grove was sold to a property developer called Anston's of York last summer. They may be able to help you find Helen. They must have a record of her current address in England.'

'Thank you, Mr Browning. That's helpful.'

'My pleasure. I always admired Anne Urwin and I'm happy to assist in anything that benefits her family.'

But you don't like Helen Urwin much, do you? Jemma thought.

After Jemma had noted down the address, she asked him one final question. 'Can you remember where Miss Helen Urwin banked? If the property developers can't help me track her down, the bank might know of her whereabouts.'

'Like her father, Helen Urwin banked with Barclays on Street Lane, Leeds.'

Not any more she doesn't, Jemma thought as she replaced the receiver.

Once they'd retrieved the car with its efficient new heater from the garage, Jemma decided to take Bobbie with her to Leeds to meet the Urwins.

'Don't you want me to go to Harrogate?' Bobbie asked. 'Someone's got to give the Reverend Slingsby the good news that we've retrieved his incriminating letters from his blackmailer.'

'Not today. That can wait. I've a funny feeling I'll need your help with this interview with the Urwins in Leeds. I need your eyes, ears and insight. There's a lot here that doesn't make sense and it's going to take two of us to unravel it.'

Bobbie sat back in the old leather seat, stretched out her toes and smiled. 'So, a more leisurely day today, eh? And rather than being rattled to the bone on a cold smelly bus, I get to travel in style and comfort. I wish I could drive.'

'I don't know about leisurely,' Jemma said, smiling. 'Although we do need to conserve some energy for our American at the Royal Station Hotel tonight. We need to be careful and thorough when we question the Urwins. Because of the lies we tell about who we are and why we're there, we only ever get one chance with our interviewees. The police can go back time and time again with their questions, but we don't have that luxury. We have to maximise every opportunity.'

Jemma changed down a gear as she overtook a farm tractor. 'In fact,' she continued, 'I'm worried if I tell any more lies this week, my nose will grow like that puppet's in the Walt Disney film.'

'Do you mean *Pinocchio*? Wasn't it lovely? You'll be taking young Tom to the cinema from now on,' Bobbie said, with a grin. 'Gabriel will shove half a crown in your hand and tell you to take him to the pictures so he and Maisie can have some peace and quiet at home.'

'She'll have to agree to marry him first.'

'Hasn't she accepted his proposal yet?'

'She seems to be softening. There's been no more interference from our Cissy, and Gabriel is going along with the house renovations, despite the distress it's causing him – and the expense.'

Bobbie laughed. 'So, the Angel Gabriel is just a typical tight-fisted Yorkshire bloke after all? I hope Maisie doesn't notice his halo is slipping.'

'Oh, he's sweetness and light with Maisie and Tom. He saves his grumpiness for me. By the way, Bobbie, talking about marriage, Ricky told me the other night that Don was married.'

Bobbie shrugged. 'Well, so are you – in your head. You still feel married to Michael, don't you?'

Jemma peered at the road ahead, snaking its way through the rolling green landscape between the two cities. 'Yes, I suppose I do.' There were primroses sprouting at the base of the hawthorn hedges separating the road from the fields. Fat woolly lambs frolicked among the cowslips and swathes of lush new grass.

265

'Then you're the same. And if Don wants a bit of company and asks you out for a drink or a meal – provided you don't do something daft like fall in love with him or have an affair – there's no harm in it.'

Jemma gave her a quick, amused smile. 'That's very broad-minded of you, considering the tantrum you threw yesterday when you discovered Ricky had photographed you dancing with a married man.'

Bobbie peered out of the window at the sky, where three Halifax bombers were droning towards the coast, scattering a huge flock of birds. 'To be honest, Jemma, I'm beginning to think we should just try and grab whatever happiness and fun we can. The Jerries might drop a bomb on our heads at any time. That could have been them up there now. And I don't want my dying thought to be: "Damn, I wish I'd enjoyed myself more in my short life".'

She changed the subject before Jemma could reply. 'Why are you so concerned about questioning the Urwins? There's obviously no love lost between Helen and this branch of her family – which is why she doesn't have anything to do with them anymore. They'll have no loyalty to her and might be happy to tell us about it.'

'We can't rely on that. Some people don't like to air their dirty linen in public.'

They were coming into the outskirts of Leeds now. Bobbie pulled out the map and directed Jemma through the suburbs to Moortown Corner.

The Urwins' home was another lovely Victorian villa down a side street, off the main junction. Except, as they quickly discovered, it wasn't the Urwins' home any longer.

The woman who answered the door told them her husband had bought the house five years ago. All she knew about the former owner, Mrs Anne Urwin, was she'd gone down to live in Chapeltown among the Jews. Jemma winced at the woman's brittle, prejudiced tone.

Bobbie was disappointed. 'So, that's it then, is it? Another dead end?'

'Not while there's a library down the road,' Jemma replied. 'I saw one at a parade of shops in Oakwood, last time I was here.'

'Normal people make a note of the pubs they drive past – not the libraries.'

Chapter Thirty-Five

Miss Annie Smiddey's private library on the Oakwood Parade wasn't as well stocked with reference books as York Central Library, but it did have an electoral register for 1937. There, in Chapeltown, among the Levys, the Solomons and the Cohens, was a solitary Mrs Anne Urwin.

'Let's hope she hasn't moved again,' Jemma said.

Chapeltown was a dirty, smoky, overcrowded and noisy part of the city, bustling with black-haired olive-skinned people in dark clothing. The women seemed to favour headscarves over hats, and the orthodox Jewish men, with their thick beards, wore black hats and long coats. Behind stacks of regulation sandbags, kosher butchers and exotic grocery shops offering unfamiliar food delicacies lined the main street. Some of the shop signage was in Yiddish. The main road was crammed with military vehicles, delivery vans and trams and they slowed to a crawl for the last quarter of a mile. Down the side streets, great factories loomed among the ugly housing, much of which was earmarked for demolition.

'So how do you want to run this interview?' Bobbie asked. 'Are we sticking with the story they've inherited some money from their elderly Jewish aunt?'

They passed a synagogue designed in a Byzantine style with a large dome and minaret. A couple of young men in kippahs leant against the Greek pillars at the entrance, laughing. Their perfect, brilliant white teeth stood out against their olive skin.

She shook her head. 'No. There's a chance Mrs Urwin is still in touch with Esther Wharton's side of the family, and she'll know we're lying. And even if she doesn't know the old lady, I don't want to raise false expectations about an inheritance for her children.'

'So, what shall we say?'

'Let's tell the truth about who we are and simply say we're trying to track down Helen for her new solicitor. He wants her to sign some outstanding legal documents in relation to the house sale last year, but Helen appears to have vanished again – and has perhaps disappeared off to the continent.'

Bobbie looked sceptical. 'What, in the middle of a war? That's no place for a woman whose grandmother was a Jewess. Let's leave off that last bit.'

Jemma shrugged. 'They'll either know she's moved to York – or they won't. And if they don't, we can ask questions about when they last saw her, etc. etc. I know it's still a twisted version of the truth but at least we won't have to act out a part today – my acting skills are drained. This is the street.' She turned down a semi-derelict road full of grimy, dilapidated houses where weeds sprouted through the broken stones of the pavement.

'Blimey, Mrs Urwin's come down in the world,' Bobbie said.

The Urwin house, with its neat, well-tended front garden and sparkling clean windows and curtains, stood out like a sore thumb among these slums.

A tall, plump young woman with frizzy fair hair and sharp pale eyes answered the door. She examined their business cards warily when they explained who they were and what they wanted.

'May we speak with Mrs Urwin, please?' Jemma asked.

'I doubt my mother can help you. We haven't seen my *dear* cousin Helen for years.' The sarcasm in her refined voice was unmistakable.

'That's a shame,' Bobbie said. 'Mr Browning was sure you might be able to tell us something that would give us a clue to her whereabouts.'

The woman's pale eyes widened with surprise. 'Oh, Alistair Browning sent you, did he? How is he?'

'He's fine,' Jemma said. 'We spoke to him this morning. Look, is your mother in? Please will you ask her if she can spare us a minute or two?'

270

The young woman hesitated, then opened the door wider. 'Very well, come through.' She led the way down a small, well-scrubbed hallway to a tiny room at the front of the house. 'We've got visitors, Mother – a pair of private detectives from York, sent by Mr Browning.'

A thin, elderly woman with pure white hair sat in a comfy chair by the narrow hearth. Her lined face broke into a wide smile of welcome and her pale eyes – which mirrored her daughter's – gleamed with pleasure. 'Alistair sent you? We haven't seen him for years, have we, Clara? I understand he's retired now. How is he?'

'He's enjoying his golf,' Jemma replied. At their hostess's bidding, she and Bobbie perched on the edge of a large, comfortable sofa. The furnishings were plush and of good quality, if a little large for the small front room of the house. They'd brought some nice pieces from their old home.

Mrs Urwin laughed. 'Alistair and Jean always did love their golf course. So, how can I help you? I've never met lady private detectives before. How very modern of you! But you young women are so modern in your outlook these days. Clara here,' she added with pride and a wave of her thin, mottled hand towards her daughter, 'is the manageress of a large administrative department in the hospital.'

Jemma and Bobbie looked suitably impressed and smiled at Clara, who stood frowning and wary in the doorway.

Jemma cleared her throat and explained that they were trying to trace Miss Helen Urwin, and how Mr Browning thought Mrs Urwin might be able to help and had furnished them with their old address, which had eventually led them here.

'I've already told Mrs James we haven't seen or heard of Helen for years,' Clara said.

'My daughter is correct,' Mrs Urwin said sadly. 'I haven't seen my niece since her father's funeral over five years ago. She went abroad shortly afterwards and never got in touch again.'

'Apart from the once,' Clara added tartly.

'Yes, my dear, but the ladies don't want to know about that.' Mrs Urwin turned back to Jemma. 'I'd no idea Helen had sold the family house in Roundhay. And you say she's been using hotels ever since?'

'Yes, and she left the last one without leaving a forwarding address.'

'She probably owed the hotel money,' Clara snapped from the doorway.

Her mother gave her a pained look. 'That's unfair, Clara.'

'Her solicitor, Mr Hepworth, is concerned,' Jemma continued.

Clara frowned. 'Isn't Alistair Browning her lawyer anymore? I thought you said you were working for him?'

Jemma turned towards her. 'No, Mr Hepworth is Miss Urwin's solicitor. She dispensed with Mr Browning's help back in 1935. But Mr Hepworth gave us Mr Browning's details, which is why we spoke to him this morning.'

'Good grief,' Clara muttered, 'it sounds like she dumped Alistair Browning at the same time she dumped us.'

Mrs Urwin frowned and opened her mouth to reproach her daughter again, but Bobbie hastily intervened.

'Miss Urwin may be staying with an old friend. Do either of you know any of her friends?'

They both shook their heads.

'I'm afraid we're badly out of touch,' Mrs Urwin said. 'I don't know anything about Helen's life. As you've probably gathered, we've been estranged for years. It's such a shame you've come all this way for nothing.'

Sensing they were about to be dismissed, and desperate to stay and hear more about this estrangement, Jemma said hastily: 'Do you have an old photograph of Helen, Mrs Urwin? Mr Hepworth didn't give us one, and it always helps if we've a rough idea what the people we seek actually look like.'

The old lady's eyes sparkled at the thought of a captive audience for her photograph albums. 'Yes, that *is* something I can do to help.' She glanced up at her daughter. 'Clara, would you please make our guests some tea?'

'Huh!' Clara said, but she turned and left the room.

Jemma nudged Bobbie, but her friend was already on her feet. 'Can I help you, Miss Urwin?' She didn't wait for an answer and followed the younger woman into the back room.

Bobbie hovered, smiling, in the doorway of the Urwins' tiny kitchen, while Clara Urwin filled the kettle. 'Can I do anything to help?'

Clara gave her a sharp glance over her shoulder. 'You can shut the door and tell me the truth.'

Bobbie lowered her voice. 'What do you mean?'

'Please don't play the innocent with me, Miss Baker. I'm not as naïve as my mother – especially when it comes to my cousin Helen.' Clara slammed the kettle down on the stove and lit the gas. 'She's upset someone, hasn't she? You private detectives have been hired to snoop around and dig up some dirt about her.'

Bobbie hesitated, then shut the kitchen door. 'How would you feel if you were right?'

Clara gave a short laugh. 'Vindicated. As you may have gathered, I don't like my cousin.'

For a moment, the two women stared at each other across the narrow space.

273

Bobbie made her decision. 'You're correct, Miss Urwin. Our client isn't her solicitor. It's someone else; someone who doesn't trust Helen within an inch of her life and wants to stop her hurting someone else – like she hurt you and your mother.'

Clara's neck and lower face flushed with anger. 'You don't know what you're talking about. You're fishing for information. I should ask you both to leave right now.'

'You'd be quite within your rights to ask us to leave. And yes, I don't know what happened between your family and Helen Urwin – but I sense it was brutal. It's something to do with the trust fund your grandfather set up for you and your family when your father died, isn't it?'

Clara brushed a stray lock of hair off her face and pulled down three cups and saucers from a plate rack. 'That's none of your business.'

'True – but something's gone badly wrong. I've seen your former home in Moortown. Please, help us, Miss Urwin. You could save another family from grief.'

Clara hesitated and Bobbie crossed her fingers behind her back.

Clara's next words came out in a torrent. 'That bitch cancelled it – the trust fund payments. Her father was hardly cold in his grave when she wrote and informed us that she'd instructed the bank to stop my mother's allowance and any further financial support.'

'That must have been hard,' Bobbie murmured. 'That money was your inheritance, it was your father's share of a successful business built by your grandfather.'

Bobbie feared for the safety of the crockery as Clara pulled out a tray and slammed a milk jug and sugar bowl on it. 'Yes, it was damned hard. My older brother, Alan, had just set up his own company and relied on financing from the trust fund to support it during that first year. My

274

youngest brother had just gained a place at Cambridge and mother couldn't afford to send him there without the money.'

'Did you seek legal advice?'

'Yes, we sought advice – but it didn't help. The lawyer said the trust fund had been a "loose arrangement" set up between our grandfather and her father, and she wasn't bound to honour it. There was some truth in that. My grandfather didn't want to split up the family business on his death – he left everything to Uncle John on the strict understanding he took good care of us, which he did while he was alive. But none of us expected him to die so young – or for Helen to turn so vicious. Then Helen swanned off abroad and it became difficult to contact her. In the end, Mother gave up fighting and sold the house in Moortown to help fund my brothers' careers. That's why we're now living in this hideous little hole and why I have to work in a miserable office.'

Bobbie glanced around at the little kitchen. 'You've made it very nice.'

Clara snorted. 'You won't say that when you and Mrs James go outside and find someone's stolen the tyres off your car. My mother never complains. My brothers have families of their own now, but they're all prospering. They plan to move Mother somewhere safer and more suitable.'

'And what about your future?'

Clara shrugged. 'I'll probably end up in some poky little bedsit in Headingley among the students.'

'When Helen betrayed you, did she give you an explanation for her cruelty?'

'No, we never heard from her again – and that hurts just as much as the financial hardship she inflicted on us. Helen's the same age as me. We grew up together and were great friends. She was a kind, generous girl and a great sportswoman in her youth. Yes, she was a bit obsessed by her

275

swimming triumphs, perhaps, and a touch vain – but she was never vindictive. Our families were close.'

'Was there an argument? Some sort of dispute?'

'No. Nothing. We supported her at the time of her father's death and encouraged her to go away for a while in the early summer to the coast. It was a part of Yorkshire she'd always loved. I even offered to accompany her on the trip, but she said she'd be fine, she had friends in Whitby.' The kettle started to sing. Clara poured the boiling water into the pretty china teapot.

'After several weeks, she stopped answering my letters and didn't return our phone calls to the hotel. By late summer we were very worried. Then the next thing we knew: bam! A formal typed letter arrived addressed to my mother, which disinherited the lot of us and instructed us to stay away from her.'

Bobbie's frown deepened. 'Something must have happened while she was away. Which hotel in Whitby did she use?'

Clara shrugged. 'I can't remember. Trust me, Miss Brown, we stayed calm and my mother insisted we remember that Helen had just lost her father. Grief affects people in many different ways. But Helen made communication and contact impossible. The next thing we knew she'd vanished abroad, leaving us to face the bitter reality she meant every hurtful word she said.'

Bobbie reached out and laid a hand on the other woman's tense shoulder. 'I'm sorry. It must have been awful.'

Clara turned and eyed her shrewdly. 'Will this information be useful for your mysterious client?'

'Yes. Very.'

Clara shrugged off Bobbie's hand. 'Then I hope your client has it in his or her power to thwart the damned woman and make her suffer.' She picked up the tea tray and led the way back to the front parlour. 'I'll thank you not to say a word to my mother about our little chat.'

Chapter Thirty-Six

When Clara and Bobbie left the room, it took Mrs Urwin a while to find the right photograph albums in the small sideboard squashed at the back of the room. And once the albums were opened, Mrs Urwin seemed determined to take Jemma on a long trip down memory lane through her marriage to Major Urwin and the childhood of her four offspring.

Jemma found herself making appreciative noises as one faded and grainy photograph after another of an infant Clara and her cherubic brothers was presented for her inspection.

Helen appeared in several of the photographs with the family. But Jemma would never have connected this chubby child with the slender and angular woman she'd seen a week ago. A later photograph showed Helen eating an ice cream and laughing with Clara at some seaside beach. By now Helen had grown into a big-boned adolescent, toned from years of strenuous exercise in the local swimming pool. Her thick raven hair was the same, as were those close-set dark eyes – but Jemma still had trouble connecting this self-assured, athletic young woman with the thin, nervous creature she'd seen at The Spinney. *Why had Helen lost so much weight?*

Jemma tried a couple of times to bring Mrs Urwin back to the subject of the family rift, but the elderly lady refused to be drawn. Jemma hoped Bobbie was having more luck in the kitchen with Clara.

'Was Helen always interested in foreign travel?' she asked. 'She must have had quite a strong urge to explore the world. It can't have been easy to find the courage to go abroad on her own when she was so young.'

'It actually took us a bit by surprise. Helen was always a confident girl, but she'd never expressed the slightest inclination to travel before. However, she'd recently given up her dream of being selected for the British swimming team, so I suppose she needed a new direction.'

279

'Wasn't there an issue with British athletes who had Jewish ancestry in the 1936 Berlin Olympics?' Jemma asked cautiously. 'I know it seems crazy now we're at war with Germany, but weren't the British selection team wary of offending their German hosts at the time?'

Mrs Urwin blinked. 'Oh, you're referring to her Jewish grandmother, are you? I honestly don't know if Helen's Jewish blood was a problem or not, Mrs James. I'd heard it said she simply wasn't good enough to make the team.'

'Either way, it must have been a terrible blow for her.'

Mrs Urwin shrugged and said without bitterness, 'Well, she became very rich when her father died – and she had her independence. That must have been some consolation.'

'Was Mr John Urwin poorly for long?'

'No, he died suddenly – of a stroke – in December 1934. He was only forty-eight years old. It was quite a shock.'

'Good grief, that is young. Did he make proper provision…?'

But Mrs Urwin cut her off. 'I just wish she'd taken Clara abroad with her when she went. The two of them were close, you know.'

'I didn't know that. Helen travelled with just her maid, didn't she? I heard a bit about the maid, from the Browning household. It wasn't very favourable; I don't think the other servants liked her.'

Mrs Urwin gave her an appraising sideways glance and a small smile. 'My, you have been busy, haven't you, Mrs James? But yes, Mellor was a dreadful young woman, rather uncouth and with a lot of ideas above her station.'

'*Mellor?*' Shock lurched through Jemma and her mouth dropped open.

'Yes, Mellor – Gladys Mellor was her full name. I've no idea why my brother-in-law employed such a rough piece of work in his household.

Someone once suggested the girl had some sort of hold over John, but that was just gossip.'

Jemma heard voices out in the hallway. Bobbie and Clara were returning.

'Do you know anything else about this maid, Mrs Urwin?' Jemma asked. 'Her family or where she was from? If we can track Mellor down, we might be able to track down her mistress.'

'No, I can't help you there – but Clara might remember something useful.'

Clara carried in the tea tray and placed it on a low table near her mother. Bobbie said nothing and sat back down on the sofa beside Jemma.

'Clara, dear, I was just telling Mrs James about Gladys Mellor, Helen's maid, but I can't remember much. Mrs James thinks it might be useful to know more.'

Bobbie tensed at the mention of Gladys Mellor, but she remained silent. Meanwhile, Clara straightened up with the teapot in her hand. 'I doubt Mellor will be much help in your search for Helen. Mellor is dead.'

'Dead?' Jemma was so shocked she almost spat out the word.

'Oh yes, that's right,' Mrs Urwin said. 'I remember now. Alan, my eldest son, told us about it.'

'Good grief, what happened? She was only a young woman, wasn't she?'

'There was some sort of accident while they were over in Whitby that summer.' Clara paused with the teapot hovering over the china cups and gave Bobbie a significant glance. 'This was another reason we were concerned about Helen. Coming so quickly after the death of her father, we felt the death of her maid may badly affect her nerves.'

'How did your brother Alan find out about the accident?' Bobbie asked.

'He was conducting some business over in Bridlington on the coast and saw a report in the local newspaper,' Mrs Urwin said. 'He hadn't a clue who Mellor was, of course. Men pay very little attention to the servants. But he recognised Helen's name in the article.'

'I'm afraid if you want to know more, you'll have to ask my brother yourself,' Clara said. 'Now, do you ladies take milk and sugar?'

The next fifteen minutes, which were spent in small talk with Clara and Mrs Urwin, were some of the most frustrating Jemma had ever known. All she wanted to do was dash back to the car with Bobbie and try to make sense of these latest discoveries. In Gladys Mellor they'd finally found the link between Helen Urwin and the Watts family. But what did it mean?

Clara gave them her brother's phone number in case they wanted to ask him any further questions about the dead maid, but she warned them he was away in Scotland on a business trip. They thanked the two women for their help and left.

'Thank goodness, it still has its tyres,' Bobbie said, as they hurried back to the car.

'What?'

'Nothing. Just something Clara said.'

When Jemma tried to start the engine, all they heard was a rapid series of clicks. 'Not again! It did this yesterday.'

'Just leave it a moment,' Bobbie suggested. 'Obviously, Saint Father of Brown is having a little laugh at our expense today.'

Jemma calmed herself, silently counted to twenty and turned the ignition key again. This time the engine roared into life.

'There must be a loose connection or something. Perhaps it needs to go into the garage?'

'It's just been in the garage to get the heater fixed! It started fine this morning.'

It wasn't until Jemma had pulled out on to the main road and they were heading back to York that she finally relaxed. 'I'm sorry for snapping, Bobbie. My head's reeling.'

'I know how you feel. It's been quite a day for revelations! Gladys Mellor was Neil Watts's older sister, wasn't she? The illegitimate one who spent some time in a juvenile prison.'

'Yes. Did Clara Urwin open up to you in the kitchen?'

'Eventually – and that's a weird story.' Bobbie told Jemma how Helen had dramatically, and without explanation, turned against her family in the summer of 1935. 'Clara claimed there was no argument or any reason for her to cut them off without a penny and throw them out of her life.'

'Unfortunately, we've only got her word for that. There may have been a bitter family dispute.'

'Anne Urwin and her daughter seemed like decent women to me.'

Jemma thought for a moment, then agreed. 'Yes, they are – and this seems badly out of character for Helen. Why help out a family of ne'er-do-wells like the Watts – but treat her own so badly?'

'I don't understand how the Urwins came to employ Mellor in the first place,' Bobbie said. 'No one seems to have had a good word to say about the girl. Surely they must have asked for references?'

'References can be forged. Perhaps Helen gives money to the Watts family because she feels responsible for Mellor's death,' Jemma suggested. 'We need to find out exactly what happened to her.'

Bobbie snorted, then gave a wicked smile. 'Maybe Helen Urwin murdered her.'

'That's a big leap of imagination, Bobbie!'

Bobbie shrugged. 'Well, it explains the guilt. And she does read crime stories. When Doctor Crippen and Le Neve were arrested aboard that steamship, they were reading Edgar Wallace.'

Jemma smiled and felt the tension begin to ease in her knotted shoulders. '*We* read crime stories and we're not murderers.'

'True.'

They fell silent for a while, then Bobbie said, 'There's something else that doesn't make sense.'

'What?'

'When I talked to the rent man and the Watts' neighbour, Mrs Sheils, neither of them knew Gladys Mellor was dead. They both told me she worked away. Mrs Sheils said she was in service. I know no one in that community likes the Watts family, but I'm pretty sure if they'd lost their eldest daughter in tragic circumstances, it would be common knowledge. A death in the family is not the sort of thing people hide.'

'You're right. This case gets more and more mysterious each day. Every time we find the answer to one set of questions, it just throws up more.'

Bobbie stretched out and grinned. 'Well, at least we've plenty to tell our client about Helen Urwin.'

Jemma sighed. 'I'm not sure it's what Mrs Banyan wants to hear. Yes, Helen lied when she claimed she had no relatives, but all she has to do is concoct some terrible story about how badly they treated her, or tried to steal from her, and she can justify the rift. Mrs Banyan wants damning evidence that'll disgrace Helen in her fiancé's eyes and make him cancel their engagement. We don't have enough for that.'

'Not yet.' Bobbie grinned. 'I haven't abandoned my theory that Helen murdered her maid. That would put the kibosh on the wedding.'

'When Alan Urwin gets back from Scotland, he might be able to tell us some more about what happened to Gladys in Whitby.'

'Failing that,' Bobbie suggested, 'we can persuade Mrs Banyan to fund a little day trip to the coast. I can't remember the last time I saw the sea.'

'We'd have to go on the bus. I've nearly used up all of my petrol ration.'

'And the library might be able to help. They keep back copies of old newspapers. We can search through the 1935 papers and see if we can stumble upon the same article Alan Mellor read.'

'Good thinking, Doctor Watson.'

'My pleasure, Miss Sherlock. In the meantime, we'd better give our tired brains a rest. We'll need all our energy tonight to seduce this American.'

Chapter Thirty-Seven

They went back to Bobbie's house to change into their best frocks for their evening at the Royal Station Hotel.

Bobbie pulled on the same shimmering dark-green dress she'd worn for their night out at De Grey's. This time she added a pair of long, black satin evening gloves. 'They were reduced in the sale at Grainger's.'

'They're perfect for cocktails at a posh hotel,' Jemma said. Her own dress was pale peach. Lightly gathered at the waist, it crossed over the bust to form a V-shaped neckline and was sculptured with shoulder pads. But the most outstanding feature was the voluminous flared sleeves, made from a pale, translucent voile and gathered at the cuff. She pulled a short-sleeved cream bolero jacket over her gown, leaving the lower section of the sleeves exposed to shimmer in the light.

'Isn't that your wedding dress?' Bobbie asked.

'I dyed it and added the sleeves to try and get more wear out of it. It's such a shame to only wear things the once, don't you think?'

'It is. That delicate colour suits you, and I love the sheen of those sleeves.'

Bobbie leant towards the mirror to check none of her hair had escaped from her sequined snood. She murmured with satisfaction and helped herself to a generous spray of Jemma's French perfume. 'Well, I think we both look wonderful – again. We need to find more time to go out on the razzle dazzle. The good citizens of York need us glamorous gals to light up their dreary war-torn lives.'

Jemma laughed. 'There speaks the new pin-up girl for the *Yorkshire Evening Press*.'

'Seriously though, if it wasn't for Terence King funding our Friday night larks around the social high spots of York, we'd never get out. All work and no play makes us dull girls. We need to make more effort to socialise.'

'You're right.'

'We shall raise our glasses and toast our fairy godfather tonight.' Bobbie reached for her coat. 'The toast shall be: *All Hail the King!* Mind you, do you think they'll even let us into the Royal Station Hotel without fur stoles? These sensible coats rather spoil the effect.'

'If the business keeps booming like it has this week, I'll buy us both a mink coat out of the petty cash tin,' Jemma promised.

Laughing, they said a cheerful goodbye to Bobbie's parents and took the short walk to the impressive pile of Victorian grandeur known as the Royal Station Hotel. Backing on to the train station, the hotel was a five-storey, high-chimneyed affair built of yellow Scarborough brick. The medieval city walls ran along one side of the building, and another had sweeping views of the hotel's extensive gardens and the minster beyond.

Inside, a beautiful gilt and marble staircase swept down in a curve to the spacious foyer, which opened out into the bar and lounge area. These lofty and elegant public spaces were lit by glittering crystal chandeliers. Tall white and gold Corinthian pillars supported the decorative plaster ceilings with their intricate friezes.

There were several men draped over the vast chesterfield sofas and elegant velvet armchairs, most of them in black tie. Mr King had sent Jemma a grainy photograph of their American businessman, cut from a newspaper article. Beneath the brim of his hat was the long face of a sixty-year-old man, with round spectacles perched on his narrow, pinched nose. He had no chin to speak of and he looked miserable.

'That's him over by the window,' Bobbie said. 'He's with the big chap and those two floozies.'

Jemma followed her gaze and saw the diminutive Mr Van Cleef, hemmed in against the luxurious gold brocade of the tall window drapes, and a chubby younger man with fleshy jowls. Both men wore evening dress and smoked Cuban cigars. Van Cleef's humourless grey eyes were fixed on one of their female companions, who seemed to be telling the party an anecdote that everyone but the American thought was funny.

Bobbie strolled closer across the luxurious plum-coloured carpet and sat down on a sofa next to a Grecian plinth topped with a vase of hothouse peonies.

Their seats gave them a good view of Van Cleef's party and enabled them to overhear some of their conversation. The younger man was the loudest and most ebullient of the group. He had the kind of cut-glass accent cultivated at an exclusive British public school. When Van Cleef spoke, Jemma couldn't catch his words, although she picked up the soft southern drawl of his accent.

The two women were also British. They were in their late thirties, and both wore beaded black cocktail dresses with an ostentatious display of feathers and chunky jewellery. One of them held a long cigarette holder from which curled a thin line of blue smoke.

'It looks like we've been beaten to it.' Bobbie smoothed out her skirt. 'Do you think they're a couple of prostitutes they've picked up?'

Jemma smiled. Bobbie was in an outrageous mood tonight. 'No, I don't. They're fellow guests at the hotel – one of the women has put her room key on the table beside her drink. They've probably only just met, but keep your ears open. We need to find out who they are – especially the other man.'

A waiter approached and Jemma ordered two sidecar cocktails. Just before he walked away, Bobbie whipped her camera out of her handbag and asked the waiter to take a couple of photographs of her and Jemma 'with the window in the background.'

He duly obliged and Bobbie replaced the camera in her bag. 'Hopefully, Van Cleef will be in these shots and we'll have something to show Terence King.' She cast a frustrated glance at the group and tried to catch the American's eye – but he ignored her. 'This might be a long night. How can we jettison those women and get into conversation with the blokes?'

'We can't.' Jemma sighed. 'Never mind *a long night*, this might be a long weekend. Mr King said if we couldn't wheedle any information out of Van Cleef tonight, we should follow him to his destination tomorrow.'

Their gleaming amber drinks arrived in conical glasses with a frosted edging. Bobbie's mood lifted at the sight of the orange twist. 'Ooh, that's the first bit of orange I've seen for a year.' She held out her glass towards Jemma.

'Is this the toast to the King?' Jemma asked.

'No, I've changed my mind about that. This is a toast to *us* and Smoke & Cracked Mirrors. What a hell of a week we've had, Jemma! We should take a moment or two to congratulate ourselves.'

Jemma grinned and clinked her glass. 'To Smoke & Cracked Mirrors!'

'And a very successful first week in our new premises.'

They took a sip and Bobbie purred with pleasure. 'This is the life, Jemma. It makes shivering for hours on Gordon Terrace worthwhile.'

'Are you enjoying the job?'

'I love it. I was born to tell lies and sneak around seedy streets in pursuit of wrong 'uns. And you, my lovely friend, are a born businesswoman.'

'I hope so – although sometimes I do feel a bit guilty.'

'Guilty?'

'Yes, sometimes I feel we should be doing more for the war effort.'

'There's other women who can do that, Jemma. Women who don't have our skills. Our clients need us. Besides which, in a roundabout way, we've helped the war effort this week. The territorial army needs Captain Newton – and we helped him to stay in his position.'

Jemma smiled. 'You should be a politician, Bobbie. You've an answer for everything. Anyway, let's hope next week is as profitable – I can't believe the money we've banked so far! It won't be long before I need you to come into the business full time. Once we can afford it, I plan to pay us both a good wage.' She named the figure and Bobbie's eyes widened in surprise.

'That's twice the amount I get for a week's work at Grainger's.'

'Which just goes to show how poorly you're paid and how female staff are undervalued.'

Bobbie replaced her drink on the coaster on the low rosewood table in front of her and sat back. 'There's no rush, Jemma. Make sure you've got enough money saved up for the rent and the bills. I'm happy to stay at Grainger's for a few more weeks yet and just help you out as and when.' She glanced over at Van Cleef's table, where his chubby and ebullient male companion was now entertaining the ladies with a story about a troublesome racehorse.

They overheard Van Cleef calling him 'Armitage'.

'Do you know what, Jemma? I've just remembered something.'

'What?'

'There's more than one way to skin a cat.'

'What on earth do you mean?'

'We've a secret weapon in this hotel – a resource we can utilise. Wait here.'

She rose and strolled gracefully out of the lounge towards the foyer. Several male heads turned to follow her progress.

291

Jemma sat back, enjoying the warmth and plush comfort of her surroundings. Bobbie was right. Perhaps she needed to stop worrying, slow down and have a bit of fun She'd had a stressful week of late nights, due to the demands of the business – especially that evening she'd spent locked in Sharrow's office during the air raid. But oddly enough, she wasn't tired. She felt excited and *alive*. There was no doubt in her mind anymore; she'd done the right thing launching this agency. And in a couple of weeks, she might even tell Gabriel about it.

Bobbie reappeared, her eyes gleaming with satisfaction. 'Leave your drink and come with me. I need your help.'

Jemma grabbed her handbag and followed her into the foyer. 'What is it?'

'It's Little Laurie Tipton – he's on duty tonight in the lift.'

When they reached the gilded lift doors, Bobbie pressed the button to call it. 'I'll do the talking, but back me up – and look at him affectionately.'

Little Laurie's slanting eyes opened wide with surprise when he saw them. A huge grin spread across his plain round face. 'Bobbie! Jemma! My, you do look lovely tonight, Jemma.'

'Thank you, Laurie,' Jemma said, stepping inside the empty lift. 'That's very kind of you.'

Laurie's fat finger hovered over the brass control buttons. 'What are you doin' here, girls? And which floor do you want?'

'Please take us to the top floor,' Bobbie said. 'We're here at the request of Mr Armitage. He asked me to meet him here.'

Laurie's eyes nearly popped out of his head. 'You mean, *Lord* Armitage? Does he want to meet with Jemma, too?' He pressed a button and the lift mechanism whirred as they ascended.

'No, it's *me* he wants to meet,' Bobbie said. 'He's not interested in Jemma.'

Laurie laughed. 'Yer aimin' above yer station, there, Bobbie.' He turned towards Jemma. 'Do you want to come for a cup of tea again with me and Ma?'

Jemma gave him her most beautiful smile. 'I'd love to, Laurie. But tell us some more about Mr – Lord – Armitage. Bobbie didn't know he was an aristocrat. Is he a regular guest in your hotel?'

'Oh, yes. He always stays here when he comes down from his castle. I suppose he ain't officially a *Lord* just yet – but he will be when his dad dies. He calls himself the Honourable Mr Whitworth-Armitage.' He burst out laughing. 'I guess if you married him, Bobbie, then you'd become *honourable* too. That'd make a change, wouldn't it?'

Bobbie ignored the jibe. 'Where's Mr Armitage from? And where's the castle?'

Laurie shrugged his shoulders in his oversized uniform. 'Dunno. Near Scotland I think.'

'What about his friend?' Jemma asked. 'The older man – the American.'

They'd reached the top floor. The lift stopped and the doors slid open into a cool, carpeted corridor of bedrooms with another lofty, decorative ceiling.

Jealousy flashed across Laurie's face. 'What do you want to know about Mr Van Cleef for, Jemma? Do you fancy him?'

She laughed and placed a reassuring hand on his arm. 'No, of course not. Mr Van Cleef is far too old for me. I just want to help Bobbie find out more about the Honourable Mr Armitage and his friend.'

Laurie scowled, unconvinced. 'You'd better get out. Mr Armitage's suite is at the end of the corridor.'

'I've changed my mind,' Bobbie said. 'I can't go in there until I know some more about him.'

'You want to go back down?' Laurie stared at her incredulously.

'Yes, please. Besides which, I like travelling in lifts. It's a beautiful little piece of engineering, isn't it? And this brass is so well polished!'

Laurie jabbed angrily at the button on the panel.

'You handle the controls so well,' Jemma said gently. 'The hotel is lucky to have your expertise.'

A sheen of perspiration appeared on Laurie's face.

'Now come on, Laurie,' Bobbie cajoled. 'You know everything there is to know about what goes on in this hotel. Who is Mr Van Cleef and how come this American is friends with Lord Armitage?'

But Laurie didn't get chance to answer. The lift stopped at the next floor and an elegant couple in evening dress stepped inside. Jemma stepped back. The small space was suddenly crowded and the air heavy with floral perfume.

'Good evening, sir – madam,' Laurie said. 'Which floor, please?'

'Take us down to the dining room, please.'

Everyone stood in silence for the short ride. Back on the ground floor, the couple departed but Bobbie stood her ground.

'We're here,' Laurie informed her. 'It's time to get out.'

'I've changed my mind. I think I'd like to go back up to Mr Armitage's room while you tell us about Mr Van Cleef.'

'I think you're just messin' me about, Bobbie. Takin' the mick.'

'No, we're not, Laurie,' Jemma said. 'It's nice to see you again and spend some time with you. I love watching how you operate this lift.'

Laurie blushed, torn between his admiration for Jemma and his suspicion that Bobbie was having a laugh at his expense. The former won out. He pressed the button for the top floor. 'Mr Van Cleef came to York to meet Lord Armitage today. He's only staying one night.'

'Do you know where he's going tomorrow?'

'No, but they're catching a train to Newcastle at ten o'clock. I heard them talkin' about it in here when I took them up to their rooms.'

'That's brilliant, Laurie, thank you.' Jemma leant down and gave him a gentle kiss on his cheek.

Bobbie could hardly hold back her laughter. 'Steady on, Jemma! Laurie's at work – and he's a trusted employee! There'll be rules about snogging in the lift!'

Laurie held his hand to the pink spot on his cheek where Jemma had kissed him. Mischief twinkled in his cat-like eyes. 'Come for a cup of tea tomorrow morning, Jemma,' he said. 'Then you can kiss the other one.'

They were all laughing when they reached the top floor and the doors slid open.

Laurie turned to Jemma with a lascivious grin on his face. 'Do you want to go up and down a few more times, Jemma? We can leave Bobbie here.'

Grinning, Bobbie stepped out into the corridor and pulled Jemma out with her. 'That's enough for tonight, Laurie – we don't want you to get overexcited and crumple your uniform.'

'Thank you for your help, Laurie.'

Disappointed, Laurie peered round the door and watched them walk away.

Jemma had trouble restraining her giggles. 'How long were you prepared to keep going up and down in that lift?'

'For as long as it took.'

'Where are we going?'

'I've no idea. Keep walking until he goes.'

Once Laurie had disappeared back inside his contraption, Bobbie leant against the wall and burst out laughing. 'Oh, Jemma! He'll be announcing your engagement if you carry on like that.'

Jemma grinned. 'He deserved a kiss. He's been very helpful.'

'I knew he'd crack in the end.'

Jemma shook her head and laughed. 'Poor little fellow. He never stood a chance, did he?'

'Did we get enough for our client, do you think?'

Jemma nodded. 'Definitely. I'll take a quick trip to the library in the morning and pull out a copy of Debrett's *Peerage*. It won't take me long to identify the Honourable Mr Whitworth-Armitage.'

Chapter Thirty-Eight

They found the stairs and descended back to the lounge. Van Cleef and his friends were still at their table. Bobbie pulled out her camera and told Jemma to pose beside the beautiful vase of peonies on the plinth. 'Just in case the waiter messed it up,' she whispered.

Bobbie took a few photographs with Van Cleef's group in the background, then picked up her cocktail and swallowed the last of it. 'I think we're finished here now.'

'Do you want another drink?' Jemma asked. 'The night is young – and our fairy godfather is paying.'

Bobbie glanced around and shook her head, her eyes gleaming with a sudden thought. 'No, it's too dull here. Let's go somewhere more exciting – like Betty's Bar.'

Jemma hesitated. Betty's Bar – or 'The Dive', as it had been nicknamed – was situated in the basement of the famous restaurant and tea rooms. It was a popular haunt of the young airmen who flooded the city, especially the Canadians. As these foreign airmen were paid two or three times the amount of the British boys, the young women of York flocked to meet them. Betty's evening bar had developed a risqué reputation as a result.

But Bobbie deserved some fun. They both did.

Jemma gathered up her coat. 'Come on then!'

They had to descend a flight of steps beneath the tea rooms to reach The Dive. The chatter and laughter drifting up the stairs nearly drowned out the jazz music played by the pianist squashed in the far corner of the semi-circular room.

Bobbie paused in the entrance and leant over to shout in Jemma's ear. 'Heavens! This is lively. I can't even see the bar!'

297

Intimately lit, with a heavy fog of cigarette smoke trapped beneath the low ceiling, The Dive heaved with uniformed men and smartly dressed young women. There were a few low tables and stools but most of the clientele stood around in groups on the chequered tiled floor. A few couples were swaying in time with the seductive rhythm of the music. The atmosphere was heavily charged with anticipation and several men turned to appraise them as they entered. Jemma felt like they were undressing her with their eyes.

They weaved their way through the crowd to the bar. A group of rowdy airmen were getting in the way of the bar staff. One of them was using a diamond-tipped pencil to etch his name on the huge mirror behind the bar, encouraged by his drunken mates, who kept deliberately knocking his arm. The whole surface of the glass was covered in the jerky scrawl of dozens and dozens of military personnel.

They had trouble attracting the attention of the staff, but their frustration ebbed away when Don suddenly appeared at their side. 'Well, if it isn't my two favourite ladies!'

Bobbie squealed and gave him a hug. 'Am I pleased to see you! Can you get us a drink, please? It's taking an age to get served.'

Jemma gave Don a welcoming smile and turned her head to allow him to kiss her on the cheek. He waved his arm and a barman magically appeared to take their order. The two women climbed on to vacant bar stools and Don leant over to talk to them. 'Are you going out dancing tonight?'

'No, we've been working for another client,' Jemma told him. 'We're just enjoying a quiet celebration now.'

Don laughed as the pianist hammered out the introduction to another lively dance tune. 'This is a strange idea of quiet. Did you get your man?'

'We sure did,' Bobbie said. 'Although Jemma had to kiss a bellhop to get the information we needed.'

Don grinned. 'Lucky bellhop.'

Their drinks arrived, and they gave Don a brief outline of their successes that week. He seemed happy to listen to their excited chatter.

'You girls are the most interesting women I've ever met,' he said.

That doesn't say much for your poor wife, Jemma thought, with a grimace. But she was grateful for his presence, which protected them from the unwanted attention of other men, and she soon relaxed. Her foot started to tap to the beat of the music.

While Bobbie gave Don a lurid account of the terrors inflicted on the poor residents of Gordon Terrace by the Watts children, Jemma glanced around. Through the gap between Don and Bobbie, she had a good view of a crowd of half-drunk airmen and the glamorous, excited women hanging on to their arms.

She froze when she saw Cynthia Ravenscar, with her dazzling Hollywood smile, standing among a group of middle-aged Canadian officers. She leant towards a portly airman of about forty-five with thinning hair and crooked teeth and touched his arm affectionately. He gave her an adoring glance then slid his arm around her waist. Leaning against his shoulder, she whispered something in his ear that made him laugh.

Jemma interrupted Bobbie, who was still in full flow. 'I'm sorry, Bobbie, but I need Don's help. Who's that officer with the woman in the pale-green dress with the feather in her hair?'

'You mean the guy with the gorgeous woman who looks like Carole Lombard?'

'Yes, that's right.'

'It's Dickie. Dickie Bell. He's my squadron leader at Linton. His sweetheart is a local woman called Cynthia.'

'Have they been together long?'

'For as long as I've been stationed here. Dickie wants to marry her and take her back to Ontario with him when the war's over. I don't think he can believe his luck.'

No, thought Jemma. *I wouldn't believe it either.*

'What is it, Jemma?' Bobbie asked.

She leant across towards her friend and whispered. 'She's the woman having an affair with Kathleen Pulleyne's husband.'

'Really? Some women just can't stay away from the guys in uniform!' Bobbie turned round for a better look. Then she too froze in shock.

'What's the matter?' Jemma asked.

'Behind them – the woman with the jet-black wavy hair on the dance floor.'

Jemma strained her neck and caught a glimpse of a woman in a patterned chiffon blouse and a glossy, black satin pencil skirt dancing with another airman, although to call their erotic, drunken swaying 'dancing' was a stretch of the imagination. Her dark hair was dishevelled and, due to her intoxication, she staggered in her high heels. If she hadn't been in such a tight and intimate clinch with the man and glued to his face in a long and passionate kiss, she'd have probably fallen over. His hand roamed over her back with the occasional foray down over her pert, satin-clad backside.

'Who is she?'

'It's Susan Quigley – Vince's wife.'

'Oh, my God.'

'I can't believe it!' Bobbie hissed. 'Poor Vince is risking his life to protect us from invasion – and she behaves like a slut! How can she do that to him?' She downed her port and lemon in one swig and asked Don to get her another.

Three of Don's fellow airmen drifted across to talk to him and cast curious glances at the two women. 'Hey, pretty lady,' one of them said to Bobbie, 'd'you fancy a dance?'

But Bobbie had fallen into a glowering sulk and rejected his offer abruptly.

Jemma and Don did their best to lighten the mood and draw Bobbie back into the conversation, but Bobbie just glared across the room at Vince's embarrassing and adulterous wife with narrowed eyes. She downed her second drink within seconds, asked for another one and mumbled something about yanking out the bitch's hair.

Jemma was alarmed. Despite Bobbie's private education and her resemblance to the glamorous Vivien Leigh, she still had her father's temper and could scrap like a backstreet alley cat when she was upset.

Bobbie started fumbling with her bag and Jemma knew instinctively what she was about to do. She reached out and grabbed Bobbie's hands to stop her pulling out her camera. 'You can't photograph her with that man!'

'I can.' Bobbie tugged harder but Jemma wouldn't let go.

'Is everything all right, ladies?' Don asked, amused by their undignified tussle.

They ignored him.

'What on earth do you think you'll do with the photographs?' Jemma whispered sharply.

'Send them to Vince,' Bobbie hiccoughed. 'He asked me to write to him and his mother just gave me his address.'

'He'll hate you for ever if you do that.'

'I'll hate you for ever if you stop me.'

'No, you won't.'

'He needs to know.'

'No, he doesn't.'

The barman placed Bobbie's third drink beside her. Distracted, she abandoned her attempt to pull out her camera and turned her attention to the alcohol. It was time to get her out of here before she made a scene.

'Would either of you like to dance?' Don asked.

Jemma shook her head. 'I'm sorry, Don, but I need to take Bobbie home. Get your coat on, Bobbie.'

'When did you get so bossy, Roxby?' Bobbie snapped.

Jemma glared back with what she hoped was the famous glint of Roxby granite in her eyes.

Bobbie knocked back her drink, slid down from her stool and pushed her way towards the exit.

Pausing only to thank Don and say goodbye, Jemma hurried after her. She caught up with her outside in the street. Bobbie's shoulders were heaving, and tears streamed down her cheeks.

'Oh, my poor love.' Jemma took her into her arms.

'It's just so *unfair*,' Bobbie sobbed into her shoulder in between the hiccoughs. 'She doesn't love him. She never did. But I love him, Jemma. I always will.'

Slowly, Jemma guided her distraught and drunk friend over the bridge towards home.

'Poor Vince! He's so brave – and such an innocent.'

Personally, Jemma had doubts about this. It took two to make a marriage work, and there was definitely something wrong with the Quigleys'.

Bobbie muttered something about writing to Vince with the truth, but the fire had left her. She was silent when they reached her house and offered no resistance when Jemma led her to her room and put her to bed.

Bobbie fell asleep immediately, still in her best frock. Her eyes were swollen from crying and her mascara had run down her cheeks, but she looked like an innocent, faintly freckled child with her head on the pillow.

Jemma listened to her steady breathing then bent over and kissed her forehead. 'Sleep it off, my love,' she whispered. 'Everything seems better after a good night's sleep.'

She undressed and climbed into the creaking camp bed squashed next to the draughty window. It smelt musty and wasn't very comfortable, but she was soon asleep.

Chapter Thirty-Nine

Bobbie was still sleeping when Jemma woke. Sometime during the night her friend had taken off her best frock, tossed it on the bedroom floor and pulled on a nightdress.

She looked so peaceful, Jemma decided to leave her. But when she reached the door, Bobbie sat bolt upright. She looked like a startled rabbit with a bird's nest hiding her long ears. 'Is it morning?' she asked.

Jemma smiled. 'Yes. Go back to sleep. I'll open up the office.'

'No, wait for me.' Bobbie clambered out of bed and reached for her clothes. 'I won't be a minute.'

It took longer than a minute for Bobbie to dress and tame her hair, of course. And when they passed through the kitchen, Margery Baker insisted they eat a bowl of porridge and drink a cup of tea before they left.

Jemma had worried Bobbie might have a bad head after all that alcohol, but she was her usual cheerful self when they strode through the streets towards Grape Lane. She didn't mention Susan Quigley or the disastrous end to their night out, but Jemma knew Bobbie hadn't forgotten or forgiven Vince's wife.

Jemma telephoned Clara Urwin's brother, Alan, but his wife told them he was still away on business in Scotland and wasn't expected home until the end of the week.

'Damn,' Jemma said, as she replaced the receiver. 'I've got to telephone Mrs Banyan tomorrow night. I would have liked to tell her more about the death of the mysterious Gladys Mellor. There's no chance of that now.'

'We've still got Plan B,' Bobbie said. 'Let's go to the library. You track down the Honourable Mr Whitworth-Armitage and I'll see what I can find in the newspaper archives about Mellor.'

Jemma soon found an entry for Van Cleef's companion in Debrett's. Whitworth-Armitage was the son of a wealthy northern industrialist with extensive interests in shipbuilding, armaments and tank manufacture, who owned at least three stately homes scattered around England. One of them was Rothbury Castle in Northumberland. Most of the Whitworth-Armitage companies held contracts with the government and one of their main rivals was Vickers in Leeds, whom Jemma assumed had employed Terence King to track Van Cleef's movements.

Knowing how much was at stake for the British arms industry, Jemma wasn't surprised these big industrialists were fighting it out to gain the attention of a wealthy American investor. She checked her watch. There was still plenty of time to phone Terence King with the results of her enquiry.

Meanwhile, Bobbie was poring over a pile of 1935 newspapers scattered across the dark oak table.

'Any luck?'

'No. They've only got the *Yorkshire Evening Press* and the *Yorkshire Post* for this period, and there's nothing in either of them about the death of Gladys Mellor. I think we need to go to Whitby library and see copies of their local newspapers. The *Whitby Gazette* – or perhaps the *Scarborough Evening News.*'

'Mm, maybe. But I've had another idea.'

When they returned to the office, Jemma telephoned Terence King.

'Good morning, Mr King. I have the information you wanted regarding Mr Van Cleef. Last night, he met up with the Honourable Thomas Whitworth-Armitage, eldest son of Lord Armitage of Rothbury, the northern industrial baron.'

Terence King groaned. 'Damn it, the situation is as bad as my client feared.'

'I'm sorry to hear that. I'm about to be the bearer of more bad news. This morning they took the ten o'clock train to Newcastle,' Jemma continued, 'from whence I suspect they'll take a connection to Rothbury Castle, which I understand is very beautiful at this time of year.'

'Damn that Armitage fellow. He's pulling out all the stops to seduce Van Cleef. Everyone knows the Americans can never resist a castle.'

'I've photographic evidence of their meeting at the Royal Station Hotel if your client would like to see it.'

'Yes, send it along with your invoice. It can't hurt. Thank you for your efficiency, Mrs James. I'll bid you a good day.'

'Mr King?'

'Yes?'

'Before you go, I'd like to ask *you* for a favour.'

'What do you want?'

'I appreciate that King's is one of the largest private enquiry agencies in Yorkshire and you've probably got lots of contacts – like myself and Miss Baker – dotted about the county. I was hoping you might have a contact in Whitby who could help *us* out with a case and save us a trip to the coast?'

He hesitated for a minute, then chuckled. 'So, you know who I am now, do you, Mrs James?'

'As you said yourself, it's important to check out the competition. Although I hope our future relationship will be mutually advantageous rather than a rivalry.' *It's a pity this will never happen with myself and Will Sharrow*, she thought.

'Quite so, Mrs James – that's how I like to work. And yes, I do have a chap – Smithson – who works for me on the east coast. But he's based down the road in Scarborough, rather than Whitby.'

'That shouldn't be a problem.'

'What do you want him to do?'

307

'I want him to scour old copies of the Scarborough and Whitby newspapers for the spring and summer of 1935. We're looking for any reference to the death – accidental or otherwise – of a maidservant called Gladys Mellor. If Smithson can also find a summary of the inquest, I'd be grateful.'

'Sounds like you've got an interesting case there, Mrs James. How much do you intend to pay Smithson?'

'Perhaps the usual rate will apply?'

'Nice try, Mrs James. But he usually receives ten shillings an hour – not six.'

Jemma winced and hoped Mrs Banyan would agree to the extra cost. 'Very well. However, I need to give you notice that in future the hourly rate of Smoke & Cracked Mirrors has risen to ten shillings.'

King chuckled. 'That's a shame. I was rather partial to your six-shilling hourly rate.'

'It was an introductory offer, Mr King. Smoke & Cracked Mirrors is playing with the big boys now.'

'You're a fast learner, Mrs James – I look forward to working with you again. I'll contact Smithson for you this afternoon. Good day.'

When Bobbie left to take the train to Harrogate to track down the Reverend Slingsby and return his incriminating letters, Jemma settled down to type out the invoices for Terence King and Kathleen Pulleyne.

Ricky had already dropped off copies of the photographs she'd taken of Cynthia Ravenscar and Group Captain Pulleyne on Coney Street. Jemma felt a flicker of pride when she examined them. She knew she'd never be as professional as Ricky, but she'd caught a clear image of the illicit couple's happy faces as they embraced. Cynthia looked radiantly happy and relaxed in Pulleyne's arms.

Jemma's pride turned to sadness when she pushed the photographs into the envelope along with the invoice and her typed report. She didn't like Kathleen Pulleyne, but no one deserved to have their dreams shattered like this, especially after only a year of marriage. And what was that Cynthia woman up to anyway, leading on both Group Captain Pulleyne and Squadron Leader Bell?

She was still thinking about Kathleen and her adulterous husband when she walked to the post box with her letters. On her way back, a sudden impulse made her turn down Coney Street and she found herself at the brash red and navy shop frontage of Cynthia Ravenscar's modern art gallery. It was open for business but empty of customers. The only person on the premises was a bored young woman sitting beside the cash register, filing her nails.

Jemma drifted around the gallery, examining the pictures, the sculpture and the pottery. She couldn't understand what other people saw in these bizarre, abstract and sometimes quite violent designs. Michael had once said that modernism tended to be an excuse for sculpture and paintings of a pseudo-barbaric and primitive type, which hid the lack of talent of amateurs. After examining the stock on display in Cynthia Ravenscar's gallery, she agreed with him wholeheartedly.

She was about to leave when the paper boy came in. A chunky, gingery young lad with a faceful of freckles, he walked over to the sales assistant at the counter and gave her a copy of the *Yorkshire Evening Press*.

'Miss Ravenscar asked fer me,' he said.

'Wait here, I'll fetch her.' The girl rose and went into the back.

Curious to see what Cynthia looked like in daylight and intrigued to know why she wanted to speak to her paper boy, Jemma lurked in front of a display of garish pot-bellied statuettes with three arms.

Cynthia soon appeared, dishevelled but still elegant in a paint-splattered smock. Even in her working clothes, the woman was stunningly attractive. No wonder she had half the men in the RAF salivating. She handed a small roll of paper to the boy, along with a handful of coins. He waved a cheery 'Goodbye', turned on his heel and left the shop.

Cynthia turned her large light-blue eyes towards Jemma. 'Can I help you, madam?' Her accent had an attractive sing-song quality. A Welsh background, perhaps? Or was she from one of the northern border counties?

'No, thank you, I'm just browsing.' Jemma walked back out into the street, curious about where the paper boy would go next. But there was nothing unusual in his behaviour as he bobbed in and out of the shops, delivering his newspapers.

Something niggled at the back of Jemma's mind, but whatever it was that concerned her refused to take shape. When the paper boy turned the corner into Coppergate, Jemma shook her head at her own foolishness and went back to the office.

Bobbie returned just before five o'clock with a smug grin on her face. Pulling off her gloves, she reached into her bag for her purse and laid thirty pounds on the desk. 'The Reverend Slingsby is a lovely man – and most generous,' she said.

'Oh, Bobbie – that's fantastic!'

'He was very relieved to get his letters back and delighted to hear he wouldn't have any more trouble from Shaun Flynn.'

'Well done!'

'Well done, *us*,' Bobbie corrected her. 'It was your brilliant idea to steal that bag from Flynn. We've made a lot of people very happy this week.'

'It's unbelievable,' Jemma said. 'I thought we'd struggle to launch this business, but everything's gone so well.' She pushed the thirty pounds across the table towards Bobbie. 'Here, you've earned it. It's yours.'

Bobbie shook her head. 'No, Jemma. I've told you before, invest it in the business. I want to be a full and equal partner in Smoke & Cracked Mirrors – this my first contribution towards the running costs.'

'Are you sure?'

'Yes.'

Jemma gathered up the money. 'In that case, we'll use some of it to pay for driving lessons for you with the British School of Motoring.'

'Really?' Bobbie's eyes widened in delight.

'Yes. You've wasted a ridiculous amount of time on public transport this week. We need to get you driving so you can take the car instead. Phone them up now and book your first lesson for Monday afternoon.'

Grinning, Bobbie grabbed the telephone directory from the bookshelf. 'You might regret this if you don't get any more clients for the rest of the month.'

'I'm happy to risk it.'

'Me driving a real car – on the real road! I hope the motorists of Britain are ready for this!'

Jemma laughed and pushed the telephone towards her. 'Just get on with it before I change my mind. It's half past five. Let's go home and have an early night for once.'

Chapter Forty

Jemma woke on Sunday morning to the sound of Gabriel and Maisie laughing downstairs. They were dressed up, ready for church, and were admiring their handiwork in her parents' old room.

Jemma wished them a sleepy 'Good morning' as she walked past on her way to the kitchen.

'It's Easter Sunday,' Gabriel reminded her. 'Are you coming with us to church?'

Jemma hesitated and remembered with a pang of guilt how she'd railed against God when Michael was first reported missing. But her anger had diminished, and she knew she had a lot to be grateful for right now. It was time to give thanks and the Easter service was always one of the pleasantest and most hopeful of the year. 'Yes, I'll be ready in half an hour.'

'Oh, Jemma!' Maisie called after her. 'Gabriel showed me the curtains you've made – they're gorgeous. Such lovely material.'

Jemma smiled. Choosing her words carefully, she said: 'There were plenty of rolls of that material for sale in the market. Do you think matching bedspreads would look nice?'

What she really meant, of course, was *when my dozy brother proposes again and you marry him and move in, do you think your sons would appreciate new bedspreads?*

Maisie beamed. 'I'm sure they'd look wonderful.'

'Oh, by the way Jemma,' Gabriel said, 'we're eating here tonight – Maisie's cooking. Will you be at work?'

'No, it's my day off. I'm going to see Fanny Rawlings later. I've neglected her since I returned. But I'll be back in time for supper.'

Fanny lived in a modern house halfway down a narrow, leafy lane that ran parallel with the meandering River Ouse. All the surrounding land and the elegant sandy-stoned manor house at the end of the lane had once belonged to Fanny and her family. Fifteen years ago, she'd sold off the manor and parcels of the land to developers, retaining a pleasant plot on the top of Ousecliffe. There, she'd built herself a new home with an extensive south-facing conservatory at the back, which commanded an excellent view of the meandering river.

Strewn with half-finished paintings on easels, paint-splattered tables and the other paraphernalia of her profession, the conservatory doubled as both her art studio and her favourite seating area.

Jemma sank into the comfy cushions of the largest sofa while her delighted old friend fussed around her with a tea tray, a plate of freshly baked scones, homemade strawberry jam, fresh cream and – unbelievably – a pat of real, golden butter. Jemma didn't ask about the butter. Fanny still maintained an excellent relationship with her former tenants, most of whom were local farmers. Blessed with the energy and athleticism of a woman half her age, Fanny would tramp through the mud and stubble of fresh-mown hayfields with her easel slung over her shoulder and her battered old paintbox in her hand. Rumour had it several local farmhouse kitchens proudly displayed a Frances Rawlings watercolour above their fireplaces. It was an arrangement that worked well for everyone. The canny local farmers had a valuable piece of artwork and Fanny had the freedom to roam wherever the muse took her and a plentiful supply of butter and fresh cream.

'Now, you'll have to tell me the gossip.' Fanny sank into the chair opposite and reached for the teapot with her bony, age-spotted hand. 'Let's start with your gorgeous brother. I've heard rumours that he's spurned my affections and is paying court to Maisie Langford, the lovely redhead from The Grey Mare.'

Smiling, Jemma updated Fanny about Gabriel's hopes to entice Maisie into marriage and their joint project to refurbish and modernise the cottage.

'I've always like Maisie Langford,' Fanny said. 'I know she's a few years older than your brother, but that sort of thing doesn't matter when you're in your forties. She'll make him an excellent wife. Marriage to Gabriel will give her the respectability she craves and young Tom a much-needed father. In fact,' she added with a mischievous smile, 'if he won't have me, I can't imagine anyone else more suitable for Gabriel than Maisie. But I shall never give up hope until the vows are exchanged.'

Jemma laughed. 'I'm glad you approve.'

'Now, tell me about this new business project of yours that you mentioned when I saw you at the post office.'

Happy to oblige, Jemma told her about Smoke & Cracked Mirrors, their new office on Grape Street and the success they'd enjoyed so far.

Fanny clapped her hands with glee. 'How fascinating! You clever, clever girl! Your father would be so proud of you!'

'I hope so,' Jemma said, blushing. 'I haven't told Gabriel about it yet, though – he thinks it's an unsuitable job for a woman.'

Fanny waved away Gabriel's objections. 'Nonsense! Detection work is in your blood. If York City Police are too stuffy to employ female officers, it's their loss and you've no choice but to find an alternative outlet for your passion. Mind you,' she added, with a wicked twinkle in her intelligent grey eyes, 'should any of our neighbours from Clifton ever come to your door for help, please remember to share the details of their problems with your oldest friend.'

Jemma laughed and an idea popped into Jemma's head. 'Actually, Fanny, there's something you might be able to help me with. I can't quite put my finger on it, but I sense a mystery hovering around one of your fellow artists, Cynthia Ravenscar. She owns the modern art gallery on Coney Street. Do you know her?'

Fanny sat back. A knowing look settled on her pale, lined face and she nodded wisely. 'Oh, I know the young glamour puss and there's no mystery there, Jemma. A woman as beautiful as that will always attract admiration, jealousy and controversy in equal measure. Wherever she goes, problems will follow.'

'How long has she run the gallery? I don't remember it being there last year.'

Fanny licked jam off her fingers. 'December, I think. She's took the York art scene by storm just before Christmas. Most of the silly old duffers adore her, of course. Well, who can blame them? She's the most gorgeous thing we've had in our society for years! They're even prepared to overlook the irregularities of her work.'

'Irregularities?'

Fanny put down her plate. 'Oh, yes. I can't talk about the sculptures, of course – but most of those paintings in her gallery aren't hers.'

'They're not?'

'Heavens, no, Jemma. Go and have a closer look at the brushwork and see the different ways the artists used the light. The techniques vary in nearly every canvas – there's no artist alive who's that versatile. Every brushstroke is a signature in art.'

Jemma glanced at the easel with Fanny's latest painting, a half-finished wintry landscape of the Ouse meandering through the Vale of York.

Fanny followed her gaze and smiled. 'Yes, my name is there in each wind-bent blade of grass and each incandescent fragment of river ice.'

'But she's signed all of the paintings.'

Fanny shrugged. 'She might be doing some friends a favour – selling their work for them. After all, she's got a prime position there on Coney Street and obviously wealthy backers. Have you seen her fabulous sports car, by the way?'

Jemma raised her eyebrows in surprise and shook her head. 'She must make a lot of money, but the gallery was empty when I went there yesterday afternoon. Is it successful?'

'I couldn't say. I don't know much about business, that's why I have an agent. But I've never seen more than a trickle of curious customers enter the premises.'

Fanny leant forward and patted her leg. 'Now, tell me some more about what you've been doing with yourself. I want to hear more about that dashing Canadian who escorted you to De Grey's.'

When Jemma returned home, it was to find piles of old newspapers, bent pieces of iron and broken gardening tools in a wooden trolley in the garden. Gabriel and Tom were adding large pieces of an oily old motorbike engine to the pile. Gabriel looked resigned but a little sad as he said goodbye to the remains of his first Triumph.

'Blimey! This is a momentous day,' Jemma said, grinning. 'Do we need to say a few words and hold a funeral service before it goes?'

Gabriel scowled at her, and she didn't hang around to hear his reply. Remembering her promise to find more salvage for Tom, she hurried about the house, dragging junk out of the cupboards and drawers. Maisie was in the steamy kitchen, crashing about with the pots and pans and hovering over another enticing casserole.

After supper, Jemma helped Gabriel to wash and dry the pots. Tom announced his intention to take the salvage back to his storage place and Maisie went out into the hallway with him, fussing about his coat and scarf.

'I've enjoyed tonight,' Jemma told Gabriel. 'Maisie and Tom are good company for us. Hurry up and persuade her to marry you.'

He frowned and gave her a cool sideways glance. 'These things can't be rushed, Jemma.'

'If you leave it much longer, you'll be going down the aisle in a bath chair.'

'You cheeky little wretch!' He flicked water at her from the bowl and she ducked, laughing.

Chapter Forty-One

Jemma decided to give Maisie and Gabriel some privacy and call at Bobbie's for an hour or two. It couldn't be easy, she realised, to have a romance with a ten-year-old boy in constant attendance. Time alone for Gabriel and Maisie must be a rare treat.

She climbed in the car but when she reached the city centre, she changed her mind and turned down into Coney Street. Almost of its own accord, the vehicle rumbled over the wet cobbles and came to a halt a few yards from the gallery.

She turned off the engine and chewed her lip thoughtfully. Despite Fanny's casual dismissal of her suspicions about Cynthia Ravenscar, something still niggled in the back of her mind.

Beside her on the pavement, the mirrored surface of the puddles from the recent shower reflected the tall gabled buildings and their blank, unseeing windows. She had no idea if Cynthia was at home or not.

Keeping one eye on the gallery, she pulled out her brand-new copy of *Sad Cypress* and settled down to read. She'd treated herself to it as a reward for all her hard work last week, although the eight shillings she'd had to pay at the bookshop nearly sent her scurrying back to the library shelves. Paper was a precious commodity in wartime England and books were eye-wateringly expensive.

Half an hour later, a taxi pulled up outside the gallery. Jemma put away her book and waited. Cynthia left the premises in her beautiful white fur coat and an exquisite, feathered hat and climbed in the back of the cab.

Jemma reached for the ignition switch but once more her car rewarded her with that sickening series of rapid dry clicks. 'No! Don't you dare! Don't do this to me!'

This time the car refused to start on her second attempt – and her third. At the end of the street, Cynthia's taxi slowed and turned left towards Lendal Bridge.

Jemma cursed under her breath then gave a cheer when, glancing in her wing mirror, she saw an empty taxi rumbling over the cobbles towards her. She sent up a quick prayer of thanks to Saint Father of Brown for this deliverance, leapt out of the car and flagged down the taxi. She wrenched open the door and threw herself in the passenger seat beside the driver.

'Where to, lass?' he asked. He was a chubby man with a round, jovial face. His chin had long since disappeared into the rolls of fat around his neck.

'I know this sounds crazy, but I want you to turn left at the end of the street and follow the taxi ahead of us.'

'So, it's "follow that cab!", is it?' the driver laughed as he pulled away. His vehicle smelled of toffee mingled with body odour and stale tobacco. 'Sounds like somethin' out o' that Fred Astaire film, *Top Hat.* You're not Ginger Rogers in disguise, are you?'

Jemma eyes were riveted to the road ahead. 'No – I can barely dance.'

'Shame that. I love a bit of Fred and Ginger, don't you?'

'Yes, of course. Can you drive a little faster?'

Fortunately, the streets were quiet, and Cynthia's cab had continued in a straight line along the main road. They caught up with it at a set of traffic lights on the Tadcaster Road.

Her driver reached for another toffee from the bag on his dashboard and gave her a curious sideways glance. 'So, what's this about then, lass?'

'It's my sister,' Jemma said. 'She's forgotten her door key. I must catch up with her and give it to her.'

They passed Knavesmire and the racecourse, then the cab slowed and turned down one of the exclusive residential streets.

'Pull back a bit,' Jemma instructed her driver.

'Bossy little thing, aren't you?' He grinned and slowed to a crawl.

Cynthia's cab drew to a halt outside the gate of one of the largest houses.

'Drive past them and pull up on the other side of the road, near that post box.'

Her driver did as he was told, and Jemma spun round to watch Cynthia climb out of the cab and disappear up the driveway.

'Friend of the Wing Commander's is she, your sister?' the driver asked.

Startled, Jemma spun round to face him. 'Wing Commander?'

'Aye, Wing Commander Robson from RAF Church Fenton.' He jabbed his finger in the direction of the house. 'He's a regular customer o' mine.'

Jemma chewed her lip thoughtfully. RAF Church Fenton was the base for several fighter squadrons of Hurricanes and Mosquitoes, a vital cog in the machinery of war.

'Didn't you know where your sister were goin' tonight?'

'Yes, of course. She's a good friend of Wing Commander Robson's wife.'

'Wife? He ain't got no wife.' His small eyes regarded her suspiciously from beneath the fleshy folds of their lids. 'Like I said, he's a regular customer o' mine.'

'Yes, of course – I forgot. I must take her the key.'

Jemma hesitated for a second, trying to decide what to do next. Her spontaneous decision to follow Cynthia Ravenscar was a bit of a disaster. The taxi driver didn't believe a word of her lies and the sooner she got rid of him the better. But she was stranded on the wrong side of the city without her car and she'd no idea how frequent the buses were on a Sunday night.

She had a vague notion she needed some time to poke around. But whatever she did, she needed to do it soon. The sky still had a dark, pinkish glow, against which the shapes of the buildings and trees stood out in relief, but it would be pitch black soon and there was no sign of the moon.

'Look, I'll pop into the house and give my sister the key and stay and chat with them for a while. Can you come back for me in about half an hour and take me back to my flat and car on Coney Street? The darned thing wouldn't start.'

'All right.'

She reached for her purse and paid him. He thanked her brusquely and drove off once she'd climbed out.

Jemma stood still for a moment, trying to calm herself. Her mind reeled with this latest discovery.

What the devil was Cynthia Ravenscar up to?

A flirtatious obsession with men in uniform was one thing – many young women up and down the country were having the time of their lives with the military right now. But Cynthia Ravenscar wasn't the stereotypical shallow, man-eating blonde. Jemma had seen intelligence and a quiet assurance in those unblinking blue eyes during their brief conversation in the gallery.

Yet the woman had spent time with three different high-ranking officers from three different airbases in the space of the past four days: Group Captain Ian Pulleyne, Squadron Leader Dickie Bell and now Wing Commander Robson.

Jemma felt a wave of unease sweep through her. As a responsible citizen in wartime Britain, she couldn't ignore this. She had to report the woman. But did she have enough evidence to accuse Cynthia of being Yorkshire's very own Mata Hari?

Her unease intensified when she glanced down the street. Her taxi driver hadn't driven away. He'd turned the vehicle around, returned and parked up. He was watching her aimless wanderings up and down the pavement through his windscreen. *Damn it.*

She gave him a forced smile and a cheery wave, then crossed the road. *You're worried about the wrong woman*, she thought.

A sloping driveway ran up the side of the large, detached house, which was silhouetted against the darkening sky. Jemma walked up the driveway and disappeared out of sight around the corner of the building.

The garden, whose sweeping lawn was bordered with mature shrubs, spread out from the back of the house before disappearing into the gloom. It was darker back here and quieter, except for the hoot of a small owl in one of the oaks. Her ears strained and she held her breath. It wasn't until she heard the taxi drive away that she exhaled.

When her eyes grew more accustomed to the darkness, she recognised the outline of a large set of French windows, dominating the back wall of the building. A small chink of yellow light slid out from an eighteen-inch gap in the bottom of the curtains and pooled down on to the stone terrace.

Wary of knocking over a flowerpot, Jemma inched slowly towards the light, squatted down on her haunches and peered inside. She was rewarded with a view of Cynthia's long slender legs, elegantly crossed as she sat on a sofa. There was no sign of the Wing Commander, but she heard the faint strain of classical music from a gramophone record and the murmur of conversation. Cynthia's right foot, encased in a beautiful high-heeled silver shoe, began to swing in time with the beat of a Rachmaninoff piano concerto.

Realising that her uncomfortable vantage point was yielding nothing except a close examination of the woman's footwear, she made her way back to the street to ponder her dilemma. There was no doubt in her mind that Special Branch needed to know about Cynthia Ravenscar. The best way to alert them was through Gabriel. But that meant she would have to tell Gabriel about Smoke & Cracked Mirrors. Immediately. Tonight.

She crossed the road, checked her watch and thought about Gabriel and Maisie enjoying a bit of peace and privacy back home. The last thing she wanted to do was ruin their evening by announcing that she'd ignored Gabriel's warning and launched a female enquiry agency. But she didn't have any choice.

She was still wondering what she could do to limit the damage to her relationship with her brother when a black car turned down the street and drew up beside her.

Two men climbed out, one of them a police constable in uniform. She knew a few of the officers at Clifford Street police station but this wasn't one of them.

'Good evening, madam,' said the man in plain clothes. 'I'm Detective Sergeant Cooper. Can you tell me what you're doing here, please?'

'I'm… I'm waiting for a taxi to come and collect me.'

'Do you live here?'

'No.'

'So, why are you here?'

'I've been visiting a friend.'

'Which friend? Which house?'

Horror flooded through Jemma as realisation dawned. Her taxi driver had reported her to the police for spying on Wing Commander Robson. Any moment now, DS Cooper would drag her up to the front door and ask the airman if he knew the crazy woman loitering outside his house. This would be embarrassing – but the real problem was that Cynthia might recognise her from their brief encounter in her gallery the previous day. And the last thing Jemma wanted to do was give the wretched woman any warning that she was under observation.

There was only one option – try to bluff it out.

'I'd rather not say.'

'Why not?'

'Because I don't want to. Look, is there a problem, officer? I didn't know waiting for a taxi was against the law.'

DS Cooper smiled. The moon came out from behind a cloud and his teeth gleamed in its light. It didn't make him look friendly.

'I think we both know you're not telling the truth, madam. I'm from Special Branch. We've had a report you've been acting suspiciously. What's your name?'

'I'm Mrs James – Jemima James – and I'm pleased to meet you, officer. I need to speak to someone from Special Branch. I think we should continue this conversation back at the police station on Clifford Street.'

If he was surprised by her confidence, he didn't show it. 'My thoughts entirely.' He turned to his colleague and beckoned him forward. 'Sergeant.'

The uniformed officer walked towards her, a set of handcuffs glinting in his hand.

Horrified, she held up her hand to stop him. 'Oh, good grief, no!' She knew she had a lot of explaining to do tonight – to a lot of people – but she was damned if she'd allow them to drag her into Gabriel's place of work in handcuffs. 'You don't need to arrest me – or use those. I'll come with you voluntarily. There's something I need to tell you. I've got valuable information.'

The men hesitated.

'Just take me to Clifford Street. We need to talk – urgently. I'll come quietly.'

'Very well.' Cooper opened the back door of the car. Without hesitation, Jemma slid into the seat. He climbed in beside her.

———

325

At least they haven't arrested me – yet. She exhaled a sigh of relief as the vehicle drew away from the Wing Commander's house.

Chapter Forty-Two

Keep the advantage, she thought, as they sped back towards the city centre.

'Right, there's something you need to know. I'm the proprietor of Smoke & Cracked Mirrors: York's Ladies' Detective Agency.'

There was a stunned silence, then both men burst out laughing.

'Pull the other one, missus,' said the constable. He glanced back at her through the centre mirror. His eyes were amused. 'Lasses aren't PIs.'

'Oh yes, we are,' Jemma replied. 'Not all private detectives are old and stooped like Will Sharrow.'

There was silence in the car. They knew who Will Sharrow was. *Just wait until they find out I'm the sister of Inspector Roxby*, she thought. But that wasn't a card she wanted to play. She wanted to keep Gabriel out of this debacle.

'Look, for the past few days I've been shadowing a woman called Cynthia Ravenscar. It's part of one of my assignments.'

'Who the hell is she?' asked the sergeant.

'The woman currently in Wing Commander Robson's house. I think she's a German spy.'

The two men exchanged a smirk in the centre mirror and Jemma wondered if she'd said the right thing. They weren't even halfway to the station. They might turn the car round and go back to check her story. 'I've been following her for several days now...' she added hastily.

'Trying to divert attention, are you, Mrs James? Save it for the station,' Cooper snapped.

The constable dropped them off outside the tall red-brick Victorian building on Clifford Street that housed both the city's police station and the magistrates' court. Cooper took her up the stone steps to the main entrance.

The duty desk sergeant had his head bowed over a pile of papers when they entered but Jemma recognised him immediately. Sergeant Ackroyd had worked with both her father and her brother.

'Which interview rooms are free, sergeant?'

'Number three.' Ackroyd glanced up and started with shock when he saw Jemma with Cooper. 'Jem—?' he stuttered.

She raised a finger to her lips and shook her head to cut him off. She didn't particularly like Ackroyd. He was a bellicose man with two volumes, shouting or moody silence, but he was loyal to her brother.

Cooper led her down the dimly lit narrow corridor to a small, bare room, which reeked of cigarette smoke. The high windows were barred and the scuffed white walls were greasy with filth and stained yellow with nicotine. A single light bulb dangled from a wire in the ceiling.

Without waiting to be asked, Jemma sat down on a chair at the rickety table and rummaged through her bag. She pulled out her notebook and a handful of business cards, and slid one of the cards across the table. 'There. Like I told you in the car, I'm a private investigator.'

Fair-haired, with a thick blond moustache and light brown eyes, Cooper was in his mid-thirties and was good at masking his emotions. He picked up Jemma's card and shrugged. 'As I'm sure you've worked out, Mrs James, you've been accused of espionage. Your PI agency might be a cover for treacherous activities – anyone can print business cards. Why were you loitering outside Wing Commander Robson's house?'

'Did the taxi driver tell you I flagged him down on Coney Street?'

He hesitated a moment before he replied. 'Yes.'

'My car wouldn't start. I was following a woman…'

'I'm not asking you about the woman. I want to know why you were spying on Wing Commander Robson?'

While she hesitated, he reached across the table, grabbed her notebook and flicked through the pages. His actions made her annoyed and uneasy.

'I wasn't spying on him, I was spying on Cynthia Ravenscar. She runs an art gallery in Coney Street, and she led me to—'

Suddenly he made a loud exclamation and jabbed his finger at an entry in her notebook. 'What the hell's this? *Squadron Leader Dickie Bell, RAF Linton?* – written with a question mark!'

He flicked back a page. 'And here – *Group Captain Ian Pulleyne, RAF Elvington: 7 p.m. 7.30: Coney Street. 8 p.m.: Dean Court Hotel, restaurant.*'

'As I'm trying to explain…'

'Just how many of them are you stalking, Mrs James?'

'I'm not. I'm…'

He leapt to his feet so quickly his chair nearly overturned behind him. 'Stay here.' Taking her notebook with him, he stormed out of the room. A few seconds later, a uniformed constable sidled through the door and leant against the grimy wall.

'Where's he gone?' Jemma asked in frustration. 'I'm trying to explain but he won't let me get a word in edgeways.'

'Just wait patiently, ma'am. He'll be back in a minute. I've got instructions to arrest you if you try to leave.'

'Arrest me?' Jemma said in horror. 'That's ridiculous. I haven't done anything – I'm trying to do you a favour.'

Her guard said nothing.

'Can I have a cup of tea while I wait?' she asked.

'No.'

Jemma sat back in her uncomfortable chair and tried to calm her annoyance. Things had just taken an unpleasant turn for the worse but losing her temper wouldn't help.

Cooper wasn't a minute; he was gone half an hour. Even her blank-faced guard was shifting restlessly from one foot to the other by the time he returned.

Cooper brought a fat, middle-aged air force officer with him, whom he introduced as Lieutenant Hall. He had a swollen red nose and a mottled purple face and wore the black and red flashes of the military police below his rank slides. He limped over to a seat at the table and when he sat down he rubbed his belly. Jemma groaned inwardly. That was another classic symptom of gout to add to his limp and his ruddy features. This was all she needed. An interrogation from a bad-tempered, gout-suffering member of the military police.

Cooper slapped a buff-coloured file on to the table and glared at her. 'Well, Mrs Ivashchenko, that's quite a cover story you've concocted about this female detective agency.'

Jemma gasped in shock. 'It's not a cover story. It's the truth. And my name is not Ivashchenko. It's James.'

'Your name is Mrs Ivashchenko. You're the wife of Mykhail Ivashchenko, an enemy alien.'

Jemma's jaw was so tense with anger, it hurt to speak. 'I am – was – the wife of Michael James, a naturalised British citizen and RAF wireless mechanic. The charge of enemy alien is – was – ridiculous. He was seven years old when he came to Britain, for heaven's sake! And the last time I checked, we're not at war with the Ukraine.'

Hall leant over the table and she smelled the alcohol on his breath. 'Don't you get cocky with me, woman! You know damned well that the Ukraine is Russian and they're colluding with Germany to carve up Europe once the war is over. Now stop messing about and tell us where he is!'

'Who?'

'Your husband, Mykhail, of course.'

'Michael?' she stammered. 'But Michael's dead.'

Both Hall and Cooper laughed. Short, unpleasant laughs.

'Of course, he's not dead. He's your handler. You're passing on air force secrets to him for his Russian paymasters.'

It was Jemma's turn to laugh – but her laughter was tinged with hysteria. 'You're out of your minds! It's Cynthia Ravenscar who's the spy – not me! And I've told you before, Michael is dead – missing in action. If you don't believe me, check your own records.'

'I did,' Cooper said quietly. 'That's why we know of your link to Ivashchenko. He's an enemy alien who absconded.'

'Absconded? What are you talking about?' The hairs stood up on the back of Jemma's neck. She thought her ears were failing her.

'Where is he, Mrs Ivashchenko?' Hall demanded.

'Michael's missing in action, presumed dead. You sent me a telegram – in January.'

Cooper frowned and shuffled through the papers in front of him.

But Hall just slammed his fist down on the table. 'Where is he?'

This was getting ridiculous. 'Missing in action, presumed dead!' Jemma screamed back. 'Stop calling me Ivashchenko. My name is James. Jemma James!' The nightmare had spiralled out of control.

She heard DS Cooper's voice drift towards her as if travelling a great distance down a silent high-sided wooded ravine.

'AC Michael James was reported absent without leave on the 12th of January.'

'Absent without leave?' she stammered. 'AWOL?'

331

'He failed to report for duty at the company known as Bletchley Wireless Manufacturing in Buckinghamshire.'

Jemma felt herself swaying. *Don't faint. For God's sake don't faint.* 'Absent without leave?' she repeated helplessly

Cooper nodded.

'But you sent me a telegram. You told me he was dead.'

Cooper shuffled uncomfortably. 'It looks like they sent you the wrong telegram.' He shrugged. 'It happens sometimes. There's a war on.'

Jemma felt her grasp on reality slipping away. All those weeks, sobbing herself to sleep every night. All that grief – wasted. The overwhelming sense of loss. Day after day, dragging herself through a life with no purpose. His devastated parents, uncle and brother... everyone bowed under an avalanche of grief.

'Just to be absolutely clear,' she whispered, 'Michael's still alive?'

Cooper couldn't meet her eyes. His nod was almost imperceptible, but it was a nod.

'You *incompetents*,' she hissed.

'Stop pretending,' Hall snapped. 'You've known all along Ivashchenko was alive and hiding among his Ruskie friends. Just tell us where he is!'

She ignored him. She'd had enough of Lieutenant Hall's silly games now – the stupid man couldn't even get their name right. Excitement fluttered in her stomach and made her shiver.

'Michael's still alive,' she murmured, trying the words out for size. The last two syllables came out in a breathless rush of excitement. The rhythm was beautiful. She whispered them again for good measure: 'Michael's still alive.'

This was all that mattered. Happiness swelled inside her, and she had an incredible urge to shout out those words from the rooftops. But the glowering, puce face of Lieutenant Hall, inches from her own, brought her back down to earth with a bang. Yes, Michael was still alive. But these idiots had lost him. And she'd need Gabriel's help to find him again.

'Mrs Ivashchenko…?'

'Fetch my brother. I want him fetched here from his home in Clifton. Now.'

Hall laughed, leant over the table and snarled in her face. 'You're in no position to make demands, woman!'

'I'm in an excellent position to make demands. My brother is Inspector Gabriel Roxby of York City Police. Fetch him.'

There was a stunned silence. Then DS Cooper swore under his breath.

'If you don't believe me, ask Desk Sergeant Ackroyd. He's known me since childhood.' Jemma laid her head down on her arms on the rickety tabletop and closed her eyes. Hall called her name – her proper name this time – but she ignored him and kept her head down.

She heard the men muttering among themselves. The door opened and closed behind them as everyone left the room.

Finally, alone, she began to cry. The tears poured down on to the stained table and pooled in the circle she'd made of her arms.

But she wasn't crying for Michael anymore. These were tears for herself, for Uncle Ivan, for Michael's parents and for his brother, Paul. These were tears of relief, tinged with self-pity. And tears of disbelief that they'd endured such a horrendous nightmare because of a bloody stupid administrative error.

Oh, darling, where are you?

It didn't matter.

All that mattered was that somewhere, Michael was alive.

——

Chapter Forty-Three

She heard Gabriel before she saw him. He was yelling at someone out in the corridor. She was glad she wasn't on the receiving end of that tirade and hoped he was venting his spleen on Cooper and Hall.

The door burst open and Gabriel, dressed in his full uniform, strode across the floor towards her. Behind him, DS Cooper and Lieutenant Hall hovered awkwardly in the doorway.

She blinked up at him, unsure where to start, what to say. She'd never seen him look so furious. His sharp eyes took in every detail of her pale, swollen, tearful face and dishevelled appearance.

'Dear God, what have they done to you.' He pulled her to her feet and into his arms for a hug.

'Michael's still alive, Gabriel,' she whispered.

'I know – I've just been told.'

'And I lied to you. Bobbie and I set up a private enquiry agency.'

'I know about that too. I've known for weeks.'

She bubbled up and burst into tears again. He gave her his handkerchief and made her sit back down. 'I'd be a poor sort of police officer,' he whispered in her ear, 'if I hadn't worked that one out. Can you bear it for a bit longer? There's some questions I need to ask these clowns before we go home.'

She nodded.

Gabriel gave Cooper and Hall a scathing glance and gestured for them to sit down at the table. 'So, let me get this straight. My brother-in-law, AC James, was instructed to report to Bletchley Wireless Manufacturing on January 12th but never arrived.'

'Correct,' Lieutenant Hall sniffed officiously. 'I'm not at liberty to tell you anything about his new posting or Bletchley.'

'As he never arrived there, I've no interest in the damned place or his role at Bletchley,' Gabriel snapped. 'But what I do want to know is how hard you searched for him.'

'The RAF military police searched everywhere for him but there was no sign of AC James.'

'Where? Where did you search?'

Hall shuffled uncomfortably through his buff-coloured file. 'At his last known address and the other places he frequented.'

'I'll need a list of those,' Jemma said. Her confusion and shock were clearing.

Cooper and Hall looked at her in surprise.

Gabriel nodded. 'Make sure there's a full list of the places you searched on my desk by next Friday. Did the MPs check the hospitals and local morgues?'

Hall began to stutter. 'Morgues? Why should we check the morgues?'

Gabriel gave him a withering look. 'For God's sake, man, don't tell me I've got to spell out standard procedure in a missing person's investigation. It was only last week we dragged the body of a soldier from Aldershot out of the Ouse.'

'Checks were made,' Lieutenant Hall said vaguely. 'I'm sure that included the morgues.'

'Clearly *not enough* checks were made,' Gabriel snapped. 'Not if you came to the ridiculous conclusion that AC Michael James was an enemy alien who'd gone over to the Russians and his wife was a fifth columnist.'

'I need a list of everywhere you've already checked,' Jemma repeated.

'Write that down,' Gabriel instructed DS Cooper. 'You will give my sister everything she needs.'

Hall frowned. 'Why?'

'Because I'm going to find him,' Jemma said simply. 'You've failed. So, I'll do it.'

There was a short silence while all three men absorbed those words.

'I also need to know the name of the last person who saw Michael... before he vanished,' she continued. She'd been going to say *the last person who saw him alive* but couldn't voice the possibility that Michael may yet be dead. Gabriel's comment about the dead squaddie in the river had struck her like a bucket of cold water. 'I'll need his – or her – address or telephone number so I can speak to them.'

The door opened and Desk Sergeant Ackroyd appeared with a cup of tea. 'Here you are, lass.'

'Thank you,' she murmured. It was incredibly sweet, but Jemma gulped it down gratefully and felt energy flooding through her once more.

Once Ackroyd had left the room, Gabriel turned angrily on DS Cooper. 'Were you goons in Special Branch also responsible for those idiots who were watching my house?'

Cooper looked embarrassed. 'We had no idea it was your home, sir. We just knew Mrs James had left Middlesbrough and moved into that cottage in Clifton. We wanted to see if her husband turned up. If we'd known...'

'Save it for the inquiry,' Gabriel said wearily. 'It's like an episode of the bloody *Keystone Cops*.'

'Inquiry, sir?'

'Yes, inquiry, Cooper. You've incorrectly let Michael James's entire family – which includes my sister, his wife – think he's dead for the last three months. Trust me, there'll be a bloody inquiry.'

Cooper looked alarmed.

'Did you also send those three thugs round to my former lodgings in Middlesbrough?' Jemma asked.

The ensuing silence confirmed her suspicions.

337

Gabriel pushed his chair back. 'I think we're done for now. Come on Jemma, I'll take you home.'

'Just a minute, there's something they need to know.' She reached across the table and retrieved her notebook. 'Now sit quietly and *listen* – without interrupting me.'

It was easy to tell them about Cynthia Ravenscar now they'd stopped interrupting her every few seconds. Lieutenant Hall even scribbled down a few notes.

'I have it on good authority, from an art expert, that the gallery on Coney Street is an unprofitable venture and that the paintings are painted by a variety of artists. It's probably a front to mask her espionage. Someone with a lot of money has set up a beautiful woman with a respectable art gallery in the centre of our city to ensnare senior air force personnel.'

Gabriel laughed – but it wasn't at her. 'It looks like my little sister has done your job for you, lieutenant.'

Lieutenant Hall shuffled with embarrassment in his seat. 'You say Group Captain Pulleyne from Elvington is caught in this woman's honey trap? That's ridiculous, I went to his wedding only last year. Ian wouldn't get involved with a woman of that sort.'

'You haven't seen her,' Jemma said, 'she's stunning. Anyway, I have photographs of them kissing on Coney Street. The negatives are with my developer but I'm sure I can get you some prints.'

'Give us his name and we'll pick them up,' DS Cooper said.

Jemma thought of Ricky's horrified reaction if Special Branch and the military police suddenly turned up on his doorstep and almost burst out laughing. 'No, you won't. I'll bring copies here to Clifford Street. I've also watched Cynthia giving messages and money to her paper boy. If I were you, I'd follow him and find out to whom she's reporting.'

'You think this delivery lad is part of the gang?'

'No. I think he's just an excited teenager who enjoys getting a few extra coins for running an errand.' Exhaustion suddenly swamped Jemma, mingled with irritation. Gabriel was right; she was doing their thinking for them. She turned to her brother and told him she was ready to go.

Lieutenant Cooper insisted that Jemma signed a copy of the Official Secrets Act before she left the station and he instructed her to stay away from Cynthia's art gallery for the foreseeable future, until they'd investigated her allegation. She was more than happy to agree to this but, ironically, she and Gabriel found themselves back in Coney Street only a few minutes later when a police car drove them back to her abandoned car.

Jemma waited in the back of the police vehicle while Gabriel lifted the bonnet and peered at the engine. Then he sat in the driver's seat, turned the ignition and her car roared back into life. Gabriel appeared at the window of the police car, wiping the oil off his hands with an old rag. 'Your spark plugs were loose.'

A loose spark plug, Jemma thought. If it hadn't been for a loose spark plug, she wouldn't have taken that taxi, attracted the attention of the police and found out the truth about Michael's mysterious disappearance.

An old saying of her mother's came into her head: *Our lives spin on the edge of a sixpence... no one knows where it may fall.*

Gabriel told her he was driving home. She sank wearily and without complaint into the passenger seat beside him. 'How did you find out? About Smoke & Cracked Mirrors.'

The sides of his mouth twitched with amusement. 'I saw your advertisement in the newspaper. It was soon after you'd told me you and Bobbie had discussed starting an agency. Suddenly York had lady detectives. I don't believe in coincidences, Jemma. Never have done. Besides which, I parked up on Grape Street one afternoon last week and watched you returning to your office.'

———

339

She gave a weak smile. 'I'm so sorry I deceived you. I didn't think you'd approve.'

'I don't – but it's your life, Jemma. Some time, you'll have to tell me all about it.'

'Not tonight, please,' she said wearily.

'No, not tonight.'

She smiled. 'Thank you – and I'm sorry I ruined your evening with Maisie.'

He gave a short laugh and slowed the car to turn onto Bootham. 'Yes, that *is* something I'll never forgive you for. In fact, I plan to make you suffer for that.'

She spun round in alarm. 'Why? What have I done?'

'You've ruined the most romantic night of my life. Maisie had just agreed to be my wife when the damned phone rang, and Sergeant Ackroyd told me my sister had got herself arrested for spying. It's a wonder the poor woman didn't walk out on me there and then. She must wonder what the hell she's marrying into.'

Jemma gave a squeal of delight, leant across the handbrake and kissed him on the cheek. 'Congratulations!'

He grinned. 'Don't think I'll ever forgive you for that, Jemma James – or let you forget.'

'When's the wedding?'

'In about four weeks. Maisie has always wanted a spring wedding. Just do me a big favour and try and stay out of trouble – and the police cells – on the big day, please?'

'Oh, my goodness – that means by May you won't be a grumpy old bachelor any more.'

'Less of the *grumpy*, you cheeky mare.' He fell silent for a moment and his smile disappeared. 'You do understand, don't you, Jemma, that if

Michael does turn up, he'll be in a lot of trouble? Going AWOL is a serious offence.'

Jemma swallowed hard and finally gave voice to the fear gnawing at the back of her mind. 'It's the trouble he's in right now that makes me uneasy. Something bad has happened. You think so too, don't you? We both know that if Michael was still in England, wild horses wouldn't keep him away from me and his family.'

Gabriel frowned and kept his eyes on the road ahead. 'While there's no dead body on a mortician's slab there's still hope, Jemma. You'll have to hang on to that thought. But yes,' he added quietly, 'his disappearance is one hell of a mystery.'

'I'll find him,' she said. 'I'm good at solving mysteries.'

Gabriel took his hand off the wheel, reached across and squeezed her arm. 'We'll find him together, sis.'

Chapter Forty-Four

The first thing Jemma saw the next morning was Bobbie's face peering round her bedroom door.

'Oh good, you're awake.' She walked into the room and handed Jemma a cup of hot tea.

'What are you doing here, Bobbie?'

'Gabriel fetched me about half an hour ago. I'd just arrived at the office when he strolled in – bold as brass. He told me to get my coat because you needed me. He brought me here. Did you know he's driving around in your car?' she added with a twinge of jealousy.

Jemma scrambled into a sitting position and reached for her alarm clock on the bedside table. She'd forgotten to wind it up last night and it had stopped. 'Good grief! What time is it?'

'Nearly ten. Gabriel said you needed a lie-in – and probably a day off – after the shock you had last night.' She sat on the bed beside Jemma, her face etched with concern. 'Is it true, Jemma? Is Michael still alive?'

Jemma nodded, then, faltering at first, she told Bobbie the whole story. Bobbie took her hand in her own and shook her head in disbelief.

'You'll have to keep quiet about Cynthia Ravenscar, though,' Jemma said. 'I'm not supposed to discuss this with anyone. They've made me sign the Official Secrets Act.'

Bobbie reached out and gave Jemma a hug. 'Never mind that treacherous cow, it's you I'm concerned about. This is an emotional roller coaster, Jemma – and it's a cruel one. One minute Michael's alive and going to Scotland – then he's dead – then he's alive again. To be honest, I don't know how the hell you're coping with this.'

'I was elated at first, but I'm worried silly now. How can someone just vanish like that – in Britain?'

343

Bobbie patted her arm thoughtfully. 'We'll find him. It'll probably be the biggest mystery we ever solve, but we'll find him. Now, what do you want to do today? I'm quite happy to stay here with you, or I can go back to the office and sit beside the telephone for the day if you want. I've got my first driving lesson later.'

Jemma threw back the blanket and slid out of bed. 'Sitting at home brooding is the last thing I need. But first I must telephone Michael's mother – which will be a difficult call. After that, we'll head into work. I promised to telephone Mrs Banyan today.'

Bobbie called round at Ricky's to request more copies of the photographs of Pulleyne and Cynthia Ravenscar for Special Branch. After that, she skipped off to her driving lesson. Her excitement brought a weak smile to Jemma's lips.

While she was gone, Jemma distracted herself with the Helen Urwin case. She pulled a sheet of blank paper towards her and made a timeline of all known events in the recent life of the woman. She'd hoped it would focus her thoughts, but it just made her more perplexed.

The summer of 1935.

Everything boiled down to the summer of 1935.

In a few short months, after leaving her family home for a holiday in Whitby, Helen had jettisoned her closest relatives from her life and dismissed the loyal staff at her family home. She's also sacked her solicitor and then – surprisingly for a young woman who'd allegedly never expressed any interest in foreign travel – disappeared abroad. In addition to that, over the past five years she'd changed her bank, sold her family home to developers and turned up in a different city on the arm of Edward Anston.

It was almost as if the woman had been determined to sever every connection with her old life in Leeds. Every connection, that is, apart from her link to the notorious Watts family on Gordon Terrace.

While Jemma was chewing her lip and pondering this enigma, the telephone rang. She jerked back to reality and picked up the receiver.

'Good afternoon, Mrs James,' said a cheerful male voice. 'My name's Smithson and I was employed by Mr King on your behalf to investigate the death of a woman called Gladys Mellor in Whitby in 1935. I went to the library this morning and read through the back issues of the local newspapers. I've a preliminary report for you. The *Scarborough Evening News* was very informative.'

'Thank you for calling so promptly, Mr Smithson. What can you tell me about Miss Urwin's maid?'

'Firstly, she didn't die in Whitby,' Smithson said. 'She drowned on 4th June at a scenic beauty spot called Hayburn Wyke, not far from Scarborough. It's a pretty little place – although rather isolated and rocky. There's a waterfall tumbling down to the beach and you can only get there by a meandering path through the woods.'

'She drowned?' Jemma knew Hayburn Wyke. Her father had taken her there one sweltering day when she was twelve. She remembered the dappled sunshine on the quiet twisty path that led through the dense woodland towards the head of the waterfall and the final steep descent to the rocky shoreline. The woods had been full of bluebells and the drone of sleepy bees, drifting from one flower to another.

'Yes, the results of the post-mortem came out at the inquest and the newspaper reported these in detail. Mellor's body had been in the water for a while by the time the lifeboat arrived and had been bashed around by the rocks. There were abrasions to all her limbs and a head injury – but she definitely drowned. There was water in her lungs.'

'Who raised the alarm?'

'It was a group of hikers. They arrived at the scene to find Miss Urwin exhausted and distraught. Apparently, the two women got into severe difficulties from underwater currents. Miss Urwin was the stronger swimmer but even she struggled. She'd just managed to pull Gladys Mellor up on to the shingle when the hikers arrived. One of them rushed to the nearby inn and phoned the coastguard. The lifeboat arrived quickly but it was too late to save Mellor. They took the body back to Scarborough in the boat because it was an awkward spot for an ambulance.'

Hence Helen Urwin's significant charitable donations to the RNLI.

The clue to this mystery had been there from the start.

Jemma tried to imagine the shock and horror experienced by the young woman when the mangled and lifeless body of her companion was taken away. As an experienced swimmer, Helen's inability to save the other woman's life must have left her with a profound sense of failure and guilt.

'The inquest was held two weeks later at the coroner's office in Scarborough,' Smithson continued.

'Scarborough? But I thought the women were staying at a hotel in Whitby.'

'Apparently not. They'd just arrived in Scarborough at the Crown Hotel the night before the accident. Miss Urwin had fancied a change, so they'd moved down the coast.'

Smithson continued to tell her the details of the inquest, but Jemma was barely listening. The Helen Urwin *mystery* had evaporated in front of her eyes like the early morning mist on a sunny day. There was no mystery here. Any subsequent odd and strange behaviour on the part of Helen Urwin, like financially overcompensating Mellor's relatives, could easily be explained and excused following such a traumatic experience.

'...then they released the body for burial at St Mary's church in Scarborough.'

Jemma swung back to reality. 'Gladys Mellor was buried in Scarborough?'

'Yes, at the parish church of St Mary's.'

Jemma frowned. This tiny detail bothered her. She'd assumed Mellor's body would have been transported back to her family in Leeds for burial. Helen Urwin could easily afford to pay for that.

'Anyway, that's the gist of it,' Smithson concluded. 'I'll send you my written report through the post.'

Jemma thanked him and they discussed payment arrangements before Jemma ended the call. She sat quietly, chewing her lip. To use an unfortunate expression, her investigation into Helen Urwin was now dead in the water. The woman was beyond reproach. Even the suspicious Mrs Banyan would have to accept Helen and her marriage to her brother.

Yet Jemma still couldn't let it go. There was an anomaly somewhere; something niggled. The same tenacious instinct for an incongruity that kept her on the trail of Cynthia Ravenscar now pulled her towards Helen Urwin.

She had one last lead to follow.

She picked up the telephone receiver and asked the operator to put her through to the RNLI at Scarborough.

'Is it an emergency?' the operator asked.

'Oh no,' Jemma said hastily. 'It's just an administration query.'

'In that case I'll put you through to the honorary secretary.'

When the honorary secretary answered the telephone, Jemma explained that she was a journalist who wanted to write a promotional piece for the *Yorkshire Post* about the RNLI and particularly wanted further information about the tragic drowning of a young woman from Leeds five years ago.

He promptly gave her the telephone number of the Scarborough coxswain, Mr John Owston.

A few moments later she found herself chatting with Mabel, a pleasant, down-to-earth fisherman's wife with a broad Yorkshire accent. 'John's out in the back yard mendin' his nets and lobster pots,' she told Jemma. 'Do you want me to fetch him in, love?'

Jemma reminded herself that the RNLI was a voluntary organisation, funded by charitable donations, and the lifeboats were usually crewed by local fishermen.

'No, please don't bother him. I'm... I'm a journalist and I'm just enquiring about the tragic death of a young woman called Gladys Mellor, who drowned at Hayburn Wyke about five years ago...'

'Ooh yes, I remember her – the poor young thing.'

'You do?'

'Oh yes, our John were the coxswain of the lifeboat on that shout – but she were already dead when they got there. It were still upsettin' for John and the other lads though.'

'I'm sure it was.'

'Her funeral were a sad little affair as well.'

'Your husband went to Gladys Mellor's funeral?'

'Aye, we both did. If the RNLI are called out and the victim is local, we often pay our respects. He were the coxswain, you see? I went wi' him.'

'Why was it a *sad little affair*, Mrs Owston?'

'Well, there were no one there apart from us, her lady boss and the hotel manager. A real shabby affair, it were. I said to my John, it weren't right. How come such a young lass had no one else in the world to mourn fer her? Where were her family?'

Where indeed? Jemma thought. 'You said Miss Urwin, her employer, was at the funeral. Was she very upset?'

'Oh, aye. She never stopped blubbin' all the way through. She wore a thick black veil but I knew she were upset. We tried to have a word after to – you know – pass on our sympathies, like. But she could barely speak – and it were clear she weren't eatin' properly. It affects them bad, you know, when they witness the drownin's.'

'Yes, I'm sure it does,' Jemma said quietly. 'It must be horrific to be part of that.'

'Are you sure you don't want to speak to our John?'

'No, please don't bother him – you've been very helpful, Mrs Owston. But may I ask you one last thing? You said Miss Urwin wasn't eating properly. How did you know?'

'The funeral were two weeks after the drownin' but already her coat were hangin' off her shoulders like it were too big for her. It were a hot day and she had the buttons undone. Her nice black dress were swampin' her, an' all.'

Jemma gasped aloud as the anomaly at the heart of this case was finally resolved. Her mind whirled with the enormity of what she'd just discovered, and her jaw dropped in shock. It took her a few seconds to regain control of her mouth and remember to thank Mrs Owston before she ended the call.

Jemma was still sitting in a trance, her mind whirling, when Bobbie flounced back into the office, giddy and excited after her first driving lesson. 'Good grief, you look awful. What's happened? Is it Michael? Is there some news?'

Jemma shook her head. 'No, Bobbie. I've just found out how Gladys Mellor died. She drowned in the sea near Scarborough while out swimming with Helen Urwin.'

'Whoa! That's a shock!' Bobbie sank into a chair, her eyes riveted on Jemma's face.

'It's not as shocking as what happened next. I think the woman who drowned was actually Helen Urwin – and the woman who crawled out of the sea on to the shingle in her bathing costume was the con woman and convicted criminal, Gladys Mellor.'

'What!'

'I think Mellor stole her employer's identity. She may also have murdered Helen Urwin.'

Chapter Forty-Five

They had to involve Gabriel, of course.

Jemma knew this would be the last thing Mrs Banyan would want, but the situation was now out of her control. Murder and identity fraud were police business. Besides which, only the police could access the evidence Jemma knew they needed to prove her theory.

Grabbing their coats, bags and the photographs for DS Cooper, they walked out into the rain and pushed their way through crowds of umbrella-toting pedestrians towards Clifford Street police station.

Their route took them through King's Square, where Jemma had first seen the blackmailer Shaun Flynn, and they passed the secret gated entrance of Holy Trinity Church, where they'd told Clarissa Deburgh her husband was still alive. It seemed a lifetime ago now. Every one of those little triumphs was totally eclipsed by this new, momentous discovery.

'I still can't believe she pulled it off,' Bobbie said, as they weaved round a pile of damp sandbags, half blocking the pavement. 'It's the most audacious thing I've ever heard! Do you think the murder was premeditated?'

'I don't know,' Jemma admitted. 'It may have been a genuine accident. All we know for a fact is that two young women arrived late at night at one of Scarborough's most prestigious hotels and the next morning, one of them drowned in the sea. If it was Helen who'd died, this was a fantastic opportunity for someone as devious as Mellor. All she had to do was crawl out of the sea, pick up Helen Urwin's clothes and handbag and claim *she* was the wealthy heiress.'

'But what about the hotel staff?'

'They'd only met the women briefly – they didn't notice anything wrong. Apart from their build, the two women were very similar in appearance.

The imposter we saw at The Spinney bears a strong resemblance to the young Helen Urwin in her aunt's photograph album. It was such a good likeness I never questioned it at the time. In fact...' A new thought overwhelmed Jemma and she stopped in her tracks. 'They might have been sisters.'

A soldier with his head down against the rain nearly walked into her. He stepped into the road to avoid a collision. 'Careful, lass!'

'Sorry!'

'Sisters? Oh my God!' Bobbie exclaimed. 'It's Helen Urwin's father, isn't it? That neighbour, Mrs Sheils, told me Dora Mellor's fancy man was a wealthy chap who'd set her up in her own house. John Urwin was Gladys Mellor's father!'

'Maybe,' Jemma said thoughtfully. 'It would certainly explain a few things. Edna hinted to me that John Urwin had had affairs throughout his marriage, so an illegitimate child isn't out of the question. No one knows why John Urwin employed Mellor – especially after her conviction. But Anne Urwin told me there was a rumour the girl had some kind of hold over her brother-in-law.'

'It's hard to get employment after a stint in prison.' Bobbie scowled. 'My dad knows this only too well.'

Jemma nodded. 'Mellor may have gone to John Urwin out of desperation and demanded help from him.'

'That must have been galling,' Bobbie said. 'To find yourself working as a servant for your own father and having to wait on your spoilt and wealthy half-sister. It would have made me murderous.'

'She wouldn't have shown it,' Jemma said. 'Mellor was an actress and a con woman. She probably hid her resentment and focused on charming Helen Urwin and wheedling her way into her confidence. If Mellor *was* her half-sister, I doubt Helen Urwin knew about it. Her father may have given his illegitimate daughter a job in the house – but I'm pretty sure he would have demanded that Mellor didn't reveal the truth to Helen.'

They walked in silence for a moment, mulling it over. 'What do you think happened next?' Bobbie asked.

'I think Mellor went back to their hotel, practised forging Helen Urwin's signature and planned her next move. Two weeks later, Helen's body is buried in Scarborough beneath a headstone marked with the name *Gladys Mellor*. None of the Watts family attend the funeral because they know the truth: they've colluded in this with Gladys Mellor from the start.'

'Do you think she bought their house for them on Gordon Terrace?"

'Definitely – and every now and then, Neil Watts takes a trip up to York and his half-sister gives him money, which is what I saw on the riverbank.'

Bobbie nodded. She looked more convinced now. 'Meanwhile, Mellor opens a new bank account, finds a new solicitor and transfers Helen's fortune. She sends a series of curt, impersonal, typed notes to Helen's family and the staff at the house, dismissing everyone from her life who might spot the deception.'

'Exactly. Not one of them saw her again after June 1935. The only person who saw anything out of the ordinary was a sharp-eyed fisherman's wife who noticed that Helen Urwin's expensive clothes didn't fit Mellor properly at the funeral. But even she didn't understand what she saw. This was the opportunity of a lifetime for Mellor; she thought everything through carefully. But even she couldn't do anything about the fact she was smaller and less athletically built than her employer.'

'She must be a phenomenal actress,' Bobbie said. 'I still don't understand how a backstreet girl from Leeds managed to transform herself into the wealthy and well-educated upper-class woman we saw at The Spinney.'

They'd reached the imposing façade of the police station. Jemma hesitated for a moment on the pavement outside. Memories of the distress of the previous evening flooded back, but she buried them. 'Oh, it's amazing the difference a few elocution and deportment classes can make. Mellor now had the money and leisure time to reinvent herself. She would have employed tutors. We know for a fact she took French lessons.'

'Mrs Banyan wasn't fooled by her though, was she?'

'No. She recognised Mellor's lack of good breeding.'

'Do you think she took those fancy deportment classes while she was touring the continent?'

'Who says she ever went to the continent?' Jemma countered. 'Just because she didn't return to the house in Roundhay doesn't mean she ever left the country. The woman has lied about everything for the last five years. The only thing that still confuses me, though, is where does Teddy Anston fit into all this? Mellor doesn't need his money and took a huge risk getting close to that man – especially as he has such an astute sister.'

'Ah, well. Even murderers can fall in love,' Bobbie said harshly. 'Think of Dr Crippen and Le Neve. And Mellor didn't expect Mrs Banyan to move back to York, did she? We've Hitler to thank for that.'

Gabriel was busy when they arrived, and they had to sit on a hard bench in the public waiting room under the curious gaze of Desk Sergeant Ackroyd. 'I thought you'd have seen enough of this place last night, lass,' he said.

Jemma smiled. 'I can't seem to stay away.'

Gabriel looked pale and alarmed when they were shown into his bland and cluttered office. His desk was overflowing with paperwork. 'What is it, Jemma? I've got a meeting with the superintendent in twenty minutes. Hello again, Bobbie.'

'Hello, Gabriel. We won't take long,' Bobbie slid on to an uncomfortable chair opposite his desk and jabbed a finger in Jemma's direction. 'Miss Sherlock here has uncovered a devious five-year-old murder. I suspected she was a murderess all along,' she added with a wink, 'but your smart little sis has worked out the details.'

Gabriel swallowed hard, pulled a notepad towards him and picked up a pen. 'I think you'd better start from the beginning.'

Fifteen minutes later, he was scribbling down frantic notes. 'If this woman *is* Gladys Mellor, what makes you think she murdered Helen Urwin?'

'I don't have any proof,' Jemma said, 'but it seems odd that there's a drowning incident and it's the woman who's the Olympic-class swimmer who dies – not her skinny maid.'

'The North Riding Constabulary would have investigated the incident in Scarborough.'

'Yes, but they knew nothing about the history of the two women – only what Mellor chose to tell them.'

'The dead woman suffered a head injury, according to the post-mortem,' Bobbie added. 'Mellor might have bashed her on the head from behind with a rock and pushed her unconscious body face down into the sea. Maybe that's how she drowned.'

'It's a very isolated little spot,' Jemma said desperately. She could sense Gabriel's scepticism.

He put down his pen and glanced at the piles of urgent case files awaiting his attention. 'You don't have any evidence of murder, Jemma. And your theory that Mellor has taken on Helen Urwin's identity is based on circumstantial evidence alone. As far as I can see, you don't have a shred of real proof to back up your claim that a crime has been committed.'

'But the evidence is out there! And you – the police – can get it. For a start, there's witnesses in Leeds who knew both Helen Urwin *and* Gladys Mellor. Apart from the Urwin family, there's also Mr Browning, the solicitor, and Edna, his housekeeper.'

'On top of this,' Bobbie added, 'Mellor was arrested by Leeds City Police for stealing pension books from dying old ladies at Leeds General Infirmary. Her fingerprints will be on file somewhere – and there should be a mugshot of her with her criminal record.'

'If Bobbie and I can see that photograph of Gladys Mellor, we'll know for sure.'

Gabriel put down his pen, checked his watch and frowned. Reaching for his cap, he pushed back his chair and stood up. 'Right. I've got to go. You can see yourselves out, I assume?'

Jemma's heart fell. Surely, he wasn't dismissing them? He rose and strode across to the door.

'Of course,' Bobbie drawled, 'Jemma and I can always charm our way into the Watts' home in Leeds and steal their family photograph album. I mean, what could possibly go wrong with such a plan?'

'Didn't that vile black marketeer threaten to disembowel your little dog, Bobbie?' Jemma asked.

Gabriel spun round and glowered at the pair of them. Jemma remembered Ricky describing the icy flint of granite in Gabriel's eyes. She saw it now. 'You both stay away from the Watts family. Do you hear me?'

'Yes, sir,' Bobbie lowered her head to hide her grin.

'I'll make enquiries with the Leeds City Police and get hold of the mugshot of Gladys Mellor. In the meantime, you two must keep quiet about this – and stay away. You keep what you've learnt to yourselves and don't tell your client anything. Is that understood?'

'Yes – we won't say a word.'

He smoothed back his hair and rammed his cap on his head. 'If this Mellor woman is as sharp as you make out, it won't take much to spook her and send her running. Keep your client in the dark.'

'Thanks, Gabriel. We appreciate your help.'

His expression softened and he gazed at them both in disbelief. 'As if I don't have enough on my plate – now I get a visit from Sherlock Holmes and Dr Watson. Do me a favour, girls, go back to the library and read your crime stories. I can do without any more excitement this week.'

Chapter Forty-Six

It took Gabriel and Leeds City Police nearly a week to track down the mugshots of the con woman Gladys Mellor.

For Jemma, the days dragged along painfully. On edge about the case and fretting about Michael, she struggled to sleep. It didn't help that the air-raid sirens went off three times that week – twice in one night.

When she telephoned Mrs Banyan, she managed to buy some time by simply telling her client they'd tracked down Helen Urwin's family in Leeds but hadn't yet had a chance to visit them. Mrs Banyan was indignant that her future sister-in-law had lied about this, but Jemma stressed they needed more information before they confronted Helen about her deception. She also said she wanted to investigate the death of Helen's maid in Scarborough, whom she thought was related to the Watts family. Convinced that more scandalous revelations would follow, her intrigued client agreed to another week's work and promised not to confront Helen about her deception – yet.

Bobbie went back to her job at Grainger's, and Jemma found the long hours waiting in the office for more work to come through the door lonely and depressing. Bobbie always called into the office after her shift to see if there had been any further developments or new cases – and usually went home disappointed.

Smoke & Cracked Mirrors only had one more enquiry that week – an elderly man who was convinced his wife was having an affair with an ARP warden and wanted her shadowed. Jemma did the job easily and realised with a sigh that these lulls in business were inevitable.

She had too much time to think and inevitably her thoughts kept returning to Michael. The initial elation she'd felt when she found out he was still alive had long since vanished. She knew something had gone badly wrong and the unknown nature of that 'something' left her with a gnawing lump of anxiety in the pit of her stomach.

She was still determined to learn the truth but had a terrible suspicion she would find herself widowed for a second time. But she had no choice; she either found Michael and dealt with whatever new horror she uncovered or spent the next seven years like Clarissa Deburgh, living a half-life as neither a widow nor a wife.

Fortunately, there was plenty to distract her at home. The wedding was booked for the end of April and Gabriel and Maisie were now refurbishing the front parlour as their own private sitting room. Jemma helped out with another new set of curtains and cushion covers. Maisie and Tom ate with them every evening and she found comfort in their company. Jemma was touched when Maisie nervously asked her to design and make her a wedding dress.

Bored and frustrated with the long hours she spent alone in the office, Jemma brought her sewing machine into work and spent her time cutting out panels of ivory satin and sewing sequins on to Maisie's veil.

She was just clearing away her sewing on Friday evening when she heard Bobbie's familiar footsteps on the stairs. Her friend wafted into the room with rosy cheeks and the smell of fresh air. 'I see that damned art gallery is still open for business,' she said, 'and Cynthia Ravenscar is still roaming free.' She waltzed into the kitchen to put the kettle on.

'I guess they're playing the long game with her – watching cautiously until they know all her contacts.'

Bobbie came back into the room and nodded. 'They'll wait until they've identified everyone involved in her spying ring before they pounce. One day, she and her gallery will just disappear. Is there any news about our other cases?'

'Well, Kathleen Pulleyne telephoned me to thank me for the photographs and to let me know she doesn't intend to pay her bill.'

'What!' Bobbie's face was a picture.

Jemma grinned as she flicked the catches to fasten the lid on her sewing machine. 'She said she was sure we wouldn't mind waiving the fee as we were such *old friends*.'

'How dare she! The—' Bobbie's expletive-ridden explosion made Jemma's mouth twitch with amusement.

'Where the devil did you learn language like that, Roberta Baker?' said a familiar voice from the doorway. For a big man, Gabriel could move quietly when he wanted to.

'My brother,' Bobbie retorted cheerfully. 'It's good to see you, Gabriel. Do you have news for us about Mellor, and would you like a cup of tea?'

'Yes, to both – please.' He lowered himself into one of Jemma's armchairs, tossed his cap on her desk and ran his fingers through his white curls. 'You've got it very cosy in here, Jemma. That's a great photograph of you and Bobbie. Taken by Ricky Wilde, was it?'

'It might have been,' Jemma murmured, smiling.

By the time Bobbie reappeared with three steaming cups of tea, he'd pulled a pair of photographs out of his pocket and laid it on the desk. 'Is this her? Your con woman?'

Bobbie and Jemma gathered round the police mugshots. There was a side view and a front view of a scowling, thin-faced girl with a big nose and fairish hair.

'Yes,' they said in unison. The photographs were about ten years old but the female staring out at them from the front view was a younger version of the woman they'd seen at The Spinney masquerading as Helen Urwin.

'Her hair looks lighter,' Bobbie said, 'but it's her.' She gave Jemma a look of admiration. 'You were absolutely right, Miss Sherlock. You've uncovered a despicable fraud.'

'The police records say she has gingery hair,' Gabriel said. 'Are you absolutely sure this is the woman you saw?'

Jemma nodded and felt a quiver of excitement and satisfaction run through her. 'Red hair runs in the Watts family. Mrs Banyan suspected she wasn't a natural brunette and dyed her hair darker. So, what happens now, Gabriel?'

'Right now, I'm going home, but tomorrow I plan to pick up Cousin Clara Urwin and bring her back to York to identify the woman in person. If she confirms that she's a fraud, I'll arrest Gladys Mellor on the spot and take her back to the station for questioning and fingerprinting.'

'Wow!' Bobbie said again. 'I want to watch that!'

Gabriel frowned. 'It's not a theatre show, Bobbie. These are serious crimes.'

'I know, but it's rather frustrating not to be there at the dramatic climax. Don't you agree, Jemma?'

But Jemma wasn't listening. Her hand quivered with excitement as she reached for her notebook and flicked back through the pages. Everything had finally come together, and they'd made it happen. Never in any of her daydreams about this agency had she imagined they would become involved in such a unique and momentous case. 'Tomorrow, between four and six o'clock, the woman who claims she's called Helen Urwin is due to play tennis with her fiancé, Teddy, at the Tang Hall Tennis Club,' she said. 'I think the courts are in the grounds of the Tang Hall Hotel on Fourth Avenue.'

'How on earth do you know that?' Gabriel asked.

'A few weeks ago, her diary accidentally came into my possession. I made a few notes about her future engagements.'

Gabriel shook his head in disbelief. 'I wish I hadn't asked. But that's helpful, thank you. I'll arrange everything so Miss Urwin and I confront Mellor at the tennis club.'

Bobbie grinned. 'That'll put her off her serve. It'll be game, set and match for Gladys Mellor tomorrow.'

'Will you open a murder inquiry into Helen Urwin's death?' Jemma asked.

'We'll have to see what happens when she's questioned, and I need to speak to the North Riding Constabulary in Scarborough – but yes, probably.' Gabriel drained the last of his tea, rose to his feet and left.

'Oh, Jemma!' Bobbie said, after he'd gone. 'I do wish we could be there tomorrow to see her face when Gabriel turns up with Clara Urwin. It seems such a shame after we've done all the hard work on this case that we miss the best bit. Lord Peter Wimsey and Poirot are always there at the conclusion to confront the villains with their crimes.'

'I'm more worried about Mrs Banyan,' Jemma said thoughtfully. 'This will be a dreadful shock for her and her family – especially her brother and her father.' She tapped her fingers thoughtfully on the table. 'I think I should go and warn her.'

'Really? Can I come?'

Jemma made her decision and nodded. 'Yes. I know Gabriel said to keep away from our client, but we owe her that much. Come here after you've finished at Grainger's and we'll drive out to The Spinney. We should get there before six o'clock – hopefully about the same time Gabriel arrests Gladys Mellor at the tennis club.'

Chapter Forty-Seven

'No servants' entrance for us this time,' Bobbie said with a wink, as Jemma rang the doorbell at the front entrance of The Spinney.

Jemma peered thoughtfully at the climbing rose clambering over the porch above their heads. 'I just hope Mrs Banyan's at home.'

The maid, Daisy, opened one of the two arched doors and listened impassively to their request to see Mrs Banyan. If she recognised them as *Mary* and *Ann*, the two casual waitresses who'd worn ridiculous outfits and worked alongside her at the engagement party a few weeks before, she gave no indication. She led them into the oak-panelled entrance vestibule, asked them to wait and went in search of Mrs Banyan.

A few moments later, Daisy took them into the elegant sitting room whose large bay windows overlooked the sweeping gravel drive at the front of the house. The last time they were there, it had been heaving with guests. Only now could Jemma properly appreciate the tasteful furnishings, the luxurious carpet and the antique rosewood furniture, whose glossy surfaces had been so lovingly polished over the decades that she could see her reflection in their patina. Even the wooden cabinets housing the gramophone and the wireless set had been crafted by artists.

Mrs Banyan was sitting on a velvet chesterfield sofa with a pile of magazines and her embroidery basket. A small fire crackled in the grate of the herringbone-tiled fireplace opposite, whose twisted oak side columns supported a magnificent carved timber overmantel.

She peered at them over the top of her reading glasses. 'Mrs James. Miss Baker. This is a surprise. I thought I'd made it quite clear you weren't to come to the house in case Helen recognised you?'

'I'm sorry, but we need to talk to you urgently and I know she's out at tennis. Do you have a few minutes to hear what we have to say?'

Mrs Banyan took off her spectacles and put them in a leather case. Ever the picture of elegance, she wore a beautiful cream mohair cardigan over a patterned green silk tea dress. 'I have a minute or two, yes,' she conceded warily. 'My father is resting before Teddy and Helen join us for dinner.' She waved her hand towards the pair of leather chairs either side of the fire. 'Please take a seat.'

Conscious of the heat of the fire, Jemma undid the buttons on her coat and sank into the chair. 'I'll come straight to the point, Mrs Banyan. Our investigation has taken an unexpected twist. We've found out that the woman you know as Helen Urwin isn't who she claims to be.'

Mrs Banyan snorted in an unladylike manner. 'Ha! Well, that's no surprise. I said this all along.'

'She's a con woman called Gladys Mellor, who was formerly in the employment of the *real* Helen Urwin as her maid,' Jemma continued.

The smirk drained from Mrs Banyan's face.

'Five years ago, a young woman drowned in suspicious circumstances while swimming in the sea off Scarborough with her maid. When she was buried, she was named as Gladys Mellor, but we believe it was Helen Urwin who drowned, and Mellor stole her identity.'

Slowly, Jemma explained the whole story to her horrified and incredulous client. When she'd finished, Mrs Banyan could barely contain her shock – or her anger.

'Well, I have to say I'm impressed, Mrs James!' Mrs Banyan exclaimed. 'When I asked you to investigate the woman and find out about her suspicious past, I never expected such a thorough job – or such a shocking outcome. Obviously, Teddy will have to dissolve the engagement now. The marriage can't possibly go ahead.'

Jemma cleared her throat. 'There's more, Mrs Banyan. In view of the seriousness of the deception and the fraud, I had no choice but to involve the police.'

'The police! Good God!' Mrs Banyan turned pale. 'What on earth did you do that for? There'll be a terrible scandal! Our family name will be in tatters. You should *not* have gone to the police.'

'I'm sorry, but Mellor has swindled the Urwin family out of a large inheritance that should have been theirs. Heaven knows how many other laws she broke when she misled the coroner and allowed them to bury Helen Urwin under the wrong name. In addition to this, there's the suspicious nature of Helen Urwin's death to consider.'

'What suspicious nature?'

Bobbie frowned. She looked irritated by Mrs Banyan's self-centred reaction. 'There's a strong possibility Mellor killed Helen Urwin.'

Mrs Banyan's beautifully manicured hand flew to her mouth. She sat back abruptly on the sofa as if she'd been struck across the face. 'A murderess? Surely not!'

For a moment, they sat in silence waiting for Mrs Banyan to grasp the enormity of the situation. They heard her children playing outside in the garden and the ormolu clock ticking on a shelf on the overmantel.

Jemma glanced at the elegant little timepiece. It was well after six o'clock. Gabriel would have confronted and arrested Mellor at the tennis club by now. Bobbie followed her gaze, rose quietly and went to stand at the bay window, looking out over the sweeping gravel drive.

'A murderess?' Mrs Banyan repeated. The skin at her throat jerked as she swallowed. 'And to think we welcomed that woman into our family home!' Her face flushed as the shock turned to anger. 'Good grief! I let that, that *woman* – that fiend – play with my daughters!'

'The police will investigate the full extent of Mellor's crimes – not us,' Jemma said. 'I've passed the case on to Inspector Gabriel Roxby at York City Police. He's already tracked down a photograph of Mellor and we've confirmed she's the same woman we saw here at your house, posing as Helen Urwin. Today he took Helen Urwin's cousin, Clara, to the Tang Hall Tennis Club.'

Jemma's ears pricked up at the sound of a car coming down the drive.

Was it Teddy Anston returning to his family home after witnessing the arrest of his fiancée?

'If Clara Urwin confirms the woman is Gladys Mellor, she'll be arrested for fraud.'

Bobbie leant forward over the window seat, craning her neck to see the occupants of the car. 'Er, Jemma...'

'Arrested?' Mrs Banyan exploded. 'In front of the tennis club? The police couldn't make this more public if they wanted to!'

Car doors slammed and Jemma heard feet crunching on the gravel. 'It's out of our hands, Mrs Banyan. This is a serious matter. It's police business now.'

'Jemma,' Bobbie said urgently. 'They're back.'

Mrs Banyan stood up. 'Is it Teddy? I must go to him. The poor lamb will be *devastated.*'

'No,' Bobbie said slowly, 'it's *both* of them: Teddy *and* Gladys Mellor.'

Shock washed over Jemma like a bucket of icy water. She scrambled to her feet then hesitated, unsure what to do.

What the hell had happened? Why was Mellor still a free woman?

Bobbie crossed over to her side. The door to the sitting room was partially open. They heard the front door open and muffled voices in the entrance vestibule. The hairs stood up on the back of Jemma's neck as Mellor's high-pitched nervous laughter drifted down the hallway.

Where the devil were Gabriel and Clara Urwin?

Jemma leant forward and grabbed Mrs Banyan's arm. 'Don't say anything – please. The police will be along in a minute, I'm sure. Just pretend you don't know.'

'Isabella? Are you—' Gladys Mellor strode confidently into the room, still wearing her tennis whites and shoes and swinging a racquet by her side. Her pale, lightly freckled face was flushed from the exercise and fresh air. A cardigan was slung casually over her thin shoulders.

She stopped abruptly when she saw Jemma and Bobbie. 'Oh, I'm sorry, Isabella, I didn't know you had company. I've got a message for you from Carol, but it'll keep—'

Suddenly, her smile vanished, and her eyes flicked up to her left as she tried to recall a memory. Inwardly, Jemma groaned and braced herself for what was coming next.

'Wait a minute... aren't you two the casual waitresses we hired for our engagement party?'

There goes the theory that no one remembers the staff, Jemma thought.

'No, we're here about a charity—'

'Yes, they are,' Mrs Banyan snapped. Jemma cringed, dreading to hear what her furious client would say next. 'Except they're not. This is Mrs James and her associate, Miss Baker. They're a pair of private detectives I hired to find out about you and your background, *Gladys*.'

Mellor's tall, thin frame swayed slightly, then tensed. Her eyes flashed like those of a hunted animal. 'What did you call me?' she hissed.

'I'm not surprised you recognised them from when they pretended to be servants. After all, it takes one to know one, doesn't it, *Gladys*? And you were a servant, weren't you? Helen Urwin's servant.'

Mellor's thin face had never been pretty but now it distorted with ugly hatred. 'I don't know what you think you know – or what lies these women have told you—'

'What's going on, Isabella?' Teddy Anston appeared in the doorway, still holding the car keys in his hand. His eyes flitted over the tense tableau of the four women. 'Helen?'

Mellor turned towards him sharply. 'Give me the car keys, Teddy. I'm going home. Your sister has taken leave of her senses.'

'You're not going anywhere.' Bobbie stepped forward menacingly. 'The police are on their way here to arrest you.'

Teddy blinked. 'What the deuce!'

Suddenly, Mellor grabbed the keys out of his hand, hurled her tennis racquet at Bobbie's head and belted out of the room.

Bobbie ducked the missile, which smashed into a small Sèvres porcelain vase on the rosewood side table behind her, shattering it to pieces.

Mrs Banyan screamed as Bobbie – and Jemma – flew after Mellor, pushing the startled man out of their way.

They thundered down the wooden floor of the hallway. Bobbie caught up with Mellor by the main entrance, grabbed a large handful of her thick dark hair and yanked her head back.

The woman screamed, spun round and punched Bobbie in the eye. But Bobbie clung on tenaciously and hauled Mellor down to the parquet flooring by her hair. With Jemma's help, she threw Mellor over on to her face then scrambled on top of her and jerked her arm up her back.

'Don't move or I'll break your bloody arm!' Bobbie yelled.

Teddy rushed towards them and tried to pull Bobbie off Mellor. But Jemma threw herself in between them and Bobbie clung on for dear life.

Then the front door opened, and Gabriel and a police constable stepped into the house.

Gabriel's mouth twitched at the sight of the undignified fray at his feet. 'Scrapping again, Bobbie?'

Bobbie's grin was crooked beneath her swelling eye. 'Gabriel! Glad you could finally join us!'

'Thank goodness you're here, officer!' Teddy Anston yelled. 'These women have just attacked my fiancée!'

'Wait a moment, sir.' Gabriel nodded at his constable, who stepped forward and indicated to Bobbie to get out of the way. He grabbed hold of Mellor and hauled her to her feet. The fight had gone out of the woman now; she was sniffling and crying. Teddy stepped forward but she turned away from him.

Gabriel turned and gestured to an ashen-faced woman to step inside the house. It was Clara Urwin. She'd frozen to the spot in the open doorway. 'I'd like to introduce you all to Miss Clara Urwin,' Gabriel said. 'She grew up with her cousin Helen in Leeds. Do you recognise this woman, Miss Urwin?"

The police constable twisted Mellor so that she faced her accuser, and everyone held their breath.

Clara's features contorted with grief and rage. Emitting a strangled, breathless sob, she stepped forward and slapped Mellor so hard across the face the sound resounded round the hallway like a pistol shot.

'What the hell have you done with my cousin – you bitch!'

Chapter Forty-Eight

The police constable dragged Mellor across the gravelled drive at The Spinney towards the waiting police car. She turned back to Teddy, shouting out how much she loved him, how he was the best thing that had ever happened to her and how she needed him to forgive her. Even Mrs Banyan had had to turn away from her distress and her tearful pleading. Everyone was glad when the car door slammed and shut out her sobbing.

Leaving Mrs Banyan to comfort her distraught brother, they returned to Clifford Street with Gabriel, who asked another officer to drive Clara back to Leeds.

Before she left, Clara hugged Bobbie and Jemma and thanked them both for the part they'd played in solving the mystery of her cousin's disappearance. Her pale eyes were clouded with shock and the strain. 'I feel dreadful now about all the names I've called poor Helen over the years.'

'You weren't to know she was dead,' Jemma said gently. 'You've been the victim of a horrific deception.'

'No, but I should have realised she would never turn on my family like that.'

Jemma and Bobbie were thoughtful as they watched Clara walk away. 'I guess it'll take time for the Urwins to adapt,' Jemma said.

'Yes, but at least whatever is left of Helen Urwin's fortune now rightly belongs to Clara and her brothers.'

Jemma nodded. 'I'm pleased for them – especially Mrs Anne Urwin. I'm sure her children will make sure she's comfortable in her old age.'

Back in Gabriel's office, he told Jemma and Bobbie it was likely they'd be called as prosecution witnesses at Mellor's trial and he asked them to make official statements.

'Ooh, that'll be good publicity for Smoke & Cracked Mirrors,' Bobbie said cheerfully. She wasn't quite so happy, though, when he asked her to write an additional statement about her experience with the black marketeers at the Forde Grene.

'Leeds City Police have picked up Neil Watts and his black marketeer pals and we need your evidence to convict them.'

'They threatened my little Timmy,' Bobbie muttered sulkily. 'What if they come for him?'

Gabriel ignored her protest and pushed the statement form towards her. 'Write it. Mr and Mrs Watts have also been brought in for questioning. My colleagues in Leeds want to know how much they colluded with Mellor in her crimes. If they're found guilty, they could be imprisoned, and their younger children taken into care.'

'Yeah!' Bobbie said, as she picked up the pen Gabriel offered her. 'Mrs Sheils will be pleased about that.'

'In fact, now Mellor knows most of her family have been arrested, she's singing like a canary down in the interview room with my detective sergeant. She's admitted to stealing Helen Urwin's identity – but claims the Watts family knew nothing about it and is trying to protect them.'

'So, she does have some redeeming features,' Jemma said quietly. 'She genuinely loves her family – as well as Teddy Anston.'

'Don't get sentimental, Jemma,' Bobbie warned. 'Has she confessed to the murder yet?'

Gabriel shook his head. 'She still says Helen's death was an accident, but she did admit that the moment she saw Helen wasn't breathing, she realised fate had offered her an incredible opportunity. She claims she's Helen Urwin's half-sister – so you were right about that, Jemma. She says she was entitled to take on her sister's comfortable life and wealth for herself – she believes their father would have wanted this. She also says the fates conspired in her favour and they wanted her to live out her sister's life.'

'Rubbish,' Bobbie said sharply. 'She's a murderer. Did you see the force with which she hurled that tennis racquet at my head? The woman is a vicious killer.'

Jemma and Gabriel smiled.

'That'll be for a jury to decide,' Gabriel said.

'But more to the point,' Bobbie continued, 'where were *you*, Gabriel? Why did I have to make a citizen's arrest?'

'Clara Urwin and I were delayed by bad traffic on the road from Leeds. We got held up by a military convoy.'

'Don't you have horns or bells or something on those ruddy cars of yours?' she grumbled. 'You'll have to do better than this, Gabriel. I won't always be on hand to do your job for you.'

It was nearly dark when the two women finally walked out of the police station.

Bobbie bounded down the steps to the street, but Jemma followed more slowly, enjoying the still mildness of the evening. The night air carried the hint of new growth and the fresh shoots of spring. Over in the trees surrounding Clifford's Tower, a nightingale warbled out its song. Jemma sensed a new beginning, a faint ray of warmer weather and of hope.

Bobbie was still bubbling over with excitement. 'What a case! Our first month in business and we stumble across an unsolved, unreported murder!' When they climbed into the car, she turned in her seat and gave Jemma a spontaneous hug. 'If I wasn't sporting another shiner, I'd suggest we dine out to celebrate. But I'll have to scurry home and hide my face instead. And I'd better not meet Little Laurie on the way because he's already convinced my dad's thumping me.'

Jemma smiled. 'You've got no regrets then?'

375

Bobbie laughed. 'Of course not! Who needs a weekend social life – dancing, or the company of good-looking men – when a girl can spend Saturday night giving evidence down at the nick instead?'

Jemma laughed. 'I'm sorry you were injured, Bobbie.'

'Oh, I wouldn't have missed tonight for the world! Watching Gabriel arrest that damned woman and seeing her face was the best thing I've witnessed for years.'

'I'm glad you stopped Mellor escaping – God knows how long it would have taken the police to find her if she'd got away.' Jemma turned on the engine and looked at her friend. 'Will Grainger's let you into work next week with that shiner?'

'Possibly not. They think it puts off the customers.'

'Then hand in your notice and come into the business full time.'

Bobbie spun round to face her, bursting with excitement. 'Is it time?'

'Yes, it's time. We've got enough money in the bank to support us both for several months and we've also got another case: a missing girl to find. A wealthy family from Beverley telephoned me today. Their granddaughter's run away with her cad of a boyfriend and they think she's in York.'

'Yeah! I'm going to be a full-time private detective!' Bobbie threw her arms around Jemma and gave her another hug.

'There's something else you need to know,' Jemma said, once she'd disentangled herself from Bobbie and pulled away from the kerb.

Bobbie gave her a shrewd sideways glance. 'I thought there might be. You've had news about Michael, haven't you?'

'Special Branch have given me the name of one of Michael's fellow students at the polytechnic in London where he was on his wireless operator course. They think he was the last person to see him before he vanished. I've got to go down to London and meet him. While I'm there, I'll spend some time making enquiries.'

'In polite society, one doesn't say one intends to *go down to London*, Mrs James,' Bobbie reminded her primly. 'One says one is *going up to town.*'

Jemma laughed.

'So, you need me to run the business while you search for Michael?'

'Yes. You can always get help from Ricky if you need it – and if necessary, you can always give some casual work to one of the other female store detectives from Grainger's.'

'Blimey – staff! Things are looking up! Will you leave me the car?'

'Yes, I'll leave you the car.' Jemma smiled at her enthusiasm. 'We've built something special, Bobbie. I can still hardly believe it, but our little agency has a future, a golden future. You and Smoke & Cracked Mirrors are the best things to happen to me this year.'

'We've done well, haven't we?'

'Yes, we've done well. Very well.'

For a moment they sat quietly at the traffic lights, remembering the mixed emotions they'd shared over the past month, the baffling mysteries they'd solved, and their eclectic and sometimes downright bizarre first group of clients.

Then the air-raid siren exploded around them.

'Oh, God! Not again!' Jemma wailed. She pulled over and parked the car. People streamed on to the street as the pubs and restaurants emptied and everyone ran to the public shelter beneath the library.

'I'll kill that bloody Hitler if I ever meet him!' Bobbie said, as they ran for cover.

DANCING WITH DUSTY FOSSILS

The York Ladies' Detective Agency Mysteries

Book #2

By

KAREN CHARLTON

May 1940

As the battle for supremacy in Europe rages in France, York's beleaguered police are baffled by a series of crimes at the city's museums.

A bungled break-in at the prestigious Yorkshire Museum is quickly followed by the murder of Lance Richards, a sub-curator at the neighbouring Castle Museum, who is bludgeoned to death.

The main suspect for the murder is the dead man's co-worker, Anthony Gill, a quiet and unprepossessing clerk. But he doesn't have an alibi and is stubbornly uncooperative with the police. His desperate lawyer employs Jemma and Bobbie, from *Smoke & Cracked Mirrors, The York Ladies Detective Agency*, to investigate the crime on Gill's behalf and prove his innocence.

Meanwhile, the women join forces with King's Detective Agency in Leeds to find evidence for a high-profile divorce case between wealthy aristocrat, Baron Stokesley, and Jodie, his Hollywood starlet wife.

In a twisting series of events, which take the women from cramped hotel bathrooms to danger in the wine cellars of historic country houses, Jemma starts to suspect that their cases are entwined.

Vengeful passions and a dark crime lie beneath the civilised, genteel, and slightly dusty veneer of those elders who preserve our history.

But which of the thousands of antiquities owned by the museum is the murder weapon?

And if Anthony Gill didn't murder Lance Richards, who did – and why?

Available on Amazon

Author's Note & Acknowledgements

Smoke & Cracked Mirrors evolved from an idea I discussed over lunch with one of my Thomas & Mercer editors, Jane Snelgrove. I'd wanted to write a historical novel about two female private detectives for a while, but it was Jane who persuaded me to set the series in the beautiful, historic city of York.

I grew up in nearby Leeds, and York had always been part of my adolescent playground. York was the favoured destination for school trips and Christmas shopping sprees with my friends. It was also the place I enjoyed one of the most romantic afternoons of my life, when my teenage boyfriend and I took a stroll in the gently falling snow along the medieval city walls.

I don't know why but I'd never actually considered York as a location for a novel. I think sometimes we take for granted the amazing things on our own doorstep and need to see them through the eyes of strangers to really appreciate them. I owe many thanks to Jane for suggesting York as a location and encouraging me to write this book.

I first came across the shady world of private detectives back in Scarborough in the 1980s. One of my fellow thespians at the local drama group owned his own agency. He told me about the 'false pregnancy' cages shoplifters wear beneath their coats to hide stolen goods. We also went to a local nightclub, where we took photos with a suspected insurance fraudster jigging about on the dance floor behind us. Those memories stayed with me and found a new home in this novel.

Smoke & Cracked Mirrors was researched and written during the coronavirus pandemic of 2020. I've always been a great one for tramping the streets of the locations in my novels and exploring the buildings I use (especially the pubs and taverns). So, researching during a national lockdown with all the restrictions was a frustrating experience.

Fortunately, I was aided and abetted by several kind and knowledgeable people, including my friend Jill Boulton, who's a native of York and a motorbike expert; Dave Cocks, who is the coxswain at the Redcar RNLI, and my father, Tony James. Dad's passion for steam engines and trams helped me recreate the sights, sounds and smells of Britain's wartime transport systems while Dave made sure I accurately represented the Scarborough RNLI of the 1940s.

Many thanks must also go to my editor, Jenni Davis, for her help with the initial drafts of this novel. And to Sandra Mangan for the proofread.

I would also like to say a huge 'thank you' to the staff at York Central Library. When I contacted them by email during lockdown, they went out of their way to send me links to information that answered my many and varied questions about the city during the Second World War.

Once the restrictions eased, and I visited the library, they handed me the *1939 York Street Directory* and fished out several large photographs of the original interior of their beautiful building. They also pointed out that many of the curved red-leather chairs and tables were original and allowed me to take photographs of the art deco interior. Help and information like that is priceless when trying to recreate historical authenticity.

I also want to thank the lady who owns the *Little Apple Bookshop* on High Petergate. During those first few days of June, when we were allowed back out on to the streets, this enterprising lady donned a full set of PPE and cautiously opened her shop. We customers queued up on the pavement and told her what we wanted over the table she'd used to block the doorway. In my case, it was local history books about York during the Second World War, the type written by local authors that you can't buy on Amazon. She wouldn't let me handle any of the books, but she found three that matched my criteria and read out the blurb on the back and the chapter headings. It was the most personal and unusual service I'd ever had from a bookshop; I bought the lot.

The staff at Betty's Café and Tea Rooms were also incredibly helpful when I told them I intended to set a couple of scenes in my new novel in their premises. They whisked me upstairs to the Belmont Room, found me a great table with a super view of the entire room and one of the managers spent several minutes talking to me about the history of the establishment and its fixtures, fittings, traditional crockery and silverware. I was also given a guided tour of their basement restaurant ('The Dive' in the novel) and shown the famous mirror with the servicemen's names etched into it.

Trawling through online newspapers for 1939-40 was fascinating and so was learning about the infamous Baedeker Raid on 29th April 1942.

During this horrific bombardment, seventy German planes dropped hundreds of bombs, killing ninety-two people and injuring hundreds of others. Over a thousand buildings and homes were destroyed, including many historic medieval buildings and churches.

However, prior to that, despite the fact there were over eight hundred air-raid warnings, there'd only been the odd bomb dropped here and there, mostly on the farmland surrounding the city. During the 'phoney war' of 1939/40, the Luftwaffe killed more farm animals in the North Riding of Yorkshire than it did people.

Those newspapers also gave me a fascinating insight into the role played by the beleaguered York City Police, whose force was decimated when their younger officers enlisted. Those snippets of information I gave you about Gabriel's work – the traffic carnage caused by the blackout and the escaped prisoners of war – were based on real incidents. The newspapers also reported that York City Police strongly resisted a call from the female-led York Watch Committee to employ women officers.

The streets and the majority of the buildings I've described still exist; York is an incredible historic city and is well worth a visit if you haven't been. A maze of narrow, cobbled streets, where ancient churches and medieval timbered taverns rub shoulders with elegant houses built in the seventeenth century and even older artisan cottages. The city is dominated by the majestic Minster and encircled by honey-coloured medieval walls, along which you can walk. An American friend who visited York with me back in 2017 said it was like stepping into an 'alternative reality'.

Researching the lives of Britain's earliest female private detectives was also a fascinating experience and I can strongly recommend Susannah Stapleton's book: *The Adventures of Maud West: Lady Detective* (see the Bibliography below). I bought this book for research, but it turned out to be one my most enjoyable reads of 2020 as well as very inspirational. And yes, the hefty O'Sullivan handbook, *Crime Detection*, does exist, although copies are hard to locate; I had to import mine from the USA.

Finally, to you, the reader, thank you for reading my book. If you enjoyed *Smoke & Cracked Mirrors,* please leave a review on Amazon. If you would like to read the opening chapter of the next book in the series, *Dancing With Dusty Fossils*, it's at the end of this book. There is also a Reading Guide for those of you in a book club which I hope will be helpful. I would also like to encourage everyone to visit my website to sign up to my occasional newsletter. It's the best place for advance notice about forthcoming releases, writerly updates and competitions.

Karen Charlton

5th January 2022

Marske,

North Yorkshire

www.karencharlton.com

Bibliography

Martin Edwards, *The Golden Age of Murder* (HarperCollins 2015).

Annie Gray, *From the Alps to the Dales: 100 years of Betty's* (Profile Editions 2019).

Val McDermid, *A Suitable Job for a Woman,* (Poisoned Pen Press 1999).

F. Dalton O'Sullivan, *Crime Detection* (The O'Sullivan Publishing House 1928).

David Rubinstein, *War Comes to York* (Quacks Books 2011).

Susannah Stapleton, *The Adventures of Maud West: Lady Detective* (Picador 2019).

Van C. Wilson *Alexine: A Woman in Wartime York* (Van C. Wilson 1995).

Van Wilson, *Rations, Raids and Romance: York in the Second World War* (York Archaeological Trust 2008).

Van Wilson, *The Changing Face of Clifton* (York Archaeological Trust 2011).

DANCING WITH DUSTY FOSSILS
The York Ladies' Detective Agency
Book #2

Chapter One

Friday, May 17th 1940
York

The old wireless in the corner of the Dunn's sitting room crackled as Britain's new prime minister, Mr Winston Churchill, gravely told the nation about the tremendous battle raging on the continent and how the Germans had broken through the allied lines and were ravaging the open and defenceless countryside of France and Flanders.

Maud Dunn groaned, murmured the names of her sons, and clutched the threadbare arm of her chair until her arthritic knuckles turned white. She turned her anguished face towards her husband and her voice cracked with emotion as she spoke: 'Our lads are in trouble, Charlie.'

On the other side of the hearth, Charlie Dunn's jaw clenched around the stem of his pipe as he fought back a wave of nausea. He'd seen this coming for days; the newspapers had been full of dire warnings. 'Steady, love,' he said, gently, 'they'll be alright. The Green Howards have trained them well.'

Maud shook her head and her voice rose hysterically. 'They're surrounded! They're runnin' for their bloomin' lives!'

Charlie rose stiffly, crossed the hearth rug and put a comforting hand on his wife's shoulder. 'Aye, well in that case it's good job they're fast runners then, ain't it? No-one could ever run faster than our lads...'

His voice trailed away helplessly, and his anxiety was replaced with a flash of anger. *How the devil had it come to this? Didn't their family suffer enough last time around?*

He'd lost a brother in the aerial bombardment on the Somme and Maud lost one in a hail of machine gun fire at Ypres. It was only by sheer luck that Charlie himself had returned unscathed after two years in the trenches. Apart from their two sons, they also had three nephews fighting with the British Expeditionary Force in France.

Fighting? No, Maud was right – they were running for their bloody lives. How many of them would come back? He held his wife tighter.

Maud shook her shoulder free from his grip. 'You're hurtin' me, Charlie.' She leaned forward as the sonorous tones of Winston Churchill sought to reassure the nation.

The telephone out in the hallway began to ring. They both started with shock.

'Who the hell can that be?' Charlie snapped. 'Tonight – of all nights?'

Maud dabbed her eyes with her apron. 'You'd better get it. It must be important.'

It was important. It was Clifford Street police station.

'Mr Dunn?' the officer said. 'We understand you're the caretaker at the Yorkshire Museum. We've had a report that a group of young lads have scrambled over the wall into the Museum Gardens at the bottom of Marygate.'

Charlie rolled his eyes and swore under his breath. 'Not again! I'm sick of telling them they've got to repair that damned wall. Bloody young scamps!'

'Our witness thinks it might be more serious than just trespass, Mr Dunn. They're carrying a crowbar; it looks like they intend to break into the museum. Have you got the keys? We'll send down a couple of officers.'

Charlie sucked in his breath and thought of the hospitium, filled to the rafters of its medieval roof with Roman, Viking and Saxon treasures. He didn't want to leave Maud right now, but he had no choice.

'Meet us with the keys at the Abbey Gatehouse entrance on Marygate in ten minutes,' the officer continued, 'With any luck we'll catch the little beggars in the act.'

Aye, and I'll tan their bloody hides for them when we catch them, Charlie thought as he reached for his coat and hat.

Despite his stiff joints and the dangers of the uneven pavement, Charlie strode angrily down the quiet, blacked-out streets towards the museum, cursing the old gentlemen who'd planted the botanical garden around it.

Built two hundred years ago, on the site of the ruins of one of the grandest abbeys in the country, the sprawling, ten-acre site, with its swirling islands of exotic and mature shrubs and thick-trunked old trees provided far too many places for the trespassing youngsters to hide.

He saw two officers waiting at the Abbey Gatehouse entrance. There was no police car parked nearby. They must have hot-footed it from Clifford Street to get here before him.

The Abbey Gatehouse, home of the elderly Keeper of the museum, was already in darkness. This didn't surprise Charlie. Mr Collinge was nearly seventy, frail, and always retired to bed early, exhausted with the responsibility he carried for the gardens, the ancient ruins and the vast treasure trove of priceless antiquities and fossils under his care.

'Evening, Officers.'

One of the policemen was a stout, rough looking chap with a scowling face and hands like hams that toyed with the truncheon dangling from his belt. His uniform was too tight, and the brass buttons strained over his stout, muscular body. *He's the kind of fellow to scare the living daylights out of the thieving little sods,* Charlie thought with a grunt of satisfaction.

But his anger flared again when saw the face of the other officer in the moonlight. The fellow was under thirty. *Why hadn't he signed up?*

'Thanks fer comin' out, Mr Dunn. Have yer got the keys?' the younger officer asked.

Charlie ignored him and turned to his companion. 'I know one of yer inspectors,' he told him. 'Clever chap. Inspector Gabriel Roxby. D'you work wi' him?' He pulled the heavy iron keyring out of his pocket and unlocked the gate. As he did so, he glanced back and saw the officers sharing an amused glance.

'Yeh, we know the archangel,' the older officer replied, smirking.

Discomfited by their lack of respect, Charlie pushed open the spiked, wrought iron gate. It screeched on its hinges in protest. A noise loud enough to wake the centuries-dead monks in the graveyard of the ruined abbey, never mind warning the youngsters that they were on their way to get them.

'Needs oilin',' the older officer commented gruffly, as he pushed his way through.

'Yeah, the whole damned place is goin' to wrack and ruin,' Charlie admitted. Unsure whether to lock the gate behind them, he hesitated. The officers crunched through the gravel beneath the medieval stone arch that linked the Abbey Gatehouse with St Olave's Church while Charlie pondered his dilemma.

There were now four airbases with thousands of airmen surrounding the city on the flat land of the Vale of York and most of these chaps spent their time off getting drunk in the city. The last thing Charlie needed was to round up the trespassing youngsters and then find a squadron of intoxicated airmen had sneaked inside the grounds through an open gate to sleep off the drink beneath the exotic magnolias and chestnuts.

In the end, he just pulled the screeching gate shut behind him and quickened his pace to catch up with the policemen. He'd never liked this place after dark. There were too many ghosts haunting the Abbey ruins for a start. Apart from the dead monks, they said King Henry VIII had once stayed here – at the old Abbot's House – and had nailed the heads and dismembered body parts of honest Yorkshire rebels above the gates. He scurried beneath the overhanging, straggly branches of a Scottish Dawyck beech tree. It rustled eerily in the wind. *Why did they grow this foreign stuff?* He wondered. *What's wrong with a good old English oak?*

The officers had already turned the corner of the path by the time he'd caught up with them.

'How many of them are there?' he asked, breathlessly. The solid black mass of the medieval Hospitium loomed into the dark sky ahead, obscuring the stars. Charlie could hear its ancient timbers groaning in the wind.

'How many what?' asked the older officer.

Charlie glanced at him, frowning. 'Kids. In the grounds.'

'Oh, them. Half a dozen, we think.'

The wind dropped and for a moment the Hospitium stood silent and – apparently – undisturbed. The moonlight glinted off the glass in the mullioned windows. None of them were broken or appeared to have been forced and the heavy oak doors were firmly closed.

'Wait here,' said the older officer. They left him shivering on the path and disappeared into the gloom to check out the sides and the rear of the building.

Charlie's ears strained to catch a sound of the intruders. Any sound.

His eyes squinted and peered into the darkness, trying to pick out movement. *Who'd have thought there were so many shades of black in the world?*

The older officer suddenly appeared out of nowhere, making Charlie start. 'Can't see anythin',' he said. 'We'd best go inside and check.'

Sighing, Charlie led the way up the twisting wooden exterior steps towards the main entrance of the Hospitium. If they couldn't find any evidence of a break-in here, they'd have to go round the main Museum building too, which was far bigger. It was going to be a long night.

The second officer joined them on the platform outside the main entrance. As Charlie unlocked the door, the sound of boyish laughter and shouting drifted towards them on the breeze.

He spun round, glanced up the slope towards the main museum building and saw several lithe shadows flitting across the path amongst the trees.

'There!' he said, pointing. 'There's the little bastards!'

He opened his mouth to holler at the kids…then his world went an even darker shade of black…

Buy *Dancing With Dusty Fossils* on Amazon.

BOOK CLUB READING GUIDE

This reading group guide for *Smoke & Cracked Mirrors* includes an introduction, discussion questions and ideas for enhancing your book club meeting. The suggested questions are intended to help your reading group find new and interesting angles and topics for your discussion. We hope that these ideas will enrich your conversation and increase your enjoyment.

Introduction:

York, England: 1940

When her husband goes 'missing in action', Jemma James returns to the city of her birth to set up a private detective agency with her best friend, Roberta 'Bobbie' Baker with whom she shares a passionate love of detective stories.

These enterprising young women are soon embroiled in a series of mysterious cases, shadowing blackmailers and bigamists, and investigating the perplexing history of a wealthy young woman who seems determined to wipe out her past. And it's not long before they stumble across an unsolved murder...

But the dead don't stay dead for long in historic York.

As the 'phoney war' draws to a close and the sky above the soaring twin towers of the twelfth century Minster darkens with menace, Jemma learns that even she is not above suspicion in wartime York.

Topics & Questions for Discussion

Plot & Mystery Elements

"investigating the perplexing history of a wealthy woman who seems determined to wipe out her past..."

1. The story of Helen Urwin and Gladys Mellor is the most mysterious case Jemma and Bobbie undertake. Discuss the mystery aspect of this plotline. How effective was their investigation and how soon did you realise the connection between the two women from Leeds? Were you able to predict certain things before they happened, or did the author keep you guessing until the end?

"But the dead don't stay dead for long in historic York."

2. There are three characters in this novel who effectively rise from the dead: Jack Deburgh; Jemma's husband, Michael James, and Gladys Mellor.

Which storyline did you enjoy the most? Which was the most intriguing – and why?

"Yorkshire's very own Mata Hari"

3. There was a strong undercurrent of distrust in wartime Britain, and it was often directed at the wrong people. As Jemma finds out to her cost, no-one is above suspicion.

Did you enjoy the story of the treacherous Cynthia Ravenscar and from your own experience and knowledge, were foreign nations and those associated with them mistreated during WW2?

Structure

4. Rather than focusing on one large mystery, this novel is multi-layered and infused with several mini cases which reflect the real-life workload of private detectives. How satisfying did you find this approach?

5. Agatha Christie wrote in her autobiography about her dislike of mysteries having a romantic subplot. Consider Bobbie's doomed love for Vince Quigley and Jemma's heartache over her missing husband. Do you agree or disagree with Christie's point of view? Did the relationship issues in *Smoke & Cracked Mirrors* enhance or detract from the novel?

Characters

Jemma and Bobbie

6. They met at school and share a mutual love of crime novels, but life has thrown a different set of challenges at the two women. Despite their close bond there are subtle distinctions between them. Which character did you like best and why? Were you satisfied that they both had the talent and the strength of character needed to become successful private detectives? And is there anything in their lives which may shatter their trust in each other in the future?

Inspector Gabriel Roxby versus Ricky Wilde

7. The archangel and the spiv; the saint and the sinner. How did they compare? Which was your favourite male character out of the two and why?

The clients

"I don't think any of our clients are trustworthy", says Bobbie.

8. At times, it does seem that their clients are a secretive bunch who are quite happy to sidestep the law. Which were your favourites? Are there any amongst them whose case you would have refused to take on? If so, why?

Recurring Themes

Misogyny & Sexism

'It's an unsuitable job for a woman', says Gabriel.

9. Both World Wars brought dramatic change and more freedom of choice to the women of Britain, but sexism and prejudice still prevailed. Like Bobbie, women were grossly underpaid in every job compared to their male colleagues and the stubborn refusal of York City Police to employ female officers is a historically documented fact.

Apart from these examples, how else were the women in this novel restricted by their era? In your opinion, which of them showed the most disregard for convention?

Justice & the Law

10. During WW2 York City Police lost a third of their officers to the armed forces but reported crime rose by 57%. The war brought with it a raft of new restrictions and regulations which many people chose to break or circumvent and the reduction in the policing of the city made it far easier for them to get away with their crimes.

What impression of WW2 policing does the author recreate in this novel?

As discussed above, several of Jemma and Bobbie's clients break or sidestep the law. Were you satisfied with how the author let them handle these events? Are Jemma and Bobbie upholders of the law?

Setting and Description

York

"King's Square was so named because it was alleged to be the site of a Viking palace, but it had never been a glamorous part of the city centre. For centuries it was dominated by a small church, which eventually crumbled into disuse and was used as a holding pen for animals about to be slaughtered by the Shambles market butchers. As a child, Jemma had always begged her mother to avoid the area because she loathed the squeal of the terrified animals and the smell from the insanitary piles of entrails and pools of coagulating blood on the cobbles..."

11. Before the advent of modern tourism, York was a quiet provincial city that relied heavily on light industry and often struggled to maintain the hundreds of historic buildings and monuments within the encircling arms of its medieval walls. Did the description the author provided help you visualise this? Do you feel this brought this historic medieval city alive?

Wartime Britain

12. In the Author Notes at the end of this novel, Karen Charlton tells us: *"During the 'phoney war' of 1939/40 the Luftwaffe killed more farm animals in the North Riding of Yorkshire than it did people..."*

How did you feel about her depiction of a provincial city at war? Were you conscious of the war in the background?

And Finally...

13. Did you enjoy the humour that the author tried to insert in this novel? If so, which were your favourite scenes and most amusing characters?

Enhance your book club experience

1. Check out the author's website: **www.karencharlton.com** On the blog page you will find a series of articles and links to others on the Internet about how she came to write *Smoke & Cracked Mirrors.* Sign up for her Occasional Newsletter.

2. Contact Karen Charlton via her website to arrange a Question and Answer session, via Skype for your book club. www.karencharlton.com

3. Follow author, Karen Charlton, on Facebook and Twitter for regular updates about Karen's writing, research and historical characters.

ABOUT THE AUTHOR

In addition to The York Ladies' Detective Agency Mysteries, Karen Charlton is also the best-selling author of The Detective Lavender Mystery series, which is set in Regency London and features Bow Street's Principal Officer, Stephen Lavender, and his humorous sidekick, Constable Ned Woods.

A former English teacher, with two grown-up children and a small grandson, Karen lives in a remote North Yorkshire fishing village with her two cats and writes full-time. She's a stalwart of the village pub quiz team.

Karen always enjoys a good mystery and loves historical fiction and historical dramas on TV. She's an avid reader herself and loves to hear from her own readers. You can easily contact her via her website. For the latest news about her fiction, her public appearances and some special offers, sign up for her occasional newsletter on the home page: **www.karencharlton.com**

Made in the USA
Las Vegas, NV
16 February 2023

67612753R00219